FRACTURES BETWEEN

FRACTURES
Between

BEATRICE MCKINSEY

Cover design by Lyric Itinerant
Cover illustration by Kare Valgon
Interior design by Dash Jones

First paperback edition: December 2025

ISBN: 979-8-9936479-1-3 (paperback)
ISBN: 979-8-9936479-0-6 (ebook)

10 9 8 7 6 5 4 3 2 1

*This story is dedicated to my wonderful partner,
who supported me on every step of this journey.*

*Thank you to all of my beta readers, including but not
limited to my partner, my brother, Jen Claire Smith,
Lacie M. Lou, and many others at Critique Circle.*

FRACTURES BETWEEN

1

"Happy birthday!" Theo yelled, leaning out the driver's side window and waving furiously.

Summer, her best friend in the entire world, ran down her driveway, then stopped a few feet away. She gave a low, appreciative whistle, hooking her thumbs into her jean pockets. "Wow. You got me a shitty minivan. I'm touched, really."

Theo sighed, and reached up to adjust her glasses. "Just get in already."

"Ooh, so demanding. I'm sixteen now, shouldn't I drive?"

"You don't have your license yet. Plus you don't know where we're going."

Summer grumbled to herself, but she climbed into the passenger seat anyway. She casually rested her elbow out the window, her leather jacket shiny in the setting sun.

Tension slithered through Theo's chest, her heart pounding faster, her breath hard to catch. This was happening more frequently every time she hung out with Summer recently. It was stupid, nothing but delusions and fantasies. She needed to push through and be normal. "I uh. Love your hair. It's really pretty."

Crap. Was that normal? It felt like too much. Theo felt her cheeks heat up, and she looked away.

Summer ran a hand through her hair, lifting it up, revealing the undercut beneath, and the recently dyed bright streaks of red. "I already sent you pictures."

"Yeah, well. It looks even better in person."

Silence hung between them. Theo winced. She wished she was brave enough to do something so cool with her own hair. It was straight and black and boring, and her mom would lose her mind if she dyed it.

"Well, where are we going, anyway? This had better be good."

"It's a surprise." Theo narrowed her eyes. "And we're not going anywhere until you put your seatbelt on."

Summer snorted. "Whatever, *Theodora,*" she said, enunciating every syllable. But she put the seatbelt on all the same.

Theo carefully checked her mirrors, then looked behind her and pulled out of Summer's driveway. Driving was still new to her, and the freedom it offered her was unprecedented, the limits of which she was still discovering.

Theo tried to be a good kid. She got perfect grades, was perfectly well behaved, and did everything right. Her mother trusted her enough to lend her the van.

The only black mark on her otherwise spotless record was Summer Sullivan.

The world around them grew dimmer as the sun dipped below the horizon. Theo turned her headlights on, and followed the route she had carefully memorized. They passed the edge of town, houses growing sparser, then turned onto a country road bordered by cornfields crown as tall as the van.

"Hey, let's put on some music," Summer said, fiddling with her phone.

Theo's heart pounded in her chest. She licked her lips. "Nope. In fact, you should turn off your phone."

"What? Why? Is this going to be some bullshit about spending time away from screens?"

"It's not that." It was hard to hide her grin, so Theo bit her lip. "You don't want your location services to have a record of where we're going."

Summer's eyes went wide, and she looked from Theo to her phone, then back again. "Hold on. Are you fucking serious?"

Theo couldn't hold it back any more, and her grin spread wide and glorious. She'd been planning this for a month.

"You, Theodora Smith. Little Miss Perfect." Summer leaned in close, her smile devilish, and said in a stage whisper. "If I didn't know any better it sounds like you're suggesting we do something *against the rules.*"

"Not just against the rules." Theo took a deep breath. A part of her was still screaming internally. "Straight up *illegal.*"

Summer let out a faux-gasp, then burst out laughing. "Holy shit. Here I thought we were just going to see a movie or something lame like that."

"You like seeing movies!"

"I mean, sure. But nothing good is out right now." Summer turned off her phone, fully powering it down. "Never thought I'd see the day."

"Yeah, well." Theo sat up a little straighter, feeling warm inside. "Maybe I'm a lot cooler than you think."

"Maybe." Summer flashed her teeth. "Guess we'll see."

By the time they reached their destination, it was fully dark. Theo switched the headlights off as they pulled into the driveway. Before them loomed an old farmhouse, casting deep shadows in the moonlight.

"We're here." Theo let out a held breath, her hands shaking as they tightly gripped the wheel. Even though there was no logical reason for it, a part of her still expected flashing red and blue lights to pop up behind her any moment.

Summer pursed her lips and stared out the window into the darkness. "Where the hell are we?"

Theo fussed with her glasses. Summer *would* actually like this, wouldn't she? "We're at an abandoned farmhouse in the middle of nowhere."

"That sounds... way more murder-y than I was expecting," Summer said, with a real hint of unease beneath her joking tone.

"The place is condemned, actually," Theo said, rushing to explain. "I heard about it from my uncle. Gonna be torn down next week."

Summer narrowed her eyes. "I don't get it. What does this have to do with my birthday, Theo?"

Had she completely missed the mark on this? Theo felt sweat beading on her forehead, and she began to shrink back under Summer's disapproval. "I, uh. Well, you know, we can..." She took a deep breath. "We can do whatever we want here. Nobody will know or care."

Silence hung between them. Theo felt even smaller. This was such a stupid mistake. She'd ruined—

Recognition finally dawned in Summer's eyes. "Holy shit."

Relief flooded through Theo, and she let out a soft sigh. "Yeah."

"Holy shit!" Summer repeated, and a wide grin split her face. "We can wreck the shit out of this place!"

Theo grinned back, biting her lip. The whole idea of doing something so brazen still terrified her, but if it made Summer happy...

Summer climbed out of the van, picked up a hefty looking rock from the driveway, took a quick glance around, then wound up and whipped it through a window.

It shattered, the sound ringing through the night air and making Theo wince.

"Fuck yeah!" Summer pumped her fist into the air. "Okay, this rules. God, I could kiss you. Come on, let's go!"

Theo squeezed her eyes shut tight and took a deep breath. She wished Summer wouldn't say things like that when she clearly didn't mean them. But wouldn't it have been so incredible if she did? If Summer had tenderly reached over, brushed Theo's hair behind her ears, leaned in, and—

This line of thought was not going to lead her anywhere useful. She was doing this to make Summer happy, not to get anything out of it.

Theo grabbed her backpack and joined Summer outside of the van. then they circled around to the back of the farmhouse, avoiding the overgrown front porch, and found the back door. White paint flaked off of it, revealing old, dry wood.

Summer climbed up two tiny steps to the door and tried to yank it open, but was met with the resistance of a lock. "No keys? Sweet. I've always wanted to do this."

"I do have the—"

With a triumphant yell, Summer raised her foot and kicked as hard as she could with her thick combat boots.

The door frame splintered with a crack, but it wasn't enough. Reeling and off balance, Summer windmilled her arms, tipping backwards.

Theo moved to catch her, the impact of Summer's full weight eliciting a grunt of effort. The strawberry scent of her hair tickled at Theo's nose, once conjuring up all fantasies that Theo was determined to dismiss.

Summer remained oblivious to the impacts she made, physical or otherwise. Grumbling under her breath, she extricated herself from Theo's arms to climb the stairs and kick at the door several more times, this time being a bit more careful with her footing.

The door finally shattered inwards on the third kick with a loud crack, and Summer cheered. "Too easy."

Theo glanced around nervously. This place *was* pretty isolated, but sound could carry in the countryside. She hoped there were no nosy neighbors sitting on their porches with binoculars.

Summer coughed as she stepped into the house. "Smells like shit in here."

Theo stepped in to join her. It smelled moldy, mostly. The backdoor opened into a tiny little kitchen with black and white linoleum on the floor and ugly countertops in a faded green. The fridge was a hulking number, straight out of the fifties.

"Hey, maybe someone left some beer behind." Summer tried to pull the fridge open, but it refused to budge.

Theo stared at it frowning. "Oh! That's one of those really old models that can lock. They stopped making them like that because kids could crawl in and get stuck."

"Huh." Summer stared at it thoughtfully. "Think there's a dead body inside?"

"I think the worse possibility is that there might be rotten food in there. It smells bad enough in here as it is, so maybe we shouldn't—"

Summer yanked on the lever that locked the fridge. It snapped off at the rusted base, leaving her holding a fairly solid looking metal club.

The fridge door swung open menacingly.

To reveal nothing but an empty fridge with no power.

"See? It's fine. You're always worried about nothing." Summer hefted the club in her hand, getting a feel for its weight, then smacked it against the side of the fridge. It made a hollow boom.

"Sorry," Theo mumbled, folding her arms over her stomach.

Summer didn't seem to notice or care as she spun, swinging her club across the countertop in a wide arc. The swing shattered several drinking glasses, then finished its arc by hitting a toaster and sending it clattering across the room and sporting a large dent.

With a cry of joy, Summer grabbed more glasses out of the cabinets, then started tossing them up in the air and trying to smack them like baseballs. She missed more often than not, but broken glass soon littered the floor.

Theo smiled, watching the sheer joy of her rampage, and wisely stepped out of the radius of broken glass. She'd worn her good boots for a reason. It was same reason she'd packed a first aid kit in her bag.

"Alright," Summer said once she'd emptied the cabinets, and tore one of their doors off for good measure. She shook broken glass out of her hair, then pointed her club towards Theo. "What else we got?"

"Let's find out."

The door from the kitchen led them into what had once been a living room, and it became immediately obvious why this house had been condemned. Theo had heard as much from her uncle, but it was still daunting to see in person.

"Holy shit," Summer said, a tinge of awe in her voice.

It was hard to see. The moonlight that had been sufficient in the kitchen was blocked by thick curtains on the windows here. But it was impossible to miss the giant hole in the center of the floor and the matching hole above it.

"Water damage," Theo explained, her voice feeling loud in the silence. "I think a pipe upstairs burst, then eventually a heavy bed crashed through both floors into the basement."

Summer took a step forward, the floorboards creaking ominously under her weight. "What's even down there?"

In the dim light, the hole seemed an endless void, but Theo had come prepared for this too. She fished through her bag and pulled out a flashlight. With a click, she pierced through the darkness to reveal a regular looking basement. An absolutely massive four poster bed lay shattered down there, its mattress covered in mold. The rest seemed to be bare stone and a lot of tools and rusty old farm equipment.

Summer gave a low whistle. "What a mess. Can't blame them for wanting to tear it down."

The smell of dust and mold was thick. Theo sneezed three times in a row.

"Oh, check that out!" Summer pointed towards an old TV in an undamaged corner of the living room. It was was absolutely massive, wide enough where it could serve as a table. It's cloth covered speakers had holes poked in it by tiny fingers, and it had a thick screen that probably only displayed black and white images.

"I always wanted to do this." Summer wound up, then smashed her club into the screen with all of her might.

Which apparently wasn't enough. The club bounced off and slipped from Summer's grasp. It went flying, clattering down into the basement below.

"Ow. What the hell?" Summer shook her hands, looking annoyed. "How fucking thick is this glass?"

"My great grandma had an old TV like that. When she passed I remember it took, like, three guys to lift it out of there."

"Hmm." Summer peered at the TV thoughtfully, then snapped her fingers. "Come on, help me out here."

With some effort, Summer wedged herself in between the TV and the wall, and started pushing. Theo hesitated for a few moments, but after an insistent look from Summer, relented and joined in.

Together, they pushed the TV forward and toppled it into the basement below. They were rewarded with the sound of shattering glass.

"Take that, TV." Summer's eyes sparkled, and she flashed a smile at Theo. "Come on, let's go find something else to smash."

Summer's rampage was a glorious thing to behold. She broke furniture, shattered windows, and kicked holes in the wall. It was pure, cathartic destruction with (hopefully) no consequences.

At Summer's encouragement, Theo even broke a few things herself. Though she didn't really think she was getting the same enjoyment out of it that Summer had.

Eventually, they found themselves upstairs, in the room with the big hole in the floor. Someone's bedroom, at one point. Any furniture that had remained had been tossed into the void and all that was left was a closet on the opposite side of the hole, still unexplored.

Summer collapsed against the wall, panting heavily. "Didn't think this would take so much out of me."

Theo grinned. She'd prepared for this. She fished through her bag, pulling out a can of soda and an energy bar. She handed them over before grabbing her own and sitting next to Summer.

"I've helped my uncle do demo before. Remodeling houses is fun at first but it very quickly just becomes hard work."

"That's not the same." Summer scowled, taking a swig of her soda. "This is destruction for its own sake, not to do a job or whatever."

"I know." Theo leaned against Summer, nudging her playfully and secretly enjoying the brief moment of physical touch more than she probably should have. "That's why I brought you here, and didn't ask you to help my uncle."

"Yeah, well." Summer grew quiet, and stared into the distance. She munched on her energy bar, thoughts clearly percolating in her head.

A dusty, moldy, broken house wasn't exactly the most serene of locations to rest in, but there was a sense of stillness to it all the same.

"This rules," Summer mumbled, looking away. "Thanks, Theo. I needed this."

Theo felt her cheeks heat up. "Of course. That's what... I mean, I wanted you to have a happy birthday. You deserve it."

Summer snorted. "You're the only one who cares about something stupid like that."

"Someone should."

Theo's heart ached. She remembered when they'd first become friends, somewhere around fourth grade. Theo had invited her to her birthday party. She came, but Summer had looked so utterly... lost. Confused. Hurt. Theo had eventually come to realize it was nothing she had done, but rather what she had: a normal family life.

"Alright, well." Summer stood up, and stretched. She tossed the empty can down into the hole, and Theo had to bite back a chastisement for littering. That didn't matter here. "Come on, I wanna see what's in that closet."

"Are you sure?" The shattered floor around them was narrow, didn't look particularly well supported, and was rotten besides.

"It'll be fine. You just gotta test it before putting your full weight on it." Summer demonstrated by inching along the side of the room, occasionally putting her weight down to test the boards underneath. They groaned ominously, but nothing splintered or sagged. Without too much effort, she pulled open the closet door. "See? Piece of cake. Get your ass over here."

Theo sighed, then made her way over as well, following in Summer's footsteps, trying not to look at the yawning chasm to her side.

The closet was small and cramped, and it was full of dresses that were very out of style. Maybe from the sixties or seventies? Many had holes in them as well.

"I wonder who lived here before. What was she like?" Theo said, idly picking through the clothes.

"That," Summer said, digging through a box in the back of the closet. "Is exactly what I'm hoping to figure out." She pulled out a small, faded book, holding it out triumphantly. "A diary."

An icy fear bit into Theo's heart. "I don't think we should look at that," she mumbled.

Summer rolled her eyes and snorted. "Don't wuss out on me now. You said you wanted to know, right? Give me that flashlight and let's find out." She unceremoniously snatched the flashlight from Theo's hand, sat down on the floor cross legged, and started reading.

"Dear Diary," Summer read out loud. "Today, Alesha and I went down to the lake to skip stones."

All Theo could think of was how utterly mortified she would be if Summer read her own diary. How disgusted would Summer be, if she knew how Theo really thought of her? "Come on. It's something private. It's not right to pry."

"Who cares, this is ancient. Besides, this is all kind of boring, anyway." Summer started skimming through the pages. "She's just talking about this one friend she hangs out with all the time, and—woah, hang on."

Summer's eyes went wide and she skipped back a page, reading more carefully.

"What?" Theo leaned in closer. The handwriting was small, and hard to make out properly, but she caught out some key phrases like 'I kissed her last night,' and 'papa will kill me if he finds out' and 'I hope God can forgive me.'"

"Shit," Summer muttered. "Rough time to be a dyke."

"Okay, that's enough." Theo snatched the diary out of Summer's hands, and stepped deeper into the closet. It all hit too close to home.

"Hey!" Summer stood up, turning around to face her. "Come on, I wanna know how it ends."

Theo gestured around them. "You already know how it ends. This place is full of stuff that hasn't been touched in fifty years. My uncle said that back in the seventies, the family that owned this place just up and drove off one night. Her dad probably found out, took her away. Nothing but a stupid, awful, tragedy."

Summer narrowed her eyes. "So then maybe we get as much info as we can, track her down, see if she's out there somewhere on social media or something. That'd be cool, right? Reunite some old lady out there with her childhood diary? Find out what happened to this Alesha? Come on, that's storybook shit. You love that sappy nonsense."

"Just let it rest, Summer. Come on, let's go break some more stuff."

"Why are you being so weird about this?" Summer tried to snatch the diary from Theo's hands, but she pulled away. "What are you, homophobic or something?"

Theo trembled, trying her best to keep it together. "I don't want to pry into someone's life like that. It's wrong."

Summer took a step forward, the shadows in the room making her look sinister. "That's not it. I know you too well. This isn't some bullshit about right and wrong, there's something else going on here. What, do you know these people? Is this your great aunt's house or some shit?"

"It's not." Theo couldn't stop shaking. "Can we please drop this and move on?"

Summer's gaze was intense, studying Theo as she looked her over. Summer was no idiot. Theo was normally so good at hiding things, hiding this. But right now, Theo felt stripped bare, her heart vulnerable and easy to see.

And she must have seen it, because Summer's eyes went wide, and she took a step back. "What? No, no way. You've gotta be fucking kidding me."

The tears falling down Theo's cheeks betrayed her. She took a step forward and reached out to Summer. "It's not like that, I'm just—"

A few more steps back let Summer dodge Theo's grasp. She ran her hand through her hair as a wild expression took hold on her face. "Holy shit. It all makes sense now. I'm such a fucking idiot. This whole goddamn time."

Everything was falling apart. Theo's worst nightmares were coming true.

Theo fell to her knees, her head hung low. She couldn't bear to look at Summer's face, to see the disgust she knew would be here.

"I can't believe it. Seriously, do I have this right? Theo, are you in—"

Something in the floor snapped.

Summer let out a scream.

Theo lunged, and caught only air as Summer fell into the darkness below.

Dear Diary,

Today was my first day as a fourth grader! I knew most of them already but there were some new kids too!

One of those was a girl named Summer. She's got pretty blonde hair and green eyes. She moved here during the summer. Haha, like her name!

She seemed kind of angry at first and yelled at a girl who tried to talk to her so I thought maybe she was bad news or a bully.

But then when I was walking home after school I was next to Summer and I saw that she had a copy of the second Magical Steed *book in her bag! I started talking to her about it and she was a little mean at first but she started talking back and we kept talking about all our favorite books the whole way home, until she had to go down a different street.*

I hope she wants to be my friend!

Theodora Smith
8/27/2007

Theo woke up screaming.

She sat up, her heart pounding in her chest and her tanktop drenched with sweat. She fumbled for the bottle on the hotel nightstand. Her anti-anxiety meds. Trembling, she poured a few out into her hand, then swallowed them easily. Washed them down with the water she'd left out the night before.

The pills wouldn't actually have an effect so quickly, but the mere act of taking them always made her feel a little better. She took deep, measured breaths, and slowly managed to calm herself.

Nightmares about Summer's death had become increasingly rare, after an entire decade of distance from that night. Theo supposed, however, that if anything was going to ignite them once more, it would be moving back to her hometown.

Was this all actually a terrible mistake? Could she handle this move and her new job without shattering into a million pieces?

Theo's phone buzzed on the nightstand, and she picked it up. Her mom was calling.

"Morning sweetie! How're you feeling?"

"Hi, Mom. I'm fine. Just woke up."

"The Petersons are expecting you at ten, so don't dawdle too much now."

Theo glanced at the clock. It was already nine. Less time to shower and get ready than she would have wanted. "You know this whole situation is still absurd, right? Renting my childhood bedroom from the couple that owns it now? I mean I kind of knew Peter in highschool but not well."

"Peter is a really sweet boy, and his husband is a delight. You'll be in good hands!"

"I'm sure they're great mom, but still. It's gonna be weird."

"Are you sure you can handle being there?"

Theo bristled at that. "I'm fine, mom. It was a long time ago. I've grieved. I've moved on."

"I'm worried about you, sweetheart. Your father and I—"

"Look, mom, I need to get ready, okay? Brush my teeth, eat breakfast."

Her mother let out a long sigh. "Okay, okay. But call me later tonight, okay?"

"I will."

"Love you."

"Love you too."

Theo hung up, then stared at her phone blankly for a minute.

She hated it when people coddled her, constantly checked in on her, treated her like delicate glass that could shatter at the slightest tap.

She especially hated it because she was afraid they might be right to do so.

But it would all be fine. She'd fought so hard, and been through so much therapy to become the person she was today. She wouldn't let the past haunt her any longer.

It was time to go home.

~

As Theo drove through the streets of her hometown, she was surprised at how much things had changed.

The entire downtown area had been completely renovated. No longer a simple midwestern main street full of old brick buildings, it had been turned into a large plaza with shops on every side, trendy cafes and a great big fountain in the middle. All to accommodate the boom the local university had been experiencing, turning the place into a proper college town.

She'd expected to feel a pang of loss when confronting the fact that the storefronts from her past were no more, but as she drove by, getting only a glance, she mostly just felt a little jealous.

The town as she remembered it had mostly been populated by failing businesses and sad bars. She would have loved to have grown up in this version of her town. It would have been great to explore and hang out in, as a teenager. The high schoolers and college students she could see milling about in the plaza attested to that.

At least her new job at the university would give her the chance to explore it properly soon enough.

For now, she continued her drive past the town center and into the residential areas, which were considerably more recognizable. Rows of houses, many of them more than fifty years old. Big yards. Familiar streets. She'd set her phone to navigate, but there had really been no point.

How many times had she ridden her bike up this road to get to Summer's house after school?

She pulled onto her street, then parked out in front. Her house had been repainted from a faded white to a soft, almost pinkish color. Several new trees had been planted in the front yard. The old black walnut in the back that Theo had spent countless hours climbing up and reading in was gone. A chain link fence had now surrounded the backyard.

No longer home sweet home.

Theo pulled off her glasses, then grabbed the cleaning cloth she kept in the car to rub them down. They weren't dirty, not really, but it was a way for her to pause, to gather herself, to steel herself for what was to come.

Maybe she should stop being so dramatic about this. It was only a house.

Theo exited the car, grabbed her bag, followed the path up to the door, stopped herself from instinctively opening it, and then rang the doorbell.

Rather than the simple *bing-bong* she'd been expecting, the doorbell busted out a high pitched and sped up *La Cucaracha*. Soon after came the furious barking of a dog.

"Just a second!" Someone called out from inside, in a bit of a sing-song.

A few moments later the door opened to reveal a ruddy faced man with a thick ginger beard and a now-quiet dog at his side. He was a bit on the heavier side and wore an apron tied around his waist, covered in flour. His eyes sparkled, and his smile was blindingly bright.

"Heya Theo! Long time no see!"

Theo had known Peter in high school, though admittedly not well. He'd been popular and well liked. Very friendly, a bit of a class clown. Head of the GSA. He was the kind of guy anyone could get along with, and in a way that had intimidated Theo, back in the day.

And now he lived in her house.

"Hi, Peter," Theo said, doing her best to smile.

The dog sniffed around her feet, its tail thumping against her leg wildly. Some kind of collie.

"This is Buddy! He'll be your best friend, I'm sure." Peter laughed, then took a step back, gesturing widely. "Come in, come in! Go ahead and set your stuff down in the living room."

Theo crossed the threshold, stepping into a home that was both familiar and alien at the same time.

Gone was the old wood paneling on the walls, replaced with modern drywall. Photos of friends and family adorned the walls. Mostly people Theo didn't recognize. The furniture was rustic and well worn compared to the modern stuff her mother had always preferred.

"Must be a bit weird, huh?"

Theo flinched. Peter was a little too close. He'd had a habit of that, she remembered. "All things are ephemeral."

Peter giggled. "Wow, deep! I like that. Sorry we changed the place so much, but you're still welcome here. I've got a nice pie in the oven to celebrate! Was hoping to have it done before you got here, but you know how it is." He spoke with a pronounced lisp, a trait that had gotten him bullied in high school, but it never seemed to bother him.

Theo opened her mouth to politely refuse, but paused. All she'd managed to eat this morning was a complementary breakfast muffin from the hotel. "What kind of pie?"

"Peach! There's a peach truck that comes up from Georgia to our tiny little corner in Illinois, selling 'em by the crateload. Absolutely delicious! Aaron and I always go through so many, but some of 'em get baked into pies. Oh, Aaron is at work right now. You probably won't see him until tonight."

One of the photos on the wall caught her eye. Peter in a tux, at the altar together with another man. Aaron, she had to assume, was taller than Peter and dark skinned. The pair had love in their eyes as they looked at each other, a beautiful moment captured perfectly.

Theo nodded. "Okay."

"Right, right." Peter clasped his hands behind his back and rocked back and forth on his heels. He always seemed to be bursting with energy in a way that spilled out onto everyone around him. It was exhausting. "You know where your room is, of course. Rest of the house you're free to use, other than our bedroom, and Aaron would prefer it if you didn't touch his craft room. He's very finicky about that."

Silence hung between them as Theo failed to conjure up a response. Peter continued to rock back and forth. "So…"

Theo grunted and adjusted her glasses. "Sorry, I'm a little out of it. It's been a long—" she paused, glancing at a clock on the wall. "Morning, I guess."

"Hey, I totally get it! Lot of memories here, I'm sure." Peter's eyes flashed with pity that stabbed her like a knife. "And you've got a big day tomorrow. New job! It's over at the university, right?"

"Yeah." Theo bit her lip. She was always annoyed when her mother had front loaded an introduction, when people knew details about her before she had a chance to share them herself. "I'll be working in the astronomy department."

"Ooh!" Peter's eyes sparkled. "You get to use that big telescope?"

Theo shrugged. "I think I'm mostly there to do admin work, but maybe on a day it's not being used for anything important."

"That's so cool! I love astronomy. I'm a Leo, for the record." He winked at her.

She had no idea if he was joking or not.

A timer beeped from the kitchen and Peter's eyes went wide. "The pie! Make yourself at home!"

He ran off, leaving Theo alone.

She let out a long sigh. Maybe this was all a mistake. Maybe she should have gotten an apartment somewhere. But as good of an opportunity as this job was, it didn't pay enough for her to manage without roommates. She didn't want to accept any more of her mom's money.

Steeling herself once more, she made her way up the stairs, to first door on the left, to her childhood bedroom.

Wouldn't it have been crazy, if it was exactly as she'd left it? With its dark blue wall paper and the glow in the dark stars on the ceiling? Its posters of various astronomical phenomena, along with one of Taylor Swift. A desk with her laptop set up in the corner, a TV on the wall, a few gaming consoles underneath. A little window AC, because the central air had never really kept up. An entire wall full of books.

But no. It was all gone. It'd all been packed up long ago when she'd moved away. When she'd fled from a place full of too many reminders of Summer to get away from it all. To heal and recover.

It was a guest room, now. Light beige walls. Generic dentist office artwork hanging on the walls. A queen bed. No style, no personality. A temporary stop.

Theo stepped inside, feeling numb. She set her bag down, then flopped down onto the bed and stared up at the ceiling.

Oh.

They'd left the stars.

~

There was a weight to this place, her old home, crushing and overwhelming. It hung in the air and threatened to push her down and smear her psyche into a fine paste.

Theo decided to counteract that by taking actions that had no weight to them at all. She unpacked a few things. She got out her laptop. She got the wifi password from Peter, ate some peach pie, browsed the internet, played some simple games, and read a book.

In the early evening she went down to eat dinner with Peter. The salmon bake was delicious. Aaron wasn't there, he had to work late tonight. She made small talk, simple, easy, never veering close to anything heavy. Peter did most of the talking, really.

Then it was back up to her room. She scrolled through short videos, one after another. They were a trap for the mind, impossible to escape from. The algorithm provided a continuous feed of distraction and escapism. It was better than the alternative.

Her therapist would scold her, certainly, but when something was too heavy to carry, it made sense to take it apart and carry it piece by piece, didn't it? She would put off carrying the big weight. She'd start her new job and settle into a routine. She'd deal with small things as they came, and not—

Her laptop died.

Theo blinked, her eyes tired from the strain of staring at a screen for so long. She pulled off her glasses and rubbed at them. It was dark out. Nearly midnight. Probably for the best if she went to bed.

She started looking through her bags for her laptop charger.

Five minutes later, the contents of every single bag were strewn across the floor with no charger to be found.

Theo groaned, pinching the bridge of her nose. She hadn't even bothered to take her laptop out at the hotel. She sent a text to her mom, asking her to look for it and see if it had been left at home.

She could continue to stare at her phone instead, but no. It was time to sleep. She had to wake up early.

She changed into her pajamas, brushed her teeth, and brushed her hair. She turned off the light, took off her glasses, and settled into bed. It was honestly more comfortable than she remembered her childhood bed ever being.

She rolled over onto her side, staring out the window, into her backyard.

Vague shapes loomed in the darkness, hard to conceptualize without her glasses. How often had she laid here, staring out the window at the stars, the faint pinpricks of light that captured her heart and sent her imagination soaring?

As her eyes adjusted more and more to the darkness, she saw it. A silhouette against the sky, a building on top of a hill.

It was still there.

~

Theo's carefully crafted defense systems and rationalizations were less effective when it was late and when she was exhausted.

So she found herself creeping through the darkened house, still mindful of where the stairs creaked with every step. A sense of guilt washed over her, as it had when she was a teenager sneaking out of the house at Summer's behest, praying that her parents were already sound asleep.

She slipped on her shoes and made her way outside. The air had a slight chill to it, autumn peeking around the corner. Insects sang their sweet serenades from every corner. The sky was vast and full of stars. She'd missed how many more stars could be seen in a town like this.

The new chain link fence made for a good, large space for Buddy to run around in and do his business, but her backyard extended far past that. They were on the edge of town, bordering farmland and wilderness.

Theo climbed the large hill in her backyard, heading for the woods up top.

As she climbed, it occurred to her that she wasn't actually sure if this hill and these woods were still a part of the property. Had her parents actually even owned the land, back in the day?

Maybe it didn't matter. As a child, she'd claimed these woods as her own, through effort and exploration, through blood, sweat, and tears.

When she crested the top of the hill, more winded than she would have liked, she stared up at it. A squat, square building, that overlooked the neighborhood. It was a fort, a hideout. It was a place for a child to play, to build their own space, to become master of their own domain.

The door was locked. But she knew where the key was, didn't she? A small circle of twelve stones around the right side of the building. A simple riddle scratched into the wood. A key, hidden under seven o' clock.

God, she'd been such a nerd.

She turned the key and pushed open the door into a memory. The place was just as she'd remembered it. The smell of dust and wood. A beanbag in a corner next to a table. A stack of books and manga long forgotten. A cooler, which gave her a brief moment of panic before she remembered that they hadn't kept food in it, only soda.

The image was there, clear in her mind's eye, of Theo and Summer, together on the beanbag. They giggled as they read through a manga

Theo had borrowed from her older brother. She remembered it being kind of stupid and horny, but it had made Summer laugh, which was all Theo wanted.

Grief was a strange and terrible thing, a serpent lying in wait to strike you and fill your veins with fire, if you happen to step a little too close to it. That fire burned through Theo now, a searing pain in her soul. She trembled as her eyes blurred over with tears.

But… there was something else there, too. A warmth that didn't burn, but merely embraced her. It brought a smile to the corner of her lips. These were good memories. She'd loved every minute she spent with Summer. She deserved to be remembered, not locked into an inescapable pit of tragedy.

That was why she had come back, wasn't it? To find a balance between what was, what could have been, and Theo's terrible mistake that had ruined everything.

She flinched at the unwelcome thought. She knew what to do next. Taking deep breaths, she counted slowly to herself. She had to forgive herself, understand that it wasn't her fault, accept it, and move on.

It was easier said than done, but Theo had been working at this for ten years. She knew she was capable. She would get better, no matter what.

Her heart rate slowed. She wiped at her eyes. Sneezed. It really was dusty in here.

Her gaze fell on a shiny metal case in the corner and her eyes widened. She'd forgotten all about it.

She knelt in front of it, carefully opened it, and revealed the once-expensive telescope inside.

It had been a gift from her father for her eleventh birthday. She'd spent so many nights out here, staring up at the stars. As much as she'd tried to share it with Summer, Summer had never really found the same joy and majesty in it that Theo had.

Tonight would be perfect for it, wouldn't it?

Theo climbed the ladder that led to the roof and opened the hatch. The cool breeze greeted her and the vast array of stars loomed overhead. They were hers for the taking. No moonlight to spoil things.

It was easy to set up the telescope. She drew on old muscle memory and familiar pieces slid together. She adjusted the focus. Her prescription had changed a bit in the past ten years.

And then there it was: Mars, the red planet. It was blown up in all of its magnificent glory, as if it was right in front of her face. So close she could almost reach out and hold it in her palm.

She'd proudly told Summer she would be the first woman on Mars. That they could be the first women on Mars together.

Even if Summer had lived, neither of them would have been cut out to become astronauts. She knew that now. But some dreams still lingered, like a decoration on an old shelf that brought a smile to your face every time you looked at it.

Theo pulled away from the telescope, blinking, looking at the sky in its entirety again. Was Summer up there somewhere, looking down at her? She wasn't particularly religious, and she didn't actually believe that. Not really.

But in the infinite majesty of the cosmos, she could understand the draw, the comfort of that belief.

Venus was next. Then Jupiter, then Saturn. Then the stars themselves and distant nebulae. Each brought her, a broken young woman, across trillions of miles of emptiness. The sky was hers. A vast and beautiful cosmos, normally invisible to her pathetic eyes. It all fit together in her mind, a kaleidoscope of galactic bliss.

Movement caught her attention. Theo blinked, rubbing at her eyes. How long had she been at this? An hour? Two? She reached into her pocket to check her phone, but froze. Something in the sky was moving. It didn't really seem like a plane, either.

She adjusted the telescope, bringing it into focus.

A ball of light, a shimmering tail behind it.

Theo let out a soft gasp. It was a comet. But that didn't make sense, did it? Comets were pretty rare. At least, comets that could be easily seen were. She hadn't remembered seeing anything in the news about one passing by, either.

It was beautiful. Theo felt a warmth inside of her. The perfect improbable little capstone to her impulsive little sojourn. Coming back here had been the right choice.

"I wish I could have seen this together with you, Summer," Theo whispered.

The comet flashed, a great crack split the sky, and the world was rent asunder.

Theo stumbled backwards, shaking her head. The sky was normal, unbroken. Her eyes were playing tricks on her.

But no, not entirely. When she looked into the telescope again, the crack was there. The lens had broken.

Obnoxious. But the telescope was old, and had survived a lot of winters out here. Expanding and contracting via temperature would have put a lot of stress on the material. She was lucky it had worked as well as it did.

Theo sighed, then disassembled the telescope and returned it to its case. It had been a beautiful dream, but she had to return to her normal life.

Once she climbed back down into the hideout, she made to head back to the house, back to her bedroom that was not her bedroom, but she paused, her hand hanging over the door handle.

She...

Theo collapsed onto the beanbag, a decade worth of dust exploding into the air. She grabbed one of the nearby manga= and cracked it open.

Just a little reading before bed couldn't hurt, right?

3

Dear Diary,

Summer won't talk to me. :(
    It was so much fun talking to her when we walked home but now when I try to talk to her in class or at recess she tells me to go away. She told me that if I knew what was good for me I'd frick off. (she didn't say frick. =O)
    I don't understand what I did wrong.
    I really want to be her friend though.

Theodora Smith
8/28/2007

The sound of her phone alarm jolted Theo awake. She sat up, disoriented and half-blindly looking through askew glasses.

Her back hurt, her nose was runny, her eyes were puffy. Allergies from all the dust, probably. She'd passed out in the beanbag, which had ended up being way more uncomfortable than she remembered.

With a deep yawn she stretched, cracking her back, before she finally turned the phone alarm off.

No nightmares last night. That was a plus.

Still, she had a new job to start today. After her nostalgia party last night, it was time to return to the present.

Morning dew soaked through her shoes as she trudged her way back to the house. She'd set her alarm early enough that she should still have plenty of time to get ready.

She didn't see Peter when she made her way back inside. Now it was time for a quick shower—the upstairs bathroom had been remodeled, and honestly it was way nicer. She'd forgotten to grab her toiletries before getting in, so she borrowed some body wash and decided to just leave her hair unwashed for now.

The problems started once she got out of the shower and made her way back to the room, only to find that her bag was missing.

Last night she'd torn it apart looking for the laptop charger, and had never bothered putting everything back inside. Taking in the rest of the room, all of her stuff was gone, not just the bag and its former contents. Even her clothes were missing.

Theo felt a sinking feeling in her gut; she changed back into the pajamas she'd been wearing before the shower. This had to be some kind of misunderstanding, right? This would be the worst, most passive-aggressive way to tell someone you changed your mind about renting them their room.

Maybe Peter had just cleaned a little too enthusiastically? She'd have to have a conversation with him about boundaries if so.

As she made her way downstairs, she called out, "Hello? Peter? Are you there?"

Thinking about it now, though, she remembered that in their brief chat over dinner last night he'd mentioned having to wake up super early for his job. Something about a bakery?

She heard footsteps coming down the stairs, and made her way back over to the stairwell.

A tall man stood on them, looking down at her, eyes wide.

Theo bit her lip. He looked just like the guy she'd seen in the photo. "Hi, um. You must be Aaron. It's nice to meet you. Do you know if my stuff got moved somewhere?"

Aaron stared at her blankly for several long moments.

"I do kind of have to get to work, and—"

"Who the hell are you, and what are you doing in my house?" Aaron growled, his voice low and dangerous.

Theo took a step back as her adrenaline spiked. "I... what? I'm your new roommate. Theodora Smith? Peter told you, right? I'm renting the guest room?"

Aaron shook his head. "I don't know what kind of scam you're running, lady, but I'm not renting out my guest room. Get out of my house before I call the cops."

This... couldn't be happening. It was insane. "C-come on, this has to be some kind of misunderstanding, right? Call Peter, he'll explain everything."

He took a step down the stairs, a heavy stomp that made her flinch. "Get. Out."

"Okay, okay!" Theo opened the front door, and practically fled outside. She could clear this all up later.

And of course, her car wasn't there either.

She stared at the empty curb in disbelief. Had it been stolen? Or towed? Maybe there were city regulations about street parking she'd forgotten or never learned in the brief period she lived here as a teenage driver.

Theo pulled out her phone. She could call Peter herself and sort this all out. Or her mom. Mom had been the one to arrange this whole thing anyway.

Deep breaths. She could handle this.

A blinking menu popped up on her phone.

SIM INVALID.

She tried anyway, but got nothing for her efforts; her phone wouldn't let her place any calls. She couldn't use her data, either.

She paced the sidewalk in front of her childhood home. Something was deeply wrong, but she didn't have time to worry about that right now. Her brand-new job started in thirty minutes.

It wasn't that far. She could walk.

She was almost certain she'd spotted a clothing boutique in the main plaza when she drove by yesterday morning. If she hustled, she could get there, buy some new clothes, and get to the university while only being, by her vague calculations, about twenty minutes late.

Not the end of the world. She could salvage it.

～

Summer laid back on her bed, staring at the conversation on her phone and trying to fight the growing sense of emptiness inside of her.

Summer: hey I had a lot of fun this weekend you wanna hang out next saturday too? Could go to the park or something

Leslie: oh

Leslie: sry Ive been seeing someone I rly like and were gonna make it official so that was the last time

Summer: sure np

It was to be expected. The whole thing had only been a friends-with-benefits arrangement to begin with. Casual sex, no strings attached.

Still. Summer had kind of started to like Leslie and found herself wanting to hang out with her in the daytime too.

But at the end of the day, nobody ever seemed to make Summer their first choice.

Her brooding was soon interrupted when seventeen pounds of cat jumped onto her stomach.

"Damnit, Chester! I already fed you."

Her orange chonker didn't seem to care, and started kneading her shirt, purring loudly.

Summer scritched him behind his ears. She'd take her unconditional love where she could get it.

"What do you think, huh buddy? She probably wasn't worth it anyway."

Chester responded by butting his head against her hand, demanding more pets.

Summer let out a soft sigh; she couldn't help but smile a little bit. Her life was one full of fuckups and mistakes and heartbreak, but at the end of the day, she was still alive. She had friends, people she cared about. Sure, she was stuck in a rut with no way out in sight but... well. It could always be worse.

As long as she didn't fuck anything else up.

Theo's credit card wasn't working either.

But that was okay! Her mother had given her a bunch of cash before she'd left, kept in a compartment in her phone case. Theo thought it had been a bit overbearing at the time, but now she could only feel gratitude for the forethought.

The boutique was hellishly expensive, though, and she burned through pretty much all of the emergency cash. Why would anyone pay two hundred dollars for a cardigan under normal circumstances?

So it was that Theo arrived at the astronomy department in the university, wearing the most expensive outfit she had ever owned, thirty minutes late for her first day on the job. She was out of breath, and a little sweaty to boot.

"Hi," Theo said, resting her hands on the receptionist's desk. She hoped she didn't sound as manic as she felt. "I'm Theo Smith, here to start my new job as the administrative assistant?"

"Oh!" The secretary was a young woman, maybe around Theo's age, with styled dark brown hair and a perfect smile. Her name tag read 'Riley'. She smiled pleasantly, but it began to fade as she looked through her computer. "I'm not seeing you listed here on my calendar…"

Theo's face fell. "You have *got* to be kidding me. Not this too!"

Riley looked her up and down, and broke back out into a sympathetic smile. "One of those mornings, huh? Don't worry, I'm sure it was just a mistake. I'll reach out to the manager."

"Thank you." Theo's shoulders slumped, and she let out a sigh of relief. "You're a lifesaver."

"I get it, I do. My first day I was such an absolute mess I was sure I would be fired. But Jerry's a good boss, you don't have to worry."

"Every possible thing that could go wrong this morning has." Theo laughed bitterly. "Except for meeting you, I guess."

Crap. Had she actually said that? She mentally pulled back on the reins. She needed to be way less gay. That wasn't what she was here for.

Riley studied her intently, a small smile growing on her lips. "Well, we're going to be coworkers, apparently, so I suppose I might as well earn some brownie points while I can."

Theo's face flushed. She didn't trust herself to say anything else under the intensity of Riley's gaze, so she just nodded and gave an affirmative grunt.

For her part, Riley didn't let up. She continued looking her over, while twirling a lock of hair around her finger. "I like your cardigan."

Dangerous. This girl was dangerous. Theo swallowed. "Thanks. There's kind of a whole story behind it. I'll tell you later."

"Looking forward to it."

The appearance of a middle-aged man in a white button down shirt saved her from any further awkwardness. He approached with a cheerful smile and shook her hand. "Nice to meet you, Theo. I'm Jerry. I can't say I'm not glad to see you here, but I must admit I am pretty confused."

Theo tilted her head to the side. "What do you mean?"

Jerry raised an eyebrow. "Well, I received an email from you last Friday saying that you were rescinding your acceptance of our offer. Kind of really left me in a lurch. Been spending all morning removing you from our systems and putting out new job postings."

What an absolute nightmare. Theo pinched the bridge of her nose and groaned, "I'm terribly sorry, sir. Something weird is happening to me. I think I'm the victim of... identity theft or something? Maybe targeted harassment? My phone and credit cards aren't working, my car is missing, it's been a whole crazy morning. I promise you, I never sent an email like that, and I do really want this job."

"Your car is missing? That sounds pretty serious."

Theo winced. "I'm really hoping it just got towed? But it's been one thing after another. Haven't really had the chance to actually deal with any of it."

Jerry nodded solemnly. "Right, right. Well, the job is still open, and there's a reason we chose you over the other candidates, so if you want it, it's yours."

"I do."

"Great." He smiled warmly. "I've got some system changes to undo but I'll show you to your desk, and get you logged in. Follow me."

Finally. Something was going right.

She followed Jerry down the hall towards her new job, her new life.

She glanced back over her shoulder.

Riley smiled, and gave her a little wave.

Dangerous.

The first half of her day at her new job was relatively uneventful. Theo was given the tour, introduced to a few other coworkers whose names she was sure she would eventually remember, shown various systems, and given some documentation to read.

Actually accomplishing anything wasn't on the menu for today. Which suited her just fine, after the craziness that was her morning. Once work was over, she'd get to a store, get her phone working again, call her mom, and try and get this all sorted out.

Sure, there were a lot of problems, but they could all be solved. She needed to take things one step at a time.

Sometime around one, Riley knocked on the door to her office, face lit up with a radiant smile. "Heya! Have you taken your lunch break yet?"

Theo looked up from the direct deposit form she'd been staring at. It might be better to verify that everything with her bank was still good before she submitted it. Her stomach rumbled, and she winced. "I haven't yet. Had to skip breakfast this morning too, with everything that happened."

"Well that's no good! Come on, there's a great little cafe within walking distance. It'll be my treat!"

A part of Theo wanted to refuse. To turn her down. To say something like, 'Hey you're really cute, and I'd love to get to know you better, but you definitely don't want to get to know me better because I've got enough baggage that if you stacked it all on top of each other it would reach to the moon'.

But maybe Theo was a weirdo, and was reading way too much into a vaguely flirty interaction from a cute girl. Riley was a new coworker. There was no reason they couldn't be friends.

"Okay. Sure."

Riley bit her lip. "Kind of a big pause there. If you've got other plans, that's totally fine."

Theo shook her head. "Sorry, no, that sounds great. I'm just a bit out of it at the moment."

"Gotcha." Riley's smile returned, her teeth perfect and white. "I've been told I can come on a little strong, so if that's ever the case, let me know and I'll back off, okay?"

"I'll let you know if it comes to that." Theo paused, then smiled. "But I kind of doubt it will."

Riley giggled and led her back out through the building. The day was sunny and warm, and the town plaza was an absolute bustle of activity.

The cafe Riley brought her to was called Over the Moon, and Theo couldn't miss the pride flag hanging in the window. It would have been hard to imagine in this town, back in the day. How much would something so simple and innocuous have meant to her when she was fifteen?

Ten minutes later, they sat together at a booth inside, sandwiches and lattes acquired. The quiet murmur of other conversations filled the air, along with the smell of fresh bread and coffee.

"So," Riley said, in between bites of her sandwich. "Are you new in town?"

Theo let her gaze linger out the window, staring at the new fountain and all of the students milling about. "Yes and no. I grew up here, but left ten years ago. This is the first time I've been back, and... it's changed a bit."

"Oh wow! Didn't realize you were a townie." Riley sipped at her latte, made a face, and then blew on it some more to cool it down. "I did my undergraduate degree here, and then I went straight into grad school. So I guess I've been here five years already? Even some of the changes I've seen during that time have been pretty surprising, but seeing it all at once must be wild."

"It's..." Theo searched for the right words, but didn't quite find them. She shrugged. "A lot, I guess. It's all a lot. Haven't really been here long enough for things to sink in. What are you studying?"

"Physics. Or, well, astrophysics, more specifically." Riley glanced towards the astronomy building and the large telescope contained within. "My secretary-work there is only a part-time thing, but I'm there super often for class-work and to study as well."

Theo's eyes widened. "Wow, really? That's so cool! I've always loved astronomy, telescopes, and the stars. I really wanted to study it myself, but I couldn't hack the science classes required. One of the reasons I wanted to take this job was so I could still contribute in some way. I might not be able to grasp advanced physics, but I am an absolute wizard with Excel."

"Good. You have *no idea* how much we need that." Riley laughed, her eyes sparkling. "If you want, I could show you the telescope sometime. Access is pretty tightly scheduled, but I could get you a peek at what I've been working on."

"I'd... love that, honestly." Theo's heart soared a little. Very dangerous. A girl this cute, and apparently super smart? Was she into girls? Was she even single?

Stop, stop. She needed to remember what had happened with Sarah. And Irene. And Denisha. Three perfectly wonderful women whose hearts she'd broken because she couldn't keep herself together, because she'd dragged them down with her and made their lives worse.

She wasn't healthy. She wasn't ready for a relationship. She wasn't good for other people.

But, a small voice in her head seemed to whisper. Maybe this time would be different. Maybe she'd been through enough therapy now. Maybe this new start would really result in a new her.

Silence hung between the two of them while Riley quietly ate, but her intense gaze never left Theo. Her eyes were beautiful and brown, her lashes long, her eyeliner game on point.

"So, uh," Theo said, her voice hesitant, feeling incredibly lame for what she was about to say, "what do you do for fun? Do you have a—" Girlfriend. Say girlfriend. "boyfriend?"

Riley raised an eyebrow, then took another sip of her latte. The temperature must have improved, as she now made a cute humming sound of satisfaction. "I don't have a lot of free time between work and school, but I get out occasionally. Hang out with friends." She paused, a small smile playing at her lips. "I'm the president of the university's GSA as well, so that takes up a bit of time. But no, I'm not seeing anyone at the moment. My last girlfriend cheated on me, which, well, really sucked."

Theo tried her best to keep her face neutral and not let the mix of excitement and terror show. Her excuses were crumbling away like a sandcastle before the tide. "That does really suck. I've been through some similar stuff before." Which could have all been avoided if Theo was a more stable, better partner.

"Yeah." Riley's eyes grew a bit distant, the pain clear in her expression. "It does."

Silence hung between them, now awkward, rather than full of tension. Theo finished the last bite of her sandwich, her plate clattering in her haste. "Still. GSA president is pretty cool. I… always wanted to join the GSA in my high school, but I was too scared."

Riley's smile returned. "I get that. We get a lot of newcomers who are so utterly terrified and taking the first steps into queer identity offline." She paused for a moment, drumming her fingers against the table. "What they're not ready for is just how boring we are. Your average queer teen discord server is way more exuberant, has way more drama, and has way better memes."

Theo burst out laughing. "I can imagine that. Discord was barely a thing yet, back when I would have needed it the most, but I did find my

way into a few IRCs. I never told anyone else about them. Not even—"
A hitch in her voice, a slight pause. But she could push past it. "My best
friend."

"IRC huh? Real old school." Riley's eyes narrowed in exaggerated
suspicion. "Just how old are you, anyway? Your skin is great, either way."

A sip of her coffee helped her not react to the compliment. "I'm
twenty-six. My dad really loves computers though, so he taught me how
to use them when I was little."

"Wow, so ancient." Riley giggled. "I'm twenty-three. Still, if you left
town ten years ago, I guess you would have still been in high school. What
took you away? Where'd you go?"

Theo stiffened, the sound of broken glass shattering through her mind.
Well, it was a perfectly normal question, it was bound to come up eventually. She tried not to let it show on her face.

Riley picked up on it anyway and pulled back slightly. "Sorry, is that a
sore subject? We don't have to talk about it if you don't want to."

What a pain. Why did it always have to come back to this one defining
tragedy, a great shadow she could never escape from? Theo shook her
head. "It's… some stuff happened. Bad stuff. Then I couldn't handle being
here anymore, so my parents picked up and moved us to Minnesota."

"I see." Riley's eyes glistened with sympathy, a look filled with insidious
poison that threatened to eat her alive. She hesitated for a moment, then
reached out and rested her hand on top of Theo's.

Theo could already see the words forming on Riley's lips. *If you ever
want to talk about it, I'd be happy to listen.*

Enough of that. Theo cut her off and pulled her hand away. "It's not
really something I want to get into. I've spent too long being defined in
everyone else's eyes by my trauma. I'm sick of it. I've come back home to
bury my past properly and move on."

"O-okay." Riley bit her lip, looking unsure of herself. The enthusiasm
and confidence she was normally brimming with were missing. Caught
up in a field of landmines all named Theo.

Theo let out a long sigh. She *always* did this. Ruined everything.
Killed the mood.

They were saved when Riley's phone buzzed and she pulled it out
of her back pocket. She studied it for a moment, then pursed her lips.
"Guess we'd better get back to work."

"Guess so."

Riley stood up and stretched, the movement revealing a glimpse of her midriff. "Do you wanna do this again sometime?"

Theo tried not to stare too hard. An open invitation. She should push back now. "Sure. I had a lot of fun, so I'd love that."

God, she was an idiot.

Riley lit up with a beautiful smile that nearly assuaged all her doubts and fears. "Great! I really would love to get to know you better, Theo."

~

There really was nothing like a workout to help clear the mind. Summer walked down Main Street, sun shining on her from above, her arms feeling pleasantly tired from their exertion.

She passed by the Over the Moon Cafe and stopped, trying to do some mental math. She was hungry, but money was tight. It would be better if she went home to eat instead.

But then again, getting dumped was an occasion to treat yourself, wasn't it?

Not that it could really be called getting dumped, when they had barely been a thing to begin with.

Whatever.

Summer stepped through the doors, enjoying the rush of air conditioning that washed over her.

"Great! I really want to get to know you better, Theo."

A familiar voice cut through the din. Summer turned to see Riley standing up from a booth where a dark-haired woman sat as well, her back to Summer.

When Riley made eye contact with Summer, her cheerful expression immediately morphed into a deep scowl.

Well, it wasn't like Summer didn't deserve that kind of reception.

"What are *you* doing here, Summer?" Riley asked, an accusatory edge to her voice. She crossed her arms over her chest.

Summer let out a long sigh. It really was a miserable day, overall. "I'm here to get food. It's a small town, Riley. We're going to see each other around occasionally."

Riley turned her nose in the air, and let out an emphatic, "Hmph! Well, I was just leaving anyway. Come on, Theo."

Theo, huh? A date? Well, good for her. "I am sorry, you know. I never meant to hurt you."

"Theo?" Riley asked, a note of concern entering her voice. "What's wrong? You're shaking."

Summer blinked, taken aback by the sudden change in the situation. The woman in question did appear to be trembling. "New friend?"

"Shut up!" Riley snapped. "This isn't about you."

Fair. She probably deserved that. She should probably cut her losses and go somewhere else.

The woman she had called Theo stood up and frantically whipped around to stare at Summer, wide-eyed.

Wait. Theo? It couldn't really be...

Summer took a look at the woman in question as horror slowly dawned on her. She had the same long dark hair, the same big glasses, the same slightly crooked nose, and dimples in her cheeks. She was an adult woman now, filled out. Beautiful, really.

A completely inappropriate thought and unfair to have, considering that back in middle school Summer had bullied Theo so badly she'd been forced to move away.

Truly a miserable day.

The way Theo's eyes had gone wild with panic, fear, and horror certainly suggested that she recognized Summer as well.

What the fuck was she supposed to do? Apologize? What good would that even do? She couldn't imagine she would want to hear it if she was on the other end. Still...

"Theo?" Riley said, putting a hand on Theo's shoulder. "Hey, what's going on? Do you know her?"

"I'm sorry," Summer murmured, though her words caught in her throat, and she wasn't sure they ended up intelligible at all.

If Theo heard them, she gave no indication. The girl sunk to her knees, head clutched in her hands. Tears streamed down her cheeks, and she shook so violently the nearby table rattled in response.

"I think... she's having a panic attack," Summer muttered, her own heart already pounding in her chest. She'd certainly had her own share, and even helped others, Riley included, through them as well.

"No shit, Sherlock," Riley snapped. "What the fuck did you do to her?"

Summer bit her lip, then shook her head. "A lot. I... I'll go."

Riley shook her head. "No. She's having a lot of trouble breathing. I'm gonna call 911. I'll stay with her and try to calm her down. You wait outside and direct them in when they show up."

"I... yeah. I can do that."

It would be the least Summer could do to atone for her sins.

~

Summer made her way outside and leaned against the wall. Nothing to do but wait. Slowly, she slid down the wall and slumped into a seated position. She wrapped her arms around her knees and pulled them in tight.

What an atrociously miserable day.

Except no. What right did she have to complain? Summer wasn't the one who had been brought face-to-face with her childhood bully after, what, ten years? Fifteen?

After about ten minutes, the ambulance showed up. Summer did her job and directed them inside, and they came back out, guiding Theo to the ambulance.

She still seemed completely catatonic, unresponsive to the world around her.

Was what Summer did really that bad? Like, she knew it was bad, but... damn. She'd always kind of hoped that Theo had been able to move on and live a happy, healthy, and productive life in spite of the damage Summer had done.

So much for that.

Her hands twitched at her side. She could really use a cigarette right now. She'd quit last year, but at a time like this...

The door to the cafe opened, and Riley stormed out. Her hands were balled up into fists, and she shook, her eyes burning holes into Summer.

"What. Did. You. Do?" She spat through clenched teeth.

Summer pinched the bridge of her nose, letting out a long sigh. "What didn't I do?"

Riley growled and grabbed the collar of Summer's jacket, pulling her closer. "Are you so determined to ruin everything nice that might happen in my life?"

With a sigh, Summer pulled free of Riley's grip. "Look, I'm a big fuckup, I know that, but it's not like I did this on purpose. I haven't seen Theo in over a decade. I hurt her pretty bad, but… I really thought I'd never see her again."

"So you're the reason she had to leave town," Riley snapped, jabbing an accusatory finger into Summer's stomach.

Summer grimaced. Riley's fingers were sharp. "Yeah. I bullied her. Bad. For almost three years. I eventually got suspended, and she moved away. End of story… until now, I guess."

Riley stared hard at her, but her fury eventually wilted. She looked away, running her hand through her hair. "God, fuck. She just moved back to town and started working at the astronomy department. She's cute, pretty sure she's gay. Why did you have to be involved?"

"I'm sorry. I've always wanted to apologize to Theo and make it right somehow. I really was a broken kid, you know? Lashing out at others, grasping any form of power I could. That didn't make it right, but I still regret all of it."

"Uh-huh." Riley crossed her arms over her chest. "And would that apology actually be for her benefit? Or would it just make *you* feel better?"

Summer shrugged. "Probably the latter. It's why I never did it. Reached out, I mean. Judging by her reaction today, that was probably the right choice."

"I'd say so."

The ambulance was long gone at this point. The lump in Summer's throat remained. "Still. If you see her again, could you pass it along? That, uh, if she wants to hear it, I'd like to apologize anyway. Wouldn't blame her if she doesn't, but…"

Riley huffed. "Yeah, yeah. I'll see what I can do." Her phone buzzed in her pocket, and she cursed. "God, I gotta get back to work. At least Jerry will understand."

"It's fucked, isn't it? Having to go back to work after something like this, like you're supposed to pretend it's all normal?"

"Yeah." Riley glanced at her, her gaze softening somewhat. "But what else can we do?"

"Dunno."

Summer watched for a while as Riley turned away and jogged back towards the campus.

She'd come here for lunch, but her appetite was pretty shot after everything. Back to her own life, her own problems.

Dear Diary,

Today I was playing alone at recess when I heard some shouting. Summer was there on top of the jungle gym, and there were three other girls. Alissa, Harmony, and Stella. They wanted to have the jungle gym all to themselves but Summer wouldn't budge! Then they pushed Summer off. Summer got real mad and started chasing the girls and they ran right to a teacher. The teacher gave Summer detention! I saw the whole thing and it was really unfair. I went over to the teacher and told him the truth but he didn't believe me so I got angry and then I got detention too.

    Detention is really boring too you just have to sit there and do homework and not talk to anybody.

    Momma said I did the right thing and that she's proud of me.

Theodora Smith
8/29/2007

Theo sat in a hospital bed, doing paperwork and not talking to anybody.

    There was nothing quite as sobering as the banality of waiting for an hour to see a doctor, being told something you already knew, and then having to fill out insurance forms.

    Although, the anti-anxiety meds they'd given her probably helped even out her mood as well. Amidst all of the chaos this morning, she hadn't realized that her own were missing.

    The paperwork gave her mind something to focus on, to release its tension and signal that all of the stress hormones her body was producing weren't actually helpful.

    Whether or not her insurance would actually work was questionable, but Theo filled out the forms anyway.

When she finished, she set the form aside and took a sip of water. It would probably be at least another thirty minutes before she could be discharged. If you weren't actively dying, the ER didn't work particularly fast.

It was time to fully consider what had happened. What she'd seen.

There were really only three main categories this could fall into.

One: Theo's perception could no longer be trusted. Her mind was playing tricks on her in some way. She was hallucinating.

It… didn't seem very likely. In all her years of therapy, she'd picked up at least some knowledge of psychology. Full visual and auditory hallucinations, even in extreme cases of schizophrenia, were exceedingly rare. Seeing something that crisp and clear, with no prior symptoms beforehand, and with no other breaks from reality… it didn't add up.

Any psychedelics capable of producing a hallucination like that would have messed with her perception in other ways, and would have had other symptoms.

Addressing it in her mind felt like a weight off of her shoulders, and she relaxed slightly. She wasn't crazy. Her mind was still her own. She had to believe that.

That led her to the second possibility: That there was a perfectly mundane, and maybe cruel, explanation.

Maybe Summer had a twin sister, separated at birth, that had also been named Summer? Maybe it was someone disguising themselves as Summer in order to gaslight and terrorize Theo specifically? Maybe Summer had faked her death somehow, and was still alive?

The thought of it made Theo's chest tighten and her heart race. The idea that anyone could be so deliberately cruel, and to her specifically, was… terrifying to contemplate. It was a level of evil that defied understanding.

But she couldn't discount it entirely. She already thought she could be the victim of identity theft. *Something* was clearly happening.

Were these things related? Or were they a series of unlikely coincidences?

That brought Theo to her third and final category: That something explicitly fantastical or supernatural had occurred.

There were a wealth of possibilities here. Had she seen a ghost? Some sort of demon or shapeshifter? Was Summer really a vampire? Had she warped in from some parallel universe? Was she a time traveler? An advanced android made to look like her? Some kind of convincing illusion or hologram?

Magic. Technology. If you discarded what you knew to be true in order to find an explanation for the unknown, then really, any explanation would work.

There was a certain appeal in surrendering to fantasy. To stop thinking.

But at the end of the day, she didn't have enough evidence. She could sit here and spin her thoughts in circles endlessly, and still arrive no closer to the truth.

She had to get out of here to find Riley, talk to her, and ask what she knew.

And then she would have to find Summer Sullivan.

~

Theo had a lot of problems to deal with.

She had nowhere to stay, barely any money, no working phone, no car, and no belongings.

A part of her understood, logically, that these all needed to be dealt with, and soon. She needed to get to the phone store before it closed so she could call her mom and call the impound lot. She should address her hierarchy of needs by order of importance and urgency.

But she chased ghosts instead.

It was nearly five by the time she was released from the hospital. It would maybe be about a half-hour walk back to campus.

Would Riley still be there? She was Theo's only lifeline at this point, her only hope.

Theo would beg her for help, beg her for information, crush her under the weight of Theo's baggage, smother the burning spark of a new connection and replace it with desperate neediness, as Theo abused her goodwill until Riley's reservoirs of kindness and charity and pity ran dry.

Theo walked down main street, and it was an absolutely gorgeous day outside. The sun shone bright in the sky, but there was a hint of autumn in the breeze, so it wasn't absolutely sweltering. There were people all about, getting off from work or running errands. Students were getting done with classes as they loitered around and formed larger groups to go hit up the local bars.

It felt wrong, somehow, for everything to be this peaceful and joyous while Theo's internal anguish raged like a hurricane. She could barely keep it together. She could barely put one foot in front of the other.

Other people must have sensed it in her. Maybe there was a particularly wild look about her, but when strangers glanced in her direction, they quickly looked away and gave her a wide berth.

That was fine. She could be the resident crazy lady. Why not?

She was drenched in sweat by the time she made it back to campus, her muscles sore.

It wasn't even that she was that out of shape, but it turned out being incredibly stressed was exhausting.

She trudged up the steps of the astronomy department and pushed open the doors. The welcome breath of air conditioning was there to greet her, a small relief.

But of course, Riley wasn't there.

Theo collapsed onto a nearby bench, burying her face in her hands. Deep breaths. Where could she go from here?

She needed a new phone. She remembered she'd driven past a cell phone store on the way into town, but it was on the outskirts. Too far to walk, really.

Could she get a rideshare? Did the town have those now? Well, not without a phone. But maybe, if her office was unlocked, she could use her work computer to order one. Except she didn't have a working card, and they didn't take cash.

Damnit, damnit. Okay, but maybe using her work computer she could log onto Discord, message her brother, get *him* to message her mom, and they could set up some kind of voice call. Did her work computer have a microphone?

It was a plan. Something she could do. She just had to move.

It took her about five minutes to calm her breathing, to force her legs to stand up, and to shamble down the hallway to her new office.

A computer sat in front of her, the internet at her fingertips. She could reach out and communicate with someone who could help her.

Instead, she searched for Summer Sullivan.

Plenty of results. Too many. It was a common enough name. She narrowed the results down to her hometown.

No obituary. But she did find a hit. A LinkedIn page.

And there she was. Summer Sullivan. Similar to how she'd looked in the coffee shop, though it was a more professional looking photo.

Her resume wasn't particularly impressive. GED, no college. Various odd jobs, a lot of volunteer work, but what did Theo care about that, really?

She opened the picture, magnified it as far as it would go. The details came out pixelated.

But it was still unmistakably *her*. Her best friend. Her first crush. Those same brilliant green eyes.

The woman she'd killed, through her own stupidity, a decade ago.

It didn't make sense. None of it made any sense.

But, well, she'd have to make sense of it, wouldn't she? Her mind wasn't playing tricks on her. She could rule that out. Probably.

A few more searches, to really narrow things down:

```
summer sullivan obituary
summer sullivan obituary 2014
summer sullivan death 2014
```

Nothing. There was nothing. But why? There should have been news articles, an obituary, any evidence whatsoever of her passing. Theo knew, because she'd spent hours and hours staring at them, reading them again and again and again until their contents were seared into her brain.

But it was all gone.

"Theo?"

Theo blinked, then turned to see Riley standing in the doorway, her face full of concern.

"Oh, uh. H-hey." Theo cleared her throat and quickly tried to wipe the tears from her face.

Riley bit her lip, looking her over for a few moments, before nodding. "Hold on one second, I'll be right back."

Theo wanted to ask her to stop, to stay, but she wasn't quick enough, couldn't make her throat work properly or her limbs move.

Riley was back in under a minute though, with a glass of water in hand. "Here," she said, setting it down in front of her. "You look like you could really use it."

Her movements felt automatic, but when the cool water touched her lips, Theo found herself gulping it all down greedily. That was right, bodies needed things to be able to function properly, to think properly.

"I'll get you some more," Riley said, taking the empty glass with a small smile.

Theo drank it slower, this time, in small sips. Riley pulled up a chair next to her.

Theo's computer screen betrayed her, rendering her desperate search fully visible to Riley.

But Riley didn't push, didn't ask for any explanations. She just offered kind silence.

Was that worse, somehow? Now Theo felt guilty, a desire to fill that silence, to open her heart.

But there wasn't time for that. Theo needed answers.

"What can you tell me about Summer Sullivan?"

~

Summer trudged up the steps to her apartment, her brain fried after her shift at the gas station.

It was late. The streets were mostly empty now, bathed in the soft light of streetlamps. In the distance, she could barely make out the hum of live music, being played in one of the bars further down Main Street.

On a night where she didn't have to work, she might have been down there herself. Even if the bands that played this town all sucked, even though she was maybe getting a little too old to keep partying with the college kids.

Outside of her door, she found a paper sack waiting for her, stuffed full of leftover bread and donuts. She sighed happily. Perks of living above a bakery. Even if her entire apartment smelled like bread sometimes.

Peter was a good guy.

Unlocking the door and stepping inside, she was greeted by the patter of tiny paws, then Chester was there, purring loudly, rubbing against her leg.

"Yeah, yeah, I know," she said, unable to keep the smile off her face. "You'll get dinner soon enough."

She kicked off her boots, tore off the plain black polo that served as her work uniform, and tossed it into a corner. She reached up under her undershirt and undid her bra for good measure, then rolled her shoulders and got in a good stretch.

Then, a diet Coke from the fridge for her, and a can of tuna for Chester.

She booted up her ancient laptop that sat on the old card table serving as her kitchen centerpiece. So many useful things could be found in the spring when the college kids moved out of their dorms.

There were a few emails waiting for her, mostly involving scheduling for her work at the youth center. Once she marked those down in her calendar, she stood at a crossroads: she could make the conscious decision to do something she actually wanted to do, like watch a new TV show, read a book, or do some drawing... Or she could stare at social media, looking at funny memes, getting mad at the state of the world, and watching short videos of buff ladies chopping wood until her eyes were tired and she stumbled into bed at three in the morning and woke up again at noon tomorrow to do it all over again.

Summer sighed and rubbed at her eyes. She was pretty good at avoiding the trap of the algorithm. Most of the time. But after everything she'd dealt with earlier today, maybe she deserved a little mind-numbing escapism.

"God, I'm such an asshole," she murmured to herself.

Chester finished eating, then sauntered over and hopped into her lap. Seventeen pounds of orange fur and chonk.

She scritched him behind his ears. What right did she even have to feel bad about this? It was Theo's life she'd ruined. She was the one who was actually suffering from all of this. Summer had no right to complain.

Maybe she shouldn't be chasing escapism after all. Maybe she needed other people right now. But who amongst her friends would be so accommodating at eleven at night on a Monday?

Summer stared at the contacts list on her phone, biting her lip. Riley would have done it. She had been that kind of friend, but Summer had ruined everything.

As she continued to stare, she realized she had a notification from Riley. Which was weird, considering she was pretty sure Riley had her blocked.

She opened it to find a new message waiting for her, sent several hours ago.

"She wants to talk to you."

Dear Diary,

Today at recess I saw Summer sitting alone on the swing set, so I went and sat on the swing next to her. I said hey but she didn't say anything, so I just kept swinging. After a whole bunch of time she finally asked me why I was dumb enough to get detention too. I told her that you should always tell the truth and that was all I did.

She got quiet again but then asked if I wanted to go catch frogs down by the creek with her after school. I told her I'd have to talk to my mom.

We only caught one frog but it was very fun! I got very muddy.

I think I maybe made a new friend!

Theodora Smith
8/30/2007

Reconciliation, apparently, couldn't wait until the morning.

So it was that Summer found herself strolling into a park at midnight, her shitty beater car parked behind her on the street.

It wasn't much of a park, in the shadow of the water treatment plant, but it had a small playground for kids and a baseball diamond that was now mostly unused, ever since they built the new mega sports complex on the other side of town a few years back.

In Summer's memories, it mostly held space as the place she used to sneak off to at night to smoke behind the bleachers. She was glad at least that those days were behind her.

Riley had been frustratingly vague over text message as to what exactly this was about, what Theo actually wanted from her. Was she supposed to apologize? Sit there and take it while Theo told her how much she hated her and how Summer had ruined her life? Was there a gang of brutish friends and family waiting in the shadows to get revenge for the former cruelty of a preteen girl?

Summer deserved a lot of whatever might be coming to her, but there were limits to even her self-flagellation. She'd been in fights before. She carried a taser for a reason.

But as she drew closer, she was sure those fears, at least, were unfounded. Nobody was slinking around in the darkness, ready to pounce.

There was just a girl she had hurt so much, sitting on a swingset, her feet idly kicking the sand.

Whatever beating Summer was about to take, it'd be purely emotional.

After a brief moment to steel her nerves, Summer made her way over to the swingset, sitting down on the one next to Theo. "Hey."

Theo didn't respond. Her hands were clasped tightly together in her lap, her knuckles white.

Summer turned to look at her, studying how the girl she'd once known under the light of the stars, making note of how much she'd changed. Everything had been too chaotic to really process anything back at the cafe.

Theo looked haggard and strung out. Her long dark hair was messy and there were dark circles under her bloodshot eyes.

Summer bit her lip and waited, pushing off the ground and swinging a little bit.

That wait stretched to a minute, then two, then five. Summer burned to fill the silence, to talk, to apologize, to say something, do anything. But her therapist had always stressed how important it was to wait and listen to what others had to say, especially when reconciling with someone you've hurt.

So Summer waited.

Tears trickled down Theo's face and her breath came in shaky, measured beats. Like someone trying to control her emotions and failing.

When she finally did try to speak up, her voice caught in her throat. She had to try three more times before she finally managed to make her words work. "Do you remember? The last time we came here?"

"Huh?"

"We were maybe fourteen. You told me that you'd found a dead body down by the river. I believed you, and I was terrified. I kept begging you to call the cops. You kept teasing me and said we had to go see it. When we got there, and I saw a leg sticking out of that sewer pipe, I nearly fainted. And then it was just one of those stuffed Halloween porch scarecrows. You laughed and laughed. Honestly, it was a mean prank. I was pretty upset, but then you picked up the scarecrow and started making funny voices with him and I couldn't stay mad at you, because how could I?"

Summer stared at Theo, her mouth hanging open. Of everything she'd been expecting here… what was this supposed to be? "I… what? What are you talking about?"

A shudder ran through Theo, and she bit her lip. "Do you remember that?"

"No. I…" Summer shook her head. "Theo, you moved away when I was like, twelve. And while a mean prank like that does sound like me… I never pulled that one on you."

Theo made a sound somewhere between a laugh and a sob. "Of course. Of course. What a fucking joke."

She laughed harder, tears streaming down her face. Then her hand shot out and grabbed Summer's wrist. "Hey, you're real, right? You're actually here. You're a flesh and blood human person."

Her nails dragged across Summer's skin, then she pinched, hard.

"Ow!" Summer yanked her wrist free, rubbing it with her other hand. "What the fuck was that?"

Theo turned to her, a wild look in her eyes. "Pinch and it hurts. Guess I'm not dreaming."

"I think you're supposed to pinch *yourself* to see if it's a dream." Summer let out a long sigh and stood up. "Look, I have no idea what you're talking about, but it's clear that whatever is going on, you're not ready for this. I should go."

"No!" Theo shouted, her voice full of desperation and panic. "Please. Don't go."

Summer stood there, her back to Theo, her stomach a roiling pit of emotions. How long had she thought about what she'd say to Theo if she ever saw her again? Workshopped her apology in her mind. Why couldn't she remember any of it now?

"I'm sorry," Summer whispered. There was a huge lump in her throat, but she pushed past it. "I was so, *so* cruel to you when we were kids. Because of everything going on at home, I felt powerless. I was angry.

Exerting some kind of power over you gave me a sense of control I lacked elsewhere in my life. That's not an excuse. I know it doesn't make anything better. It's just… what happened. I'm sorry. I've wanted to apologize to you for a long time, but I didn't want to re-traumatize you in the process. Here we are, though, so I'm saying it. I'm sorry."

Silence. Summer remained there, shaking. A part of her wanted to say more. To turn around and beg for forgiveness. To offer herself up for punishment. But that was all self-serving. She'd said her piece. She could wait for a response.

Theo laughed again, hollow and bitter. "You don't have to apologize to *me*, Summer."

Summer clenched her fists, then turned around. "Please. You don't have to accept my apology, or forgive me… but please don't just brush it off as if it was nothing."

"That's not it." Theo smiled, and it looked a little creepy, not quite reaching her eyes. "You don't have to apologize to me because I'm not the one you hurt. I'm not the same Theo you knew."

That was… Summer blinked, then took a deep breath. "Okay…" she said, hesitant. Was this some kind of disassociation thing? Multiple personalities? God, she was not equipped for this conversation. "I'm not sure I understand what you're saying. Could you explain it more clearly?"

As if she was talking to an upset child. It felt condescending as soon as it came out of her mouth, and it probably was.

Theo moved to speak, then paused, her brows furrowed as she thought something through. "What I'm about to say is going to sound crazy. It is crazy, but, well, I have some evidence. I think I'm from another world."

Summer stared at her blankly. "What?"

"You say you used to bully me. Really badly. Enough that you got expelled, and I moved out of town. Apparently when I was like twelve. Riley told me some of this too, but… is that the gist of it?"

"…Yes?"

"Well, I don't remember any of that. In my memories, we met in fourth grade, and became instant best friends. We spent all of our time together. Up until your sixteenth birthday, when I—" She choked on her words, then looked away. "You died in a terrible accident."

The hair on the back of Summer's neck stood on end. The kind of feeling you got when you realized that an off-leash dog is genuinely hostile, and doesn't simply want to play.

She shifted her weight a bit, inching away from Theo. "Okay. Um, sure. Is there anyone I could call for you? Maybe your mom or something?"

"Don't look at me like that," Theo said, her voice sounding tired. "I'm not crazy. Or, well. I'm pretty sure I'm not crazy. But look. Here. See?"

She pulled out her phone and started flipping through her photo gallery. It took a little bit, but she finally settled on something. "This will do. July 13th, 2014. You had come up on a vacation with me to the Wisconsin Dells, and we took a selfie wearing those stupid cheese hats."

Summer took the phone, not really sure what to expect, but then there it was: a picture of herself and Theo, smiling happily for the camera.

It was herself as a teenager, her hair still blonde, poking out from underneath the cheese hat. Her arm was wrapped around Theo's shoulder, a teenage version of Theo she'd never seen, though honestly still pretty similar to the girl she remembered.

And Summer had never been to the Wisconsin Dells in her entire life.

"What the fuck," she murmured, shaking her head. "This is… Photoshop, right? Some kind of AI thing?"

Theo rolled her eyes. "The picture metadata has the date. And feel free to scroll through, there's more."

Summer did just that, scrolling backwards through the camera reel. Lots of selfies of her and Theo together. More than a few of just Summer, lounging around, playing video games, reading manga. One particularly striking one had her standing on a scenic overlook, framed by the setting sun, looking back at the camera with a smile.

She couldn't remember ever smiling that much as a teenager.

Her heart was pounding in her chest. None of this made any sense. Either Theo was the world's most dedicated and creepiest stalker, or…

"How? Why?" she managed to spit out, her voice shaky.

Theo shook her head. "I don't know. For me, yesterday, everything was normal. I moved back to this town. Then I woke up, and things were different. It was like I didn't exist. My new roommate didn't recognize me. My stuff was gone. My car was gone. My phone wasn't working. My credit card wasn't working. It was all weird, but a normal, *possible*, kind of weird. But then I saw you at the cafe. Someone who's supposed to be dead."

Summer sat back down on the swing, running her hands through her hair. "What the fuck."

"And now we have different memories of each other. So I don't really know what happened or how, but my best guess is that I… somehow crossed over into an alternate universe or something. Maybe a parallel reality where things happened differently?"

"That's impossible. That's just sci-fi bullshit."

Theo shrugged. "I agree, but, well, I'm here, and *something* clearly happened."

Summer pursed her lips, trying to put it all together in her head. "So you're saying… the Theo I bullied… the one I hurt, is still out there, somewhere? There's two Theo's?"

"I don't know for sure, but I think so. I think the other me accepted the same job I did, but backed out at the last minute. No idea why, or who she is as a person though."

Deep breaths. Summer looked up at Theo. Looked at her again this time, as a young woman she'd apparently never actually known. She watched the panic and pain flicker in Theo's eyes every time she looked at Summer.

She looked back down at the phone again, at the photo of herself, smiling. That happiness was dead and gone, apparently. Stolen from the world too soon. "Fuck. This is all just… fuck. I'm so sorry."

"I already told you. I'm not the one you need to apologize to."

Summer shook her head. "It's not that. I mean, I guess that's still a problem, but… how you must have felt when you saw me. That's worse than anything I could have imagined. Like, Jesus Christ. How are you even functional right now?"

"I'm not," Theo said, looking away. "I'm fraying at the edges. I feel like too little butter spread over too much waffle. Honestly, I've kind of been like this for a long time. Childhood trauma does that to a motherfucker." She laughed. "But yeah, no. Not doing great."

"Okay." Summer stood up and started pacing back and forth. "Okay. This is a lot to process. I'm barely handling it, but you're doing worse. Okay. Maybe we need to both take a step back. Get some sleep. Take some time to think things through. Deal with it in the morning. Where are you staying? I can give you a ride."

Theo bit her lip.

Summer groaned. "Right. You don't have a place to stay, because you're from a parallel reality. Okay. Um. Riley might be willing to—"

"No," Theo said forcefully. "I've imposed enough on her already today. She deserves better than to have to deal with my bullshit."

Honestly, Summer couldn't argue with that. Riley did deserve better. "Okay." She pulled out her phone. God, it was so late. "Who the hell do I know that would still pick up…"

"If you can get me to a hotel, that would be enough. I might still have enough cash for one night."

Summer opened her mouth, sighed, then shook her head. "No, that's stupid. I don't think hotels even let you book without a credit card on file these days anyway."

"Alright then, fine. I bet I could get away with sleeping in the office."

"Come on, that's even stupider. Let's just…" Summer pinched the bridge of her nose, already regretting what she was about to say. "You can crash at my place."

Theo stared up at her, expression unreadable. "I don't want to make you have to deal with my bullshit, either."

"Yeah, well, a little late for that." Summer shrugged. "There's something clearly fantastical going on here. I can deal with a little bullshit. We'll figure something better out in the morning."

It took a long time for Theo to respond, but she finally gave a small nod and whispered, "Okay."

Crap. Was this the wrong move? Summer was the spitting image of Theo's dead best friend. Maybe the right thing to do would be to stay as far away as she possibly could.

But… well. She was a part of this now, whether she liked it or not. She didn't want to hurt Theo any more than she already had. So she'd follow Theo's lead on what she was comfortable with.

That would have to be enough.

~

As Theo stepped into Summer's apartment, she could immediately see that it was a total shithole. The tiny little kitchenette lacked a stove or oven. The rest of the place was split between a cramped and narrow bathroom, and a single bedroom, dirty clothes strewn across the floor.

"Give me like five minutes to clean up." Summer said, pushing her way into the bedroom and closing the door. "You can have the bed."

Right before the door closed, Theo was sure she caught a glimpse of something large and purple on Summer's nightstand.

Which made sense, Summer was an adult woman, who presumably lived alone, and god Theo did not have the brainpower to process this right now.

"Where are you going to sleep?" Theo asked, raising her voice a little so it would carry through the door.

"I've got a plan," Summer said. "Don't worry about it."

Theo worried about it anyway, at least a little. She thought back to when they were younger. She and Summer had sleepovers all the time. They'd usually share the same bed. It was totally platonic, no matter how much Theo might have wished otherwise.

She couldn't even dream of asking for something similar now. It would destroy what fragile remnants of her psyche were still intact.

She looked around the apartment, trying to take in the personal touches of the woman Summer had grown up to become.

The fridge was the main canvas, covered in magnets and stickers. Photos of Summer with a large group of kids. Logos of various bands. A large bi flag. A sticker of a cartoon egg with a cracked head and the caption 'Egg Breaker'. Several stickers that said 'Protect Trans Kids.'

A laugh bubbled up from Theo, unbidden, a little crazed. What an insane way to learn that Summer maybe hadn't been straight either.

"Alright, that should be good," Summer said, opening the door back up. "There's some phone chargers by the bed. I set out a clean pair of pajamas too, it looks like we're about the same size. Feel free to grab water or whatever you need, help yourself to any food as well. I'm gonna run out and grab a few things from the corner store."

Something brushed against Theo's leg, and she looked down to see a big orange tabby. "Mousey?" she asked reflexively.

Summer winced. "Mousey passed away a few years back. This is Chester."

Theo reached down to scratch behind his ears. "Nice to meet you, Chester." She glanced up at Summer, her lips pursed. "Where exactly are you sleeping? It doesn't look like there's anything else in here."

"It's fine, don't worry about it." Summer flashed her an all too familiar grin that made her feel faint. "There's a little nook where I curl up and nap sometimes."

"Okay. Sure." Theo made her way into the bedroom. There were a number of band posters on the wall. Another bi flag hung above the mattress, which didn't even have a box spring.

"Thank you," Theo murmured.

"Of course, no problem." There was a sense of guilt in Summer's eyes. Maybe she thought this was a way to make up for the things she'd done to the other Theo.

But well, Theo was projecting a lot here too. So what did it matter?

"Alright. I won't be gone long. Holler if you need anything." Summer left, leaving Theo alone in a stranger's room.

Would she even be able to sleep tonight? Theo would try anyway. She put on the pajamas, plugged in her phone, climbed under the covers, turned out the light.

She thought it would be too much, that she'd lie here for hours processing this living nightmare she was dealing with.

But exhaustion won. Her worn out brain couldn't handle anymore.

As she drifted into sleep, she was struck with a sense of familiarity. A memory that she hadn't even known that she still remembered.

It smelled like Summer.

Dear Diary,

I turned 11 today!

We had a nice, fun little party at my house, with my grandparents, and aunts and uncles all coming over to visit. Summer was my only friend there, but I'm really glad she made it.

Of all the presents I got, my favorite was the telescope my dad got me!

It's cloudy tonight, so we couldn't do anything with it, but Summer is going to spend the night tomorrow, and hopefully we can look at the stars together!

Theo
6/30/2009

Theo woke to the sound of her phone alarm.

She fumbled around, trying to turn it off, but ended up knocking it off the nightstand instead.

With a groan, she sat up in bed, blinking the sleep out of her eyes. She should have turned off the alarm, given how late she got to bed.

Which… should she even go to work? Did it matter? She was in some kind of parallel reality. She should be figuring out how to get home, not worrying about her career.

But what if she was stuck here for a while? What if she could never go back at all? She'd need money, a place to stay.

Would she even be able to do that much? She wasn't legally a person in this world. If there was another Theo, they probably shared the same social security number. If Theo tried to open up another bank account, get another credit card, it'd probably get flagged as some kind of identity theft.

The phone was still screaming at her. She bit her lip. These thoughts, these problems were too big to tackle right after waking up. She needed to step back. Exist in the present for a moment.

In a present where Summer was still alive.

Except that wasn't true, was it? Summer—Her Summer, was dead. Nothing would change that. This Summer was a different person entirely.

Theo turned off the phone, stood up and stretched. Rubbed her eyes. Reached for her anti-anxiety meds, which weren't there. Another problem that would likely become a much bigger problem if she didn't solve it soon.

She made her way out into the kitchen, and was immediately greeted by Chester. Poor guy was probably used to having free reign of the bedroom, but had been locked out last night. Summer wasn't in the kitchen or the bathroom.

She found a new toothbrush, still in the package, lying on top of the bathroom sink. How thoughtful.

Brush her teeth. Shower. Use Summer's shampoo and conditioner. Her body wash and moisturizer. Smell like Summer.

At least she felt a little more like a human being afterwards, instead of a lump of meat stuffed full of stress and anxiety. She slipped the borrowed pajamas back on, not sure what she should do for clothes otherwise. She only owned the one outfit, and it definitely needed to be washed after the events of yesterday.

Summer returned at that moment, to save her from her deliberation. She opened the front door, dark circles under her eyes, her hair disheveled, wearing only a tanktop and a pair of sweatpants. "Morning," she said through a yawn.

Theo's breath caught at the sight of her. Part of it was the spike of trauma that came from seeing a walking ghost. The other part, well.

With everything else going on, Theo hadn't really had the presence of mind to actually *look* at Summer until now.

She'd grown up, in so many different ways. Taller, more filled out, and she carried herself with an easy confidence and swagger that leant a purpose to every movement she made. Such a difference, from the awkward teenage girl she remembered, always trying to overcompensate for everything.

Summer stretched her arms above her head, her tanktop lifting to reveal her midriff, and Theo couldn't help but notice her visible abs, and lean strength. Did she work in physical labor? Did she spend a lot of time in the gym? The latter seemed hard to imagine, but... ten years could change a lot.

"You alright?" Summer asked, voice hesitant.

Theo blinked, and shook her head, pulling herself out of her thoughts. "Sorry, just... you know. Everything. I'm fine. What about you? You look like you slept terrible."

"Nah, it's fine. Was a late night, that's all. Went and took a walk around the block to clear my head. You eaten anything yet?"

"No, not yet." It was surreal. Standing in a kitchen, talking to Summer. As if nothing was out of the ordinary. As if talking to the dead was normal.

Theo took a deep breath, and pinched herself on the arm, hard, focusing on the pain.

"Cool. When you get dressed we can go downstairs and get something from the bakery. Oh, and you can meet Pete. Great guy."

"I don't have anything to wear. And I have to go to work in an hour."

Summer blinked. "Oh right. Capitalism. Is that... really the highest priority, considering what's going on?"

Theo shook her head. "Probably not. But if I burn my bridges now, and then it turns out I'm stuck here..."

"Didn't even think about that. Shit. Alright. Guess it makes sense to play it safe. Feel free to borrow whatever you want from my wardrobe. I've got at least a few things in there that should be appropriate."

"Thanks." Theo paused, thinking for a moment. "Don't you have to go to work too?"

"Nah. Well, I do, but I work second shift. At a gas station. Not the greatest but, I scrape by."

Was that sad? It felt sad. She thought back to being a teenager, discussing the future with Summer. Theo had always had such big dreams. She'd go to college and study astrophysics. Summer would come with her, of course. They'd get an apartment together, like Best Friends do.

But Summer had always been listless about it. She'd struggled to picture any future at all. Her teachers scolded her. They told her she'd be stuck in a dead end job at a gas station if she didn't buckle down and apply herself.

Of course, Theo had robbed her of even that possibility.

"You okay?"

Theo realized that her fists were clenched, her whole body tense. She forced herself to relax, unclenching her jaw. "Yeah. I'm fine. I'm probably going to do stuff like that a lot, considering, you know. Everything. PTSD sucks."

Summer grimaced. But it wasn't a grimace of pity. It felt like a grimace of understanding. "Yeah. It does."

They sat in silence for a moment, and then Theo turned away, closing the bedroom door behind her.

Summer had a lot of band t-shirts, crop tops, various alternative fashion styles. But Theo was able to find a nice pair of jeans, and a cute sweater. It was a little warm for it, but the air conditioning in the astronomy building had been on the strong side, so it would do.

She came out a few minutes later to find Summer sitting at the table, petting Chester.

Theo put on the best smile she could manage at the moment. "You said something about a bakery?"

~

Summer brought Theo to the bakery downstairs. The door gave a fun little jingle as they walked in, and the smell of fresh baked pastries washed over them.

"Hey Peter!" Summer called out, grinning widely. "How's the morning treating you!"

Peter laughed jovially from behind the counter. "Summer! My favorite upstairs neighbor. I don't usually see you up this early. And you've brought a friend, too." He shot her a sly look.

Better cut that assumption off quickly. She gave a quick shake of her head. "This is Theo. I'm, uh. Helping her get back on her feet."

"Nice to meet you, Theo. You can call me Peter! And..." He trailed off, staring at Theo a little closer. "Hang on a second..."

Summer turned to look down at Theo, who shifted uncomfortably.

Crap. Was this someone else Theo had some weird alt universe history with?

"I know you!" Peter slapped his fist into his palm, his face lighting up. "We went to school together. Theodora Smith, right? You moved away in what, fifth, sixth grade? But, I never forget a face."

Theo rubbed at the back of her head. "Yeah. That's me alright."

"Gosh. Time flies." Peter shook his head, still smiling. "Well, welcome back! Town's changed a bit since then, as I'm sure you've noticed. Here, let me get you something. Consider it a homecoming gift."

"Oh no, you don't have to—"

But Peter had already grabbed a danish from below the counter. "Any food allergies I should know about?"

"I have the thing where cilantro tastes like soap, but nothing else."

"Excellent!" He handed the danish over to Theo. "My treat. You know, I remember I always wanted to be your friend when I was little. But it never seemed to work out."

"You did?" Theo frowned, then glanced over at Summer. Probably something more relevant to the other Theo's memories. "I uh. Was a bit awkward as a kid, so sorry."

Peter's eyes widened a bit, and he shook his head. "Oh, no, no, I didn't mean it like that, it was nothing to apologize for. If I remember correctly, you moved away because of bullying, right? I only heard rumors, but... I was pretty angry about it. I helped organize a whole anti-bullying campaign and everything. Dunno that it was effective, but I believed in it at the time."

"That's... very sweet of you."

Now it was Summer's turn to feel awkward. She remembered that campaign. She'd come back from her suspension, to find that the entire school had turned hostile to her. The fear she'd once inspired in others had vanished, replaced with contempt. It was a lesson she'd needed to learn, but god it had been a kick in the gut at the time.

Peter frowned, looking at Summer. "Wait, wasn't it actually you who..." He blinked, and looked between Summer and Theo again. "Huh. Well, I guess we've all grown a lot as people since those days."

Summer winced. She wished that was true. But she hadn't actually bullied *this* Theo. The real one assuredly still hated her guts, for good reason. There was no absolution to be found here.

Theo glanced at Summer. "It's... complicated. But we're working on it, I guess." She took a bite of the danish, and the way her face lit up afterwards was kind of cute. "Oh damn, this is really good. Kind of forgot how hungry I was."

Peter laughed, the sound rich and jovial. "It's nice to meet you again,

Theo. If you ever need anything, anything at all, just let me know. I can always—"

The door to the shop opened up.

Aaron walked in, as tall and muscular as always.

There was a beat of silence, and then Peter finally called out, "W-welcome! Good to uh, see you, Aaron!"

The confidence and cheer that Peter greeted everyone with had vanished, replaced with a nervous energy, and Summer could see his blush hiding under his ginger beard.

Summer rolled her eyes.

Aaron smiled, in a way that he didn't for most other people. "Morning, Peter. Can I get two dozen donuts? Gonna bring 'em to work."

"Wowza," Peter said, completely unironically. "You must be the most popular guy at the factory, with how many donuts you're always bringing for everyone!"

"Uh, yeah." Aaron rubbed the back of his head. "People can't get enough of them, I guess."

"Uh-huh," Summer muttered. She crossed her arms over her chest. "'People' can't get enough of these donuts, which is why you specifically come here every morning to get them."

Aaron blinked, then turned to look at her. "Oh, hey Summer. You're up early. And…"

He squinted his eyes, his expression growing hard. "Hold on. You're the crazy lady who broke into my house yesterday."

Summer turned around to see that Theo had ducked behind her. Her face was bright red.

"Um, hey," Theo said, raising her hand in a little wave. "I'm uh, terribly sorry about that."

"What's this?" Peter asked, head tilted to the side.

Theo folded her hands together in front of her, looking like she wanted to be anywhere else but here. "I was, um. I have a sleep disorder. And your house was, well. My old childhood home. I think I was… sleepwalking? And very confused when I ran into you. I had um, run out of my meds, so I was, um…"

Summer frowned. Theo had mentioned something about that last night. She should have asked for more details. Theo was apparently a terrible liar.

She stepped forward, imposing herself between Aaron and Theo. He was ultimately a big softie at heart, but he could be quite intimidating. "Sorry about that. It's kind of a long story, and well. A lot of personal medical stuff. I'll be keeping an eye on her from now on, you won't have anything to worry about."

Aaron sighed and shook his head. "I mean, it's whatever. As far as I can tell she didn't take anything. I didn't bother to call the cops. Just… it scared the crap out of me."

Theo bowed her head. "I'm sorry."

"Maybe we can start over. I'm Aaron Peterson." He held out his hand.

"Theo Smith." She stepped out from behind Summer, shaking it.

"Well that's great, looks like we're all friends here," Peter said, with an edge of forced cheer to his voice that usually came naturally to him. "I've got your donuts here, Aaron."

Aaron turned back to Peter, a genuine smile returning to his face. "Thanks. I'll, uh, see you around."

With his donuts in hand, Aaron paid, then left, leaving Peter behind with a dopey smile.

"So," Summer said, resting her hand on her hip. "When are you going to ask him out?"

Peter groaned, and rested his forehead on the top of the counter.

Theo glanced at the door, then back at Peter. "Wait, what? I thought you two were married. This wasn't all just some elaborate bit?"

"Married? Gosh, no." Peter let out a sigh, staring out the door. "I don't think he'd ever want to have that kind of life with someone like me."

Summer pinched the bridge of her nose. "He's *clearly* into you, Peter. He comes here like every day."

"I've got a lot of regular customers!"

She sighed. "Whatever. Theo's got to get to work. Don't have time to give your dumb gay ass a pep talk."

Peter rolled his eyes. "Love you too, Summer."

Summer headed for the door, Theo at her heels.

Theo called back. "Thanks again for the pastry. It was nice to meet you!"

"See you around, Theo!"

Once outside, they made their way back up to the apartment, opening the door to her kitchen.

"Wow," Theo said, grinning. "I'm almost positive they actually were married in my reality. Guess some chain of events made it so that didn't happen here."

Summer shook her head. The whole thing was still so hard to believe, to wrap her head around. "Makes sense, I guess. It feels inevitable, for them. They both need a swift kick in the ass to get around to it."

"It's kind of adorable."

"It's infuriating, is what it is." Summer sighed. "Lemme grab my wallet and keys, then I'll give you a ride to campus."

Theo frowned, then shook her head. "It's only fifteen minutes. I'll walk. It'll help me clear my head."

Summer paused. "You sure?"

"Yeah. You've done enough for me already."

Could Summer *ever* do enough to make up for the things she'd done to Theo?

Except this wasn't the same Theo, and she couldn't let herself forget that. Nothing she did here would earn her any forgiveness.

~

Theo still had a lot of problems to deal with.

But after all the chaos that was the previous day, they seemed a lot more manageable.

She wasn't haunted, she wasn't crazy. Of her myriad predictions, the most dire hadn't come to pass.

She had a working hypothesis that seemed plausible. And she had some thoughts on where to start looking for the how and why, and what next.

But in the meantime, she had simple mundane problems to tackle. And those too, were imminently manageable.

Other than of course, the problem of Summer Sullivan.

Was… she really a problem? She was just a person. Completely unrelated to anything she knew, other than by appearance. And the sound of her voice. And the way she smelled.

And Summer had been gracious enough to listen to her and believe her, and help her. That wasn't a problem. She was a confidant. Maybe even a friend.

All of that was still a little too overwhelming. She would focus on the mundane stuff for now.

This time, she was fifteen minutes early to her new job. She'd made an absolutely terrible first impression, but maybe it was still salvageable.

Riley was working at the front desk when Theo stepped through the door. She had on a stylish pink jacket, and she was wearing a pair of glasses. She looked up, smiling brightly when she saw Theo.

"Heya!" Riley waved, her voice cheerful. "Glad you could make it back today. How's it going?"

Theo paused, hovering in the doorway for a moment. Riley had been so kind to her yesterday, helping her, telling her about Summer, sitting and chatting with her about nothing in the hours it took Summer to respond to the request to meet. An absolute gem of a person.

With the lack of a response, Riley's smile faltered, somewhat, but she kept it going, waiting patiently.

Theo waved back, forcing her own smile. "Hey. It was… a long night. But I'm still alive, and willing to give a hundred and ten percent. Yesterday was a fluke, and it definitely won't happen again."

Riley nodded slowly. "Sure. And like I said before, Jerry's an under-standing guy. There's nothing to worry about.

An awkward silence fell over them. Theo made her way closer to the desk. She wanted to say something, explain herself, impart understanding, so she didn't seem so pathetic. But there was no way she could be honest without seeming crazy.

"That's um, a cute sweater," Riley said, biting her lip. "I used to have one just like it."

Theo blinked, and tugged at the sweater she was wearing, a light beige with some floral patterns in its stitching. "Oh. Thanks? I'm just borrowing it."

"Borrowing…" Riley narrowed her eyes slightly, and she leaned for-ward a bit, sniffing the air. "Oh. That might literally be my sweater. You must have crashed with Summer last night. I guess… you were able to resolve your differences, huh?"

There was a slight edge to Riley's voice, that she hid behind her prac-ticed smile.

Theo winced. "Yeah, we uh, had a lot to talk about. Was pretty late when we finished, so she let me crash at her place."

"Very generous of her. I don't remember her having a spare bed though."

"She let me take the bed, said she was sleeping in some corner or nook somewhere." Theo pursed her lips. "I was a little too absorbed in my own problems to ask earlier, but it does kind of seem like you dislike Summer. Can I ask why?"

Riley raised an eyebrow. "Weird to hear that coming from you. But you're right. I'm not the biggest fan of Summer right now."

Theo licked her lips, then gave voice to the worry she'd been avoiding in her heart. "Was Summer the ex you mentioned? The one who cheated on you?"

"Not... exactly." Riley let out a long sigh and looked away. "Summer and I did date for a little bit. But that was years ago. She helped me figure out a lot of things about myself, and it was a pretty amicable breakup. We were good friends... but then my ex cheated on me with her."

"Fuck." A strange mix of relief and disgust settled in her gut. How could Summer do something like that to someone? But Summer had already done so much worse, to the other Theo, hadn't she?

Riley rested her chin on her palm, and drummed on the desk with her other hand. "Look, in Summer's defense, my ex lied. Said we'd had a big blowout fight, and that I'd hit her, that we'd broken up. She came to Summer full of tears and flattery."

Theo shook her head. "That's not an excuse. Even if you had actually broken up, it'd be a huge dick move."

"Yeah. You're right. It was." Riley pursed her lip, and it trembled slightly. "But the truth is, I like Summer. She sucks a lot sometimes, and I'm still super mad at her. I'm not ready to forgive her yet... but I want to be, eventually. It's complicated."

"Believe me. I know complicated, when it comes to Summer Sullivan."

Riley looked up, a soft smile on her face. "Guess we've got something in common, then."

Jerry took that moment to walk into the room, and he called out, "Theo, hey there. Got a minute to talk?"

Theo stiffened, and a flutter of panic swept through her. Maybe her fuckups yesterday were more serious than she thought.

Jerry smiled at her. "Relax, you're good. I just want to have a conversation about what we can do to help accommodate you with whatever you might need to succeed."

"Oh. Sure, I can do that."

Riley looked up at her, grinning? "See? He's a big softie. Do you wanna grab lunch again?"

Theo felt herself relax. "I'd like that. Except, well. There's a few errands I need to run. If you could maybe give me a ride, I'll treat you to some fast food?"

"Sure, sounds good to me. See you at one?"

"See you."

~

Summer stared at the clock on the wall, tapping her foot impatiently. Only a few more minutes until her shift at the gas station was over and she could clock out.

"Alright, alright, this one's going to do it, you'd better watch."

"Uh-huh." Summer spared a glance for her coworker, Minha, who currently had a rubber band stretched between her fingers, a paper projectile carefully balanced on the makeshift slingshot.

Minha squinted, her aim careful. She released, and the little paper triangle soared through the air, smacked right into the top of a pringles can, which clattered off the shelf onto the floor.

"Yes! I am the champion!" She cheered. She held her hand out for a high five.

Summer slapped it half heartedly, but she couldn't keep the grin from her face. "You sure are. I'm not picking that back up though."

Minha stuck her tongue out, then went over to fix her mess. She was all of five nothing, cute as a button, athletic as hell, and dumb as a box of rocks. But she was probably one of Summer's closest friends, and made working in this dead end job tolerable.

She was also, luckily, straight as an arrow. They could just be best buds, without any of the complicated dyke drama that so often soured Summer's other friendships. Drama that was usually Summer's fault, one way or another.

The door to the gas station opened with a chime, and Summer turned to see Chet walking in, here to relieve them and take the night shift.

He took one look at the dozens of paper projectiles littering the floor and said, "I'm not cleaning that up."

"I'm on it, I'm on it!" Minha called, already jogging off to get the broom. "I totally nailed it though!"

Summer laughed, and gave an exaggerated shrug. "If at first you don't succeed…"

Chet rolled his eyes. "You could try actually working."

"Uh-huh. I'm sure you get soooo much done at the night shift. It's so utterly busy, hardly a moment off your feet."

He grunted. "You know as well as I do that when the bars let out it can get pretty hectic in here. Maybe I'll tell the boss what you've been up to, he'll give you a taste of the graveyard again."

Summer raised her middle finger. "Fuck off, narc."

"Slacker."

A beat passed, and they both laughed. Summer punched him in the arm lightly.

She didn't actually like working with Chet that much, but their antagonism was mostly a friendly one.

At least she hoped it was. Where was the line, and when did it cross over into bullying? Given her track record, she probably shouldn't push things so much.

Minha finished sweeping. "Let's get out of here," she said, taking a bite out of an ice cream sandwich.

Chet raised an eyebrow. "Did you pay for that?"

"The box was damaged!"

With a heavy sigh, he went to actually clock in, and Summer and Minha left him to manage the gas station alone.

They walked together down the street, the cool night air welcome.

"You wanna hit up a bar?" Minha asked.

Summer shook her head. "Nah. It's Tuesday. Only people out drinking are the sad old townies."

"What, too afraid you'll end up like them someday?"

"Shut up." Summer leaned over and nudged Minha with her shoulder. She of course, shoved back, and packed a surprising amount of force into her tiny frame.

"Come on. I've got tomorrow off, I wanna do *something*," Minha whined.

Summer grimaced. "Sorry, but you're on your own. I've got some stuff I need to take care of."

"Boooo." Minha's lips curled into a pout, which was adorable. She paused for a moment. "Is this more stuff about Heather?"

"What? No way. That was a one-time mistake. This is something else. It's… complicated."

"How so?"

Summer bit her lip. She normally told Minha just about everything, but… what was she supposed to say about Theo? It was still such a big thing to try and wrap her head around. She'd done a bit of searching on the internet this morning, but everything she found was either science fiction or some advanced physics paper theorizing that such a thing could technically be possible by using a bunch of terms she couldn't understand.

Minha clicked her tongue. "Alright, fine. I'll guess. Let's see, what could be worse than you banging Heather while she was still dating Riley… oh I know. Did you seduce some married woman?"

"Just how low of an opinion do you have of me?"

"Or wait!" Minha snapped her fingers. "I forget since you're always with women, but you're bi, right? Maybe you seduced the husband, too! And neither of them know about the other! Gosh, what a tangled soap opera your life must be. How do you keep track of it all?"

Summer shoved her again.

Minha laughed, the sound of it a delightful cackle.

It was hard to keep the grin off her face. "But seriously," Summer said. "I'm helping out a friend. She's going through some stuff, which I'm not at liberty to talk about."

"Geez, should have just led with that." Minha rolled her eyes. They came to a stop light, and Minha yawned. "Whatever. Going alone will be lame, so I guess it's tiktok and chill for me tonight. Later, Summer."

Summer waved goodbye, and watched as Minha left down the cross street.

Only a few more blocks to go. Would Theo still be waiting there for her? Summer was glad to help her however she could, but being around Summer was probably traumatizing as all hell. Not to mention the possibility that Theo could simply blip back into her own reality at any time. It wasn't like they had any idea how this worked,

Her fears were misguided, and turned into new fears, when she opened the door to her apartment to find her kitchen a disaster.

_7_

Dear Diary,

Tonight was amazing!
  Summer was really grumpy about it at first, saying that it was dumb, that it was pointless, but she sure shut up once she got to see Venus for the first time!
  We spent hours looking at all the stars and planets and the moon and I had my skychart out and was able to name them all.
  It was magical.
  Like it was just the two of us, together in another world entirely by ourselves.
  We're camping out in the fort tonight, Summer's currently passed out on the beanbag while I'm writing this. I'll curl up in the sleeping bag soon, I promise.
  But... I really hope we can keep doing stuff like this forever.

Theo
_7/1/2009_

Theo looked up to see Summer staring in the doorway, looking baffled.
  "Hey!" Theo said, smiling to see her despite herself. What a confusing jumble of emotions it was every time she saw Summer, The sheer joy of being able to talk and interact with her again. The guilt, because it wasn't really her. And the fact that, despite wearing dark slacks and a tucked in polo as a work uniform, objectively unsexy fashion, Summer looked so _damned good._
  "Uh, hey." Summer raised an eyebrow as she stepped into the kitchen and closed the door behind her. "You uh, look like you've been busy.
  Papers littered the table, and Theo had hung up a corkboard, which

she'd stuck several notes to already. She blinked a few times, and felt her cheeks color. "Riley helped me run some errands. I got a new sim card, and picked up some office supplies with the last of my cash, so I'm flat broke until my first paycheck. I guess I thought it was important to organize thoughts about this whole 'other world' thing, you know?"

Summer laughed, and shook her head. "Sure, sure, I get it. I tried doing a little bit of searching myself, but didn't find anything useful. Unless, maybe, you got hit by a truck? That came up a lot."

Theo snorted. "No trucks, so I don't think this counts as an isekai."

"I don't know what that means."

Oh. A small needle inserted into her heart. It wasn't much, but there were an awful lot of needles in there already.

Her Summer knew what that meant. They'd poured through manga, watched anime together, made fun of the genre in all its silliness. But that had all mostly been at Theo's behest.

"Did you feed Chester?" Summer asked, oblivious to her inner turmoil.

Theo took a deep breath, and let it out slowly. "I didn't know what to give him. He's been very talkative though. I'm pretty sure that means he's literally starving to death because he's never eaten in his life."

Summer laughed, and shook her head. "He'd like you to believe that. But it's all good, you're not expected to feed him or anything. Just wanted to make sure he wasn't trying to double dip." She unlaced her doc martins, then started going through the cabinets. "What about you? Did you eat?"

It was far too easy to ignore minor details like 'being hungry' when Theo was focused on something. "Not since lunch."

"Cool. I'll make some mac and cheese."

"Getting the real five star experience here, I see."

Summer turned to her, resting a hand on her hip. "Sorry, but I'm not much of a cook. I can order pizza if you want something else."

Theo winced. "No, sorry. Mac and cheese is fine." What was she doing, sassing Summer? To her, Theo was a complete stranger that she was going out of her way to help. She had no reason or obligation to help Theo at all, so she should be grateful. They didn't have a rapport, they didn't banter.

"Sure, sure." Summer set a pot of water on a small hotplate, then made her way into the bedroom, closing the door behind her. When she came out, she'd switched out of her uniform into shorts and a large, loose t-shirt.

And no bra, Theo noticed before quickly averting her eyes. God, what was she doing? A part of her felt like she was sixteen again.

Summer stretched, her back popping audibly. "So, what's with the conspiracy board?"

Better to focus on the situation at hand, rather than old and dead fantasies. "It's not a conspiracy board. It's a way to organize all my notes and the information I've gathered. Normally I would have used my laptop, but it's still back in my home world."

"This is an insane thing, so it's a conspiracy board." Summer opened her fridge and pulled out a bottle of beer. "You want one?"

Theo shook her head immediately, a tightness in her throat. "No, thank you. Alcohol interferes with my medication. And… even without that, I don't really like drinking."

Summer studied her thoughtfully. "Do… you want me to not drink around you? It's not a big deal, I promise."

"No, no, that's fine. And it's your house, I couldn't…" Theo trailed off, the words stuck in her throat. She wrapped her arms around her stomach and looked away, unable to finish her words.

Silence hung in the air for a few moments, followed by the sound of the fridge opening, and a beer being put back on the shelf.

God, Theo was pathetic.

Summer stepped next to her, her thumbs in her pockets, and she leaned over, studying the papers scattered across the table. "So, what do you got? Any brilliant insights?"

Theo licked her lips. "Uh, not exactly. Well, I've ruled out a few things, I guess. And, the fact that Peter wasn't married in this reality made me wonder what else could be different. Butterfly effect and all that. But I spent some time trawling Wikipedia, and it seems like our worlds are pretty much the same, in terms of major historical events. Same presidents. Same wars. Same plague. Same celebrity deaths. What variations there are must be much smaller and on a personal scale."

"Huh. Didn't even consider that." Summer scratched her head. "Guess the butterfly isn't that powerful after all."

"It's… both comforting and a little disheartening at the same time. Good to know I don't have a completely different history to try and navigate here but… it kind of hammers home that one person can't really make a difference, huh?"

"Not people like you and me, anyway." Summer sighed, then pulled away from the table to study the corkboard on the wall instead. "So, our worlds suck equally. That's something I guess. What else you got?"

Theo pulled her phone out. "I've confirmed that there's definitely another me in this reality. Found some references in news articles for a high school science fair, found her social media. Honestly, I wouldn't be surprised if she uses the same three passwords I do, so I could probably hack into her email or bank if I needed to. But... feels wrong, somehow."

She showed the photos she found to Summer, who stared at them impassively.

"She looks like you. Dunno what I was expecting. Maybe a different haircut?"

Theo shrugged. "This one suits me fine."

"Right. Well, let's avoid the two of you ever meeting, because who knows if you'll cause some kind of paradox and melt into goo if you touch each other."

"I highly doubt that's how this works, but avoiding her is probably good for multiple other reasons." Theo adjusted her glasses. "But... that's about all I have that's concrete. Everything else is speculation."

"Hmm." Summer made her way back over to the pot of water, now boiling, and dumped noodles into it. "Not much to go on, there. You said you woke up one morning, and you were here?"

"Well..." Theo paused, getting her thoughts in order. "The biggest question I'm grappling with right now, is; Was this a random event, something that happened by chance? A phenomenon that could be exploited? Or was there... a will, of some sort, behind what happened?"

Summer glanced over her shoulder, eyebrow raised. "What do you mean by a 'will'?"

"Like, did some person, or some*thing* want this to happen? Is there a point to it? A god? An angel? A devil? Some kind of alien? Some sort of eldritch horror? Is this a science problem? Or a me problem?"

"Devils and aliens, huh? I dated a girl for a hot minute who was super into aliens and UFOs. Was cute at first but she took it a little *too* seriously, you know? But what do you mean by a 'me' problem?"

Theo twitched slightly. Which was stupid. Of *course* Summer had a dating history, she knew that already. Theo had her own dating history. It wasn't any of her business. "Have you ever seen 'It's a Wonderful Life'?"

Summer frowned. "…No? Well, I don't think I've ever sat down and watched it, but I kind of know the gist of it. It's all about an angel showing a guy how the world would be without him, right?"

"Well, it's mostly about community and also how much banks suck. The angel bit is actually pretty short, and only happens at the end of the movie."

"Really? Shit, that actually sounds kind of cool."

"Eh. Anyway, that's kind of the question. Is there some kind of entity that brought me here for a reason? Am I supposed to learn some kind of lesson about myself, by seeing this world in which we never became friends, in which you never died?"

"Or," Summer said, crossing her arms over her chest. "Is it like life normally is—a series of mostly random, unrelated events caused by the choices we make, with no overarching narrative connecting them?"

"Yeah. That."

"Huh." Summer rubbed at her chin. "Which would you prefer?"

"I…" Theo faltered, and stared down at her notes. "Both are terrifying."

"Cool." Summer poured the noodles into the strainer, then back into the pot, before mixing in the cheese powder. "Dinner's ready."

Theo stacked her notes into a pile and set them aside, then the two of them ate together in silence.

Flavor wise, the noodles were adequate, but once Theo started eating she remembered that her body required sustenance in order to function. Keep going, push forward, never look back, run until you drop. When she stopped, she had to actually feel it all. The ache in her muscles. The strain in her brain, run ragged by emotions, pushed further by attempts at deduction.

If she didn't keep going, she would fall apart, a dinner plate shattering into pieces when it finally hit the ground. All she had to do was fall forever, and she'd be fine.

They finished, and Theo was quick to grab Summer's bowl and her own, and take them to the sink. "Let me wash them, at least."

Summer gave a half shrug in acknowledgment, and then leaned back in her chair, hooking her feet on the hinges beneath the card table.

No dishwasher here either. But a pot, a strainer, two bowls, and two forks was hardly a monumental task to hand-wash. Easy enough.

"I think we should focus on the assumption that this is some sort of phenomenon, rather than an entity who wants you to learn something," Summer said from behind her.

Theo glanced over her shoulder, eyebrow raised. "How come?"

Summer gave a slight smile. "Well, its a matter of where effort is best spent, y'know? If you do have to come to some sort of emotional revelation then... what's the plan of action there? It's not like you can speedrun something like that. So if that's what you need, then it'll probably happen on its own while you're spending time investigating the other possibility."

"That's... an astute observation. Huh." Theo snapped her fingers, applying a rhythm to her suddenly racing thoughts. "Well, it's also a possibility that if there's some sort of entity involved, they're not actually doing it for my benefit. Maybe its random cruelty, or they'd need something else, like a virgin sacrifice or something. But even if that's the case, then it's still likely the entity will make themselves known, sooner or later. So investigating some sort of unrelated phenomena still seems like a better use of time."

Summer snorted. "If it's a virgin sacrifice we need, I *definitely* don't know anyone who qualifies."

Theo crossed her arms over her chest. "You don't know anything about me. I could be a virgin."

"Nah. You fuck. I can tell."

She felt her cheeks heat up, and she found herself leaning a little closer to Summer. It almost felt like flirting, didn't it? But... no. She needed to hit the breaks on that as hard as possible. She cleared her throat, and mumbled, "okay, sure."

Summer grinned. "Anyway. Weird phenomena. Where do we start? Like it's some kind of wormhole or something, and we've got to reverse the polarity of a tachyon beam and bounce it off the deflector dish?"

Theo blinked. "You watch Star Trek?"

"Sure. My ex—UFO girl, actually, got me into it. It's good shit."

Another thin needle inserted into Theo's heart, like acupuncture of the soul. She'd tried over and over again to get Summer to watch Star Trek with her, but Summer had a stubborn streak a mile long, and if she arbitrarily made up her mind about something, nothing could change it. In this case, that Star Wars was superior, and that Star Trek was boring and dumb, which she'd concluded having never watched an episode.

Theo pinched the skin on her arm, twisting and wrenching hard, letting the pain of it pull her out of a far deeper pain.

Summer noticed, her face scrunched up with concern. She opened her mouth but... didn't say anything and closed it again.

She loved Summer for that.

Which was a wretched, unacceptable thought. She broke its bones with a baseball bat, and threw it out back beside the dumpster, never to be considered again.

Instead, Theo sat back down at the kitchen table, her breathing carefully controlled and measured.

"So," Summer said, her voice a little wary. "Walk me through exactly what you remember, step by step, as much detail as possible. From when you last remember being in your world."

Easy. Simple. Theo started recounting her day. Waking up in the hotel room from a nightmare. Talking to her mom. Driving through town, seeing how it had changed. Meeting Peter and Buddy. Dinner with Peter. A night spent carelessly browsing the Internet.

A pull of nostalgia. A trek to her little fort, her hideout, her sanctuary. The manga she used to read with Summer. Her telescope, still working. Skygazing on the roof. The stars, vast and beautiful above her. Mars. Venus. Jupiter. Saturn.

"And then... I saw something a bit strange. Moving through the night sky. And when I focused the telescope on it, it turned out to be a comet."

Summer perked up at that, still furiously scribbling notes. "A comet, huh? Could be something. Comets are weird and mystical, right? Lots of portents and prophecies ascribed to them."

Theo shook her head. "It's just a ball of rock and ice hurtling through space. It gets that distinctive look with the tail when it gets close enough for the ice to melt. Nothing mystical about it, just physi—"

Hold on. There had been something else, hadn't there? Her sentiment, her overwhelming nostalgia. She'd wanted something, said something in that moment, while gazing upon this visitor from beyond the solar system.

I wish I could have seen this together with you, Summer.

There it was. An expression of desire, followed by something strange. The comet had seemed to flash, her telescope had broken. It didn't make sense compared to any known physics, but there was a clear pattern.

If she was right, she had a clear path home. All she needed to do was to view the comet together with Summer, and her wish would be fulfilled. Then she'd probably be whisked home once more.

And she'd never see Summer again.

Her breathing came in short, ragged gasps, her ears ringing. A panic attack was slithering up her spine, wrapping itself around her, crushing her organs, choking out reason and sense.

"Theo?" Summer asked, her voice full of concern, but it sounded distant, muffled.

Theo wrenched control of herself with brute force, wrestling that serpent to the ground, strangling it, breaking its spine. She trembled, but forced a smile onto her face. "Sorry. I'm uh, feeling a bit overwhelmed by it all. I think I need to go lie down for a bit. The comet is maybe a good lead, though. I'll ask Riley about it tomorrow."

Summer bit her lip. "Sure. You uh, need anything else before bed?"

"No, I'm good. But thank you. You've been a big help." Theo stood up, her steps careful, balanced. Not wobbly.

"Anytime," Summer said, like she actually meant it. But why, though?

Theo couldn't bear to face that question. She made it into the bedroom, and closed the door behind her.

Summer's bed was waiting for her, with its poisonous, familiar scent. Theo fell into it, wrapping herself in its tangled web, covering herself, drowning in it.

She pressed her face into the pillow, and screamed as quietly as she could.

⁓

Summer sat alone in her kitchen, unsure of what to do with herself.

It was a little too early to go to sleep, still. And with the way her muscles protested, she wasn't exactly champing at the bit to return to her sleeping arrangements.

Someone else in her space made it hard to relax. Her books and drawing supplies were all still in the bedroom, so she wouldn't get anything done there.

And Theo was... well. She still didn't know what to make of Theo. If they'd met as strangers, had no past with each other on either end, Summer was sure she'd have liked her. She was cute, funny, a good conversationalist. Definitely queer. Summer would flirt, and Theo would flirt back, and they would fall into each other, make some undeniable memories, and Summer would fall desperately in love until Theo wised up, realized that Summer was a loser with no future, and moved on. That was how the story always went. She'd made peace with it.

But they weren't strangers. Summer had ruined one Theo's life. And this Theo had been devastated by another Summer's loss. It was too much, too complicated, too much baggage. It would all have to be completely hands off.

Chester rubbed up against her legs, purring.

"Hey buddy," Summer said, leaning down and scratching him behind the ears. "What do you think of our new roommate, huh?"

From her vantage point, Summer noticed that Theo had left her phone on the kitchen chair.

Summer frowned, then reached out and grabbed it. Did she have a charger out here, somewhere? Would be good to set Theo up for tomorrow.

As she moved the phone around, the screen lit up with a notification from some mobile game, and she was presented with the lock screen.

Summer stared at it for a few moments, chuckled to herself, then punched in her own birthday, just for fun.

It worked.

She immediately shut the phone off, her heart pounding in her chest. She'd only been joking, she hadn't meant too—

Summer glanced towards the bedroom door and bit her lip.

It wasn't like there was anything on Theo's phone she was interested in, anyway.

Except…

It would be wrong, wouldn't it?

But didn't she also have a right to know?

Her mouth dry, Summer opened the phone back up, and unlocked it again. She went for the camera app, and scrolled back to the very first photo.

It was a blurry picture of Summer, circa 2010, looking annoyed at being photographed. Not even a teenager yet, her hair still its natural blonde. Long and wavy, before Summer had worked up the nerve to try out styles that suited her better.

She kept swiping, and saw a selfie of Theo and Summer. Then a few pictures of various stuff around a nice home, new books, a video game. A birthday cake, that said Happy Birthday Theo.

And then a family picture. Theo, and Summer, and two people who could only be Theo's parents. An older teenaged boy who must have been her older brother.

And in this photo, of Summer standing with someone else's family she looked... awkward and uncomfortable, for sure. But there was a spark in her eyes all the same, a hint of a genuine smile underneath her feigned indifference.

Who was this girl, really, this other version of Summer? One who had a best friend, and a confidant. A family that welcomed her with open arms, gave her a place to be herself, a place to be safe.

Summer kept scrolling through the photos. Context was clear that this birthday party likely resulted in Theo getting her first smartphone. And she used her newfound powers of a camera at every opportunity. There were a lot of pictures of various objects, foods, sunsets. But just as many of Summer.

Watching a life she could have lived, in small snapshots. A happier life, a better life.

She'd done her best to try to become a better person, as an adult. She'd unpacked her own trauma with therapists. She'd done her best to reconcile with those she'd hurt. She wasn't perfect. She still fucked up, still made mistakes, still hurt people. But she'd built a life, a moral framework, something to hold on.

Her change had taken a lot of hard work, a lot of time. It had taken maturity, perspective, able to look back on her past actions and understand her own behavior, instead of lashing out.

Or, that's what she'd thought it required, anyway. Apparently, if the right person had reached out to her, at the right place, at the right time. If she had reached out, accepted someone else's outstretched hand instead of spitting on it... it all could have been avoided.

Summer felt tears brimming in her eyes. She closed out of the camera app, locked the phone once more, and set it back on the table.

What a weird feeling, to be jealous of yourself, even when she was dead.

8

Dear Diary,

I lied to Summer today.
I thought if I told her the truth, she wouldn't want to be my friend anymore.
I don't want that to happen.
I hope she never finds out.

Theo
10/31/2010

Theo woke up to the sound of her alarm, but it was distant, muffled.

She sat up in bed, rubbing at her eyes, trying to shake away her confusion.

She felt... well rested. For everything that was happening, for everything she was going through, she'd expected to be plagued with nightmares, to be tossing and turning all night.

Instead, it was some of the best sleep she felt like she'd had in a long time.

Blackout curtains on the windows kept things dark. Important, for someone working second shift.

Her phone alarm was coming from outside the bedroom, in the kitchen. Had she left it out there?

The alarm cut off, and a few moments later, there was a soft knock on the door. "Hey, your alarm was going off," Summer called from outside. "Also, I made eggs."

"Be out in a sec!" Theo stood up, stretched, and turned the light on. She looked through Summer's closet again, finding a nice blouse, and another pair of jeans, then set them aside for after she showered.

When she stepped out into the kitchen, she paused, taking in the simple sight of Summer standing in front of her hot plate, cooking eggs in a pan.

She remembered once, waking up in her bed after a sleepover, when they had the house to themselves, and going downstairs to find a kitchen full of smoke, Summer having catastrophically failed in her attempt to make breakfast. They'd ended up eating bowls of cereal instead.

The memory would normally come with all sorts of pain but... here and now, it brought a smile to her face instead.

Summer smiled back, which made Theo's stomach flutter a bit. "Morning." The dark circles under Summer's eyes did nothing to diminish her cheerful demeanor.

"Morning." Theo let out a yawn, and stretched, pressing her hands against the top of the doorframe. "That smells good."

"Just eggs. Don't got any cheese to go with it, or anything else really. Cash is a bit tight for me, but I was thinking maybe once you get your first paycheck we might want to go grocery shopping. Assuming you're staying, anyway. Maybe this comet thing will pan out."

Right. The comet. A wish she'd made. It was so obvious; such an easy fix. Theo bit her lip. "I'll see what Riley has to say, I guess. But... right. I still don't have a bank account. And I don't think I can convince my boss to give me cash. Hmm."

"You wanna use my bank info?"

Theo made her way over to the kitchen table and sat down. Her phone was resting on it, plugged into a charger. That was sweet of her. "Would that be okay?"

"Sure. If it's only a temporary thing anyway, I can withdraw whatever gets deposited and give it to you in cash. Saves you from fucking up other Theo's credit score or whatever."

Summer dumped the scrambled eggs onto two plates, then made her way over to the table and placed one in front of Theo. She sat down across from her, and started digging in.

Theo took a bite of her eggs. They were a little overcooked, honestly, but eggs were eggs. She chewed slowly, her mind racing. It felt so... weirdly domestic, sitting here eating breakfast with Summer. She could easily picture this in her life, had her Summer lived. The two of them, sharing an apartment, eating breakfast, discussing their plans for the day.

It was a different Summer. But it still felt a little like everything she'd ever wanted.

"Is it really… okay?" Theo asked, trying to be nonchalant as she ate, and failing. "Me staying here? I really appreciate all you've done for me, and it means a lot, but I could always try and figure something else out. I don't want to be a burden."

Summer raised an eyebrow, swallowed, and took a drink from her glass of water. "You're not a burden, Theo. But also, I totally understand if you want to find something else. I can be difficult to get along with even normally, and I don't imagine my face being a living reminder of someone else helps with that."

Crap. That wasn't what she wanted. Theo sucked in a breath through her teeth. "It's not that, I promise. It's hard, sometimes, sure. But that's my problem to deal with. And… I don't know. You're so similar to her, and also so different, sometimes. Maybe it's selfish of me, but I kind of want to get to know you. But you shouldn't have to deal with that either, and all of the expectations I have."

"Mmm." Summer set her fork down, and met Theo's gaze, her emerald eyes intense. "Look, it's not every day I meet a girl from another dimension. I want to help you, Theo, however I can. I get that it's messy, but… I get the impression we're both being too midwestern and polite here, so let me be clear. As long as you're okay with it, I'm okay with you staying here."

Theo wanted to look away, but couldn't. "Okay. As long as you're okay with it, I'm okay with staying here."

Summer grinned. "There. Problem solved."

"Okay. Problem solved."

~

"A comet?" Riley asked, looking up from her computer.

Theo leaned over the desk, resting her elbows on it. "Yeah. I was stargazing with a backyard telescope a few nights ago, and I thought I saw a comet. Just interested to know more about it. What it's called, how long it's visible, that kind of thing."

"Huh." Riley clicked her nails against the deck. They were cute, long, and had patterns of constellations on them. "I think I remember seeing a notice or something about that, in terms of like, visible astral bodies for the month. Let me check."

She started typing on her computer, her face scrunched in concentration. A stray strand of hair had fallen loose from her ponytail, and she blew it out of her face. It was incredibly cute.

"Okay, here it is." Riley turned the monitor, so that Theo could see it. There was a blurry picture of a comet there, along with a bunch of listed statistics.

"It's BTKC21. Not exactly one of the big fancy ones people care about. But hey! A comet is a comet, right?. Fun to look at, especially if you've never seen one before."

Theo stared at the blurry photograph, suddenly feeling incredibly silly. Was she completely off base here? It was just a random space rock. How could it possibly grant wishes, listen to her will, transfer her to an alternate dimension?

But at the same time, she *was* in an alternate dimension. So something had to have done it, and this had the most direct causal link. It wasn't like she had any other leads. "How long is the comet visible?"

Riley turned the monitor back, scrolling down slightly. "Looks like… the last day of easy visibility from this hemisphere should be September 22nd. Assuming good weather, anyway."

That was… a little over 4 weeks from now. Summer's birthday. And the day she'd died. It all made sense, in some sort of twisted way.

She could take Summer, show her the comet, her wish would be fulfilled, she'd presumably be sent home, and this whole dream would be over. If it didn't work, there would still be more time to figure out if she needed to do anything else with the comet.

Simple. Easy. Over in a flash, only a few days of strangeness, and then back to her own world, her own life.

"Theo?" Riley asked, sounding concerned.

"Yeah, no, sorry, I was thinking about something." Theo forced a smile. "Thanks so much for the information. BTKC21, right? Guess comets are kind of a dime a dozen, but it was really cool to see unexpectedly, you know?"

"Sure, definitely. My Dad showed me a comet with our backyard telescope when I was like eight and well," Riley gestured around the room. "here I am."

Theo's smile became a lot more genuine. "Yeah. Same, honestly. My

Dad bought me my telescope for my eleventh birthday, and, god. There's so much wonder in it, you know?"

Riley bit her lip. "If you want… like I said. I have access to the university telescope. I could schedule some time with it, we could look at the comet together."

"I—" Theo started, but then cut herself off. What the hell was she doing, anyway? Riley was cute, and sweet, and Theo liked her. But she was going to be gone soon. This wasn't her reality. Even if all the normal self deprecations Theo would use to pull the brakes failed, this one was huge enough to derail the train entirely.

Even if, under normal circumstances, there was nothing more she'd want to do.

Theo's expression must have betrayed her, because Riley looked away, and let out a sad sigh.

"Nevermind. I'm sorry, I must have really misread some things here. Please ignore me."

"It's not that." Theo groaned, and pinched the bridge of her nose. "Look, I'm the one who should be sorry. I'm going through a lot of stuff right now, my mental health is in the toilet, and I can't… be the kind of person I want to be, I guess. And I'm barely capable of being a good friend, let alone any other kind of relationship."

Riley kept her eyes down, and idly traced circles on the desk with her finger. "It's my fault, really. I have a tendency to daydream a lot, and when I meet a cute girl that goes into overdrive. And then my assumptions turn out to not be mutual and I'll get sad and cry about it later and then things will be fine. Just the way I am."

Theo's heart wrenched at that, and a part of her wanted to do whatever she could to staunch that pain. But that would be worse, in the long run. "It's not… *not*, mutual. Under better circumstances, I'd be all for this. For you. I just… mean it. I can't handle it right now."

"I understand." Riley looked up, still smiling, even if it was sad. "Is that… door opened a crack, maybe sometime in the future when things are different? Or should we close it entirely?"

"Close it entirely." Theo took a deep breath, and forced herself not to look away. "I'd still like to be your friend, but I understand if you wanna back off a little."

Riley nodded. "Well, I'd like that too, Theo. Luckily, I'm very good at compartmentalizing, I promise." She gave an exaggerated wink.

Theo snorted with laughter. "Sorry for being so dramatic."

"I dunno. I kind of like it." Riley's eyes twinkled. "There's an intensity to you, must drive the girls crazy."

"Uh…"

Riley laughed. "Right, sorry. I'm pretty flirty with people I'm friends with, too. But I'm shelving all expectations and hopes that it goes anywhere. And I can tone it down, if you want."

"No, it's fine."

"Right." Riley smiled her perfect smile. "Good talk. You still wanna grab lunch later?"

"Sure do. But I guess I'd probably better get to work."

"See you later."

Working second shift sucked.

And while that was pretty much a constant, Summer always felt that the most keenly when there was someone at home waiting for her.

More than a few of her relationships had fallen apart because they were unable to handle the strain of only seeing each other briefly in the mornings and then only for an hour or two before sleeping at night, never time to go out, to do anything fun. Especially since Summer was so often scheduled on weekends.

But what could she do? Her willingness to work shitty hours was one of the only reasons she'd managed to keep this job. And it wasn't like she had the education to get anything better.

That was her lot. She'd accepted that long ago.

Still, there was a small thrill that ran through her when she opened the door to her apartment. When there was someone there, who saw her, smiled, said hi, seemed happy to see her. Especially when that person was a gorgeous woman with long dark hair that would be perfect for running her fingers through, and an intense gaze that seemed to strip all of Summer's defenses bare.

But this wasn't the kind of arrangement where Summer could get excited about that. She needed to remember that.

"How was work?" Theo asked from where she sat at the kitchen table. There was no flurry of notes this time, no frantic energy of discovery.

Summer shrugged, then knelt down to pet Chester. "Shitty. Some drunk guy puked in the freezer, and I lost rock paper scissors and had to clean it up."

Theo's face fell. "Is that… a usual occurrence for you?"

"Nah." Summer waited a beat, and then grinned. "Normally I'm the one who wins."

Her joke fell flat, and Theo looked at her sadly. Oh well. The horrors of retail were best coped with via comedy. Summer changed her focus, and sniffed the air. "Is that—"

"Oh, yeah!" Theo sat up a little straighter, beaming. "I cooked some ramen for you, and put some eggs in it and everything."

"Wow, fancy." Summer found the ramen in a pot, and then a clean bowl to put it in. "Thanks. Did you eat already?"

"Yeah, I had some ramen too."

Summer sat at the table and started eating. God, when was the last time someone had made her food, even something as simple as ramen?

Chester meowed loudly, rubbing against her leg.

"Yeah yeah, you're next buddy."

Theo fidgeted in her seat, something clearly on her mind.

Summer raised an eyebrow. "So, anything from Riley, about magic comets?"

"Right. Yeah, I talked to her." Theo carefully folded her hands together on the table, and looked away. "I'm pretty positive the comet is the culprit. It'll be visible until September 22nd, and it won't work again until then."

"Huh?"

Theo bit her lip. "Well, the night I came here the comet was in alignment with Mars. And on September 22nd it will be in alignment with Venus. I looked up some mythology stuff too, and Mars has a whole connotation with traveling, and Venus has one with coming home. So, uh. Yeah. Seems pretty straightforward."

Summer stared at Theo, her lips pursed. Something about Theo's demeanor felt off. It almost felt like she was lying. But… it wasn't like Summer knew Theo well, to know her tells. And Theo had every reason to be awkward and uncomfortable in her presence.

"Okay…" She said, carefully. "So we gotta wait until then. Easy enough, I guess. Still, it sounds a little farfetched. Might be worth pursuing other angles in the meantime, just in case."

"Sure, of course." Theo rubbed her hands together, clearly agitated. "I mean, I'll handle it, you don't have to worry about it. Keep poking at other options and whatnot."

Summer finished eating her ramen. This whole conversation still felt off. "Are you sure you don't want—"

"Hey!" Theo said, a little too forcefully, a little too loudly. "I don't want to think about magic comets anymore. Seems like there's some waiting to do so… I dunno. Can we maybe get out of here? Go somewhere? Do something?"

Not what she had expected. Summer watched Theo carefully, trying to understand her agitation. "Sure, if you want. Where do you wanna go? I assume not a bar?"

Theo took a deep breath, and relaxed visibly. "I could do a bar, if that's what you want. I won't drink, but it's really not a problem. But also, like, I dunno. What spots do you like to go to, around town? Parks? Shops? Nightlife? Anything weird and interesting? I'm down for whatever."

"Not much open this late." Summer doubted that Theo was *really* down for whatever, but she didn't think she'd need to push her, in any case. "I know somewhere chill though, if that's the kind of mood you're in."

"Sure. Chill is good."

9

Dear Diary,

Yesterday we went camping, just got back!

    It was incredible fun. We ate smores, and my brother played some songs for us on his guitar.

    Summer complained a bunch about the heat and the bugs, but late at night when everyone else was asleep she woke me up and told me she had something cool to show me.

    She took me down to the lake, and the moon was full and reflecting off the water and it was all so beautiful.

    Then she picked up a rock, whipped it into the water and it bounced like five times!

    She got a bunch more impressive throws after that. Then she started teaching me how to do it, how to hold it properly, how to pick the perfect rock.

    Most I ever managed was three bounces, but it was still so much fun. I'm getting excited all over again thinking about it.

Theo
8/11/2011

Theo had lied to Summer.

It was all she could think about, as she sat in the passenger seat of Summer's car, staring out the window and watching the town turn into farmland turn into wilderness. That she'd lied, utterly, blatantly, selfishly. Mars and Venus were in alignment? What complete bullshit.

She should come clean, tell Summer the truth, take her to view the comet, and end this whole farce.

But the simple fact was that she didn't want to do that. She wasn't ready to go home.

So she'd lied. She'd put off going back to her own reality until the last day the comet would be visible, in a little under a month.

And now she'd stay with Summer. Leech off of her generosity. Soak in her presence like it was a drug, like she'd fallen off the wagon after a decade of being clean. Drown in her own indulgence.

Selfish. Pathetic. Disgusting. Creepy.

"We're here," Summer said, putting the car into park.

Theo blinked, pulling her awareness out of her mire of self loathing, and back to the world around her.

They were in the state park a few miles outside of town, parked close to a large lake. She'd come here often enough when she was younger, camping with her family, sometimes with Summer. This particular spot was unfamiliar to her.

"I come here sometimes when I want to be alone, or want a chill place to hang with someone, you know?" Summer sounded a little embarrassed, and climbed out of the car.

Theo stepped out as well, stretching. The air coming off the lake was cool. "Is this a fishing dock?"

Summer shrugged. "Yeah, pretty much. Definitely see people come here a lot during the day. Empty at night though. Come on."

Summer started towards the dock, down steps carved into a hill, until they were level with the lake. The dock swayed and creaked underneath them. Summer reached the end of it, pulled off her boots, rolled up her leggings, and stuck her feet into the water. "It's pretty, isn't it?"

Theo opted not to get her feet wet, but sat down next to Summer, folding her legs underneath her. The sky was clear, and full of stars. A little less light pollution. The still water of the lake reflected the sky above, an infinite cosmos above and below. A sliver of a crescent moon peaked over the horizon.

Somewhere up there was a comet, barely visible with the naked eye. If Summer happened to glance at it, would Theo blip out of existence? Somehow she doubted it, but she would deserve it.

"Yeah. It's beautiful."

Summer leaned back a bit, propping herself up on her elbows. "Is this kind of what you had in mind for something chill? I've got a few other ideas, if you'd like."

Theo shook her head. "This is perfect. Thank you." She'd push it all down, her pain, her terrible sin. Enjoy this for what it was. An impossible chance to connect with Summer again, even if it was temporary. Engrave it into her memory, her soul. What could have been.

"Cool, cool." Summer gave her a soft smile.

A silence fell between them, but the world was far from silent. Trees rustled in the breeze. Insects and frogs sang their sweet serenades. Somewhere distant, a splash from something jumping into the water. The distant hooting of an owl claiming its territory.

"So," Theo said, glancing over, summoning up a spark of playfulness. "How many other girls have you taken down here to try and impress?"

Summer started, glanced at her, then looked away. "Ah, well." She rubbed at the back of her head. "It's not like that, this spot helps me relax, that's all."

Theo laughed. "I know, I'm just teasing. Although I guess, boys too? You're bi, right?"

"Yeah." Summer paused, then frowned. "Well, maybe. I'm not entirely sure, honestly."

"It's always been only girls for me, but... comphet is a hell of a drug."

Summer shook her head. "It's not that. It's more that nearly every guy I've dated has ended up, well. Not being a guy. So I wonder sometimes."

"Oh. Sounds complicated."

"A little. Though honestly it was super funny after like, the third time it happened." Summer grinned, then stood up. She walked back to the shore, and started looking for something. Eventually she picked up a flat stone, and tried to skip it. It sunk into the water with a loud plunk.

Theo turned to face her from where she was sitting. It was a little chillier than she'd been expecting. She should have brought a jacket. "You've mentioned a lot of ex's... I guess nothing has really worked out for you?"

Summer remained silent, as she searched for another stone, and tried to skip it too. It also failed. "Depends on how you define 'worked out', I guess. I tend to keep things pretty casual. We have fun. We part on good terms. There's more to success than 'you get married and have kids and stay together until you die', you know?"

"Is that what you want?"

"Dunno. Don't have much else to compare it to." Another stone. This one managed one bounce before sinking. "I'm not exactly someone most people can envision a future with, you know? I can kind of be an asshole, I'm stuck in a dead end job. After being with me, my ex's always seem to have a better grasp of who they are, what they actually want out of life. I suppose that's not a bad role to be in."

Theo bit her lip. She'd always dreamed of a future with Summer. But that was the twisted perspective of a baby lesbian with a crush. She was an adult now. If she looked at things objectively, had met Summer as a stranger, would she really think that? Or would she maybe be a fun, casual fling, and nothing more?

A dangerous place to let her thoughts go.

Summer looked up, and met Theo's gaze, her emerald eyes reflecting the starlight. "What about you? Is there a sweetheart waiting for you, back in your own reality?"

The question caught her off guard, and Theo blinked several times, gathering her thoughts. "No, there's uh. Nobody. The few relationships I've been in have... all ended messily. Turns out all my trauma and baggage means I don't make for a very attentive or good partner."

"Mood."

They sat in silence for a bit longer, as Summer continued trying and failing to skip rocks.

Theo pulled her knees in close, shivering. "It's funny. Kind of thought I might be able to have a thing with Riley. New job, new coworker. She was cute, gay, single. But then I met you, and realized that I'm in another reality, and, well. That's as big of a dealbreaker as they come, you know?"

Summer shrugged. "Shame. Riley's great, even if she hates my guts for good reason. Honestly I bet the two of you would work out pretty well together. Maybe there's another Riley in your reality, you can meet up with her when you get back. Tell her she comes highly recommended. Four and a half stars."

"What's the last half star?"

"Terrible circulation, her hands and feet are frozen. Nothing quite like being woken up in the middle of the night because you accidentally brushed your thighs against a block of ice."

Theo burst out laughing. She held up her own hands. "I've got the same problem, I'm afraid. Guess that half star will be permanently out of my reach."

A beat passed between them. Crap. Had she said that? That was too much. She was dancing on the edge of a pit, one wrong step and she'd fall into a hell she could never come back from.

"Just occurred to me," Summer said, frowning. "Is time passing at like, the same rate in your world? Is it gonna be one of those things where you come back the moment you left, or are you gonna show up and find that you've been missing for a month and there's like cops looking for you and stuff."

If Summer had noticed her slip up into blatant flirting, she'd thankfully decided to ignore it. Still, that was a sobering thought. "I hadn't thought about that. Crap. My family will be so worried..."

A casualty of her selfishness. How much would her mom worry, if Theo was missing for a full month? Gone with no trace. Would Peter and Aaron be considered primary suspects? Their own lives turned upside down by her adventure in another world?

She could turn that all around, right now. It had only been what, three days? Easy enough to explain her absence without anyone getting too worried.

"Well, I hope for their sake it's the former. Gonna be hard to explain otherwise." Summer made her way back up the dock, standing next to Theo.

Theo pulled her arms and legs in even closer, burying her head in her shins. She had to come clean. She had to—

Something covered her shoulders. The smell of old leather. Summer's jacket.

If she told them the truth, her family would understand. She could bring proof. She already knew her photos would carry between realities. Theo took a deep breath, then stood up, slipping her arms into the jacket properly. "Thanks."

"Sure. Forgot that it gets a bit chillier down by the lake, should have said something before we left."

Theo pulled out her phone. "Hey, come here. I wanna take a selfie."

Summer raised an eyebrow, but leaned in close, pressing her body against Theo's, her breath hot against Theo's neck.

The lighting was dim, but her phone had a pretty decent night photography mode. With a longer exposure it corrected the image so that their faces were visible, night sky and lake visible behind them.

She'd have to take a lot more photos, infallible proof. That this was all real. That it was all worth it.

"Thanks for bringing me out here," Theo said. "Honestly, just what I needed." She wandered back down the dock, to the shore where Summer had been skipping rocks. She reached down and shifted through the pebbles there, feeling them in her hand, testing them for weight, shape. Finally she found one that was perfect.

A simple flick of her wrist. And then one. Two. Three. Four. Five. Six bounces, before it finally sunk into the water.

Summer whistled appreciatively. "Damn, that's nice. Who taught you how to do that?"

Theo looked to her, a soft smile playing at her lips. "You did."

~

It was harrowing, the way life kind of went on, after something that felt so big, so monumental. Theo was living a lie, stealing something that didn't belong to her. Polluting this world with her presence.

But she still woke up in the morning. She chatted with Summer. They went downstairs to the bakery, got some pastries. Chatted with Peter, watched him awkwardly fail to flirt with Aaron. Watched Aaron be just as awkward back.

And then Theo was off to work. To her new job, which wasn't really her job, which she'd be leaving in a month. She had lunch with Riley, and enjoyed it, even if Riley had dialed things back a little. Then she was back home to Summer's apartment, finding ways to kill time until Summer got home. The guilt gnawed at her, and made it hard to relax, to focus on browsing the Internet, so she ended up cleaning the entirety of Summer's bathroom. To justify her presence in Summer's life, in some small way.

And then Summer was home. They ate dinner. Decided to stay in tonight. Summer had a TV in her bedroom, a hand me down from a friend who'd upgraded to a better one. She hadn't specified if it was another friend she'd slept with, and Theo couldn't bring herself to ask. She shouldn't even care. It had nothing to do with her. Less than nothing.

But despite maybe being a good fifteen years old, the TV could still handle an HDMI cable plugged into it from Summer's laptop, and so they watched some K-drama Theo had been meaning to check out.

Honestly it was pretty mediocre at best. But that didn't really matter. She was watching it with Summer. Theo in her borrowed pajamas. Summer in shorts and a tank top that really showed off her figure. Her muscles were well defined, and Theo couldn't stop herself from peaking at the way her back flexed when she moved or stretched. Summer had mentioned going to the gym as a part of her morning routine, probably after Theo went to work.

And then it was late, and Summer went off to… wherever it was she slept. And Theo was alone, in a bed that smelled like Summer, her body aching with yearning.

But taking care of herself in Summer's bed would be a step too far, a violation of trust, of boundaries. Too pathetic. Too creepy.

So Theo slept.

And woke up the next day to do it all again. Breakfast. Casual conversation. Off to work. It was Friday, which meant payday. Theo was able to get her paycheck properly deposited to Summer's account. They went grocery shopping. Summer drove them to the Walmart in the next town over, since the local grocery store wasn't open that late.

Together they walked through the aisles, buying staples, and more junk food than was strictly necessary. They griped about how expensive food was getting, about how evil Walmart was as a corporation, how they ruined local communities. It was, of course, a toothless critique, considering how they were still actively shopping there.

Theo also went out of her way to buy Summer some new kitchen accessories, including an air fryer. Some additional cleaning supplies. More phone chargers. A box fan for her room. Anything Summer wanted, or even so much as glanced at, and Theo bought it.

It felt so *easy* with Summer. Like putting on a comfortable, well worn pair of shoes. Slipping into an old and familiar dynamic. Easy conversation. Easy banter. Like they'd been friends for over a decade. Summer was different. But she was also the same. It was easy to see the trajectory that led from the girl Theo had once known to the woman she was now.

And for Summer's part, she seemed to fit right in on her end. Even though she had no reason to, no substantial connection to Theo other than guilt. She was probably like this with everyone, Theo knew, but a part of her wanted to pretend that she was special. That they had some sort of connection, that transcended reality, life and death.

Theo's capabilities for self delusion were truly astounding.

Their grocery trip over, their fridge stocked, Theo got ready for bed, brushing her teeth. Staring at herself in the mirror, the eyes of a liar reflected in her glasses.

"Hey," Summer called from the kitchen. "You wanna do anything tomorrow? I've got Saturday off."

A whole day. Not just bouncing into each other at the margins of where their lives intersected, but deliberately spending time together. A date. Not really a date. Theo spat out toothpaste, gargled water, spat again. "Sounds good to me. What do you usually do on your days off?"

Summer shrugged. "Hang out with friends, usually. Since my schedule is so fucked during the week, gotta get it in while I can, you know? If you'd prefer something more low key, that's fine too."

Theo stomach twisted itself into knots with anticipation. "I'd like that. To meet your friends."

Anything, to increase the amount of space she shared in Summer's life, even if only a tiny bit.

Dear Diary,

Summer got into a fight with her mom again.

I've never really met her mom, so I don't know her well. But Summer gets so, so angry. She was staying over tonight, and ranting about it. Honestly I could barely follow her train of thought. Something about not making dinner?

And Summer goes on and on, staying mad, getting more and worked up, shouting, mom had to yell at us to quiet down, and then Summer just kind of... broke. She started crying, which I almost never see her do. I didn't really know what to do so I hugged her close.

I wish there was something more I could do for her. We're best friends. She's practically my sister already? It would be nice if mom could adopt her or something.

~~I dunno. Would it be weird? Maybe that's too weird.~~

After she finished crying Summer got really distant and snippy for the rest of the night. The whole sleepover was kind of ruined.

I don't know what to do.

Theo
6/2/2012

"Yeah!" Fuck yeah! Get 'em Minha! Go go go!"

Summer stood up, cheering wildly as she watched Minha slip past the defenders and kick the ball past the goalie. Others in the crowd cheered as well, though attendance was sparse.

"Wow," Theo said from beside her, a wry smile playing at her lips. "I didn't know you were this enthusiastic about sports."

"I dunno that I am." Summer sat back down, grinning. The energy of sports games was always infectious, and she was glad that Theo seemed to be having a good time too. "But I like to support my friends, and I try to know enough about sports to hold a conversation. Can get you pretty far and make new friends you wouldn't otherwise."

"How very mercenary of you."

Summer laughed, then shrugged. "Hey, it works. Kind of like taking up smoking in order to get more breaks."

Theo blinked. "You smoke?"

"Quit last year. Still hard, though."

"Gross." Theo made a face. "But, that's good. My dad smokes, and he's tried to quit so many times, but it never quite sticks." She paused, then her brow furrowed in thought. "I wonder if my dad in this reality managed it. So many things could be different, you know?"

"Huh. Never thought of it like that. Kind of makes you curious."

"A little. Probably not worth sticking my nose into, though."

Summer spared a rare thought for her own mother, which instantly drew a sour expression to her face. Was her mother any different, in Theo's world, or still the same terror? How had she fared, after Summer's death? Maybe she had her come to Jesus moment and turned her life around? Far more likely that she self destructed even farther.

She decided she didn't want to know the answer, and banished the thoughts by cheering louder instead. "Come on, lets go! Show them who's boss!"

Theo adjusted in her seat, angling her body more to face Summer. "It is nice though, seeing you… so outgoing and cheerful about this." She had a low cut blouse on, her cleavage very prominent from Summer's angle. Which definitely wasn't something Summer should be paying attention to.

Wait, had she reminded Theo to put on sunscreen? Damn, if this was anyone else, Summer would offer to help put it on herself. Make it playful and fun and flirty.

She needed to focus. What had Theo said again? "The other me. She wasn't… outgoing?"

"Oh. Um…" Theo winced. Her cheeks colored slightly and she looked away. "Sorry. I didn't mean to compare you."

"Nah, it's fine. It can't be helped, and I've got to admit I'm pretty curious. What was the other me like?"

Theo nodded and took a deep breath. She gripped the fabric of her jeans, and didn't meet Summer's gaze. "I was the shy and awkward kid, and Summer was the outgoing and confident one. At least, that was how it always seemed to me at the time. She would open up with me, take charge, be full of confidence. But—and believe me, it took a lot of conversations with my therapist to fully understand this—she shut the rest of the world out at the same time. She was angry, and had so much derision for everyone and everything else out there. Getting her to unironically relax and enjoy something was like pulling teeth."

Summer felt a gnawing pit in her stomach, and she swallowed. "That, uh. Sounds like me alright."

"Sorry."

"No no, it's fine. I asked, after all." She sighed, and shook her head. "I apologize if this is insensitive, but… I think she must have been lucky, to have a friend like you."

Theo didn't meet her gaze, and she reached over and pinched the skin on her own arm, twisting it. "I find that hard to believe. And, well. Look at you. You're thriving, and I wasn't involved."

Summer snorted. "'Thriving' seems like a generous term for it. I'm getting by. But… I dunno. It was a long and hard road to get to where I am now. I'm proud of that, but when I was little… I really wanted someone, anyone to care. I put up a lot of walls, was an absolute little shit, but I wanted someone to climb those walls, push past my defenses, and care about me anyway."

"You were just a kid." Theo fidgeted in her seat. "I guess I did kind of do that. I had to be really insistent in the beginning, before we became friends. But… it feels wrong, that I had to. You deserved better from all the other people in your life."

"Ain't that the truth." Summer ran a hand through her hair. "Just being a kid isn't that much of an excuse. Look, you… the other Theo. She did reach out to me. I rejected her pretty harshly at first, but then I decided I could use her. I was cruel, and mean, but also pushy. I got her to do my homework for me. Other things. I kept escalating, she was a giant pushover. I used her as a tool for my own benefit, and as a punching bag for my own frustrations. Maybe I had a shitty childhood, but that's no excuse. I'm responsible for my own actions."

Theo grew silent, her head down.

How cruel, to know that fate can take such wildly different paths. Was this Theo slightly more persistent and friendly? Was the other Summer less of a bitch? Or was it a simple matter of timing? Who knew.

The crowd grew tense, anticipating something. Summer turned her attention back to the game, and—"Oh come on, what the fuck was that! That's a blatant foul! Do your job, ref!"

Theo burst into a fit of giggles.

"Theo?"

Laughing even harder, Theo shoved Summer, pressing their sides together.

Summer blinked in confusion, but shoved back, and felt a smile return to her face.

"Sorry," Theo said. She took off her glasses, and wiped at her eyes. "Just… the whole situation, your past, my past, it's all so fucked up and sad, and for a moment, it wrapped around into absurdity."

"I guess it kind of does." Summer chuckled.

Theo looked up at her, a dazzling smile on her face. "I just… I like talking with you. Whether it's about our fucked up trauma, or stuff like sports. That's all."

Summer smiled wide, and felt her face flush, that familiar and dangerous sense of butterflies twisting up her stomach. "Yeah, me too."

~

The game ran it course, and they won, 3-2. Summer cheered her loudest, and even Theo got into it a little bit.

They lingered in the bleachers as things wrapped up, the small crowd slowly dispersing. Eventually, Minha broke away from her team, and made her way over to them.

"Yo, Summer!" Minha called out, raising a hand as she grew closer. "Glad you could make it."

Summer grinned, then stepped down to meet her, clasping her hand. "Glad you actually won, woulda sucked shit to waste all that cheering for nothing."

"Fuck off," Minha said, laughing. She punched Summer in the arm, hard enough that it actually hurt a bit. "So, did you bring the new girlfriend?"

"For the last time, it's not like that. She's just a friend I'm helping out."

Minha rolled her eyes. "Yeah, I don't believe that for a second."

Summer sighed. "Just don't be weird. Anyway, yes. This is my *friend*, Theo." She gestured behind her.

Theo stepped forward, smiling, and held out her hand. If she was bothered by the insinuations, she didn't let it show. "Hi Minha, it's nice to meet you. Summer's told me a lot about you."

Minha shook her hand, and then as she actually got a good look at Theo, her eyes widened, and her mouth fell open. "Wait, what the fuck? *Theo* Theo? Like, Theo Smith? What the fuck?"

God dammit.

"Uh..."

"Dude, I haven't seen you in ages!" Minha said, breaking out into a wide smile. She pulled Theo into a tight hug. "Fuck, how many years has it been?"

Theo met Summer's gaze, panic in her eyes. "Sure, that's uh. How many, I wonder..."

Summer stepped forward as the hug broke apart. "How do you two already know each other?" she asked, directing her question to Minha.

Minha laughed, and ran her hand across her hair, squeezing her ponytail, her expression full of disbelief. "Theo dated my older sister all through highschool, and I think a bit of college? Dunno, they broke up, but like, I always thought she was cool."

Theo let out a relieved sigh. A piece of the puzzle was revealed. "Yep. Uh-huh."

"What exactly happened between you and Seoyun anyway? She never really talked about it to me. Kind of a shame, everyone thought you two were gonna make it."

Summer bit her lip. She could see how uncomfortable Theo was, but there wasn't a lot she could do to step in and bullshit in her place.

"Oh, you know." Theo fidgeted, holding her left arm with her right. "It's complicated. I'm uh, a different person than I was, when you knew me. And I guess it didn't work out."

Fuck, that was way too on the nose. Summer motioned to abort, but then Minha spoke up anyway.

"Shit happens. What brings you out to Bumfuck, Illinois anyway?"

God bless Minha and her lack of subtlety.

Theo laughed, and shook her head. "I grew up here, actually. But uh, got a job at the university. What about you?"

Minha gestured behind her at the soccer field. "Scholarship. But hey. You guys wanna go grab something to eat? We can catch up. Trade embarrassing stories."

"Oh, well, we, uh—"

A chance for Summer to intervene. "Don't you have a shift later today?"

"Pfft. That's in like three hours. Plenty of time to grab a bite. I only had a protein shake this morning, I'm starving."

Summer crossed her arms over her chest. "You still need to go shower. You go to work and funk up the place and Chet will blame *me*."

"Fuck Chet, he sucks anyway. And what are you, my mom? Come on, I wanna try that new burger place. Look, women's soccer needs all the support it can get, consider it a donation to the team."

"So now I'm buying too?" Summer nodded meaningfully at Theo. "Besides, we've got some *other* plans for today. Y'all can catch up another time."

Minha furrowed her brow, but then here eyes went wide, and she smacked herself in the forehead. "Oh! Duh. Shit, sorry. I get it, I don't want to be a third wheel. I'll bother you later."

"Thanks," Summer muttered.

"Have fun." Minha punctuated her words with some exaggerated eyebrow wiggling and finger guns. "I think I still have your number, Theo, so we'll figure something out later! I'mma go find some grub."

"Wait, my number is—"

But Minha had already turned and jogged off after one of her team-mates, probably to try and bum lunch off of her instead.

Summer pinched the bridge of her nose and let out a long sigh. "Sorry about that. Minha can be a little intense even under normal circumstances, but... sure as shit wasn't expecting her to know you already. Small world, I guess."

Theo had a distant look in her eyes. "Yeah. Just... a whole other life I have no context for. Hard to wrap my head around. Where is Minha from, out of curiosity?"

"Somewhere in Maryland, I think."

"See, when I moved away from this town, we ended up moving to Minnesota. But I guess other Theo went out east."

"Huh." Summer raised her hands above her head, stretching. "Well, guess that's another problem to deal with then. You wanna go grab something to eat? Without Minha?"

"Sure, I'd like that. But um… what do we do about her? I don't think I could bluff my way through a longer conversation."

Summer frowned, thinking it through. "Avoiding her would be the easiest. Although honestly if you told her that you were actually an identical twin switched at birth or something she'd probably believe it. She's not the brightest bulb."

Theo pursed her lip. "That feels kind of mean."

"Oh, uh." Summer winced. "I mean, I love Minha to death, but she… is what she is, I guess. I dunno."

"Is she… another one of your ex's?"

Summer laughed. "Nah. She's straight. Goes for tweedy hipsters taller than six feet, usually runs 'em pretty ragged."

Theo smiled. "Guess I can picture that. But… yeah. Let's grab something to eat. We'll figure the rest out later."

~

Theo collapsed onto Summer's bed, staring up at the ceiling. "Ugh, I'm beat."

Summer sat down on the edge of the bed, running a brush through her hair. She glanced over her shoulder at Theo and winced. "Maybe a little burnt too. Sorry."

"Oh. Right. The sun. Forgot about that." Theo touched her neck and shoulders, and they did feel a warm, and a little sensitive. "Doesn't seem too bad, at least."

"If it is bad, lemme know, I can run out and grab some aloe."

Theo shook her head, smiling. "I think it should be fine, but thanks." She paused for a moment, watching Summer. "And thanks for today, too. I had a lot of fun."

Summer shrugged. "Sure. It was no big deal."

It was a big deal to Theo, but she knew it wouldn't be the other way around. Just a regular day out on the town, nothing special at all. They'd eaten at a local diner. Walked around the town center, checking out all the various new shops that Theo didn't remember from her childhood. Examining tchotchkes, trying on fancy clothes, eating free samples at cheese shops and the winery. Perusing a gallery of local artists. Buying nothing.

All in all, it was a pretty good date.

"What's on the agenda for tomorrow?" Theo asked, trying to not sound too eager.

"No work, so whatever we want, I guess." Summer stretched, yawning. "My vote's for a lazy day doing nothing, though."

"Fine with me."

"Maybe binge watch something. I've been meaning to catch up on my—ah shit."

"Hmm?"

Summer fished her phone out of her pocket, and started checking it. "Damn, never mind. Forgot I do have something tomorrow. Guess you're on your own. I've already showed you where the spare key is so, you know. Whatever is fine."

Theo frowned. "What thing do you have?"

"It's, uh." Summer looked away, seemingly embarrassed. "I volunteer at the local youth center. Not a big deal or anything, I have a prior commitment is all."

"Oh." Theo felt her heart warm at that. "I mean, I'd love to come along and see that, if you don't mind."

Summer fidgeted uncomfortably. "I don't mind, but there's like, a whole process everyone goes through before you can actually interact with the kids. Background checks and interviews and stuff like that."

Theo's face fell. "Ah. Forget it then."

"Well, hmm." Summer looked between Theo and her phone. "If you wanted to come and watch, I could possibly spin some bullshit to the director there about you taking a class on child psychology or something and wanting to observe and take notes."

"Would that really work?"

"Probably. Bends the rules but doesn't quite break them in a way that might cause a huge problem, and the director likes me, so it shouldn't be too hard to convince him."

Theo leaned forward a bit, smirking. "Do you make a habit of coming up with elaborate lies to bring girls to places?"

Summer winced. "I... doesn't sound great if you put it like that, I guess. Easy enough to justify it as all pretty harmless, but... I really shouldn't be toeing that line. Sorry."

"What? No, sorry, that's not..." Crap. Theo pulled off her glasses, and rubbed at her eyes. "I was trying to make a joke. I do actually like the idea, and it does seem pretty harmless."

Of course, Theo was approaching it from the strong moral stance of 'I want to see Summer interact with kids, that sounds cute' which maybe wasn't the most convincing.

"Yeah, I guess. It's probably fine." Summer sighed, then stood up and stretched. "I always gotta be second guessing myself, you know? All that toxic shit doesn't unlearn itself, and can hit when you're least expecting it."

Theo pursed her lips, not sure what to say.

"Anyway. Should probably let you get to sleep." Summer made her way to her closet, and started fishing around in it. "Been meaning to grab this out of here though, it's just that I usually remember after you've already gone to sleep." She came out a few moments later holding a sketchpad and pencil case.

"You draw?" Theo asked, genuinely surprised.

Summer glanced at her, and angled the sketchpad towards her body, so Theo couldn't see anything on it. "Sure. It's only a hobby though, something I've picked up in the last five years or so."

"What do you like to draw?"

"Portraits, mostly. I like drawing people."

Theo smiled. "Can I see?"

Summer sighed, then flipped through her sketchbook, before turning it around to showcase a pencil drawing of Riley. "This one's more recent, I guess. Isn't too terrible."

"Holy shit," Theo breathed. "Summer, that's incredible. You're really good."

"Nah, the shading is off here, and I kind of fucked up the eyes. They're a bit uneven, and look a bit dull."

Theo rolled her eyes. "Never met an artist who could properly accept a compliment."

Summer's face was red, and she folded the sketchbook back up. "Don't go looking through this though, okay? Some of these are private."

"Pulling a real Jack Dawson, huh?"

"Who?"

Theo blinked. "Jack Dawson. From Titanic? Leonardo DiCaprio's character?"

Summer shrugged. "I saw it once like a million years ago. Don't remember the characters name. But seriously."

"I won't look through it, I promise." Theo paused, daring to be a little bold. "Do you think maybe you could draw me?"

"Maybe." Summer smiled softly. "You've got some striking features, and… well, feels rude to say it, but a haunted look to you sometimes that I'd love to try and capture."

Theo laughed. "I mean, it's true. I'm talking to a ghost, after all."

Summer laughed with her. "OoOoo," she said, making ghost noises. "Anyway, another time, with better lighting. Good night."

"Night."

~

Theo woke up in the middle of the night to nature's call

Obnoxious and annoying. She tried to ignore it and go back to sleep, but her bladder was particularly insistent.

So she climbed out of bed, keeping only one eye open a crack, stumbling through the darkened room.

She slowly opened the door to the kitchen and it creaked. Theo winced at the sound, and hoped that it wasn't enough to wake Summer… wherever she was out here. The box fan in her room helped to even out any noise, a constant hum.

Theo crept through the kitchen, eying the floor for any sign of Summer curled up in a sleeping bag or something, so she didn't stumble over her. Finally, she made it to the bathroom, and closed the door behind her, without turning on the light.

Her business concluded, Theo yawned, and made her way back out.

She reached the threshold to the bedroom, but a thought stopped her in her tracks.

Just where the hell was Summer, anyway? She'd always been so vague about her sleeping arrangements whenever Theo asked. But this apartment was so tiny. Kitchen, bedroom, bathroom. Unless there was some little laundry nook Theo had missed somewhere that Summer was hiding in, it was impossible for her to still be here.

A sense of curiosity mixed with a spike of alarm. Was she okay? Was she safe?

Well, Theo was fully awake now. No sense fighting it. She flipped on the light to the kitchen.

Sure enough, Summer wasn't hiding in any darkened corners.

She scoured the rest of the apartment. Summer wasn't sleeping in the shower, wasn't curled up in the closet. The apartment didn't even have its own laundry. There was no possible place for her to be hiding.

And then Theo finally noticed that Summer's shoes were missing, and her car keys weren't hanging by the door.

Her heart pounded in her chest. Was she staying at a hotel, for Theo's sake? Could she afford that?

Was she crashing at a friends place instead? At an ex's house?

The thought made her stomach twist. She had to get her jealousy under control. She had no right.

Maybe Summer had woken up in the middle of the night and decided to go for a walk or something. That would be normal, right?

Chester brushed against Theo's leg, purring.

She knelt down to rub his adorable face. "Do you know where she is?"

If he did, he wasn't going to tell her.

Making up her mind, Theo grabbed her phone, slipped on her shoes, and then headed outside.

The night was cool and still. It was three in the morning. All the bars would be closed. Any parties still going this late on a Saturday night would have moved somewhere private on campus, to dorms and fraternity houses.

Maybe that was where Summer had gone? Maybe she was an incorrigible party girl, and left Theo out because she didn't think it was her thing.

She could have at least asked. Theo would go, for her.

She walked down the stairs, then rounded the block, towards the parking spaces behind the apartment. She just wanted to see if Summer's car was there.

If it wasn't, she supposed there wasn't anything else she could do. She'd wait until morning, and ask Summer about it then.

It wasn't any of her business.

It wasn't her place.

It had nothing to do with her.

Theo rounded the corner.

Summer's car was there.

And so was Summer.

~

Summer woke to the sound of someone banging violently on her window.

She groaned, blinking blurry eyes. She'd finally managed to actually nod off, and now what? Some dickhead cop spotted her and decided he had nothing better to do?

"What the fuck do you think you're doing!?"

That was Theo's voice. Summer shot up in her seat, eyes wide.

Theo stood outside her window, looking absolutely furious.

Worst case scenario then. She would have preferred the shitty cop. She knew how to handle cops.

"Mornin', Theo," Summer slurred. What time was it? Still dark. She opened the car door, and stepped out, stretching, her back popping audibly. It was so sore after a week of sleeping in her car, but, oh well.

"Really?" Theo growled. "This is where you've been sleeping this whole time? No wonder you've been so vague about it. What the fuck, Summer? That's so stupid!"

Summer sighed. Theo had been through a lot, but she'd never had to struggle the way Summer had, that was certain. "It's not a big deal. I've slept in my car before."

"It's not safe! And it can't be comfortable."

"It's not comfortable, but it's safe enough. I can handle myself."

Theo was trembling before her. "What if someone came and bothered you?"

Summer rolled her eyes. "Like you are right now?"

"You know what I mean!"

"Like what, Theo? A homeless guy? Some carjacker? A random drunk college student? For the most part nobody gives a shit. On the rare occasion someone does, well…" Summer reached back into her car, pulling out her stun gun from the center console. She clicked it on so that it sparked ominously, which made Theo jump. "I can handle myself."

"Is that even legal?"

"It is if you have a permit."

"Do you?"

"What are you, a cop?"

Theo clenched her fists. "Whatever. That's not the point. The point is... there had to have been a better option than this. You should have said something! We could have figured it out, made it work."

Summer sighed. What did Theo even care? "I had a feeling you'd freak out about it, which is why I didn't say anything. It was the best option I had. That apartment is tiny, the floor smells too much like cat pee for me to sleep on. The car is familiar. Its not the best but it's more comfortable than some of my other options."

Tears brimmed in Theo's eyes. "I could have gone to a hotel. We could have bought an air mattress or something."

Crap. Now Summer felt guilty. Well, she always did, There was a visceral reaction somewhere deep inside of her, at the sight of Theo crying. "With the money you only got from your paycheck yesterday?"

Theo looked down, still shaking. "We could have shared." Her voice came out in a bare whisper.

Summer turned around, staring down the street, not looking at Theo. "You could barely stand to be in the same room as me when you first got here. I wasn't going to push that on you. Me sleeping out here isn't a big deal, honest."

Sure, she was miserable and sore, and kept having to nap in her own bed after Theo went to work. But wasn't it a small sacrifice, compared to what Theo had gone through?

Theo sniffed, and shook her head. "I could have handled... well. We could have at least talked about it."

Summer shook her head. "You were a total mess that first night, and it was easier to keep it going afterwards. Sorry, I guess. Truth's out now. Doesn't actually change anything. I'm going to go take a walk and clear my head, before going back to sleep. You should get back yourself."

"No."

Theo's hand shot out to grab Summer's, holding onto her as she tried to walk away. Her fingers were cold.

"Just come back up to the apartment. Please? We can share. I'll be fine with it, I promise."

Summer looked back over her shoulder.

Theo met her gaze, eyes still glistening, but there was a fierce determination to her expression. She didn't flinch.

Something told Summer she wasn't going to win a battle of self sacrifice tonight. She was already too worn out. Might as well relent. "Fine," she said with a resigned sigh. "I'll warn you though, I can be a bit of a blanket hog."

"That's fine." Theo took a deep, shuddering breath. "My hands and feet get super cold, so if you steal the blankets than you'll be the one to deal with the consequences when I try to grab them back."

Summer snorted with laughter. "Mutually assured destruction then. Alright."

A smile flickered at Theo's lips. She still hadn't let go of Summer's hand.

A moment passed, and they both glanced down.

Theo let go suddenly, awkward. She cleared her throat. "Come on. Let's get back inside."

Summer followed her up the stairs, her mind racing.

What did Theo see when she looked at her? The other Summer, dead and gone? That she was her own person? It must have been so confusing, such a confusing jumble of emotions. A walking, talking trauma trigger. Inviting her to bed seemed like a dangerous game to play.

Had Summer ever once shared her bed platonically? Ugh, a terrible thought. She didn't have to be such a ho about everything. She could be the perfect gentlewoman. Sure, Theo was gorgeous, and had a great smile, and every moment spent with her brightened Summer's life considerably. Any other context and sure. Summer would have made a move.

But the way things were it felt like juggling with live grenades.

She didn't want to hurt Theo any more than she already had.

They made their way back up to the apartment in silence. Chester was there to greet her, likely a little confused by the nighttime activity.

Theo kicked off her shoes, then made her way into the bedroom and crawled back into bed.

Summer hesitated in the doorway, feeling like she was on the edge of a precipice, but she finally stepped forward, slipping under the covers next to Theo. The bed was still warm.

They lay there in awkward silence, the minutes ticking by. Theo had rolled over on her side, facing away from Summer.

Could she really sleep like this? The car sucked, but Summer's heart was pounding in her chest. If she fucked up, said something wrong, moved in the wrong way, would Theo have a panic attack?

And at the same time, Theo was so *close*. The slightest movement would press their bodies together.

Theo said something, but the white noise from the fan was loud, and Summer couldn't quite make it out.

"What was that?"

Theo paused, then rolled over to face Summer. Her dark eyes were barely visible in the dim light provided by a handful of LEDs throughout the room.

"I said I'm sorry. For freaking out on you like that."

"It's fine."

"I don't…" Theo bit her lip. "I don't want you to hurt yourself for my sake, okay?"

Summer sighed, and averted her gaze. "That's a bit dramatic. It was a bit of discomfort. But you've been going through so much this past week. A little discomfort on my end to make that easier for you is a small price to pay."

Theo let out a short, exasperated sigh. "I hate that. I hate it when people treat me like I' some piece of fragile china, who will shatter into pieces if someone even looks at me funny."

"I don't think you're fragile. As far as I can tell, you're incredibly resilient. But… I mean, this situation is literally supernatural. Like, this is some crazy shit that would break anyone."

"Maybe. But still. You don't have to do so much for me. You barely even know me."

Summer averted her gaze. "Look, you're not the only one here who is really seeing someone else. Have you considered that I'm just being selfish? Using you to manage my own guilty conscience for what I did to the other Theo? Telling myself that if I can do things right by you, that somehow makes it all okay?"

Theo was silent for a long time, her gaze boring into Summer.

Finally, she spoke. "I don't think that's true."

Summer turned back to her and raised an eyebrow.

Theo smiled. "I mean, maybe it is a little. Maybe we're both hung up on our other selves. But I don't think guilt is your only motivation. I think that, maybe, just maybe, you might be a good person, Summer Sullivan."

Her cheeks grew hot, but she didn't tear her gaze away from Theo. "Doesn't feel like it, most days."

"Maybe…" Theo took a deep breath. She shook a little, under her covers. "Maybe we can try? To see each other, not as… you know what I mean. I'll try better to see you as you. You try better to see me as me?" She wriggled under the covers, and then extended her right hand.

Summer stared at the hand, her mouth suddenly dry. But she nodded. "Okay. Yeah. I'll try my best."

She grabbed Theo's hand. It was cold, but not as cold as it had been earlier. And she could feel the warmth from her own hand seeping into it.

It was too dark to fully make out Theo's expression, but she was definitely smiling. "Good night, Summer."

"Good night, Theo."

Dear Diary,

Summer got into a fight today.

She's always been really mean to Emily Peterson. Because she's a little on the heavier side, because she's a bit of a weird loner, because she doesn't have much of a filter. Summer's always making snide comments and stuff. Usually not to her face. I always tell her to stop, but she doesn't really listen.

Today she made some comment under her breath when we passed Emily in the hallway and I guess Emily heard because she absolutely flipped her shit, started screaming at Summer. And Summer of course didn't back down. They ended up fighting.

Summer got a black eye. And she got suspended, with the principal saying she's lucky it wasn't expulsion.

And afterwards Summer kept ranting to me about 'that crazy psycho bitch' and how unfair everything was and it's like, ugh. I don't know. I'm kind of mad at her for getting involved at all.

Theo
4/8/2013

Theo woke up to the sound of Summer's soft snores.

And also without a blanket.

Well, she'd been warned, after all.

Theo sat up, stretching, and grabbed her glasses from the nightstand.

Summer was curled up, wrapped in her blanket like a burrito. A little bit of morning sunlight filtered in through the blackout curtains, illuminating her face, her fiery red hair, blonde showing at the roots.

Her face was soft, her expression peaceful.

God, she was beautiful.

All sorts of negative feelings flowed through Theo at that thought. Doubt. Indecision. Disgust at herself. A sense of betrayal, for Summer's memory.

It was all so fucked up.

But she was so, so tired of wallowing in her guilt, her past. And the truth was, she was loving every minute of this. She'd promised Summer last night, that she'd try to do better.

So she rolled her negativity and self loathing into a ball, stuffed it into a small corner of her mind, closed it away, locked it and threw away the key.

It wasn't sustainable and she knew it. She was good at compartmentalizing, but this was too big. Theo would break, eventually.

But she'd deal with that when it happened. For now, she'd allow herself to pursue what she'd always wanted, in the brief window provided to her by a miracle.

She'd allow herself to be happy, if only for a moment.

A part of Theo wanted to reach over, to brush Summer's hair out of her face, to pepper her with soft kisses, to wake her up by murmuring sweet nothings into her ear.

Their relationship wasn't there. Not yet, anyway. But Theo *wanted* it to be. She could admit that much.

Instead, Theo quietly climbed out of bed. She got dressed, crept out into the kitchen and closed the door behind her. Summer deserved to sleep in.

She thought about making breakfast, but the smell of fresh bread wafted up from the bakery below, and she couldn't resist. She slipped on her shoes, and made her way downstairs.

"Hey!" Peter called out as she walked through the door. "If it isn't my favorite new-old friend. How's life treating you, Theo?"

"Good," she said automatically. Then paused, and smiled, genuine warmth filling her heart. "Great, actually. Really, really great."

Peter raised an eyebrow, his eyes twinkling. "Well now. Anything you'd like to share?"

Theo shrugged. "Dunno that there's much to say. Not yet, anyway. But I've figured some things out. About what I want."

"Sometimes, simply knowing where you're going can be a huge burden lifted." He paused, then frowned. "Although where I'm headed is a total disaster. Maybe you could help me out, actually."

"What's up?" Theo made her way closer to the counter, looking over the pastries on display.

Peter scratched at his beard, his face red. "Well, I was talking to Aaron. About board games, we're both big fans apparently! And he was talking about how he's been wanting to organize a board game night, but none of his coworkers are the type. And I told him how I had a group of people who regularly came for board game nights. And he said that'd be great, and that we should come over tonight if we're available."

Theo blinked. Peter spoke rapidly, his words spilling all over one another. It took a moment for her to process them all. "Okay. So, uh, what's the problem?"

"I don't actually have a group!" Peter groaned, and slammed his head into the counter. "I *used* to have a group. Like, a couple years ago. It petered out. But I was flustered talking to him, like I always am, and didn't correct the miscommunication until it was too late."

"Okay, so… show up alone? Then it's almost like a date-date, right?"

"No way!" Peter stood back up, and waved his hands back and forth, nearly knocking over a container of napkins. "That's so pathetic and needy! I can't have him think I'm a loser without any friends!"

"So what you really want is—"

"Can you and Summer show up with me? I'll be so much less awkward if it's a double date. Please? I'll give you free donuts for a week!"

A small thrill ran through Theo, at the fact that everyone looked at her and Summer and saw a couple. She laughed. "I don't think the bribery is strictly necessary, but I'll take it. Summer's sleeping in, but I'm sure she'll be interested. Tonight, you said?"

"Thank you thank you thank you! You're a a lifesaver, Theo. And yeah, tonight. Seven o' Clock sharp. Oh, and the address is…"

As Peter rattled off the street name and number, Theo stiffened slightly. She'd already known where Aaron lived, of course. Her old house.

Another chance to drown in memories.

But this time with Summer at her side.

~

"Hey, kiddo," Summer signed as she approached Faith. "Been a minute.

Haven't seen you in awhile."

The normally shy eleven year old lit up as Summer approached, and they smiled brightly. Their hands moved animatedly with sign language. "Summer! It's so good to see you!"

"Woah, slow down there a second. You know I'm still learning."

"Oh, right. Sorry." Faith took a deep breath, then slowed down their movements, making them clearer and more precise. "Can you teach me to draw some more?"

The youth center was full of activity, kids running around, screaming, shouting. The other adults ran around, doing their best to corral them.

It was a special place, for the kids to exist, to play, outside of the context of school. While their parents were at work, or needed time to themselves for a day.

Summer wished she'd had a place like this when she was little. Full of adults who cared about her. Things to do. So she did her best to provide that space to others.

"Look what I've been working on!" Faith pulled out their own sketch-pad, showing a series of beautiful girls, done in an anime style.

"Damn, kid." Summer grinned. "Maybe you should be teaching me instead."

Faith's cheeks colored, and they looked away. "They're not that good. The eyes look weird. Yours are always so much better."

"Well, let's practice some eyes, then."

Summer removed her own sketchpad from the grocery bag she'd carried it in, then sat down the a large table on the edge of the rec room. Some of the other kids would likely join them once they got bored with running around and chasing each other, but Summer liked the one on one time with Faith while it lasted.

Faith pursed their lips, glancing over to the corner of the room. "Who's that?"

Summer followed their gaze to Theo, who was sitting by herself, writing in a notebook. She caught Summer's gaze, smiled, and gave a little wave. "A friend of mine. She's taking a class, and wanted to observe."

Warmth in her blossomed in her chest at that, and Summer returned the smile and wave back.

A devilish grin spread across Faith's face.

"Is she your *girlfriend*?" they signed, adding extra emphasis on 'girlfriend.'

Summer rolled her eyes. "She's not, and it's none of your business even if she was."

"How come? She's super pretty."

"She's way more than super pretty, she's ultra instinct pretty. But there's more to dating someone than finding them attractive."

Faith laughed at that. "So you don't like her?"

Summer pursed her lips. "I like her just fine. But it's way more complicated than that. Adult relationships are complicated."

Faith leaned closer, relentless as always. "Complicated how? Is she straight?"

She needed to get her emotions under control, and not have them be so immediately obvious to an eleven year old. "She's not, but... look, we have a history, alright? It's complicated. And it's not going to happen."

"Shame." Faith shrugged, then pulled out their pencils. "She's still mega galaxy pretty though. I'm going to draw her."

Summer let out a sigh of relief, then chuckled. "Alright, alright. Not a bad idea, though. I'll do it too."

She started sketching the rough outline of Theo in the distance, sitting on her chair. Looking happy, peaceful, contemplative. Her notebook in hand, occasionally chewing on her pencil.

The drawing began to take shape. The girl who had crashed into Summer's life in the most unexpected way, only a week ago. Had it really only been a week? It felt like so much longer.

It was funny. An inter-dimensional traveler showing up should have been more momentous. A herald of great change, a call to adventure. But life continued on, same as it always.

But even without any grand destiny, Summer's life still felt brighter with Theo in it.

She set down her pencil for a moment, studying Theo's features, trying to figure out how to best capture her eyes behind her glasses.

Faith nudged her in the side, grinning. "Wow, you *really* like her, huh?"

"What? No. Shut up, I'm trying to draw. Don't interrupt me."

"Uh-huh. *Sure.*" They winked, and turned back to their own drawing. Damn kid.

It didn't mean anything, not really. Summer liked lots of girls. She fell fast and easy. Even if it never lasted, it was fun.

But Theo was definitely, one hundred percent off limits.

~

"Come on, hurry up, we're going to be late!" Theo grabbed Summer's arm, trying to drag her forward faster, as they walked down the sidewalk towards her old home.

Summer laughed, resisting her with surprisingly casual strength. "Relax. It's seven thirty, we're fine."

"He said it started at seven!"

"Exactly. And Peter is very punctual, meaning he's already there. Hell, he won't stop blowing up my phone, telling me to hurry."

Theo pursed her lips. "So what, you want to let him wait?"

Summer shrugged. "I mean, yeah, kind of. He's there alone with his crush right now. Maybe if we're lucky we'll walk in on them making out."

"Or he'll be so anxious about it he ruins everything."

"Also a possibility. Which is why we're arriving fashionably late, instead of ditching them entirely."

Theo sighed, and stopped trying to tug Summer forward. In response, Summer compromised, and sped up her leisurely walking pace a little bit. They kept their arms linked together.

Old streets, familiar houses. "I wonder if the neighbors I remember growing up are still in these houses."

Summer nodded thoughtfully. "There's a weight to towns like this, a momentum, that can be hard to escape from. So yeah, probably. Wouldn't be surprised if it's still the same faces."

"I don't even remember their names." Theo smiled, thinking back. "But I would help my mom make Christmas cookies every year, and we'd give out a platter to everyone on the block. Mostly older couples without kids, so I'm not sure I interacted with most of the neighbors beyond that context."

"That's a lot of cookies." Summer gave her an odd look, something distant in her eyes. "Sounds nice, though."

Theo winced. Right. Summer didn't have happy childhood memories like that. Was mentioning her own some kind of faux pas? She remembered that her Summer would get weird about it too, lashing out angrily.

But Summer smiled at her. "Any particularly cool spots in this neighborhood you were able to discover?"

"Best were the woods behind my house. And the little fort that was up there."

"A whole fort, huh?" Summer whistled appreciatively. "Well I gotta see that."

"It's not my house anymore but… can probably be arranged."

They finally arrived, in front of her home. Aaron's home. She hadn't really had much time to notice when she was being kicked out the first time, but it looked a little different than it had back in her own reality. The siding hadn't been repainted, and it was still a faded white. Must have been Peter's influence.

Peter's car was parked in the street out front, and they stepped up onto the porch together. Theo rang her own doorbell.

No dog bark awaited them. Theo wondered if Buddy had been a dog they'd gotten together. She vaguely remembered Peter mentioning he'd been a shelter dog. Hopefully in this world, he'd found another family who would love him just as much.

Peter opened the door, looking incredibly relieved. "Girls! So glad you could make it. Welcome, come on in!"

As they stepped inside, Peter leaned in close, whispering to Summer under his breath, but loud enough that Theo could still hear.

"What the hell took you so long! I'm dying here!"

Summer grinned. "Relax. A wingwoman is never late, nor early. She always arrives precisely when she means to."

"Unbelievable," Peter growled. But then he pulled back and was all smiles again. "See, Aaron? I told you they would make it."

"Did you have that quote memorized?" Theo whispered.

Summer shrugged. "What quote?"

They took off their shoes and made their way into the living room. It too, was different than the last time she'd seen it. Different furniture, different artwork on the walls, different photographs. Marks of a life shared with Peter, now absent.

Aaron was sitting in a recliner, a bowl of chips on the table next to him. "Hey. Don't worry, you didn't miss anything. Hadn't actually gotten started yet."

"Uh, right, yeah!" Peter said, looking back and forth. "Haven't even figured out what game we're gonna play yet, haha. Just been talking."

Summer shrugged. "Hey, I'm here to be social. We can play whatever, doesn't matter much to me."

Theo studied Aaron. Her past two meetings with him had been tense and uncomfortable. But now he seemed relaxed, laid back, friendly. He had a soft, easy smile to him, and there was a fondness in it every time his attention turned to Peter.

Aaron gestured towards a large dining room table, made of an expensive looking dark wood. Several boardgames adorned it. "This is what I've got. Can I get anyone anything? Snacks? Water? Beer? Wine?"

Theo recognized Catan, and Diplomacy, and Carcassonne, and then there were a few others she didn't know, but they had pretty box art. "Water would be nice."

Summer glanced at her. "I'll take some water as well."

Peter wilted slightly. "Well, I was going to say wine, but if nobody else is having any…"

Aaron smiled at him. "I'm sure the two of us can manage to polish off a bottle."

"Oh, uh. Sure, that sounds great." Peter gulped audibly.

God, he was down *bad*.

"A-anyway." Peter tugged at the collar of his sweater. "I also brought a few games, just as options. Left them in the car. But you know. Whatever is good."

This was getting nowhere fast. Theo rolled her eyes, then stomped over to the table and took a closer look. "I don't want to play the 'what should we do? I dunno!' game all night. So if nobody actually has any strong opinions on what we should play then I'm picking whatever looks like it will take the longest and has the most complicated and hard to understand rules."

Summer burst out laughing.

Aaron looked at her with a smirk. "Sounds weirdly like a hostage negotiation, but sure. Alright." He stood up, the recliner creaking underneath him. "There's one here there that's good and easy to pick up for a new group, we can just—"

"Wait!"

All eyes turned to Peter. He licked his lips. "I uh. Can I at least grab one of my games from the car? Give you all a pitch?"

"Sure, go for it," Aaron said, laughing.

Peter ran off, leaving the three of them alone.

Aaron left for the kitchen, returning with the wine and water.

"Thanks for coming, really," Aaron said. "Peter is so sweet, but he gets so nervous. I'm hoping he'll relax with you two around."

Summer grinned. "He'll get there eventually. I have some… *classified information* on how it all turns out."

"Huh?"

Theo elbowed Summer.

"Just an inside joke."

Peter came back, holding a board game close to his chest, face flushed, a little sweaty.

But there was a glimmer in his eyes as he began to explain the concept and the rules, and his excitement for the game was sincere and lovable.

It warmed Theo's heart.

~

From the back porch, Summer stared at the night sky, and at the backyard. Wide open grass, a small garden in the corner. And then hills and trees further beyond.

The door opened behind her, and Theo stepped out. "There you are."

"Just wanted to get some fresh air. Are we needed?"

Theo said down next to her, a smirk playing at her lips. "There was some vague talk about starting another game, but… they also seem pretty engrossed in conversation right now."

Summer chuckled. "Guess Peter needed a little bit of liquid courage."

"Or maybe a little time to relax and feel comfortable. Probably both."

"Yeah." Summer nodded. It had been a team based game, with Summer and Theo pairing off against Peter and Aaron. Theo had proven surprisingly competitive, quickly memorizing the rules and finding various loopholes they could exploit. Summer had been forced to throw the match in the final hour, to give Peter a much needed W.

They sat in silence for a time, serenaded by the sounds of night. The chirping of crickets. The humming of frogs. The distant sound of a car alarm going off somewhere.

"You were really cute today," Theo said softly.

Was Theo really…? Summer turned to her and raised an eyebrow.

"Oh?"

Theo flushed, and looked away. "I mean. With the kids. It was really cute. You're really good with kids."

"Ah, well." Of course, that was what she meant. Summer rubbed at the back of her head. "I dunno. Kids are easy. Just be honest and show an interest in what they're doing. All it takes, really."

"If you say so. I've always been super awkward with them. How did you get involved with the youth center, anyway?"

Summer bit her lip. It always felt weird, admitting something like this out loud. She never really knew how others would react, how it would change the way they saw her. She could lie, or deflect, but... "It was court-mandated community service. After I got out of juvie."

Theo's eyes widened. "You... went to juvie?" She sounded sad.

"Yeah. Lasted a year. Had court mandated therapy and community service. Both are what really helped me turn around."

"I see."

A long pause. Summer felt stupid. Talking about it always felt like she was reciting an answer she'd rehearsed. All the emotions tied to it were distant, and felt like they had happened to another person entirely.

"Can I ask... what happened?"

Summer let out a long sigh, and stared at her hands, resting on her knees. In her mind's eye she could picture the blood covering them. "Got into a fight with another girl. Pulled a knife, thought it would make me look cool and tough and intimidating. Ended up with us both being hurt pretty bad."

"Jesus Christ," Theo whispered. "That's... oh my god, Summer. I'm so sorry. Is..."

"She's fine. Now, anyway. Moved to Iowa, has a kid. We had a real heart to heart a few years back. Water under the bridge."

"What about you?"

Summer lifted her shirt, revealing her stomach, and the thin scar that ran across her left side. "Still got the scar to prove it."

Theo bit her lip, then gently drew her fingers closer, hesitating, her eyes meeting Summer's.

Summer didn't stop her.

Her fingers made contact, and Summer flinched. "Fuck, how are your hands so cold?"

Theo laughed. "Sorry, sorry."

But she didn't pull her fingers away, and instead lightly stroked the line of her scar.

Summer's stomach clenched, and a shiver ran through her that had nothing to do with the temperature of Theo's digits.

Theo looked up at her, her face red, her lips parted.

Was this really happening? Summer leaned closer, not willing to say anything, in case it broke the spell.

The spell broke, and Theo stood up suddenly, and took a few steps down the porch, onto the grass. "Sorry. Uh. It's nice to learn more things about you. Even the sad things."

The whiplash left Summer reeling, but she swallowed it down, and tried her best to recapture the thread of conversation. "I'm still alive, at the end of the day. That counts for something." She stood, and stretched. "We going back in?"

Theo turned to face her, eyes sparkling, grin mischievous. "Didn't I promise to show you my fort?"

"You sure that's not trespassing?"

"What are you, a cop?"

Summer laughed, then stepped off the porch. "Lead the way."

Theo ventured forth through the backyard, her eyes raised towards the cosmos.

The sky was vast and bright and full of stars. Summer wondered if she could see this supposed magic comet out here somewhere. Some strange celestial body that had transported Theo across dimensions.

One that would transport her back in less than a month.

Summer felt a pang at that thought. She was getting used to Theo's presence in her life. She fit there like she'd always belonged. But she'd known from the start that it'd be a temporary thing. A brief, crazy, wild adventure. Gone in an instant. A fond memory, the truth of which she'd never be able to share.

Oh well. That was Summer's lot in life. She'd accepted that.

The mowed backyard gave way to unmowed hill, and the tall, stiff grass scraped against Summer's jeans as she hiked.

By the time they reached the top of the hill, Theo was breathing heavily.

Summer turned to her, raising an eyebrow.

"Shut up."

"I didn't say anything."

Summer grinned. The fort was just ahead. A small, square, stout building made of wood. Grand and impressive. A place to hide away, be yourself. Something that would have been absolutely incredible to have as a child.

"Here we are." Theo gestured grandly, her voice tinged with nervous excitement. "My home away from home. Secret base, headquarters for all sorts of adventures and shenanigans."

As she approached, Summer saw that the door had a small padlock attached to it. "It's locked."

"Yeah." Theo clasped her hands behind her back, leaning close to Summer as she inspected it. "Think you can figure out the secret to get inside?"

Summer blinked. "Uh, I guess?" She wasn't really sure what Theo was trying to get at, but well. She was equipped. She fished her keys out of her pocket, found the lockpicking tool attached to the ring, then slid it into the padlock and jiggled it around until it popped open.

Theo stared blankly. "That's, uh. Hmm."

"What? Locks like this are painfully insecure."

"No, that's fine, I just..." Theo sighed, then chuckled. "You find that thing useful pretty often?"

Summer shrugged. "I wouldn't say often. But it's come in handy every once in awhile. Best part is using it to access the roof on my apartment building. Good place to hang out."

Theo's eyes lit up. "Ooh! We should totally do that." She grinned, then stepped forward and opened the door.

There wasn't much to it. A small, square room. A beanbag set up in the corner. Stacks of manga and books. An empty cooler. A storage box in the corner. The smell of dust and old wood.

"Well, alright then." Summer stretched, then made her way over to the beanbag and fell down on it, a hurricane of dust bursting forth in her wake.

Theo sneezed three times in a row, which was adorable. "Just like I left it. The night I, uh... came to this world, I guess, I ended up passing out in the beanbag there, after reading some manga. Was a big nostalgia trip for me, trying to put memories to rest, that sort of thing."

Summer grabbed a random manga from the stack, paging through it.

"Are you sure it was the comet? Maybe one of these books is magic."

"I guess I'm not a hundred percent sure. But there was… a sensation I felt with the comet. Seems more related than Fairy Tail." Theo came over, kneeling before the stack of books, looking for something specific before she pulled it out. She then collapsed onto the beanbag next to Summer.

It wasn't that big of a beanbag. They were pressed close together, Theo's weight partially on her. Her body heat was easily felt from her clothing, and the smell of Summer's own shampoo tickled her nose, coming from Theo's hair.

Summer counted to three in her mind, to refocus. "Sounds like the two of you had a great time together here."

"Sometimes." Theo smiled fondly. "More so when we were a bit younger. By the time we were properly teenagers, we were out and about more often, and when we did hang out, it was easier to just hang out in my room. Had my laptop and TV there, more comfortable seats, air conditioning. Less bugs."

There was a pull of nostalgia at all of this, for something that Summer had never known, had always wished she could know. She leaned back, staring at the ceiling. It was dark, but her eyes were adjusting, and she stared at the rough wood. "Which of these books was your favorite?"

Theo sat up. "Oh, um. Let me see. Hard to say, I guess. A lot of them weren't very good, but I devoured them all pretty ferociously anyway."

There was something there, on the wood. An indentation, or maybe scratch marks. Initials? Summer squinted, trying to get a closer look.

"Summer always said her favorites were the dark edgy stuff, like Berserk or Claymore. But there was a time she read my copy of Fruits Basket 'as a joke' and ended up staying up all night finishing the entire thing. She was a softy at heart."

"Sounds like me," Summer mumbled. She was only half listening. She'd never really gotten much into manga and anime herself, so only had a vague idea of what Theo was talking about. But… she stood up, awkwardly using the beanbag to get more height, and pulled her phone out of her pocket, flicking on the flashlight.

"Summer?"

There, in the harsh light from her phone, were two initials scratched into the ceiling.

T.S.
S.S.

Theo Smith and Summer Sullivan. "Why is this here?" she asked out loud.

"Huh." Theo stepped next to her, straining to see in the light. "I remember carving those. Had to borrow a step ladder to do it. Honestly I was a little against it, but Summer was insistent."

"No, I mean…" Summer turned to look at Theo, incredulous. "I sure as shit didn't carve anything here. But this is my world, isn't it? So why are these carvings here?"

Theo's eyes went wide, and she looked even closer. "Oh. Shit. These are all of my manga too. Like, maybe the other Theo had the same taste, but I'm pretty sure some of these I bought specifically for Summer."

Summer shook her head. "What does that mean?"

"I don't know. Maybe it wasn't me that got transported over, but the entire fort?"

"Magic fort, huh?" Summer stepped off the beanbag, and gently kicked the wall. "Doesn't seem like anything special to me."

"It makes as much sense as anything else that's happened, I guess."

"Maybe." Summer crossed her arms over her chest. "But… it feels like there's a lot we don't know here. I know you seemed pretty confident it was the comet but… how sure are you, really?"

Theo winced, and looked away. "I… don't know. It seemed like such a straightforward explanation, but maybe it's not."

"You said you were gonna look into it more. Did you find anything?"

"That is… um." Theo shook her head. She seemed nervous. "Not really. But… I guess I've been a little distracted. Sorry."

Summer sighed, then sat back down. "No, it's fine. I get it. A lot going on, and this is all pretty crazy. But… it would be bad if you got trapped here, wouldn't it? Feels like the lack of a legal identity would come to bite you in the ass eventually."

Theo sat back down next to her. "People do it and get by every single day. Wouldn't be the worst thing in the world."

"Yeah, but you've got a family back home. They're probably worried sick."

"They… probably are, yeah." Theo's face scrunched up in pain, and she looked away. "It could be I'm completely wrong about the comet. It could be that... this was all just a thing that happened. And there's no going back. Some things are just like that."

Summer shifted, facing Theo. "I don't think it's like that. There's got to be a way for you to get back."

Theo shook her head. Her voice wavered. "But maybe there's not. We don't know anything. Maybe I'm stuck here forever."

A small part of Summer, a very small part, wished that it was true. That Theo wouldn't leave. She squashed that intrusive thought immediately. Guilt flooded her and drove her to speak. "I'll do everything in my power to get you home. I promise. Even if I have to fistfight god herself."

A snort of laughter escaped from Theo. "You would, wouldn't you?"

Summer sat up, grinning, and flexed her right bicep. "I'd give it like 50-50 odds."

Theo let out a sigh, a tender smile playing at her lips. "But you're right. I've definitely been taking this comet thing for a given when I maybe shouldn't have. I'll try and do some more research. But..."

"But?"

"For now, do you maybe want to just sit here with me and read some manga together?"

"Sure." Summer smiled, then settled back down on the beanbag. "I'd like that."

Dear Diary,

IF ANY LAW ENFORCEMENT IS READING THIS IN THE FU-
TURE THIS IS A WORK OF FICTION

I had my first beer today.

Summer stole a pack of beer from her mom, and we snuck out into the woods behind my house to drink it.

Honestly it was super gross. I could only drink about half the can before I felt kind of sick and had to stop. I didn't even feel drunk or anything, it just… tasted and smelled so awful.

Summer called me a wuss, then proceeded to drink her entire can. And then another. And then another.

I don't know why she thought she had to prove something to me.

She got really drunk, and threw up. The smell is still lingering in my nose when I think about it.

I had to help her walk back to the fort, and I was really scared that if mom came out and checked on us we'd be found out.

The whole way back Summer kept saying weird things, like… how glad it was that I'm here, how special I am, that I'm the best…

~~It wasn't like her. And I don't really know what to~~

I gave her a bunch of water and let her sleep it off. She complained a whole bunch about a hangover in the morning.

I think mom might have smelled it on her when we came back to the house the next day but if she did she didn't say anything.

Theo
4/20/2013

The next couple of days passed by in a blur. They both had to return to work, their days only intersecting briefly. Worn out from the busy weekend, they spent their nights in the apartment, watching shows, playing on their phones, Summer working on her sketches.

It felt wrong, somehow. If Theo was going to lie, to refuse to go home until the last possible moment, shouldn't she be making the most of every single moment? Filling her time with enough memories to engrave upon her soul?

Instead, she was slaving away in a capitalist grind, watching Summer do the same, all to barely keep a roof over her head. It seemed so pointless, futile, a complete waste.

But, she'd rather struggle at Summer's side forever than enjoy a life of luxury and comfort without her.

God, she was down *bad*. She was constantly thinking about Summer while at work, thinking of things they could do together, imagining a life with her. It affected her performance, but what did it really matter? And then during the nights while Summer was still working, she'd pace around the tiny apartment, anxiously waiting for Summer to get home.

She'd try to distract herself on her phone, looking up information about comets and parallel worlds. She couldn't find anything concrete. People had stories on forums, but they all seemed fake. Just people role-playing. But if she told her story, it would probably sound just as fake. Especially considering the literal wish fulfillment.

Had she even been this obsessed, as a teenager? She remembered writing her thoughts in her diary, the angst she felt. Convinced her own affections were one sided and creepy. Awful attempts at poetry. It made her wince to think about, even now.

But this was all consuming. Maybe this really was all a dream. Maybe she'd died, and this was her personal heaven.

A heaven that still involved having to go to work, for some reason.

Wednesday night, Theo sat at the kitchen table, playing games on her phone, when the door finally opened. Summer stood there, looking apologetic.

"Hey," Theo said, her face lighting up. "Welcome ho—"

"Yooo! How's it hanging, Theo!" Minha said as she pushed past Summer into the apartment.

Summer groaned, pinched the bridge of her nose. She mouthed the word "Sorry."

"Oh, um. Hi Minha," Theo said, taken completely off guard. She had no idea how Minha expected her to act, what she expected her to know.

Minha put her hands on the kitchen table, leaning forward. "Come on! We're going out tonight!"

Theo blinked. "We are?"

Summer shook her head. "We're not. And I told her that, multiple times, but she insisted that she wanted to ask you herself."

Minha rolled her eyes. "Dunno why Summer's being such a wet blanket, but I *know* you're pretty cool. Look, tomorrow's my day off, and I want to have some fun. There's a college bar pretty close to here, Slurps. They do a Wednesday Night Trivia thing. You love that nerd shit. It'll be great."

"Theo doesn't drink," Summer growled. "I told you that already. Look, you got your chance to ask. Go find someone else to bother."

Theo bit her lip, looking between Minha and Summer. "I… might like that, actually."

"Fuck yeah!"

Summer blinked. "Really?"

"Yeah." She met Summer's gaze. "I told you before, I'm not that fragile. I was just in a weird place in the beginning. Hell, feel free to have a few beers if you want. I can be the designated driver."

"It's within walking distance."

"The designated walker, then."

Summer sighed. "Alright, well. If you're sure you're okay with it. Give me a few minutes to shower."

She headed into the bathroom, leaving Theo alone at the table with Minha.

Oops. She hadn't thought that part through.

Minha leaned back on her chair, balancing it on only two legs. "Goddamn, though. It's still so wild to me that you're here. Real blast from the past, you know?"

Theo folded her hands in front of her, and thought through her words carefully. She could be vague about this. Couldn't be too hard. "Yeah, I've uh, been feeling that a lot, recently."

"So many good memories from when we all were hanging out back home. I mean, I guess I was the annoying little sister tagging along, but still. Always meant a lot to me that you two showed up to every one of my games."

That sounded very thoughtful of the other Theo. She could sense a hint of vulnerability there, underneath all of Minha's bravado. "I'm glad I was able to catch one again. You've gotten better."

Minha laughed, and flexed. "You know it."

Curiosity tugged at Theo, and she decided to be bold. "Hey, I lost all of my old photo albums awhile back because of some phone nonsense. Do you still have any old pictures of the three of us?"

"Really? Damn, that sucks. But uh, sure, hold on." She pulled out her phone, and started scrolling through it. "Oh, here's a favorite. After I won State, back in highschool."

She showed Theo the picture, and sure enough, it depicted a younger Minha, smiling wildly, holding up a trophy.

And next to her, leaning in close, was Theo, and another woman that could only be Minha's sister. Seoyun, Minha had said.

The Theo in the picture was maybe eighteen or nineteen, freshly an adult. She looked happy, and her fingers were interlaced with Seoyun's.

Theo definitely hadn't looked that happy when she was eighteen. She was still deep in depression, trying to claw her way out of her grief. Struggling to stay afloat.

Was this what Summer had felt, when Theo had showed her pictures? Another possibility?

What had caused this Theo to break up with her girlfriend, anyway? What had she been like? Why hadn't it worked out?

"Yeah." Minha nodded, and pulled the phone back. "That day ruled, honestly. Top ten. Lemme see what else I got."

Theo held up a hand. "That's good. I'm good. I just… felt nostalgic for a moment, that's all."

Minha blinked, then shrugged. "Sure, whatever." She started poking around on her phone, browsing Instagram instead.

Did Minha have complicated feelings? Did she think of Theo like a sister? Was she sad, that she'd never become an official sister-in-law?

Once again Theo wondered if she was making a terrible mistake. Playing with fire, with hazardous materials. She was going to get burned, and maybe burn others in the process. Maybe it would be better if she accepted that this was just a dream, and returned home, and forgot that it ever happened. Move on with her life.

Was any of this even worth it? So she could live this domestic life, act the role of Summer's partner in her twisted fantasy, but not actually in reality? There was no reason Summer would want anything to do with her. And even if she did… she'd just be another notch on Summer's bedpost, a string of casual relationships that didn't mean anything. She wouldn't be anything special.

It was getting hard to breathe. She felt sick, like she wanted to throw up. She was freaking herself out again. Too much time spent in her own head and this was the result.

"Dude? You alright?" Minha asked.

The door to the bathroom opened, and Theo twisted in her chair, searching desperately for a lifeline.

Summer stood there, wrapped in a towel, her hair wet, looking muddy brown instead of its usually vibrant red. "Hey," she said, with a casual, easy smile. "Just be a few more minutes. Minha's not bothering you too much, is she?"

Theo licked her lips, and she watched a droplet of water run down Summer's neck, pool briefly in her clavicle before continuing down her breast, eventually hitting the towel and being absorbed. "Uh. Yep. Mmmhmm."

Minha snorted with laughter. "Not dating my ass."

Summer rolled her eyes. "Shut up," she said, then made her way into the bedroom.

Right. Nothing quite like horny brain to short circuit a panic attack. Theo took a deep breath, forcing herself to calm down. Let herself accept the delusion, felt it wash over her. This would all be fine. She'd chase after what she wanted, whether it was a fluke, a dream, a miracle, her destiny. She'd enjoy every minute she could with Summer.

It would destroy her, Icarus flying too close to the sun. But that would be a problem for future Theo to deal with.

"So," Theo said, turning back to Minha with a smile on her face. "What did you say this bar was called?"

～

Slurps had the look, feel, and smell of a small town sports bar. Small, dingy, nicotine stains on the glass. Photos and logos for the Chicago Bears plastered all over the wall. It was exactly the kind of place you'd expect to be full of crusty old alcoholics, their kids long gone, who came here every night because they had nothing else going on in their lives.

But for some reason, it was full of college students instead. Young men and women in their early twenties, loud, rowdy. There were quite a few, for a Wednesday night. Trivia must have been popular.

Theo wondered how it happened. Maybe the owner knew how to market and appeal to the younger crowd. Or maybe people thought the name was funny and memorable, and latched onto it.

Maybe they didn't check ID.

Trivia was already ongoing when the three of them arrived, but there would apparently be one more round they could sign up for.

They took a seat at an empty table.

"How does this actually work anyway?" Theo asked. "I've never done bar trivia before."

Summer had her phone out, and looked up. "Oh, it's all app based now. I've already got it downloaded, so I'll be the team leader and sign us up."

"Oh." Theo felt a pang of disappointment. "I was kind of hoping it'd be like a gameshow or something, and we'd get fun little buzzers."

Minha laughed. "Dude, that would be awesome! But nah."

"What should our team name be?" Summer asked.

"Strikers!"

Summer raised an eyebrow. "Like the soccer position you play?"

"Obviously."

"How about comets?" Theo said softly.

Summer glanced at her, smiling. "I like that."

"Comet Strikers!"

Theo laughed. "That also works."

"Alright, Comet Strikers it is." Summer filled out whatever information she needed on her phone, then set it down. "When the round starts, they'll ask a question, then we'll have about a minute to discuss amongst ourselves and submit an answer."

"Cool." Minha stood up. "I'll go get us drinks. You want anything?"

Theo bit her lip. "Actually, can I get something too? Maybe just a cider."

"Hell yeah!" Minha grinned. "Summer?"

"Grab me whatever IPA is on tap," she said, frowning.

Minha ran off, leaving the two of them alone.

"Are you sure about this?" Summer asked, leaning forward and lowering her voice.

Theo shrugged. "Alcohol messes with my medication… but I can't exactly get my prescription in this world, so I've been off my meds for over a week now. And sure, I've had a few bad experiences with drinking in the past, but…" She took a deep breath, and met Summer's gaze. "I trust you to help me make this a good one."

Summer stared at her for a few long moments before smiling. "Alright, I'll try my best. Just take it easy, okay?"

"I will, I promise."

It was loud, but not so loud that she needed to shout to be heard. The room was full of a constant hum of conversation. Easy enough to tune out. Theo leaned back in her chair, letting her gaze drift across the room.

She'd graduated what, four, five years ago now? Hardly any time at all, but it still felt like such a massive gap. The students here all felt and looked younger than she'd really expected them too.

Or maybe that was merely a difference of perception. She'd never been the bar and party type in her own college experience. It had been distant from her then, and continued to be distant now.

Her gaze fell on a table of girls, hair and makeup done up, their outfits likely brand name. All gorgeous. They seemed like sorority types, but were chatting and laughing amongst themselves.

Theo pursed her lips. From behind, the build and hair of one of the girls looked familiar. Was that—

The girl in question turned around, and sure enough, it was Riley. She craned her neck around, probably looking for a waiter or something, but her gaze fell upon Theo. Her eyes went wide with surprise, but she smiled, and gave a little wave.

Theo waved back.

Riley turned back to her group, said some things, and then stood up, and started walking towards their table.

"Hey guys. Wasn't expecting to see you here."

Summer started in surprise, turning to Riley and looking like a dog who'd just peed on the carpet. "Oh, uh. Hey Riley."

Riley's smile tightened a bit when her gaze fell on Summer. "Didn't know you were into bar trivia. You should have said something at lunch,

Theo!"

"It was kind of a last minute decision. And it was Minha's idea."

Minha came back at that moment with the drinks, setting down the glasses on the table. "Oh, hey Riley! How's it hanging?"

Theo stared at the cider in front of her. It smelled fruity, and a little sour. She thought about the first time she'd ever drank alcohol, when she was fourteen. Her stomach twisted, the sense memory of Summer's vomit filling her, the sensation of holding her hair back.

Summer had never talked about that night again, and had never bothered stealing her mom's beer again.

"I thought you said you don't drink," Riley said, turning towards Theo, a slight edge to her voice.

Theo took a deep breath, banishing the memory from her mind, her senses. Her stomach calmed. She took a sip of the cider. It was fruity, and a little sour. Not bad. She looked up to Riley, and smiled. "I'm in the mood to push my boundaries a little bit, that's all. It's good to see you though. Are those your friends back there?"

Riley's skepticism lingered for a few more moments, but she let it slide, and an easy smile returned to her. "Yeah. They're my sorority sisters."

"Oh." Theo blinked. "I don't think you ever mentioned you were in a sorority."

"Didn't I? I could have sworn it came up." Riley reached up and brushed a stray strand of hair behind her ear, looking nervous.

Summer rolled her eyes. "She didn't mention it because people, especially nerdy and queer types, often have a lot of weird ideas about sororities thanks to movies and stuff."

Riley spun to glare at Summer. "I didn't ask for your opinion."

"Yeah, right. Sorry." Summer held her hands up defensively.

Theo smiled at Riley softly. "I guess I can understand that. I don't know much about them. Maybe you could tell me about it tomorrow at lunch?"

"I... sure. I'd love that. We can..." Riley trailed off, and her eyes flickered between Theo and Summer. She bit her lip, and took a deep breath. "I'd better get back to the girls, they're hopeless at trivia without me. Guess we'll be competing in the next round."

"Sure. Later."

Riley turned and made her way back to her table.

Minha snorted, and raised her glass to Summer. "Looks like you've got some competition."

"It's not like that," both Summer and Theo said at the same time.

But while Summer said it with mild annoyance, Theo's words had an edge of desperation to them. Because she didn't want Summer to think it was true.

"Alright alright, geez." Minha held up her hands. "But hey, Riley actually spoke to you. That seems like a step up."

Summer glanced over her shoulder and sighed. "I mean, I fucked up pretty bad. I deserve far worse than a cold shoulder."

Theo took another long swig of her cider. She'd avoided thinking about the topic, because it was uncomfortable. "What really happened, between the two of you? Riley said... that you got tricked?"

"That's... not really an excuse." Summer rested her chin on her palm, her gaze directed away from Theo. "But we're here to have fun tonight, right? If you really wanna know how much of a shithead I am we can go over it later."

"Sorry," Theo mumbled.

"Alright folks," a young man said over a microphone. "We're going to start up round three here, and we're going to kick things off with a hard one. Remember, you're not allowed to look things up on your phone. What's the capital of Burkina Faso? You have one minute to answer."

"Shit." Minha groaned. "I hate geography stuff."

"Yeah, no idea."

Theo grinned. "It's Ouagadougou."

Minha's eyes went wide. "For real? I knew inviting you was a good idea."

"Before you think I'm smarter than I am, I happened to see a meme about that recently."

"Well, whatever works." Summer held up the app, ready to type the answer in. "So how do you spell that?"

"Umm..." Theo looked away, and took another sip of her drink. It really was good. "I think it starts with an O?"

Summer laughed, deleted what she'd typed so far. "Well, we'll see if we'll get points for getting close."

They didn't.

Dear Diary,

Summer has been ignoring me ever since the beer incident.
I don't understand it. Did I do something wrong?
I just want to talk to her. I want to hang out with her. She's my best friend.
I'm pretty sure most of the time she feels the same way about me.
I just… wish she didn't get so distant sometimes.

Theo
4/27/2013

Summer leaned against a post in the bar, arms crossed over her chest, watching disaster unfold.

Minha stumbled into Theo, slinging an arm around her shoulder. "Hold on, the lighting sucked in that one. Let me try again!"

Theo laughed a little too loud, and then grinned as Minha raised her arm to take a selfie. "You gotta send me these pictures!"

One drink had turned into two, and then when Summer had gotten up to go to the bathroom she'd come back to find empty shot glasses on the table. Theo and Minha had now passed Tipsy and reached Drunk.

Summer had failed in her duties. Minha could be so freaking obnoxious, and she always tried to drag everyone down to her level.

But at the same time, they were both adults, who could make their own decisions. Wasn't like Summer had any right to tell them what to do.

A familiar scent of lavender tickled her nose, and Summer stiffened.

"That was a good match," Riley said from behind her.

"Hard to compete with a genius like you. And even then it was all thanks to Theo."

They'd lost the trivia round, but only barely, coming in second place with Riley's team coming in first. Just like with the boardgame, Theo had gotten really into the competitive spirit of it. Unfortunately, the final bonus tiebreaker questions had come down to astronomy, and that was Riley's department.

Riley chuckled softly, her voice tinged with nostalgia. "Always quick to try and build others up, huh?"

Summer shifted uncomfortably, not really sure where this was going. A part of her felt the urge to simply apologize again, but she bit down on it. She'd already given what apologies she could. Adding more on top of that would burden Riley even further.

Silence hung between them, heavy, awkward. Punctuated by the loud, drunk college students occasionally erupting into cheers. Somewhere a game of beer pong had started. Minha looked like she was trying to sell Theo on the idea of playing.

"Do you think she'll be okay?" Riley asked, looking towards Theo.

Summer shrugged. "Dunno. She seems like she's having fun, but it might be a good idea if I take her home soon."

Riley nodded. "She is a bit... delicate."

"She's tougher than she seems."

Another long silence, then Riley stepped forward, into Summer's field of vision. She searched her face, looking unsure. "She's been staying with you for a while now. Have the two of you..."

Summer winced, and shook her head. "It's not like that. She's a friend who's been through a lot, and I'm helping her out the best I can. That's all."

"From what I've heard you were exceptionally awful to her as a kid. The fact that she's someone you can call a friend means she's pretty remarkable."

"It's... slightly more complicated than that," Summer hedged, looking away. A part of her wished she could tell Riley the truth, but the proof that had worked so well on Summer would fail to convince anyone else. And that would be Theo's story to share, ultimately.

"Hmm." Riley studied her carefully, leaning in closer. "Do you wish it was something more?"

Summer was silent for a long time. She could deflect. She could lie. But Riley would see right through her. She'd always been able to read her too well. "A little," she admitted. "But it's not an option. Too much baggage there, and she's gonna be gone in a month anyway. Uh, moving away."

"Wait, really?" Riley blinked several times. "Shit. She never mentioned that. And she's been doing such a good job keeping everything in the department organized. Jerry is going to be devastated."

Whoops. Well, might as well lean into it. "Some family stuff she needs to deal with, I think." Technically true.

Riley turned to stare at Theo, her eyes sad. "Why is it we both always fall for the same, unavailable women?"

Summer laughed, and shook her head. "Even with the university, only ever so many gay girls around. If I stick around too long in this town, I'll eventually completely age myself out of that dating pool too."

A beat passed, and then Riley snorted with laughter. "Sorry, sorry! For a moment I pictured you as the lesbian version of that creepy older guy who shows up at college parties."

Probably where her future was headed, but Summer grinned anyway. She scrunched up her face, put a rasp into her voice, and said "Heeeey ladies," in the creepiest way she could manage.

Riley laughed even harder, and elbowed Summer in the side. "Too real!"

Summer grinned, and for a moment, it was just like old times. Riley was her friend again. All was right in the world.

The moment passed. Riley looked away. Silence hung in the air, awkward once more.

"I'm still mad at you, you know. What you did really sucked." Riley's eyes glistened in the dim light.

"I know. I wouldn't expect anything else."

Riley took a deep breath. "*But*," she said, looking back up at Summer. "It's becoming clearer and clearer to me that Heather isn't someone that was worth keeping in my life anyway, and that you still are. It hurts. But I'll get there. Eventually."

Hope fluttered inside of Summer, followed by a wave of self loathing. "I don't deserve that," she mumbled.

"Not your decision, unfortunately." Riley grinned. "If I decide I want to be your friend again, there's nothing you can do about it. Whether you deserve it or not."

Summer swallowed carefully, biting back the deeper emotions that threatened to well to the surface. Keep it light, casual, funny. "Why does it feel like you're mugging me?"

Riley laughed, pointed a finger gun at Summer, and affected a bad gangster accent. "Stick 'em up, pal! Hand over all the friendship you got!"

It made Summer laugh, and she relaxed a bit. "I don't carry any physical friendship on me these days, it's all on my card. Which you can take if you want, but I'll just cancel it as soon as I get home. Might as well—"

The sound of a shattering glass interrupted her gag, and they both turned to see Theo standing there, broken glass on the floor next to her, looking a bit surprised.

Summer sighed. "I should probably take her home."

Riley nodded. "Looks like. Get her home safe, you hear? And don't do anything I wouldn't do."

"Short list, that."

Summer made her way over, gently resting her hand on Theo's shoulder to get her attention.

"Heya!" Theo lit up when she saw Summer. She wobbled a bit, but looked utterly delighted. "I'm so glad I decided to cut loose. Let loose. Loose, tonight. I'm having so much fun!"

"Sure, yeah, it's been good." Summer stretched, exaggerating a yawn. "I'm getting a little beat though. How about we head home?"

Theo's brow scrunched up, and she frowned. "Minha said we gotta keep the party going."

Summer scanned the room for Minha, and found her in the lap of some tall, tweedy looking hipster. "I think she's doing alright for herself."

"I'm fine," Theo grumbled, an edge in her voice. "I don't need you to babysit me."

So Theo was the type to get stubborn when drunk. That tracked, honestly. But Summer had other tricks up her sleeve. "I know you are, you look like you're having a blast. But I'm feeling a bit off, personally. I think those nachos we ordered aren't sitting right in my stomach. And... I don't really want to walk home alone. Is that okay?"

Theo's expression immediately softened. "Oh. Crap, I'm sorry. Um... sure. Yeah. Let's head out. Let me close up my tab."

Summer walked down main street, Theo clinging tightly to her arm.

"I really did have fun tonight. Thanks." Theo stumbled as she walked, and squeezed Summer even tighter. "It feels like... I dunno. Like I've been carrying a lot and I don't gotta care about it right now."

"Sure. I'm glad you had fun." Summer glanced down, Theo's hair close, the scent of it familiar, that of Summer's own shampoo.

"Mmm." Theo hummed to herself, a little off key. "Why am I getting the impression that you didn't really have fun? I'm sorry."

Summer shrugged. "I liked the trivia, but I wasn't really in the mood for anything rowdier. And I love Minha, but she can be a lot sometimes, especially after working a full shift with her."

Theo chuckled to herself. "I think she's fun. I'm jealous, that my other self has such a cool younger sister. Or had. God, I really want to know what went down there. But I have like, barely any social media footprint. It's so obnoxious, and makes me really difficult to cyberstalk."

"Isn't that a good thing?"

"Yes, but it's really inconvenient for *me* personally," Theo whined. "I know it'd be a bad idea but I really wanna know who she is, how she thinks, how she's different from me, if her relationship was a total disaster like all of mine have been or if it was slightly more amicable. How often does anyone get the chance to know how things could have turned out, you know?"

Summer's mind immediately drifted to all of the pictures of herself on Theo's phone, and she nodded. "Yeah, no. I... definitely understand that feeling."

"You know, that used to be a movie rental place," Theo said, pointing at what was now a small cafe. "I remember going there with my mom and dad when I was little. I guess before streaming quite took over everything."

"You could get older movies there for like, a quarter," Summer said, thinking back. "I didn't really have access to streaming when I was young, so I definitely rented a lot. Up until the point where I got banned for uh, not returning too many of them."

Theo snorted. "Always the troublemaker."

Summer shrugged. "Had a whole scheme in mind where I would sell the DVDs to other kids for a dollar, but turned out nobody actually wanted them."

As their walk continued, Theo pointed out stuff she remembered or that had changed, waxing nostalgic. Both of them shared memories of growing up in this small town, intersecting in all sorts of slanted ways, but never actually touching.

When they made it back to the apartment, Summer poured Theo a glass of water, and grabbed a bag of pretzels from the cabinet. "Here, get some food and water in you."

"I can think of some other things I'd rather have in me," Theo said, waggling her eyebrows.

Summer stopped, blinked several times, then turned to stare at Theo incredulously. "What?"

Theo opened her mouth, then closed it again. Her face turned bright red, and she drank the entire glass of water. "Sorry," she mumbled. "That was funnier in my head than it ended up being. I'm... still a little tipsy, if you haven't noticed."

"What? Nah, couldn't be." Summer flashed a grin, but her heart pounded in her chest. Women had certainly gotten her into bed with *worse* lines, and the thought of Theo actually following through with her comment lit a fire deep in Summer. It was bad enough that her thoughts kept drifting towards similar scenarios, when Theo was at work and Summer had the apartment to herself.

But circumstances weren't different. They were a fucked up pile of trauma and booze and bad decisions. And Summer liked Theo too much to walk the dumb and horny path.

Theo munched quietly on pretzels, her face still flushed, occasionally stealing glances over at Summer.

Summer sighed, and stretched. "Might as well get ready for bed. You gotta get up early for work tomorrow."

"... Right. Almost forgot about that. Can't even like, come up with a good excuse, considering Riley was there."

"She'd cover for you, if need be. But you're not *utterly* shitfaced, so you'll probably be fine tomorrow. Nothing some ibuprofen couldn't fix, anyway."

Theo let out an almost dreamy sigh. "Riley's so cool. Can't believe you didn't hold onto her, she seems like a real keeper."

It was Summer's turn to flush, and she rubbed at the back of her neck. "It's complicated. She was going through a lot at the time, and... well. The more important part is that she's a very driven and ambitious person, and

I'm… not. Was never gonna work long term. Glad I could still be her friend. Glad she still is considering being mine, even after what I did."

Summer paused, then cursed under her breath. She'd walked right into the next question.

"What *did* you do, exactly?"

"I slept with Riley's girlfriend. What else is there to say?"

Theo pursed her lips. "But that's not really the full story, is it?"

Summer groaned, then sat down at the table across from Theo, resting her chin on her palm. "Does the full story really matter at all? I did a bad thing. I was a shitty friend. I betrayed Riley in a way that should be unforgivable, and the fact that she's considering forgiving me anyway is utterly baffling. Any reasons or explanations I could give are just excuses. They don't justify anything."

"Summer…" Theo reached out a hand to rest on top of Summer's. "I'm not blaming you for anything. I'm a total outsider in all of this. It's not about excuses or justifications. I want to understand you better."

A lump formed in Summer's throat at the contact. Theo's hand felt warmer than normal. "Alright, fine. Gimme a second."

She sat there, letting her thoughts stew, letting the narrative piece together in her mind. How much should she say? How much context should she give for this messy drama that stretched back years?

"I never really liked Heather." Summer kept her tone careful, even. She was relaying her own perspective, as neutrally as she could. "She was always involved in some big drama or another. Her mood switched at the drop of a hat. You were either her absolute favorite person in the whole world or the worst kind of evil to ever walk this earth, with absolutely no in between."

Theo made a face. "I've… definitely met people who fit that description before."

"Mmm. Since I didn't actually go to college, I didn't interact with her much directly, so a lot of what I got was secondhand, from other people. Until she started dating Riley."

Summer sucked in air through her teeth, her whole body tensing up. "It wasn't a healthy relationship. Heather was mean, and demanding and manipulative, constantly putting Riley down, poking at her insecurities, gaslighting her. It pissed me the hell off, but it didn't feel like there was anything I could do, without coming across as a jealous ex."

Theo squeezed her hand a little tighter. "I'm sorry. That sounds really hard to deal with."

"Yeah, well." Summer snorted. "And then one night, back in... June? May? Heather showed up on my doorstep in the pouring rain. Soaking wet. Makeup ruined. Sobbing. Bruise forming on her face. She told me that she'd gotten into a fight with Riley. That Riley had screamed at her, put hands on her, thrown her out onto the street. I let her in. Listened to her. Believed her. Gave her a change of clothes, made her some hot cocoa. Let her cry in my arms. And then..."

"One thing led to another?"

Summer pulled her hand free from Theo, wrapping her arms around her stomach instead. "I hate that phrase. It's never something that just happens. It's a choice you make, at every step of the way, to continue, to escalate, to not stop. She was vulnerable. I believed her, like an idiot. I wanted to make her feel better. And when she kissed me, I kissed back. Because I thought it would help. Because a part of me wanted it too. Because I'm just that pathetic."

Theo was silent. Summer couldn't bear to meet her gaze any longer, and she wondered what judgment and condemnation was lying there.

"I confronted Riley about it the next day, full of righteous fire and fury. And she was so confused and hurt. A lot of things were said. Took awhile for the full truth to come out, but well. Heather was half telling the truth. It wasn't Riley who'd done those things. It was her other side piece."

"So..." Theo licked her lips. "She took advantage of you. Manipulated you."

Summer shook her head. "I fell for it. I should have trusted in Riley. I knew what Heather was like, and even then. I could have simply believed without *also* then sleeping with her. Could have talked to Riley calmly, rather than letting her find out in the worst possible way. Every step of the situation could have been handled better, but it wasn't, because I'm the kind of loser who sees a girl in trouble and gets horny about it."

Theo fidgeted in her chair, wringing her hands together. "It sounds like despite all the pain and drama, maybe it's for the best. If this relationship was as unhealthy as you said."

"That's the bullshit of it all." Summer clenched her teeth. "You're absolutely right. On some level, I did Riley a favor, by making it clear exactly the kind of person that Heather was. And I might do it again. Being the villain feels like a small sacrifice in comparison."

"There are... *probably* better ways to achieve the same result."

"Yeah, well. I didn't do those, did I?" Summer stood back up, walking past Theo towards the bathroom. "We should get ready for bed. You have a better idea of how much of a dirtbag I am now. So if you want me to fuck off and sleep on the floor, or back to the car, I totally will."

Theo's eyes softened, and she shook her head. "I don't think you're a dirtbag, Summer."

Summer rolled her eyes. "Well, wait till you hear about just how much of an evil bitch I was towards the original Theo."

She didn't wait for a response, and made her way into the bathroom to brush her teeth.

Twenty minutes later, they were both in bed, blanketed by darkness. Summer closed her eyes, trying to let the turmoil stirred up in her calm down. She'd shown more of her true self. Maybe Theo needed time to process it, but she'd eventually come to realize that Summer wasn't worth it.

This was only ever about Summer desperately trying to assuage her own guilt. To fill the pit of emptiness inside of her with 'good deeds'.

"Summer?" Theo asked, voice barely audible over the sound of the fan.

She didn't respond. Better to pretend to be asleep.

Theo's hand gripped Summer's bare shoulder, and she shook gently. "Hey. Summer?"

Summer sighed, then rolled over so that she was facing Theo. "What's up?"

"I..." Theo licked her lips, her expression difficult to read in the dark. "You look like you could use a hug."

"I'm fi—"

But Theo was already moving closer, sliding her arm underneath Summer, wrapping her other around from the top. She pulled Summer close, head resting against Theo's chest.

A terrible idea. It made Summer feel even worse, knowing how much she wanted this, and how much she wanted more.

But she hugged Theo back, snuggling in close. Sharing warmth, hearing her heart beat, feeling the tickle of breath on her neck.

She would drink deep of what she was offered, and enjoy what she could, for as long as it lasted.

But Summer always came to an end.

~

Theo woke up with Summer held tight in her arms.

She was still asleep, breathing softly. Their smells were intertwined, the same soap, the same shampoo.

It was hard not to think of when this had happened in the past. Summer was loathe to be vulnerable, to be this close, but there were a few nights, after particularly bad fights with Summer's mom.

Summer would come over to Theo's house. She would be upset, she'd rage, at her mother, the world, everything and everyone. Except Theo. Theo would hold her, let her cry it out, be close to her, be her rock, offer her comfort, the one thing she could hold onto in her fucked up life.

She'd then avoid Theo for a week or so afterwards, until coming back like nothing had happened, never acknowledging it.

And Theo would go over it in her mind over and over and over. Hell, she'd *yearned* for it, hoping that Summer would come back to take solace in her embrace once more. Because she was a pathetic lesbian with a crush. Because she would take whatever scraps of affection she was given and greedily hope for more.

What had Summer really thought of her, back then? She'd thought her crush was nothing but one sided pining, that Summer was straight, could never have cared for her in the same way. She'd spent ten guilt filled years of grief, so sure that Summer had been disgusted by the reveal of Theo's crush right before the end. That what Theo thought was a special connection between them was nothing but wishful thinking.

But she knew the truth, now. Summer was into women. She was just as much of a messy dyke as Theo was.

Had Summer also yearned for that closeness? Had she been afraid that Theo would reject her, if she asked for something more? Had her thoughts drifted to Theo at night, with her hand between her legs?

What more could they have become, if Theo hadn't fucked up, and gotten Summer killed?

Summer stirred in her arms, and Theo brought herself back to the present.

"Morning," Theo whispered.

"Mmm."

What was. What could have been. Useless thoughts, to pull her down below the depths and drown her. What mattered was now. Summer was right here in front of her, in her arms. By an unknown miracle, she had another chance.

And she wasn't going to miss it.

Summer's eyes fluttered open slowly, until they met Theo's gaze. They focused, and then a somewhat shy, nervous smile bloomed on her face. "Morning."

Theo couldn't help but smile back. Because she knew what she wanted. And she was an adult woman now, not a shy teenage girl. She'd made up her mind.

One way or another, she was going to seduce Summer Sullivan.

Dear Diary,

Summer break is coming up soon.

 I'm really excited about all the stuff Summer and I get to do together this year.

 We've known each other since 4th grade, which is so crazy to think about. Which means we've had 5 summers spent hanging out and having fun already, and that this will be the sixth.

 So maybe it shouldn't be so special but... it always is. I know she has just as much fun as I do.

 I really can't wait.

Theo
5/8/2013

"Hey Peter!" Theo called out.

Peter turned around, a warm smile lighting up his face. "Hey Theo! I was just closing up, but if you want some leftover bread it's all yours."

Theo grinned and leaned against the wall, enjoying the feeling of cool brick against her bare shoulder. It was hot out today, and Theo had spent her entire workday going over various ideas and plans in her mind. None of them quite clicked, though. "Nah, we still haven't finished the last batch of bread you gave us. Appreciate it though. I was actually hoping to talk to you."

"Oh." Peter blinked in surprise. "I still got some cleaning up to do, but happy to talk while I work."

"Need help?"

Peter raised an eyebrow. "Do you mean that? Because I'm not too humble to accept."

Theo laughed. "Yeah, I mean it. Not like I have anything better to do while I wait for Summer to get home."

"Alrighty then." Peter led her inside the bakery, then handed her a spray bottle and some towels. "Go ahead and wipe down the counters and tables."

Easy enough. There wouldn't be a single crumb left behind when Theo was through.

"So what can I help you with?" Peter asked as he pulled a bag from a trash can, tying it up.

Theo bit her lip, thinking. Should she launch right into it? "How long have you known Summer?"

Peter tilted his head to the side. "Since elementary school. Thought you knew that. As long as you have, really."

Right. Unhelpful. "Sorry, I meant like, as an adult. How long have you actually been friends?"

"Oh, duh. Sorry." Peter rubbed at his neck. "Maybe about two, three years now? Whenever she started living in the apartment upstairs. Wasn't exactly the moody troublemaker I remembered from school. Why do you ask?"

Theo rubbed at a particularly persistent stain, putting more pressure on it, before she realized it was part of the table. Well, she might as well spit it out. "I want to ask Summer out on a date. And I want it to be something special. I know she's had a ton of girlfriends before and I was just wondering if... I dunno. You had any insight on the kind of thing she might like."

"Oh!" He reached up and stroked his beard, giddy with joy. "Not gonna lie, I kind of assumed you two were already dating. The way you both light up whenever you see each other. The way it's already 'us' and 'we'. You two make me swoon!"

"Yeah, well." Warmth flooded Theo's cheeks, and she moved onto the next table, focusing very hard on that instead. "You're not... wrong, I guess. But it's not anything we've talked about, or made any real moves. It's only tension. Connection. I've spent a lot of my life being a useless lesbian, and I want to suck it up and actually do something about it for once."

Peter laughed. "That's so cute, Theo! Gosh. And I mean, it's not like I have any room to criticize."

Theo glanced back at him. "How are things going with Aaron anyway?"

"Oh, you know." Peter hunched inwards, his fingers twisting up in his sweater. "We're taking things slow… gonna see him again tomorrow night though."

Adorable. She was so happy for him. She wanted that for herself. "I'm glad. I know you two will be super cute together."

Peter put a hand against his cheek. "Come on now, aren't we talking about you? You want to ask Summer out. So do it!"

"It's… complicated." More complicated than he would ever know. "I just… she's really special, and I want to show her. How much I care. Something more than just a trip to a coffee shop or whatever."

"I see, I see." Peter's face grew serious, and he tapped his foot on the floor. "Summer doesn't exactly spill a lot of tea when it comes to her dating life, but to me she's always seemed like a go with the flow kind of girl. She'd probably be happy with anything, as long as it meant spending time with you."

The thought made Theo's heart soar, but it wasn't what she was here for. "I know that. And that's part of the problem. I want her to feel special, not just someone who goes along with what everyone else wants."

Peter's brow furrowed. "Hmm. Makes sense, I guess. Well, let me think. She loves the outdoors. Big fan of a good burger, too."

"Outdoors, huh? Like hiking and stuff?"

"She goes hiking out by the lake a lot, I think."

An idea was finally starting to coalesce in Theo's mind. Something she could use. "Thanks, Peter. I can work with that."

"Anytime. Summer deserves some special treatment. She gives so much of herself to everyone she meets that it's hard to see what's left over sometimes. Can you grab me the mop and bucket from the closet over there?"

Theo did so, and helped Peter clean everything for the next half hour, as she discussed her plans, refining them. It would be simple, sweet, but would require her to rush out to the grocery store as soon as she got her paycheck tomorrow, and get everything ready in time.

She would do everything in her power to make it perfect.

Summer leaned against the counter at the gas station, staring at her phone, trying to decipher the text message on the screen.

Theo: Hey. Make sure you're hungry and ready to go somewhere when you get home, because I've got some plans for dinner. ;)

Earlier that morning, Theo had asked Summer if she could borrow the car for grocery shopping. Which was a little bit of a bummer. Summer had enjoyed going when they went shopping together.

But now it sounded like Theo might cook dinner tonight? Something fancier than boxed mac and cheese or ramen. But also they were going somewhere? Confusing.

"Sounds like you got a hot date tonight," Minha said from behind.

Summer cursed and stuffed her phone back into her pocket. "It's not like that, and I'm getting really sick of explaining that to you."

Minha held up her hands. "Dude, she's totally into you, it's super obvious. And that winky face emoji? She's asking you on a date for sure."

"It's food plans. We're roommates. We plan dinner occasionally. There's no point in reading into it."

"Uh-huh." Minha rolled her eyes. "I dunno how you've got so much rizz for everyone else but are completely clamming up with a girl who literally already lives with you, and is objectively awesome as hell."

Summer grumbled under her breath. "Look, you knew Theo before. Did she ever tell why she moved out to... um. Massachusetts?"

"Maryland."

"Right, that."

Minha shrugged. "I dunno. Something about being bullied pretty bad in school?"

"Exactly. She was bullied so bad that she moved across the country to get away from it."

"I don't see what that has to do with anythi—"

"It was *me*," Summer hissed. "I'm the one that bullied her and ruined her life. So when I say things are *complicated*, can you please believe me?"

That finally got through to Minha, and she stared at Summer, eyes wide, mouth open. "Fuck, dude. That's messed up."

"Yeah, I know."

"So it's like, a whole enemies to lovers thing?"

"Oh fuck o—"

"Excuse me."

Summer blinked, then turned around to see a middle-aged woman standing at the counter with a bag of chips and a soda.

"Sorry," Summer said quickly, her face flushed. "Let me get that for you."

"Oh, no worries." The woman smiled as Summer scanned her items. "Don't mean to be nosy, but… why not ask if it's a date?"

Of course, even strangers were getting involved in her love life. Summer pinched the bridge of her nose. "Fine, whatever." She pulled out her phone, and fired off a quick text.

Summer: Almost sounds like a date, lol

Silence hung in the convenience store, everyone waiting in anticipation.

Theo texted back a few seconds later.

Theo: It is. <3

Well shit. What was she supposed to do with that?

Minha punched her in the arm, cackling.

The woman smiled, and took her items. "Have fun!"

"Thanks," Summer mumbled. She slumped on the counter, her head in her hands.

What did it all mean?

She liked Theo. Theo liked her. Was that enough?

Summer had hurt a different Theo. Theo had lost a different Summer. Wasn't it all too messy?

In only a few weeks, Theo would be leaving forever, returning to her world. Nobody ever wanted to stay with Summer longterm.

So if there was anything here at all, it would at best be a brief, passionate fling.

Summer was used to it. That was her lot, her role in other people's lives. Someone who could hopefully be a good memory, but nothing more.

A part of her was giddy for it. She wanted this. A part of her dreaded this, because it wouldn't be enough. It was never enough. A twin helix of hope and dread intertwined together in her soul.

There was nothing to do except move forward.

Summer: Looking forward to it

~

Summer opened the door to her apartment, and found Theo waiting for her.

"Heya! Welcome home." Theo sat at the kitchen table, her smile wide, but with an edge of nervousness to it. She'd put on makeup, a bit of shadow around her eyes, lips a little darker than normal. Her eyes darted to the corner of the room, where a cooler and several bags had been stacked into a pile. "So. I've got a plan, and I'm ready to go whenever, but I guess you maybe want a chance to change or decompress or whatever first. So I can wait. Whatever you're comfortable with."

Accommodating. Easy. Casual. So why was Summer's heart pounding in her chest, why did her mouth feel so dry? She'd been on so many dates before. What made this so different? She took a deep breath, then nodded. "Sure. Let me get changed."

She closed her bedroom door behind her. Alone, only a few inches of particle board separating them It felt a bit silly. They shared this room together. Shared the bed. Things were already intimate, to a degree.

But this step, this escalation felt like standing at the edge of a cliff, a yawning chasm ready to swallow her whole. The potential for disaster was so high.

But even if Summer fucked things up entirely, she could find a way to salvage things. Riley or Minha would probably offer her a couch.

Steeling her nerves, she stripped out of her work clothes, put on a nicer pair of jeans, reapplied her deodorant, found one of her favorite t-shirts, and topped it all off with her trusty leather jacket.

Should she do her makeup too? Do something nice with her hair? Her roots needed a touchup, they were getting bad. She sighed, staring at herself in the mirror. She'd never been any good at stuff like this. She'd always done her own thing, and expected others to either take it or leave it.

She'd done the same with Theo, and Theo apparently wanted to take it. So that would have to be good enough.

"So where are we going?" Summer asked as she exited the bedroom a few minutes later.

A wave of visible relief washed over Theo at the sight of Summer. She'd probably been going through her own internal panic spiral. "It's a secret."

Summer raised an eyebrow. "Is that so?"

Theo winced. "Saying it like that probably makes it seem a lot cooler than it actually is. It's nothing that special, honest. Well, I mean. I want it to be special, I just…" She trailed off, looking away and wringing her hands together.

It was nice to know that they were both nervous, both unsure. That they could navigate this, figure it out together. Summer smiled. "Sure, I get it. I'll trust you."

"Okay. Yeah. Shall we go then?"

"Lead the way."

15

Dear Diary,

~~Fuck fuck fuck fuck fuck fuck fuck~~
  ~~I think I'm~~
God I don't even know what to say about this.

We were hanging out in the fort reading manga, and I grabbed one of the ones she wanted to read, and she tried to grab it back, and we were play fighting for a bit but then she pinned me down onto the beanbag and it was like all the breath left my body and my mind went totally blank.

And then she smiled and reached down and brushed some dust or something out of my hair, and when she touched me it was like electricity shot through my entire body.

All I could think about in that moment was how much I wanted to kiss her.

And then she grabbed the manga and laughed and pulled away and the moment was over and I felt really confused and stupid and not sure what just happened.

And now I'm sitting here in my room writing this and trying to make sense of it all and googling what it means if you want to kiss your best friend and

Fuck I think I might actually be gay

I've been reading through old entries in this diary and god like 90% of them are about Summer.

Has this been going on the entire time?

What the fuck am I supposed to do?

Theo
6/22/2013

Theo's mind raced a million miles a minute as she drove to the date spot.

Had she prepared enough? Thought everything through? Was this a good idea at all? Would Summer actually like this? Was she going along with it out of some sense of pity? Was this all some terrible mistake? Would she destroy everything good she'd built during her time in this reality? Would she be forced to run home with her tail between her legs? Granted a miracle for a second chance, only for it to crumble to ash and slip between her fingers?

Her hands shook on the steering wheel. The bad thoughts crawled through her brain, a swarm of spiders, thousands of little legs, sharp and itchy. A constant annoyance, a buzz of pain and discomfort.

The lack of her anti-anxiety meds was definitely starting to take its toll.

A soft pressure on her shoulder. Summer's hand, a gentle squeeze. A warm smile, promising comfort, reassurance.

Enough of a lifeline, to pull Theo's head back above water. She took a deep breath, focusing her attention back on the present, at the road she probably wasn't paying nearly enough attention to. The spiders in her brain continued to scratch and tear, but she would ignore them. She had to.

Luckily, they had arrived.

Theo pulled into the parking lot and stopped the car. They were in the nearby state park, not far from the lake where Summer had taken her. The scenery here was gorgeous in the day, this late at night there wasn't much to look at. But there was at least enough light to see the park shelter that was their destination, full of tables and those rusty grills that everyone was allowed to use.

Summer glanced at her, raised an eyebrow, and then shrugged.

A part of Theo wanted to rush to explain, to justify her thought process, to stumble over her words as they tied her in knots until she tripped and ended up sprawled on the floor.

Instead, she simply said, "Help me with the stuff," and got out of the car.

Together, they got out the cooler, and other various supplies, and dragged them over to the park shelter. They had the place all to themselves. Theo immediately got to work on filling one of the grills with charcoal, dousing it in lighter fluid, and getting a fire started.

Thick heavy clouds blotted out the sky. Just her luck. When she'd been picturing this night, she'd imagined it under a blanket of stars, the moon shining bright. She probably should have remembered to check the weather.

But she still had other tricks up her sleeve when it came to romantic ambiance. When she'd scouted out this location earlier, she'd set up a bunch of candles around the park shelter. She set about lighting them one by one.

Except it was windier than she'd expected. The candles fought her and refused to stay lit. When she finally succeeded, the flames flickered dangerously, ready to go out at any moment.

Summer sat quietly through it all, sitting at one of the picnic tables, her intense gaze focused solely on Theo.

Theo sat opposite from Summer, her hands folded in her lap, her head hung low. Why was it so awkward? They weren't usually this awkward. Their conversations usually came easy, their banter natural.

She'd been so full of confidence when she'd made this plan, ready to finally shoot her shot. Grasp what she'd always wanted.

And now...

"Hey," Summer said, her voice low and soft.

Theo looked up, into those brilliant green eyes, eyes that were so easy to get lost in, eyes of a girl she'd seen dead, staring vacant with nothing behind them.

"This is really sweet," Summer said, biting her lip.

Simple words that stopped Theo's downward spiral dead in its tracks. She forced herself to take a step back, pay more attention. She studied Summer's expression carefully. Was she blushing? It was hard to tell, in the dim light. "You think so?"

Summer chuckled softly, and raised a hand to run her fingers through her hair. "Yeah. I mean. Of all the dates I've been on, they're always, you know. Hanging out, or whatever. Same as I'd do with a friend, but also we have sex afterwards. Nobody's ever tried to like... *woo* me before. Grilling by candlelight in the park? It's... sweet."

Theo wasn't sure how to respond to that, and she wrung her hands together in her lap.

"...Shit. I probably shouldn't be talking about other girls on a date, huh? Sorry. I'm not very good at this."

"It's fine." It wasn't fine, not really, but Theo didn't want to get into that right now. "You deserve it, though. To be wooed. I know everything about us is completely messed up, but… I want to do this anyway."

Summer studied her in silence for several long moments, before she gave a slight nod. "Okay."

The fire was probably hot enough by now, right? Theo stood up, turning away from Summer, hiding the heat in her cheeks. There were burgers to grill, after all.

She could still feel Summer's gaze on her back, burning a hole into her heart.

The heavenly smell of cooking burgers made Summer's mouth water. It had been too long since she'd eaten today.

Theo, for her part, seemed to know what she was doing. She remained focused on the grill, her concentration intense, her back to Summer.

So Summer let her focus, and kept silent. There was a tension between them, thick and heavy. Too many questions, too many things unsaid. Summer was afraid that if they were spoken out loud, it would all flicker and fade, like an illusion.

"Damnit," Theo muttered under her breath. The vicious wind whipped her hair all over the place. She was constantly having to fuss with it, tuck it behind her ears, a futile struggle that would only stay in place for a few seconds before it blew back into her face again.

Theo's hair really was pretty. Long, straight, and so dark it reflected the firelight. Summer wondered what it would feel like to run her fingers through it, to pull on it.

"Hey," Summer said, stepping up behind Theo. "Let me get that for you."

Theo let out a soft gasp as Summer grazed her fingers along Theo's neck, gathering up her hair in between her fingers, pulling it back. Summer had a spare hair tie around her wrist, and after gathering all of the strays she could manage, pulled Theo's hair into a ponytail.

Summer felt Theo shiver beneath her fingertips, felt her breath come in short gasps, could see the redness of her face illuminated by burning coals.

She stepped back, feeling a rush at how easily Theo had been affected by this slight touch. "Better?"

"Mm. Mmmhmm." Theo nodded ever so slightly.

Summer grinned, then sat back down to wait for food.

It came a few minutes later. Thick, juicy burgers, cooked to perfection, the meat well seasoned, fresh pickles, relish, ketchup, cheese, and accompanied by a side of potato chips and a soda for good measure. Classic midwestern cookout.

It was hard to look dignified or sexy while eating a burger. So Summer didn't bother. She let out a quiet moan of satisfaction as she bit in. "This is a really fucking good burger," she mumbled, her mouth full.

Theo dabbed at ketchup on her lip with a napkin, hiding her expression. But her delight was clearly still visible in her eyes. "My dad was a big fan of holding cookouts for the whole neighborhood. And he taught me a lot about grilling. Haven't had much chance to put it into practice recently though, was worried I'd gotten rusty."

Summer took another bite, making sure to actually chew it and swallow before continuing this time. "Never got to really do the classic cookout thing as a kid. But I do the whole tailgating thing every once and awhile now. Minha burns the shit out of her burgers though. Seriously, these are perfect."

A flash of pain crossed Theo's eyes, and she looked away. She was silent for several moments, opened her mouth as if to say something, and then she closed it again and shook her head softly.

Something to do with the other Summer, probably. Maybe they'd done the cookout thing together. That'd make sense.

Summer bit her lip. She didn't want to think about it too hard. So much baggage there. So little time, only a few weeks left. Did it even make sense, to try and unpack it? Was it possible for them to relax and enjoy themselves?

They continued to eat in relative silence, punctuated by the occasional comment or observation, but it was shallow, easily passed, easily digestible.

When she was done, Summer leaned back, finishing things off with a loud belch. She held her empty can of soda lightly in her fingers, letting it sway back and forth. If she set it down on the table the wind would probably claim it.

Thunder rumbled low in the distance.

"Is this really okay?" Theo asked, her voice barely above a whisper.

Summer shrugged. "I mean, I'm here, aren't I? If I had a problem with it, with you, I wouldn't have gone along with this. Simple as that, really." She paused, thinking through her next words carefully. "I was a bit surprised, though. That this is what you want. Considering, well." She gestured vaguely. "Everything."

Theo folded her hands over her stomach, and kept her eyes firmly on the picnic table. "Thought I had it all figured out. Was gonna be cool and forward and seductive. But when push comes to shove, I'm an awkward mess, a shell of a person held together by practiced defense mechanisms and some specific medication. Neither of which I have right now."

"I like you, Theo. I really do. You put this all together, made a move I was too terrified to make. And I'm impressed and charmed. What's to be scared of, at this point?"

"You, terrified?" Theo shook her head. "Come on. By all accounts you're a real playboy, aren't you? Could easily pick up any girl wherever you go."

Summer winced, and looked away. "It's not like that."

Theo paused for a moment, then looked up. "Sorry. That was uncalled for. I'm just... a bit jealous, I guess."

"I'm terrified, because, I mean. This whole situation. I'm the alternate reality ghost of your dead best friend. That's super fucked up. How could I be expected to make a move? I like you a lot, and I'm super happy that you seem to like me too, but... are you really...?"

The unspoken followup hung in the air.

Lightning tore through the sky, and a clap of thunder rumbled, shaking the plates on the tables. The sound of rain against the roof beat like a drum.

Theo took a deep breath. "Summer... the other Summer. Her and I were only ever friends. But... it's true, that I wanted it to be something more."

There it was. The truth that Summer had long suspected, but hadn't really wanted to consider. A replacement, then. For love lost and never found. A second chance.

It hurt, deep inside. But... well. That was Summer's lot. To be what others needed her to be. It was only for a few weeks. Deep down, she wanted more. Wanted Theo in her life for far more than just a moment. But that wasn't going to happen, so she'd take the moment anyway, however long it lasted.

"I'm sorry." Theo squeezed her eyes shut. Tears ran down her cheeks. "I want to say that it's fine. That I'm over that. That I can see you as your own separate person. That its you, all you. But the truth is I don't know. How can I possibly separate what was and what is?

Theo barked a short, manic laugh. "You're both so different, so similar. Is knowing you now corrupting my memories of her? I don't know, I don't know, I don't know!"

Summer circled around the picnic table, sliding onto the bench next to Theo, taking her hands in her own. They were freezing cold. "Hey. It's okay. It's all fucked. I get it. It's okay."

Theo sniffed, shaking in Summer's grasp. "It's not fair. You deserve so much better. But these past two weeks have been so wonderful. Every moment I spend with you is just... but would I care that much, if I hadn't known *her*? If we met as complete strangers, would any of this be happening right now? I want to believe that we could find each other and connect in a vacuum. But is that really true?"

"Hey, it's okay. I'm not mad or anything. I understand. Listen to me, Theo. It's really okay."

"It's not! This was supposed to be a cool, suave date. To show you how special you are. You even said it, nobody tries to woo you. You deserve it, Summer. You fucking deserve it! You deserve so much more than a broken, lying piece of shit like me!"

"Theo." Summer said, her voice clear, calm, loud. "Look at me. Trust me, okay?" She stood up, still holding tight to Theo's hands. Come with me. There you go."

Theo followed her, still trembling violently. "What are you—"

A shriek split the night as Summer dragged Theo outside of the park shelter, into the thunderstorm. It had opened up into a full downpour, and both of them were soaked to the bone instantly. The rain was warm, at least.

"W-what the hell?" Theo yelled. She tugged at Summer to escape, to get back under the shelter, but Summer held on tight, and didn't budge.

"Nothing's perfect." Summer grinned wildly, and took a step back, dragging Theo with her, further into the rain. "You're not perfect, I'm not perfect, this date isn't perfect. Nothing about this situation is perfect, okay? Doesn't mean it's not worth it."

Theo stopped resisting, and followed Summer into the rain, step by step. "There's a far cry between 'not perfect' and 'completely and utterly fucked.'"

Summer's hair was plastered to her face. She tried, and mostly failed, to blow it away. "Fine, then. It's completely and utterly fucked. Let's be completely and utterly fucked together, okay? For as long as it lasts."

"You're crazy."

"And?"

Theo didn't have a response to that.

Summer grinned, and took another step backwards, into the darkness and the storm.

Her foot slipped on a patch of mud, and for a brief moment she hung in mid air, gravity about to overtake her.

Theo lunged and wrapped her arms tight around Summer, and together they tumbled down a small hill, rolling over and over, tearing up grass and mud in their wake.

They hit the bottom of the hill, and Summer stared up at the beautiful woman on top of her, Theo's glasses askew.

Lightning split the sky, illuminating the panic and terror on Theo's face.

Summer met it with a grin, and couldn't help but start laughing.

Water streamed down Theo's cheeks, and she shook. Maybe with tears at first, but it turned into laughter.

Thunder rumbled above them.

Theo kissed her.

Dear Diary,

God I'm such a creep.

Summer took a shower at our house and when she came out she was wearing nothing but a towel and I just… couldn't stop staring. She's so beautiful.

And then she even noticed, and said "take a picture it will last longer" and fuck I wanted to disappear from the face of the earth.

Why am I like this?

We've been best friends since we were little kids. We've changed around each other plenty of times, we hang out at the pool in swimsuits. It used to be fine. Why am I being so weird? Why can't I be normal?

Theo
6/27/2013

Theo felt dizzy as she climbed the steps to the apartment. Rain continued to spray against her and she clung tightly to Summer. Step by step, almost to somewhere warm and dry.

Her lips still tingled from kissing Summer, there in the rain and mud. And the considerably more times she'd done it afterwards.

They finally crossed the threshold into the apartment, and closed the door behind them, shutting out the tempestuous elements. Safe and sound once more.

Summer immediately pulled off her muddy jacket and threw it into the corner of the room, then followed it with her shirt, leaving a sports bra. "Go ahead and get your clothes off and put 'em there, can get laundry going after we shower."

Well. Maybe safe was the wrong word. Was she ready for this? Theo's cheeks burned as she watched the half naked Summer confidently stride into the bathroom and turn on the shower.

As Summer turned back and started struggling out of her wet jeans, she paused, making eye contact with Theo, and bit her lip. "...Sorry. Making some assumptions here. We can take turns, you go first. Just don't use up all the hot water."

Theo held up her hands. "No, that's fine. I'm just... a bit nervous, that's all. But I mean... your shower runs out of hot water pretty quickly. It's efficient to share, you know?"

Summer smiled softly and nodded. She stripped out of her underwear, tossing it into the pile with the rest. She stood, her whole body on display, her lean muscles absolutely gorgeous.

A part of Theo wanted to look away, to hide. A part of her interest felt wrong, and shameful. But it was okay. Summer said it was okay. So she drank it all in and stripped off her own clothes. Her cardigan, her blouse, her skirt. Finally her underwear, until she too was open and vulnerable.

"You're beautiful," Summer whispered.

Despite how wet and cold she felt, everything inside Theo burned. She fidgeted, folding her arms over herself in an attempt to diminish how much of her body was visible. Was that really true? She generally felt that her body wasn't... *bad*, or anything. It was soft, a little pudgier in a few places than she really would have cared for. Adequate. Average.

Nothing compared to Summer's, which was stunning not just in its aesthetics, but in appreciation for the effort and care that maintaining it required.

Summer turned back to the shower, testing the water with her hand, then nodding with approval. She stepped inside and groaned with delight. "Fuck, that feels good."

Theo approached slowly. "Nothing like a hot shower after getting caught in the rain," she said, her voice cracking a bit. She hesitated, staring at Summer for a little longer before pulling off her glasses and setting them on the sink. Unfortunately, whatever else she was going to get to see of Summer was going to have to be a bit blurry.

Her nervousness evaporated for a brief moment once she stepped into the shower, and the hot water hit her cold and aching muscles. It really was heavenly.

The hot water soothed Summer's aching muscles, restored feeling to her numb fingers. Pulling Theo into the storm had been the right move to make, but it did have its physical consequences. Most of which were currently washing away.

She scooted to the side as Theo stepped into the shower with her, to let her enjoy the hot water too. It was a tiny, stand up only model. Barely enough room for one person.

The other consequences of pulling Theo into the rain had yet to be reckoned with.

A heat blossomed in Summer that had nothing to do with the shower. Summer's eyes wandered up and down Theo's body. Her soft curves, her long legs, thighs that she wanted nothing more than to bury herself in. She noticed that Theo had freshly shaved. Not something Summer cared much about either way, but... the fact that she'd prepared for tonight. Anticipated this. *That* was what got her—

Summer bit her lip. She needed to slow down a bit. Her eyes met with Theo's, and her breath caught in her throat. She wanted nothing more than to push Theo against the wall, slip her hand between her legs, feel inside of her, hear her gasp and moan and scream her name.

But, but but. Just because things had escalated didn't mean she could charge forward with reckless abandon. Making out in the rain was one thing, but the entire situation was still incredibly precarious. She had to follow Theo's lead, let her decide what she was comfortable with. Not trample any boundaries.

Theo kept her gaze locked with Summer's, her lips parted slightly, her face flushed. She sucked in a deep breath, a shudder running through her. "I..."

Not trampling, but... Summer leaned forward, pressing her arm on the wall of the shower. Her breath was close enough to move the water droplets on Theo's face. "Yeah?" she asked, her voice low.

A snort of laughter escaped from Theo, and she clasped a hand over her mouth, though the smile was still clear in her eyes.

"Something funny?" Summer asked in that same tone of voice, exaggerating it even further.

"Sorry, sorry!" More giggles escaped from Theo. "It's all so surreal, you know? Feels absurd, like it's not really happening. Like it's all a dream. Don't even think I was this nervous when I actually lost my virginity."

Summer shrugged. "Doesn't have to be a big deal. Whatever you're comfortable with, you kn—"

Theo closed the distance between them, pressing their lips together.

With a groan, Summer kissed back, the fires within growing even hotter. She took her hand off the wall, resting it on the small of Theo's back, pulling her closer.

And then Theo was gone, pulling back, a hand on Summer's chest, pushing her away. But her eyes sparkled, her expression mischievous. "Can you pass me the soap?"

So Theo was the kind of lover that liked to tease. Sure, alright. Summer could work with that. She took a moment to reorient, for the gears in her brain to adjust. Then leaned back against the opposite wall from Theo. She hooked the bottle of body wash on the floor with her ankle, and kicked it, sliding it along the floor, past Theo. "All yours."

Theo blinked, looking confused, and stared at the bottle, then back to Summer. Then recognition dawned, and she made a cute little O with her mouth. It morphed into a sly grin, and she turned around, spread her legs wide, and slowly bent over to pick up the body wash.

Everything on display for Summer, all for her.

And then Theo stood back up, and all of her wet hair fell in front of her face, making her look like one of those Japanese ghosts.

Summer burst out laughing. God, she was something else.

"What?" Theo asked, the amusement clear in her tone. She ineffectually blew at the strands of wet hair stuck to her lips. "Is there something on my face?"

"There is, yeah." Summer reached out her hand and tucked Theo's hair behind her ear.

Theo's breath caught, the playful mood once again replaced with charged tension.

Summer gently rested her fingers on the bottle of body wash in Theo's hand. "Want me to help with that? Wash your back?"

"Yes!" Theo said almost immediately. "I mean, uh. Yeah, if you want." She handed the bottle off, then turned around, taking a deep breath.

A squirt of body wash into Summer's hands, rub them together to lather them up. She pressed her palms against Theo's back, which earned her a quiet gasp. Her skin was soft, smooth. Summer took her time.

"I didn't know you had a tattoo," Summer murmured. There was a small depiction of a setting sun, near Theo's left shoulder blade. Her finger lingered on it.

Theo stiffened. "Ah. I, uh. Forget it's there sometimes. I got it in… well. In memory of Summer. Sorry."

A bit of a mood killer, that. Summer paused, studying the tattoo, grief etched into flesh. Would anyone think of her so fondly, were she to pass? She shook her head, clearing the thought. She let her fingers continue to scrub Theo's back. "It's cute. I've always wanted to get a lot of ink. Got a whole series of sleeves, and a back tattoo planned out in my sketchbook."

"That would be super hot." Theo twitched and fidgeted as Summer's fingers drifted to her sides. She raised her arms, bracing them against the far wall of the shower. "What's holding you back?"

Summer traced her fingers up Theo's sides, barely grazing her breasts, moving up past her armpits. "Cash, mostly. Tattoos ain't cheap. And uh. Some other interpersonal issues, I guess."

Theo barked a high pitched laugh that was a hairs breadth away from being a moan. "Let me guess. The best tattooist in town is another ex of yours."

A flush of embarrassment washed over Summer, so easily seen. She stepped even closer to Theo, her chest pressing against her back, the scent of strawberries filling the shower. The thin film of soap lathered on her hands made it so easy to glide them across her body, back down to her breasts, her nipples swiftly captured between her fingers. "Is it a problem if it was? Does that make you jealous?"

"I, uh, i-it does." Theo moaned in earnest this time, pressing her body backwards, tight against Summer's. "Sorry. I know I don't have the right to be, but I—Ah!"

Summer cut off whatever Theo was going to say by pinching her nipple, relishing how she writhed at her touch. She rested her chin on Theo's shoulder, and grazed her earlobe with her teeth. "Does that feel good?"

"Mmm. Mmmhmm." Theo didn't have many coherent words left in her, apparently.

Time for more. Lower, and lower. Her hands grazed Theo's hips, the inside of her thighs, the bare skin where her pubic hair would be, soft and smooth. Close, close, closer, but not quite touching.

"Fuck, Summer." Theo's breath was short and heavy, her neediness clear. She wriggled against Summer, trying to draw her hand to her clit. "I don't... I don't wanna—"

The words hit Summer like a splash of ice to her brain, and she immediately pulled away, stepping away from Theo.

Theo stood there, hands against the wall, panting heavily. "Damnit," she muttered. "Not like that." She took a shaky breath, then stood up, turning to face Summer, a sheepish smile on her face. "Sorry. I don't want to cum... here. Can we, uh. Bedroom?"

Summer's heart was beating a hundred miles an hour, but she nodded slowly. She hadn't fucked it up. "Of course, yeah."

"Cool. Yeah." Theo nodded several times, her face red, her eyes still focused intently on Summer, full of desire. "Move though, I actually gotta rinse off."

~

Theo's heart pounded in her chest, so loud that she was sure the neighbors across the street could hear it. It mixed and melded with the rumble of thunder outside, the patter of the rain against the windows.

It was finally happening. It was finally happening. *It was finally happening.*

Summer's hand was in hers, guiding her to the bedroom. A quick tug and they fell onto the mattress together, a tangle of limbs, full of warmth and wet skin and oh so exquisite touches.

She could feel Summer's lips on hers, feel her fingers run down her body, tease her breasts, pinch her nipples, promising so much more.

This was what she wanted. This was what she had always wanted. How often had she thought of this as a teenager? In her most shameful moments, dreaming of Summer late at night. Conjuring fantasies where a lingering touch or friendly hug turned into so much more. Hidden under her blanket, looking up porn on her phone, imagining that the lesbians on the screen were her and Summer.

How often as an adult, had she continued to dream of this, in her ragged grief? She'd had girlfriends, lovers. How often had she dissociated while having sex, pretending that it was with Summer, instead? How unfair that was to the women she was with, how much she still did it anyway?

Theo moaned as Summer sunk her teeth into her neck, just hard enough to elicit pain and pleasure. Electrifying, all consuming sensations filled her body, but at the same time it all felt a bit distant and numb.

But now she finally had it. Summer, in her hands, hot and reactive to her touch. She was here, she was into Theo, and she was *so fucking hot*. Maybe not the same Summer. A twisted reflection of her dreams. But it was Summer all the same, and she was wonderful and kind and Theo was down so, *so* bad for her.

Summer trailed kisses down Theo's body, slowly, occasionally nipping gently with her teeth. She lingered for a long time on her breasts, giving each nipple plenty of attention, before moving down Theo's stomach, and down even further.

Theo stared at the ceiling of this cheap apartment, while getting fucked on a cheap mattress without a box spring. Hardly the perfect setting, for something so magical, so dreamlike. But at the same time, she couldn't imagine anywhere else she'd rather be. It wasn't only Summer's shitty apartment. It was *hers*. Theo lived here too. She would happily live a life together with Summer in these small confines, as long as they could stay together.

Her thighs tingled with the impressions of Summer's lips. Summer was so close, her breath hot on Theo's clit. Theo wriggled, thrusting her pelvis into the air, begging for her touch, for sweet release. She knew she must be absolutely soaking wet. They'd probably need to wash the sheets tomorrow. Or maybe they could get them dirty again, over and over and over.

A life with Summer. That's what she wanted. Fuck her world, forget everyone who loved her back home. She should stay here forever. Couldn't she have this? Couldn't she keep this? Couldn't she survive solely on this?

Summer, finally, mercifully, blessedly, let her tongue graze Theo's clit, just a tease, but god did it feel so, *so good*.

Theo let out a cry of pleasure halfway between a moan and a sob.

There was a pause, no further pleasure coming her way. "Hey. You okay up there?"

What? Theo blinked several times, her vision blurry. "I'm fine. I, uh. Don't stop, please, I—"

Tears slipped down her cheeks, unbidden. No, no no no no! She couldn't be doing this now, not now!

"Woah." Summer was there in an instant, crawling up Theo's body, taking her face in her hands. "Hey, it's okay, I'm here. We don't have to do anything you don't wanna do, alright?"

Theo was shaking, trying her hardest to make the tears stop, but that made it even worse. "Shut up! No, I… please, I want this. Don't stop, I really want to…"

Summer laughed awkwardly. "Come on, Theo. You know I'm not gonna do that."

This was so stupid. She felt utterly pathetic. She couldn't even look at Summer, couldn't believe she was ruining something so utterly precious. "I'm sorry."

"Sssh. It's okay." Summer pulled her close, wrapping her arms around Theo's head, holding her against her chest. "I've got you. And you have nothing to apologize for. I should have taken things slower."

Theo took a deep, shuddering breath, her nose runny. She could hear Summer's heartbeat, as rapid as her own. "But I *want this*. I want you. So, so badly."

A pause, and then Summer made a pleasant hum of acknowledgment. "That makes me really happy. I want you too, Theo. A whole lot. But that doesn't mean we have to go so hard and fast, does it?"

"But if not now, when?" Theo murmured. She sniffed, the sound ugly and stupid. She squirmed in Summer's embrace, rubbing her legs together, her thighs still damp with unfulfilled desire.

Summer planted a soft kiss against the top of Theo's forehead, wrapped her fingers in her hair. "I'm not going anywhere, I promise. I'll still be here in the morning. And the day after that, and the day after that. I'll be here until—" She cut herself off, likely stopping on the same implications of the fleeting nature of their relationship that had Theo twisted up in knots. Summer took a deep breath. "I'll be here as long as you want me here."

Theo's heart began to still somewhat. She dug her nails into Summer's back, pulling her even closer, wishing they could become one being, occupy the same space. "I really do want you. So badly. I just… I dunno. I might want you *too* much. I'm so deep in my own head about it, that it's just so overwhelming, and it's spilling out of me. Out of my eyes." She snorted again. "Much rather have it spill out of my pussy, you know? Like, onto your face?"

Summer snorted with laughter, directly in Theo's ear. "Christ, that's some imagery there. But hey, I get it. It's okay. It's easy to build up expectations in your head. Hard when they come face to face with reality. We'll take it slow, alright? One step at a time."

"Yeah. Okay." Theo took a deep breath and let it out slowly. This was for the best. She'd been about to disassociate through sex with *Summer* of all people, and she definitely didn't want that. "Thank you," she murmured.

"Always." Summer continued stroking her hair gently.

"I—" Theo caught herself and stopped immediately. About to say three words that she definitely already felt, but definitely shouldn't. Too much, too fast. They'd only known each other for two weeks. "I really like you," she said instead.

"Mmm. Me too."

Theo let herself be held, let her needy desire fade to a dull ache, let the exhaustion in her be lulled by Summer's warmth and steady breath.

Even if she had to hide the true depth of her feelings.

17

Her lips

Her skin

Her eyes

Her breath

Her touch

Sets fire

My dream

Theo awoke the following morning to darkness, and the soft pitter patter of rain outside.

In a moment like this, she resented the blackout curtains on the windows, and wished she could see the sun filtering in from outside, feel its subtle warmth, and see it illuminating the sleeping form of the gorgeous woman next to her.

But the situation she was in wasn't picture perfect, and that was fine.

She watched Summer sleep, picking out what details she could. The peaceful smile on her face. The rise and fall of her chest with every breath.

It made a warmth blossom in Theo's chest. Her mind was so much more still, compared to last night. Sleep and cuddles were an absolute miracle cure. The underlying issues still bubbled underneath the surface, but...

Could she try again? The ache of unfulfilled desire still burned within her, after all. She needed to reframe her view of sex with Summer. Not as the narrative climax of some sort of cross dimensional destined love story. But as a simple act of affection and pleasure, between two women who cared about each other.

Theo breathed in deeply, the faint smell of Summer's shampoo, and the scent that was unmistakably *her* tickling her nose.

Right. She could do it this time.

She stood up, stretching, her bones popping audibly. Then she strode over to the curtains, and furled them up. It was rainy and overcast outside, but it still let a lot more light into the room than there'd been previously.

Summer let out a groan from the bed, rolling over and burying her face in the pillow.

Theo grinned, then made her way back to the bed, crawling on top of Summer, her hair draping down to tickle Summer's face. "Morning."

"Nnngh." Summer freed an arm from her blanket to brush the hair away. "What time is it?" she slurred."

"Dunno, didn't check."

"Too early then," Summer grumbled, and hunched further into herself.

Theo adjusted herself, putting a little more weight onto Summer. "Hey. Summer?"

"Hmm?"

"Do you want to finish what we started last night?"

That got her attention. Summer rolled onto her back, looking up at her, blinking sleep out of her eyes. "I, uh. Are you sure?"

"Yeah." Theo smiled, and gently cupped Summer's cheek with her hand, before she leaned down to plant a soft kiss on the tip of her nose. "I'm feeling a lot better. And the fact that I want you hasn't changed."

Summer licked her lips, sat up straight, and flexed her shoulders. "Sorry, give me like two seconds to wake up and I'll—"

"Ssh." Theo ran her hand down Summer's cheek to her neck, idly tracing her finger along Summer's collarbone. "I get the impression you like to take charge a lot. And that's... *super hot*, not gonna lie. But I kind of want to just... please you?" She winced, and bit her lip. It had sounded hot in her head, but saying it out loud made her feel stupid. "You can... lay there, and stuff. Is that okay?"

Summer met her gaze, wide awake now. She studied Theo for several long moments before a small smile played at her lips, and she nodded. "Okay."

Perfect. Theo lifted herself up, kicking the remainder of the blanket off of Summer. Once more revealing her body

With her heart pounding in her chest, Theo sat back down, straddling Summer's abs. She remembered how Summer had touched her last night, how it had driven her wild. She gently let her fingers drift across Summer's abdomen, marveling in the feel of her muscles, her strength. Gently tracing her scar, and—

Summer hissed, then twisted and lifted her knee, bucking Theo off her, and forcing her weight onto her bed instead of Summer directly.

Theo's eyes went wide. "Sorry, should I not have?"

"No, it's fine, sorry." Summer grabbed at her stomach. "Uh. Spontaneous morning sex is great and all, but it does run into a few problems."

"Like?"

Summer grimaced. "Like the fact that I really gotta pee, and you just put your weight on my bladder."

Theo snorted with laughter, and shook her head. "Wouldn't mind brushing my teeth first, honestly."

"Five minute break, then we'll get right to it?"

"Don't keep me waiting too long."

Mundane activities, to get in Summer's way. Bathroom. Brush teeth. Feed a whiny cat. It all served to dim the burning passion somewhat.

But maybe that was okay? Summer was used to passion. Hot and heavy, all consuming, burned out in an instant, gone in the morning. Standing in her kitchen, watching Theo—her girlfriend? Her lover? Her complicated situationship?—drink a glass of water, while butt naked. There was something simple and cozy about whatever this was.

It felt right.

Summer made her way to the bed, leaning back against her pillows. She spread her legs and rubbed a few lazy circles around her clit. The touch awakened the remembrance of desire from last night and she wiggled her hips and let out a soft sigh.

Theo stood at the foot of the bed, biting her lip, her eyes heavy with lust.

"God, you're beautiful," Summer murmured.

"…You said that already."

"Better get used to it."

Theo knelt down, crawling across the bed until she hovered over Summer, blocking out the light. "Hey."

Summer grinned. "Hey."

And then Theo's lips met hers, and Theo's leg pressed in between hers, the pleasure of that connection rocketing through Summer's body.

She wrapped her arms around Theo's back, pulling her closer, grinding her hips against Theo's leg. Their tongues pressed together, fresh and minty.

Theo's hair tickled Summer's face, and she held Summer's wrist, pinning her against the bed, while she continued to thrust, grinding against Summer.

Summer moaned into the kiss. A part of her wanted to twist, to throw Theo off of her, pin her down instead, make her moan and writhe. It was what everyone always expected of her. She was good at it.

But Theo seemed to want to make her feel good instead. She wasn't going to argue with—

A thought wormed its way into Summer's insecurities, and she pulled away from the kiss, panting heavily. "Hey. Just want to check but like... please don't feel like you need to do this to make up for last night or anything, I—"

Theo shut her up with another kiss. Her hands wrapped in Summer's hair, and then her mouth was on Summer's neck instead, sucking hard on the skin, enough to leave a mark. "I'm doing what I want to do. Okay?"

Summer let out a hiss, shivers running through her body as Theo's teeth grazed her collarbone. "O-okay. Yeah."

"It's been hard, you know," Theo murmured. "Haven't been able to rub one out since I've been here." She moved her hands down to Summer's breasts, squeezing them roughly. "And I've had to live next to the hottest fucking woman I've ever met."

"Shit, that sucks." Summer laughed, though it quickly turned into a yelp as Theo pinched her nipples, hard. "I just masturbate in the shower while you're at work. You coulda done the same."

Theo blinked, and she looked downwards, her expression bashful. "Yeah, well... it would have been weird."

"Guess we'll have to make up for lost time."

That seemed to set Theo off, and she grinned. She pulled her knee away, then replaced it with her right hand, as the left continued to caress and pinch Summer's breasts. "God, you're so fucking wet."

Summer groaned, and thrust her hips against Theo's fingers. She felt Theo's thumb on her clit, rubbing soft circles, before two fingers thrust inside of her.

Theo leaned further, pushing farther inside, her head dipping down to place soft kisses on Summer's breasts. She made eye contact, looking up at Summer, her bangs falling in front of her face.

"Fuck," Summer breathed, her voice nearly a whisper. She thrust her hips in time with Theo, relishing at every movement of her fingers inside of her, at the constant pressure on her clit. "I-I'm close."

"Mmm," Theo hummed, low and sultry. "This is doing it for you, huh?"

"Just don't, stop, ah. Please."

Theo stopped.

Summer let out a soft whimper, the absence of her touch a stark contrast. She wanted those fingers back, working their magic. "Hey, come on. Don't make me beg."

"I dunno, that could be fun." Theo grinned then shifted to give Summer a quick kiss on the lips. "But not what I'm going for, at least for the moment. I just..." She crawled further down the bed, until she was in between Summer's legs. "I really want to taste you."

And then Theo's tongue was on Summer's clit, and her mind went white for a moment.

She wrapped her fingers into the bedsheets, squeezing tight. "Theo, I, ah!"

Once again, Theo stopped, denying her pleasure. It didn't seem cruel this time, however. Theo pulled back, pulling her hair out of her face, adjusting her position slightly.

Her thoughts were a bit sluggish, but something broke through to Summer's rational brain. She grabbed a hair tie from her nightstand, and held it out to Theo. "Here."

Theo looked up a bit surprised, but smiled. She took the hair tie and tied her hair back into a quick, messy pony tail.

"You're really fucking hot with your hair up, you know that? You should put it up more often."

Theo grinned. "My hair is kind of brittle, and breaks easily when I put it up. But... I guess if that does it for you, I can make an exception."

"Plus, it means I can do this." Summer wrapped her fingers around the base of Theo's ponytail, and brought her face back down to her pussy.

Theo let out a loud moan. At some point she'd shifted so she could have her own fingers in between her legs.

Summer panted, moaned, and writhed under the effects of Theo's skilled tongue. She knew how to bring Summer to the brink, and then back off, leaving her wanting more, aching for it every time.

"Theo! Please, I—"

She wasn't sure how long it had been, but at some point, Summer hit her limit.

Summer let out a scream, thrusting her hip into Theo's face, holding her there as she pushed the rest of the way to an orgasm that rocked through her, her back arching, her thighs clamped around Theo's head.

She fell back to the bed, collapsing into a limp heap, panting heavily, aftershocks of pleasure still twitching through her. She was covered in sweat, could feel it pooling in her lower back, sheets damp.

"Fuck..." Summer muttered, in between gasps of air.

Theo pried Summer's thighs off of her head, and came up looking incredibly smug. "Hey," she said, a bit out of breath herself.

"Hey." Summer took a deep breath, her heart still pounding. "Give me a few minutes to recover, and I'll return the favor."

"Nah, I'm good for now." Theo crawled up the bed, and collapsed onto the bed next to Summer, rolling over to stare into her eyes. "I came at the same time you did, on my fingers. I don't think I've ever been so turned on eating pussy before."

Summer laughed. "Kind of surprising. You're clearly pretty damn good at it."

Theo brushed a strand of hair that had gotten loose from her ponytail out of her face. "I guess. Like in the past I've enjoyed doing it, but I've always been focused on pleasing my partner. With you I... I was so turned on I couldn't help myself."

"Yeah?" Summer reached out a hand, tenderly cupping Theo's cheek, then leaned in for a quick kiss.

"Mmmhmm."

They lay there in silence for quite some time, catching their breaths, cooling down, basking in the afterglow.

"Now what," Theo finally asked several minutes later.

A spike of worry wormed its way through Summer's heart. "Oh, um. I dunno. I mean... whatever you want, and are comfortable with, I guess. We can take it one step at a time?" Did she really have to think about the future right now? Theo wasn't long for this world, but she was here, right now. Couldn't that be enough?

Theo's laughter surprised her, and she shook her head. "Sorry, I meant like. Today. It's a Saturday morning. Whole day ahead of us. Do we wanna do anything?"

Oh. Right. Of course. This wasn't a discussion on the nature of their relationship, an examination of what it was, what to call it.

Which was good, because when people did take the time to examine the nature of a relationship with Summer, she always came up lacking.

Summer sighed, and glanced out the window. "Raining out, so that crosses a lot of potential stuff off the list. I can figure out some indoor stuff if you want though."

"No, no, that's okay." Theo bit her lip. "Would it be okay if we just… stayed in all day? Watched TV or something, just hang out?"

"Sure, fine by me."

Theo looked away, her cheeks flushed. "…Maybe fuck some more? After we've recovered a bit?"

Summer laughed, then rolled over and pulled Theo into a tight hug, planting a kiss on her forehead. "I'm down for whatever you are. Might wanna grab breakfast at least though. Keep up our stamina."

"Yeah." Theo kissed her back. "Plus I accidentally found your stash of toys awhile back, and, I mean…"

"Naughty girl." Summer grinned, and kissed her again.

Whatever this was, whatever they were to each other.

It was still good, for now.

~

The rest of the day passed by in a mixture of domestic bliss, and more orgasms than Theo could count.

They ate a nice breakfast of eggs, bacon, and toast, with Theo learning the hard way why cooking bacon naked was a bad idea. They settled back into bed to binge watch a show that was a favorite of Summer's. About halfway through, Summer started casually masturbating, so Theo joined her, side by side, heads resting together, Theo's leg draped over Summer's.

Afterwards, they decided to take another shower together. Theo helped Summer re-dye her hair. It came out a beautiful, vibrant shade of red, like when she'd first seen Summer two weeks ago. They returned to the show, and Summer held her when Theo cried, with an all too knowing smile of 'yeah, I knew this one would get you.'

Pizza was their lunch. They ordered from a local place that Theo had remembered fondly from childhood. Summer opened the door while wearing a bathrobe wrapped around her, and the poor teenaged delivery boy nearly had his eyes pop out of his skull. Theo couldn't blame him. The pizza wasn't very good. The sex afterwards was great. Summer found her magic wand, and they shared it together, the vibrator pressed in between them, their moans muffled by each other's mouths.

With the show over, they decided to take a break instead of jumping into nothing new. Summer pulled out her sketchpad and did a few portraits of Theo, though she refrained from doing the full body nudes, for now. Theo poked around Summer's room and they chatted, telling each other stories about their lives, both heavy and light. She eventually found an old xbox in Summer's closet, and they decided to fire it up and play an old Call of Duty game, the servers that once supported it long gone.

Theo had never really liked shooters, but it was fun, playing together with Summer. Theo got into it, decided to be competitive. Challenged Summer to see who would wear the strap.

Summer won, and Theo found herself bent over the bed, screaming into a pillow as Summer pounded her brain into atoms.

And so it was that at the end of day Theo was exhausted, sore, and happy. Utterly, deliriously happy. She couldn't remember feeling this happy in over a decade. Maybe even longer. As much as she'd loved her time with Summer in the past, it had been full of anxiety. That Summer would know her, judge her, abandon her.

But this. This was everything she wanted. A simple, but fulfilling life shared next to the woman she loved.

It was the best day of Theo's life.

And to keep it, she'd have to give up everything.

Dear Diary,

We're at the Wisconsin Dells!
    We're staying in big fancy hotel with a waterpark and everything. I always heard about this place but never knew what it was like.
    Beyond all the cool water stuff there's a ton of arcades and cool shops and like a weird puzzle quest thing?
    And I wasn't weird about Summer being in a swimsuit or anything.
    I think I've definitely gotten things under control by now. Sure, I have a crush on her, but it's just a crush. We're friends. And it doesn't mean anything, and never will.
    It's fine.

Theo
7/13/2014

Summer woke to the smell of eggs and toast wafting in from the kitchen.

If she waited in her comfy bed, Theo would probably bring her food. Nice and easy.

But then again, spending a whole day inside always left Summer restless. She stretched, her bones popping, her muscles sore, then stood up and made her way to the bedroom door.

"Mornin'," she slurred, leaning against the doorframe.

Theo had put on a t-shirt and sweatpants, and stood in front of their little hot plate, eggs nearly finished. A bright smile lit up on her face when she turned her head to look at Summer. "Hey."

"You're always cooking stuff. I can cook too, you know."

"I like it. Besides, I've never really been able to sleep in."

"Dunno what that's like." Summer let out a big yawn, then sat at the table, the metal of her folding chairs uncomfortable against her bare ass.

Theo made her way over, and set the plate of eggs and toast in front of Summer. Her gaze lingered a bit on Summer.

Summer raised an eyebrow. "Ready for round…" She paused, trying to count in her head. "Ssssix?"

"I, uh." Theo looked away, her face red. "Yes and no? Like I do but I'm also not sure if I can physically handle any more sex, you know?"

"It's definitely a workout." Summer added more salt to the eggs, and then dug in. Over easy, with the toast to sop up the yolk. Just like she preferred. "But yeah, that's fine. What do you wanna do today, instead?"

Theo sat across from her, a mug of tea in her hand. She blew on it a few times, face scrunched up in thought.

Summer never drank tea, so Theo must have bought her own at some point.

"Do you have a shift today? With the volunteering for the kids and stuff?"

"Nah. Next Sunday though."

"Hmm." Theo drummed her fingers on the table. "I'm tired and sore from yesterday, but I also kind of want to go do something? Like, I enjoy being lazy and sitting around all day, but I start to get anxious and feel grungy after doing so. Reminds me of… some of my worst days, cooped up in my room, after. You know."

Summer hesitated, but then remembered she had free reign to be physically affectionate now. She reached across the table, taking Theo's hand in her own, and squeezed gently. "I'm a little surprised. I kind of figured you were the 'sit inside all day and read a book' kind of introvert."

Theo squeezed back, smiling. "I am… but also not? I think it's just anxiety, really. Feel like I have to be doing things, or else I'm wasting something or ruining everything."

"Shit sucks."

"Yeah."

"Anyway." Summer finished off the rest of her egg and toast. "I'm happy going out and doing stuff. Any idea what?"

Theo puffed out her cheeks, and then blew air out her lips slowly. "God, what even is there to do around here?"

"Uh…" Summer pulled out her phone, checking what she knew about various local events. "Doesn't look like anything is going on this weekend.

We could see if Minha wants to hang. Or maybe rope Peter and Aaron into a double date."

"Eh. Nah. I'd rather it just be us."

"Okay." Summer kept scrolling. "Oh, that town painting event is happening next Saturday. Doesn't help us now, but could be fun."

"Oh!" Theo lit up at that. "God, I used to love going to that as a kid."

"Was never my thing, didn't really get into art until I was an adult."

Theo sighed. "Yeah. Summer always thought it was lame and for babies and never wanted to go."

A beat of awkward silence between them, as there always was at the mention of the other Summer. Push past it. "Well, I'm down. But, again. A next week problem."

"Hmm."

"Had you blipped into this reality a few weeks ago, we could have gone to the county fair."

Theo grimaced. "The rides always made me puke."

Summer chuckled. "It's gotten kind of sad, honestly. Way less people, less stuff to do, and three times the price."

"That's a shame." Theo shrugged. "We could go to another town?"

"I mean, they're not much better." Summer leaned forward, resting her hand on her chin. "Gotta go all the way to the Quad Cities to really find anything fun. Botanical gardens. Zoo. A mall that isn't *entirely* a wasteland."

Theo perked up. "Oh, maybe. Yeah, shit, let's do that. I'm down."

Summer grinned. "It's a date."

"Perfect!" Theo clapped her hands together and stood up. "I'll get right to it."

"Just need to put on pants. Oh, and I wanna grab a donut on the way out."

~

When they walked into the bakery together, Theo knew she'd been made.

Peter squealed out loud as soon as he saw them, clasping his hands over his mouth, and his eyes brimming with tears. "Oh my gosh! You two...!"

The fact that Theo's fingers were currently interlaced with Summer's was probably a dead giveaway, but she felt her face flush anyway. "Morning, Peter."

With a dreamy sigh, Peter leaned forward on the counter, and folded his hands under his chin. "I take it the date went well then?"

Summer glanced over at Theo and grinned. "Didn't know Peter was involved in this."

Theo sighed and rubbed at the back of her neck. "I wanted some ideas and some reassurance, that's all."

"I'm so happy for the both of you. I could tell you had so much chemistry with each other from the moment you met!"

"Yeah, well." Summer slipped her hand out of Theo's, and made her way over to the donut case. "Can I get one of these? The maple bacon?"

Peter nodded, grabbing some paper and moving to the display case. "Anything for you, Theo?"

"Uh, one of the cherry filled ones."

"Gotcha. Any big plans for today?"

Theo smiled. "We're actually planning on—"

The door to the shop opened, followed by a soft gasp.

"Oh shit, Faith!" Summer said as she turned around. "How's it going!"

Theo looked behind her to see a preteen kid, dressed in a hoodie with their hood up despite the heat, and a mop of blonde bangs sticking out over their face. Faith? Summer had mentioned them, she thought.

Faith pursed their lips, seeming vaguely annoyed at Summer.

Summer smacked her forehead with her palm, then started signing, presumably repeating her greeting from earlier.

Theo didn't understand any of it, of course. It was one of those things that had always seemed cool to learn, but never made particularly high on the priority list. She sighed, and made her way over to the counter and paid for the donuts.

Summer had a glimmer in her eye that meant she was being cheeky about something, and sure enough, Faith burst out laughing.

Outside the window Theo could see an older woman talking on the phone. Faith's mom, maybe?

"So yeah, this is Theo." Summer had switched to signing and speaking at the same time, though she had to noticeably slow down to do so. "You were right last time, I guess. She's my girlfriend now."

Girlfriend, huh? They hadn't actually talked about labels but… it felt right. Warmth spread throughout Theo, and she tried to keep her expression neutral.

Faith's expression lit up with joy, and they signed several things emphatically before looking over and catching Theo's eye, grinning.

Theo smiled, and waved. "Hi Faith."

There was a pause, and then Faith pulled a phone out from their hoodie pocket, and after fussing with it, held it out, a phone number prominently displayed.

It didn't take long for Theo to add the number to her contacts. "Hi Faith! It's so nice to meet you!"

Faith smiled, then started texting back. "I'm glad Summer decided to stop being a chicken, I could already tell she really liked you."

"Oh? What gave it away?"

"Just little things. The way she talked about you, the way she looked at you, stuff like that. It was adorable."

Theo spared a glance for Summer, and couldn't stop grinning. "Well, we're a pair of idiots who took a minute to figure it out."

"Let me guess, you had to do all the work?"

"It was like 80/20."

Summer leaned over Theo's shoulder, trying to glance at her phone. "Something funny?"

Theo pulled away, laughing. "Just shittalking you."

"No fair," Summer whined.

The door opened, and the woman from outside, who was almost definitely Faith's mom now that Theo got a better look at her, stood in the doorway, looking absolutely stricken. The jovial atmosphere vanished.

Faith signed something quickly, their face scrunched up with worry.

"Faith, sweetie," the woman said, signing at the same time. She bent down, to get at eye level with Faith. "I'm really, really, sorry, but… I have to go into work today. It's an emergency."

Theo shared a glance with Summer, a mutual wince.

After what looked like a heated reply from Faith, the woman shook her head. "I know, I promised. I was really looking forward to this too, it's just… This project is falling apart without me, Jackson completely screwed up our case report, and if I don't fix things by tonight we're going to lose this client entirely. We'll reschedule, okay?"

The tears in Faith's eyes were evident, and they stormed over to the corner of the room, folding their arms over their chest.

The woman let out a long, defeated sigh.

"Hey, Gloria," Summer said, waving slightly. "Everything all right?"

"Oh!" Gloria jumped slightly, and then stood up fully. "Hi, Summer, I didn't notice you there. I'm sorry you had to see that."

Summer shrugged. "It's fine. But, uh… what was up?"

Gloria winced, and rubbed at her temples. "I promised I'd take Faith to the zoo. They've been looking forward to it for months and… God, I'm the worst mom in the world."

"Believe me, that's definitely not true," Summer said, an edge of bitterness in her voice.

"Oh, right. Sorry." Gloria sighed. "But it sure feels like it some time. I don't know what to do."

Summer glanced towards Theo, a question in her eyes.

Theo smiled, and nodded. Sure, she'd hoped for a day alone with Summer, but there was no way she'd back away from something like this.

"If you want, well. This is Theo, my girlfriend, and we were already planning on going to the zoo today. We'd be happy to take Faith with, if that's okay."

Gloria gasped softly, and looked between Summer and Theo. "I… I couldn't possibly impose."

Theo stepped forward. "It wouldn't be any trouble at all. Honestly, let's be real. Zoos are fun and all to visit as an adult, but when there's a kid around to get excited about everything, it's way more magical."

"You'd really…?"

Summer nodded. "As long as Faith is cool with it." She made her way over, and tapped Faith on the shoulder.

A terse exchange of hands later and the despair melted from Faith's face, to be replaced with joy and excitement.

"Thank you so much," Gloria whispered. "I'll pay for everything, I promise. This will mean so much to them, they talk about Summer all the time."

"Yeah," Theo said, her heart blooming with warmth. "She's pretty amazing."

~

Air conditioning blasting her face, Summer drove down the highway, radio cranked, enjoying the latest pop hits interspersed with, like, five minutes of ads every time. Her car was too old for bluetooth integration, and the CD player had busted a few years back. Theo had suggested they buy a small bluetooth speaker and hang it from the rearview mirror. Wasn't a bad idea, but...

Just the casual way Theo treated things, that Summer reciprocated in time. Like this wasn't a relationship with an expiration date. They both acted like they were building a life together. Summer wished it were true.

In the backseat, Theo sat with Faith, eagerly learning as much sign language as she could. Faith was a particularly harsh teacher, as Summer knew too well, but Theo seemed to be able to handle them with enthusiasm.

Was this the way Summer was? She told herself that she was a stepping stone for women to find themselves, and that she was okay with that. It was what happened time and time again. Sure, she always wanted more, but it made sense that nobody else wanted that. Nobody to blame but herself.

And it would be like that with Theo. A replacement for her dead self, an impossible fantasy come to life in Theo's eyes. She hoped this relationship would bring Theo to a sense of closure, that when she returned to her own reality, that she'd hold these memories close to her chest and they would keep her warm.

Except...

It was the way Theo looked at her. Like Summer was the most important person in the world. Summer wanted that, for someone to see her and be their most important person. Maybe Theo was special like that. Maybe Summer was desperate enough to accept that from anyone. She didn't know, not really.

She watched Theo and Faith in the back seat, giggling to themselves, struggling to communicate in a way that Summer definitely couldn't follow while driving.

Theo looked up, meeting her gaze in the mirror, and the smile that bloomed on her face, the love in her eyes was so potent it made Summer swerve onto the shoulder briefly before correcting.

"Eyes on the road," Theo chided, laughing.

"Sorry, sorry. Should be there in like ten more minutes."

Summer's heart pounded in her chest, and she took a deep breath, to try and calm herself.

Maybe it was impossible. Maybe Theo would leave anyway. But maybe...

Maybe Summer could ask for more.

Dear Diary,

On our way back from the Dells we stopped at a rest stop.
There was this scenic overlook, and Summer went to go look at it
And I took a picture of her, and it might be the best picture I ever took.
She's standing there, looking over her shoulder back at me, smiling, but not in a posed way, and framed by the gorgeous Sunset behind her.
And... fuck.
I really am in love with her.
So, so much.
I know it won't ever mean anything.
She'll never look at me the same way I look at her.
It hurts.
But I have this perfect moment, captured forever.
And I can dream.

Theo
7/14/2014

Summer snapped a photo of Faith as they stood there, rigidly straight and unmoving, hands held high up into the air. The freakishly long tongue of a giraffe slurped up food from their palms, and Summer could tell it was taking herculean effort for Faith to not flinch away.

When the giraffe finally lifted its head away, Faith relaxed, and a smattering of applause resounded from nearby onlookers. A park employee directed them to a nearby sink to wash their hands, and a few moments later they came sprinting over to Summer and Theo, their face brimming with delight.

"Ew ew ew ew ew ew!" Faith signed repeatedly. "It was so, so gross and rough!' They shuddered. "Never doing that again!"

Theo laughed, and then signed, "Good!"

Summer grinned. "I made sure to get plenty of pictures to send your mom later."

Faith's expression fell a bit at that, and they nodded. "Thank you."

Crap. As fun as Faith was having, they'd probably still rather be spending the day with their mom. No amount of cool big sister energy would change that. Should she say something, talk with them about it? Or maybe try and distract them with more cute animals? They'd been at it for a while now, and had covered a lot of the bigger exhibits already.

Theo stared at something on her phone, a quick sign language tutorial. She smiled, then looked up to Faith, and made a little waddling motion with her hands to sign, "Penguin?"

Faith giggled, and then nodded and took off, leading the way to the penguin exhibit.

"They're a good kid." Theo leaned over into Summer's space, wrapping their arms together as they walked, her head on Summer's shoulder.

It was a little warm for such direct contact, but Summer wasn't going to complain too hard. If Theo wanted a face full of Summer's sweaty shoulder that was her prerogative. "Yeah. Faith rules. I mean, all the kids at the youth center are great, and we're not supposed to pick favorites."

"But you do anyway?"

'Yeah. But Faith's got a lot of things to struggle with. Just do my best to be a bright spot, y'know?"

Theo furrowed her brow. "So then, their mom is…"

Summer shook her head. "Nah. Gloria is doing the absolute best she can. It's just hard, going it alone. She was so terrified that she'd done something wrong or fucked something up when Faith first came out. I really managed to help talk down her anxiety and helped her understand."

"Hmm." Theo pulled back a bit, studying Summer closely.

"What?"

"Nothing. There's a sense of fondness they way you talk about her. Theo's lips twitched into a shit eating grin. "Don't suppose you're sweet on *Mommy*, are you?"

Summer felt her cheeks flush. "Come on, who are you, Minha? Among other things, that would probably be wildly unethical."

Theo laughed, and bumped their shoulders together playfully. "I'm teasing. But if professional ethics weren't a concern, would you?"

"Pretty sure she's straight."

"And if she wasn't?"

"She's like, ten years older than me."

"Would that actually stop you?"

"I mean, I dunno. Maybe?" Summer glowered at Theo. "This conversation feels like a trap."

Theo opened her mouth to respond, then closed it again, pausing to think things through. After a few moments, she nodded. "Sorry. I do have a few issues with jealousy, but I'm trying to make them into a joke instead. If it's making you uncomfortable I'll stop."

Summer rubbed at the back of her neck. "I dunno. I guess I kind of have a reputation as an easy ho that's probably deserved, but it doesn't really feel like that from my perspective. I just... like to connect with people. That's all."

"I understand." Theo nodded thoughtfully, and they paused while Faith peered over the fence at an exhibit of pangolins.

"Would you, though?"

"Would I what?"

"Gloria."

Summer pinched the bridge of her nose. "*If* it wasn't unethical, *if* she was into women, *if* the age gap wasn't an issue, *if* she was actually into me, *if* Faith was okay with it, and *if* I wasn't already dating you?"

"Yeah."

"Then yeah, sure. She's nice enough, and pretty attractive. But I can't imagine her being interested in a washed up dropout who works in a gas station."

Theo leaned up, and planted a quick kiss on Summer's cheeks. "There's a lot more that goes into someone being attractive than working a good job."

"Attractive? Sure. Long term relationship material? Highly questionable."

"That's not true at all."

Summer turned to her and met her gaze, raising an eyebrow. "Are you sure about that?"

Theo looked away and an awkward silence fell between them.

Crap. Summer had skirted too close to what neither of them wanted to address.

Her existential dread was interrupted by the furious waving of Faith, standing in front of the entrance to the penguin exhibit. Clearly they needed to hurry up.

Summer took Theo's hand, interlaced their fingers, and squeezed.

Theo squeezed back.

~

Theo stared blankly as Faith held up their phone for Theo to see. It was some kind of picture of a turtle? It didn't really make sense, but Faith seemed to be expecting something, so Theo smiled awkwardly.

"Hmm? Whassat?" Summer asked, mouth full of fries. She leaned closer to see Faith's phone, then snorted with genuine laughter. "Nice."

Faith beamed, then pulled their phone back to continue poking at it. They wore a light up headpiece bought from the zoo gift store, which had cost forty dollars and would probably break within a week.

The three of them sat at a table in the zoo restaurant, which was also pretty overpriced and the food quality was middling at best. But Faith had insisted, and Gloria was footing the bill, so why not?

Theo leaned over to Summer. "Did you actually understand that?"

"Sure. I'm around kids a lot, so I've managed to pick up some things. That one was a reference to a previous series of memes, that's mutated to the point of being incomprehensible symbolism."

"Huh." Theo reached for a fry, only to find that she'd eaten all of her own. Summer still had some left though, so she grabbed some of those instead.

"Hey!"

"That's girlfriend privileges, isn't it?"

Summer laughed, then shook her head. "Guess that's what I'm signing up for." She pressed her leg against Theo's, a quiet gesture of affection. "But whatever. You can have the rest if you want. This burger kind of blows compared to the ones you made the other night."

Theo straightened up a little at that, a surge of pride fluttering through her. "Really?"

"Definitely. That burger was like, top tier." Summer pushed her tray of half eaten burger and fries towards Theo.

"Glad to hear it." Theo pushed the tray back. "Don't want it though."

Summer raised an eyebrow. "What do you mean you don't want it?"

"It's only good if I'm stealing it from you."

"So that's how it is." Summer let out an over dramatic sigh. She took another fry herself.

Which was of course, Theo's cue to steal another one.

Faith giggled, then held up their phone again. It was a gif of two muppets sloppily making out with each other.

"I think we're being told that we're disgustingly cute," Summer deadpanned.

Theo grinned, and made the sign for "Yes."

That seemed to satisfy Faith, and they brought the phone back.

"Do you want kids?" Theo blurted out.

Summer coughed, clearly choking on something, until she took a big drink from her fountain soda, breathing heavily. "I, uh, jumping right into that, huh?"

Theo felt her cheeks heat up, but she pressed forward. "Sorry. Kind of popped out. I don't really mean anything by it, I'm just curious."

Summer ran a hand through her hair, taking several long moments to think about it. "Can't say I've ever really given it too much thought, though I guess I could see it'd be on your mind. But honestly my bloodline is probably cursed. Not a great idea."

"You're so great with kids though."

"Nah." Summer dumped the remainder of her fries into her mouth, chewing slowly, her expression thoughtful. Eventually, she swallowed, and continued. "It's easy to be great with kids when you only see them once a week and play with them. It's another thing entirely to be their... everything, responsible for them in every way possible. I've got no good examples to turn to. I'd fuck things up for sure."

"I guess." Theo thought about Summer's mom. She'd never known much about her at all. Summer almost never invited her over, so most of her knowledge was filtered through the lens of Summer's complaints. Some of it had sounded like pretty typical teenage rebelliousness. Other parts had painted a picture of deep neglect, of a woman who spent most of her time strung out on xanax, and barely acknowledged Summer's existence. Theo put her hand on Summer's and squeezed.

"What about you?"

"Dunno." Theo glanced towards Faith, who seemed absorbed in their phone. If they were bothered by a conversation they couldn't be a part of, they didn't seem to show it. "I guess I'm not opposed to the idea of being a mom on principle, though I've always had a deep seated fear and revulsion at the thought of getting pregnant. Although I think a lot of that has to do with the thought of a man being involved." She shuddered involuntarily.

"Sure. Makes sense."

"But..." Theo drummed the fingers of her other hand on the table. "Despite my own massive pile of issues, I think I've always held out a small hope that maybe someday I would finally get past them, and be ready for a big step like that."

Summer met her gaze, then reached up and brushed a strand of hair out of Theo's face. "Yeah. I could picture that pretty easily."

Theo licked her lips. "For what it's worth, I do think you'd be a great mom."

"Well. Agree to disagree I guess. Definitely not something I'm interested in considering any time soon, in any case." Summer glanced towards Faith, and grinned. "I'll keep enjoying being a kickass babysitter for now."

Faith looked up, and cocked their head to the side.

Summer started speaking and signing. "You ready to continue? A lot more zoo left."

"Yes!"

~

Summer parked her car on the street outside of Faith's house, deep in one of the newer suburban neighborhoods filled with mcmansions. She turned off her car and the headlights, then unbuckled her seatbelt and stretched a bit, rolling her shoulders.

She turned to look at Theo and Faith in the back seat. They'd both fallen asleep, with Faith resting their head on Theo's shoulder.

"Hey," Summer said softly, unable to stop from smiling. "We're here."

"Mmm," Theo grunted, and stirred slightly, but didn't seem in any hurry to actually get up.

It was utterly adorable. Summer had a thought, and pulled her phone in order to snap a quick picture.

Of course, the damn auto flash went off, and that certainly got both of their attention.

"Fine, fine," Theo mumbled. She blinked several times.

Without even opening their eyes, Faith half-assedly made the sign for, "Carry."

Summer rolled her eyes, but got out of the car anyway, made her way around, and after some finagling, scooped Faith up in her arms. They were light, and it hardly took any effort at all.

Theo followed out shortly after, still rubbing at her eyes. It had been a long day, and it wasn't like they went into today particularly well rested to begin with.

Dodging past one of those little lawn signs that meant the grass had been sprayed recently, Summer made her way up to the front door.

Gloria was there waiting, door open. "Hi Summer, Theo. Thank you both so much for doing this. I'm so sorry for all the trouble."

Summer smiled, and shifted positions slightly, to adjust how she was carrying Faith. "It wasn't any trouble, I promise. We all had a great time. Where should I put them?" She spoke in a hushed whisper, which she quickly realized was a bit silly, but oh well.

"Upstairs, first door on the left."

Easy enough to find her way. Open the door to a small bedroom, likely filled with all sorts of personal touches. It was a little too dark to see, though, and Summer wasn't going to stumble around searching for the light switch. She gently set Faith down onto the bed.

Faith made a soft, murmuring sound, then crossed their arms over their chest to sign, "Love."

Summer grinned and ruffled Faith's hair. "Later, kiddo." She stepped out, closing the door behind her, and made her way back downstairs.

As Summer rounded the corner, she could see Theo talking with Gloria. Gloria had placed a wad of cash in Theo's hand, which Theo was being very midwestern about and trying to refuse.

"Thanks," Summer said, snatching the cash and pocketing it. She could tell it was definitely way more than the trip expenses had been, but a broke bitch didn't have room to be so humble. She didn't think Theo had really internalized the reality of Summer's financial situation, not yet anyway.

Although things had been way easier with Theo around.

Theo glowered at Summer, and elbowed her in the side, but Summer ignored it.

Gloria clasped her hands together. "Would you girls like anything? Maybe some tea?"

"Oh. Umm…" Theo glanced up to Summer, looking for support.

Summer hesitated for a moment, doing her best to read Theo's expression. A slump in her shoulders, a bit of a wobble in her stance, a hint of pleading in her eyes. Summer shook her head. "Nah. Been a long day, and I think both of us are pretty tired."

"Of course, of course. I won't keep you then. And thank you again, so much."

"Anytime." Summer turned to go, waving as she went. "Seriously. Faith is a great kid."

Theo yawned as they stepped back out into the nighttime air, and walked back to the car. "I feel like we accomplished something today."

They climbed back into the car together, and then Summer was driving them back home.

"We did, a little bit. We made a kid happy. It ain't much, but it's a lot better than most days."

"Mmm." Theo reached over and gently squeezed Summer's thigh. "It's… nice. I dunno. But I suddenly feel kind of selfish all of a sudden."

"How so?"

"Like… hmm." Theo kept her hand where it was, but leaned away, to stare out the passenger window. Her reflection flickered in and out. as they drove past street lights. "I've spent the last ten years thoroughly wrapped up in my own bullshit. And maybe my reasons are about as excusable as they get. But… I feel like I've spent that whole time taking, and taking and taking, and never giving anything back. Not even something as simple as spending a day making a kid happy."

"You've got to secure your own oxygen mask before helping others, right?"

Theo snorted and rolled her eyes. "I'm so sick of that metaphor. At this point I've long polished off my own oxygen mask, and have started systematically sucking down all the oxygen from everyone else's tank too."

Summer shrugged. "Technically speaking, the oxygen masks on airplanes don't have tanks, it's actually a chemical reaction that produces the oxygen. That's why you gotta pull on them."

Her fun factoid was rewarded with a blank stare from Theo.

"What? I listen to podcasts when I work out. I learn stuff sometimes."

Theo snorted with laughter, and she shook her head. "Sorry. Didn't mean to bring the mood down."

"Nah, it's okay. I get it. I mean, the whole reason I do charity is because I used to be such a shitbag and I constantly feel guilty about it. So it's not like I've any particularly noble reason myself."

"But at the end of the day, the kids are still better off, regardless of why you do it."

"Yeah."

Summer pulled into her parking spot behind her apartment, then stepped out of the car stretching. She got a few steps away from the car, before she turned back and realized Theo wasn't following.

Theo was still sitting in the passenger seat , unbuckled, the door hanging open. Her face was red, and she wasn't looking at Summer.

"You coming?"

"Ummm…" Theo twiddled her fingers together, and then awkwardly made the sign language for, "carry."

Summer burst out laughing, and Theo's blush deepened even further.

"I'm sorry, is that too much?"

"Nah, you're good." Summer flashed her teeth. "Just bear with me though. You're a bit heavier than a stick of an eleven year old."

"Can't even be mad about that."

Summer rolled her shoulders, squatted, made sure her form was good, then scooped Theo up into a princess carry, which earned her a delightful little squeak.

Wasn't *too* bad. She could probably make it up the stairs to her apartment. She took a few steps, getting her balance, then paused. "Put your arms around my neck, support yourself a little.

Theo did just that, staring up into Summer's eyes. A fire burned in her expression that made Summer's mouth go dry.

The cool night air was contrasted by the growing heat in Summer's body, in her arms, her core, and the arousal bubbling up within her. The stairs were a challenge, but soon enough she stood outside of her apartment door.

"Shit. I didn't think this through. Doors are locked."

"Hold on. I've got this." Theo brought a hand down, dipping herself until she slipped her hand into Summer's pocket, pulled out her apartment keys, and then unlocked the door.

The whole gesture was ridiculously absurd, and they both started laughing.

Summer quieted the laughter by lifting Theo a bit higher, and kissing her.

And she kept kissing her, all the way to the bed.

Dear Diary,

We're back in school again, which means Summer is miserable again. After lunch I found her lounging around outside and she was making mean comments about all the incoming freshmen.

And I just... don't understand why. Why does she have to be so mean to everyone else? The only person she's nice to is me. And I'm glad she cares! I just... wish she could care about others too.

Theo
8/28/2014

"Morning!" Theo called out cheerfully as she stepped into the astronomy building.

"Hey Theo!" Riley looked up from her computer screen, her eyes studying Theo, and a wicked smirk blossomed on her face. "I can see you had a fun weekend."

Theo came to a stop at the front desk. "I, uh. I mean, sure. Yeah. I had fun."

"I bet." Riley leaned forward, resting her chin on her palm. "I guess things between you and Summer have changed, huh?"

Theo stared at Riley, dumbfounded. How could she possibly...

Riley burst out laughing. "Sorry, sorry. It's okay, honest. I'm happy for you."

Being seen was mortifying, even if it was by a friend. Theo tugged at the collar of her shirt, unable to make eye contact. "Is it because I'm being cheerful, or...?"

"Well, it's that, and the concealer on those hickeys doesn't quite match your skin tone. I have an eye for that kind of thing."

"Oh." Theo raised a hand up to her neck, gingerly touching the skin there. Her face was burning hot. "I mean I borrowed the makeup from Summer, so I guess it wouldn't be perfect."

Riley pulled back, stretching her arms high above her head. "Yeah, that tracks. She only gets the drugstore cheap stuff, and never had much of an eye for using it either. If you ever want, I've been meaning to head to Ulta again sometime soon. I'd be happy to help you get some quality stuff that fits you."

It was so weird, to be casually talking to her girlfriend's ex. That she herself was attracted to, and probably would have pursued if reality hadn't been fractured. Lesbian dating in a small college town was such a mess. "Maybe. I can't say I've ever had much interest in makeup myself, besides the basics. It's one of those 'oh that seems fun to learn' kinda things that always sounds cool but I never actually get around to, like playing guitar or something. It sounds like it's something you're passionate about, though?"

"Yeah, kinda." Riley beamed, her teeth perfect and bright. "It's something I first got into out of a sense of necessity, but I really got sucked into the artistry of it all, you know? I follow a ton of different makeup influencers, and do my best to practice and experiment when I have free time."

"Do you have your own channel? Your makeup looks so good, you definitely have the talent."

Riley's smile faltered, and she shook her head. "Nah. And I'm not trying to be humble here, I *do* actually think my makeup skills are good enough. But... I'm a little terrified of the attention you get when chasing social media clout, and the parasocial stuff just... gives me the creeps." She shuddered. "Most I do is share various looks on instagram."

"I get that. Probably one of the main reasons I don't have much of a social media presence either." She paused, and an old memory bubbled up from the past. "Only thing I ever really got more than a few followers on was my old AO3 account."

"Oh?" Riley's eyes sparkled with interest. "What fandom did you write for?"

"Ugh, no." Theo shook her head emphatically. "Not gonna say. Even the slightest chance that you might be able to track down the stuff I wrote when I was fourteen and I'll die of cringe here on the spot."

Besides, the memory was a bit sour, looking back. She'd only ever dared to write in secret, hadn't even shared it with Summer, and then of course, Summer's death had stolen any spark of creativity she had.

"Come on now, it can't be that bad! I'm sure we all have our fandom deep secrets."

"Yeah, well. This one is staying under lock and key." Theo paused for a beat, then grinned. "For now, anyway."

"A bit of mystery, huh? Love that."

A silence stretched between them, replacing tension with awkwardness.

"Ah, uh. Sorry." Riley looked away, and started shuffling with papers on her desk. "So, you and Summer, huh? How's that going?"

Theo bit her lip. "Good, I guess. I mean. I dunno. Amazing. Everything I ever dreamed of. It's complicated. Summer is complicated."

"She is at that." Riley let out a quiet sigh, then sat up a little straighter. "But I am happy for you. Really."

"It's just…" Theo turned away, and started pacing back and forth in front of the desk. "I'm scared, I guess. Terrified that it's all going to come crashing down, explode in my face, that I'll end up losing everything again. That this is all an impossible dream, that will be gone when I finally wake up."

Riley studied her quietly for several long moments, her brow furrowed in thought. "I'm starting to get the impression that things between her and you are a little more complicated than her bullying you as a kid."

What could she even say to that? Theo shook her head, but answered anyway. "Yeah. I guess. Long, complicated story. One you probably wouldn't even believe."

"Come on, really?" Riley raised an eyebrow. "You can't leave me hanging with something like that. I'll listen and won't be judgmental, I promise."

Could she tell Riley? "I'm serious. It's a completely insane story. You'll probably think I should be locked up in the looney bin. Or something."

Riley rolled her eyes. "First off, the looney bin isn't a kind of place that exists anymore. Second, while involuntary psychiatric holds *are* a thing, I'm not a fucking cop, and I doubt whatever you're going to tell me will make me think you're genuinely dangerous. Third, I have a friend, Cindy, who believes in UFOs and other conspiracy stuff. She's constantly asking me to use the telescope to look for them. It's a bit silly, but she's still a good person."

Theo opened her mouth to say something, then closed it, then opened it again and blurted out, "Did Summer date her?"

"…She did, yeah. Look, it's a small town, only so many lesbians to go around, you know?"

Theo snickered. "Yeah, I get you." She glanced up at the clock in the lobby, then sighed. "Alright, fine. I've got to actually go do some work, but we can talk about it over lunch, okay?"

"Looking forward to it!"

~

Summer let out a long sigh as she laid in bed and stared up at her ceiling.

The scent of Theo still lingered in the air. Her sweat, her sex, and whatever else that was unmistakably her.

Was it a comfort? Something to keep her warm, to keep her sated on the memory of bodies pressed together? Or an empty reminder that Theo wasn't here?

Summer sat up, and rubbed at her temples. How pathetic, to feel so utterly empty when, what? Theo had only been gone for a few hours?

Shouldn't she be used to being alone by now? She'd had a long time to make peace with her lot in life. And it wasn't like she was even *alone* alone. Theo was only at work, not even a mile away. She'd be coming home tonight, and they would resume their weekday schedule, only able to spend time together in the evenings, and briefly in the mornings. It wasn't ideal, but wasn't it enough?

All the rationalization she was doing didn't seem to fill the emptiness, either way.

Chester decided that moment to hop up onto the bed, and lazily sauntered over to her lap, where he crouched, purring.

Summer laughed, and rubbed him behind his ears. "Alright, sure buddy. I'm not alone."

Maybe she should give her therapist a call, schedule an appointment. But then again, the state wasn't paying for it anymore, so appointments were no longer a regular thing, more of an, 'as needed'. Was this really enough of a problem to be worth a hundred bucks?

"Alright, come on, you're hungry, right?" She got a loud meow in response, so Summer stood up and made her way to the kitchen. She had a life to get to, a job to work at, no matter what. And when she came home tonight, she'd be doing it to the arms of a beautiful woman who was, for all sorts of fucked up reasons, as desperately into Summer as she was into her.

After feeding Chester, and then herself, Summer got dressed and headed to the gym. Might as well stick to her normal routine.

When she entered the gym, she was surprised to find Minha there, doing dumbbell curls.

Minha looked up, her face lit up, and she dropped the weight onto the ground, causing a nearby gym-goer to wince and then glare at her. Not that it bothered Minha any. "Yo, dude, how's it going!"

"Hey, Minha," Summer said, coming to a stop near the bench. She shifted her gym bag so the strap dug into her shoulder a little less. "Thought you had class on Monday."

"Nah." Minha grinned her shit eating grin. "Class got canceled. Professor got into a car accident or something."

Summer blinked. "Damn. That sucks."

Minha shrugged. "Eh. He said in his email he's fine, just needed a week off. Supposed to keep doing our assignments but I'm still good for a C even if I don't, so whatever. Spot me?"

Summer sighed, then set her gym bag to the side, and moved with Minha over to a bench press, and helped her set the weights. Not a huge number all on its own, but damned solid for someone as petite as Minha.

"You ever come here with Theo?" Minha asked, after finishing a set.

"Nah, schedules don't line up. Besides, I dunno that gym's really her style anyway."

Minha laughed. "Yeah, she kinda got those noodle arms. I remember she came with us on a family hike once, and even my grandma was passing her on the trail."

"Huh." That was right. The other Theo had history with Minha. Before she could stop herself, Summer found herself asking, "What's she like? Or, I mean. What was she like when you knew her?"

"Pretty cool, I guess." Minha grunted as she picked up the weights again, starting another set. "She was… kinda quiet… at first. Didn't talk much."

She racked the weights and let out a long breath, before sitting up and wiping her forehead. "Honestly I kind of thought she was a bit of a bitch.

Seoyun seemed to like her, but whenever she was around our family she seemed kinda cold. I dunno. I had my own stuff going on, so I didn't pay much attention at first."

Summer nodded. "How old was she, at the time?"

"Uh…" Minha ran a hand through her hair, idly playing with her ponytail. "I wanna say I was just starting middle school? That was when soccer got more serious, and we were in it to win it. Which I guess made Theo and Seoyun…" She paused, counting on her fingers. "Juniors in highschool? Maybe sophomores? I forget."

"And your parents were cool with your sister dating a girl?"

Minha blinked, looking confused. "Oh, right. I mean, yeah. Mom was like, a big name feminist before she moved here, was totally normal. Anyway maybe like six months into it Theo started to open up more, started actually talking to me. She was a total nerd but kinda funny, you know?"

Summer couldn't keep the fondness out of her smile as she nodded. "Yeah, I know."

"Hard to exactly say how or why things changed, I guess. Not like there was some big dramatic event or anything. But at some point it was like I had two big sisters instead of one, which was pretty cool."

"What was Seoyun like?"

Minha pursed her lips, looking Summer up and down. "I dunno. She's my sister, you know? Kinda of bossy and demanding. Really dedicated to studying and other school shit. She cared, though. But like. Why don't you ask Theo about this? She probably saw sides of Seoyun that I didn't."

"It's more complicated than that." Summer tried to picture how it must have been. Theo, a girl who'd probably had her trust and self esteem utterly shattered. And then a highschool girlfriend, slowly helping Theo out of her shell. Did they have a lot in common with each other, good chemistry? Had it been a situation where they were the only queer girls in school and gravitated to each other out of necessity? What had caused them to drift apart?

"Somehow it's always complicated with you." Minha rolled her eyes, then laid back down to do another set. When she finished, she rolled her shoulders, panting heavily. "You should stop worrying about her ex and smash already."

Summer hesitated.

Minha's eyes went wide. "Dude, no way!"

"Goddamnit."

"Fuckin called it. Up top." Minha raised her hand, expecting a high five.

With a dejected sigh, Summer gave her one. Well, it wasn't like she was planning on keeping it a secret. And shouldn't she be proud? Theo fucking ruled.

"Tell me all about it!"

"Fuck no."

~

After her workout, Summer went back home to shower and change. But there was still some time before she had to go to work, and she hadn't had lunch yet. She could make something, but a part of her craved a good sandwich, and she'd had a little extra money to burn lately. So why not?

She made her way to the Over the Moon cafe. She hadn't stopped by ever since she first bumped into Theo there, two weeks ago. Had it really only been two weeks? Definitely the longest two weeks of her life, even counting the time she spent in juvie.

And of course, as soon as she stepped into the cafe she spotted Theo and Riley sitting at a booth together.

Summer's heart warmed at the sight of Theo, and she couldn't keep the grin from her face. "Hey," she said, sliding into the booth next to Theo.

"Oh!" Theo's expression lit up, and she leaned over to give Summer a kiss on the cheek. "Didn't expect to see you here, Summer. I, uh. Well." Her smile faltered, and she glanced over at Riley.

Riley let out a long sigh, and leaned forward on her elbows, massaging her temples.

Uh oh. She looked kind of angry. Summer looked between the two of them and saw Theo avert her gaze. "Am I interrupting something here?"

Theo scratched at her chin. "I kinda sorta told Riley everything? Like about the other dimension stuff."

"Oh." Summer turned her attention to Riley. "So how do you feel about that?"

"Like I have a migraine?" Riley continued rubbing soft circles around her temples, her brow furrowed. "Is this all real, Summer? She said you could independently verify."

Summer shrugged. "As far as I know. I've seen the pictures, and they're definitely not ones I was ever in. I don't know for sure that it's some kind of multidimensional magic comet swap or whatever. I know my memories and Theo's don't match up, and she has photographic evidence of a different timeline. I've been with her long enough that I'm sure she's not lying or delusional."

Riley looked up, her eyes boring deep into Summer's. "And this isn't like, the world's shittiest prank?"

"Of course not. What would even be the point?"

"Yeah. Yeah. Alright." Riley folded her hands over her mouth, and sat still, deep in thought.

Summer turned to Theo, keeping her voice low. "How was work?"

"Same old. Missed you." Theo pressed her shoulder against Summer's, bringing them ever so slightly closer.

"Missed you too." Summer kissed Theo on the top of the head. "Saw Minha at the gym, got to hang out for a bit."

"Give her my best when you see her again at work."

"Okay, so." Riley placed her hands on the booth, leaning forward. "Let's say I accept all of this is true. My inner scientist is screaming at me right now but whatever. I can roll with this, at least for now."

"Yeah?" Theo said, smiling. "I'm sorry, didn't mean to lob a grenade into your sense of reality. It's just... what I'm dealing with, I guess."

Riley shook her head. "I mean if it's true it's the most important scientific discovery of the century. But also if its true, like... what the absolute fuck?" She gestured to Theo and Summer in turn, her face twisted up with disgust.

Summer raised an eyebrow. "What do you mean?"

"I mean..." Riley closed her eyes and took a deep breath. "This is the mostly wildly unhealthy thing I've ever fucking seen. And I dated Heather! What the fuck, Summer? I thought you knew better."

Summer winced. "Hey, come on. It's not like that. I'm following her lead here, it's fine."

"Do you *really* think that?" Riley growled, and leaned forward, pointing a finger at Summer. "Because from my perspective it looks a lot like taking advantage of someone's trauma. Not like you don't have a history of it already."

Anger boiled up in Summer, and she did her best to keep it tamped down. "It's not like that, Riley," she said through clenched teeth. "I care for Theo a lot, and we're both aware of the issues, and the past. We're taking things slow and trying to be careful with it, and talking things through as much as possible. I can understand being wary, but…"

"But you also managed to find a solution that involves you getting laid, wow, how convenient," Riley said, her voice thick with sarcasm.

"Okay, that's just—"

"Shut up," Theo said, her voice low and cold, but still commanding silence as both Summer and Riley turned to look at her.

Theo let out a sharp breath from her nose. "Riley. I consider you a friend, but you need to shut the fuck up, right now."

Riley reeled as if she'd been struck. "Theo, I—"

"No." Theo silenced her with a finger. "For the past ten years, ever since Summer—my Summer—died, I've been treated like a broken, fragile mess, by everyone around me. And make no mistake, I *am* a broken, fragile mess. And I am sick and tired of being treated like one. By my parents, by my brother, by my friends, by my ex girlfriends. I am a competent, adult woman, who is capable of making her own decisions. And even if I'm not, too fucking bad. I'll make my own mistakes. I've chosen to throw myself into this, and if it turns out to be a bad idea, I'll do therapy about it later. I don't need you, or anyone else, to coddle me. Do you understand?"

Shocked silence hung in the air for several long moments, before Riley let out a soft squeak, and nodded.

"Good." Theo took a sip of her coffee, her posture clear that the discussion was over and done with.

"Damn," Summer muttered. She was impressed, maybe even a little turned on, and glad she hadn't stumbled into that trap herself. She would have to be careful in the future, not to try and be too protective.

Riley sat there in silence, her face red, her lips twisted in a pout, as she clearly workshopped what she wanted to say in response.

After maybe a minute of silence, Riley finally nodded, and then spoke. "I'm sorry. That was uncalled for. I think that I'm maybe… not over some things as much as I thought I was. Please forgive me."

Summer looked over at Theo, and Theo nodded back. "It's okay," Summer said. "I get it."

Riley rubbed at her cheek, not making eye contact. "I think I'm maybe… also a little bit jealous. Sorry. I know I don't have a right to be but it's like. Damn. I never stood a chance at all, huh?"

Theo's expression softened. "Sorry. I actually do… no. I don't think there's really anything I can say that wouldn't twist the knife there more, is there?"

"Probably not." Riley chuckled bitterly, sniffed, and closed her eyes. "Okay, well. Can we still be friends?"

"Of course," Summer and Theo both said in unison.

"Good." Riley opened her eyes, and nodded. "Let's push the messy relationship drama to the side then. You're from another world, Theo. That's huge. I have so many questions, and I need to look up this comet too."

Theo pulled out her phone, checking it. "It's about time we get back to work, anyway."

"Ugh and now I have to sit there and be a secretary for four more hours instead of using the telescope. And this is going to absolutely sideline my current research but fuck it. Alternate dimensions exist!"

Summer laughed, then squeezed Theo's hand and stepped out of the booth. "Guess I'll see you later tonight?"

Theo smiled, then stood up and kissed Summer on the cheek. "Looking forward to it."

~

Theo panted heavily, her naked body covered in a thin sheen of sweat. Aftershocks of pleasure still rocked through her body, and she squeezed her legs together, still savoring the sensation.

"Fuck," Summer breathed, collapsing onto the bed next to Theo, her arm draped over her forehead.

With a grunt of effort, her legs unable to support her in this maneuver, Theo managed to roll over, and rest her head on Summer's chest. The sound of her pounding heartbeat thudded comfortably in Theo's ear.

Summer adjusted her position, snaking her arm underneath Theo, pulling her even closer, her fingertips tracing idle patterns along Theo's side.

They lay like that for quite some time. Theo listened as Summer's heartbeat and breathing slowed. Her eyes closed, her mind started to drift, as sleep called to her, comfortable and warm.

"Do you think this is a mistake?" Summer asked, her voice quiet.

"Huh?" Theo blinked, pulling herself out of the start of a dream. She could see Summer was avoiding her gaze.

Summer was silent for at least another moment, to the point where Theo almost started to drift off again. But Summer eventually squeezed Theo gently before continuing. "What you said to Riley. Didn't really register at the time but… you said you wanted to be free to make your own mistakes. I just… is that what this is?"

"Oh." Theo propped herself up on her elbow, then reached out her other hand, and cupped Summer's cheek. She turned Summer so their eyes met, and then she leaned in to kiss her softly. "That's not how I meant that."

"Yeah, I know, I just…" Summer bit her lip. "It got stuck in my head, and. I dunno. It's stupid. I don't want to be—"

Theo kissed her again, stealing her words from her lips. "I don't know, honestly. How can I? It's the most unprecedented situation anyone in the history of ever has dealt with."

"Is it? Maybe this actually happens to people all the time, and we don't know about it."

The absurdity of the thought made Theo laugh, and she planted a kiss on Summer's nose this time. "Maybe. But still. I don't know. Does anyone ever really know if something is a mistake, until after the fact? A part of this feels like it might be. But I don't want it to be. It feels… magical. I want that to mean something. It means something to me, anyway."

It wasn't like she had any idea what Summer actually saw in her. Theo traced her finger down Summer's chest, through a small puddle of sweat that had gathered in her clavicle. "Is that okay?"

Summer looked at her, her brilliant green eyes shining. "Yeah. Sorry. Just got a little tripped up in my own head for a minute."

"Believe me. I know how that goes." Theo kissed Summer one more time, then laid her head back down on Summer's chest, ready to let Summer's heartbeat lull her to sleep.

If this was a mistake, it was going to be a beautiful one.

Dear Diary,

We were grabbing snacks from the gas station and Summer saw some sketchy guy loitering nearby and joked about going to buy drugs from him and I practically had to drag her away. I know she was joking but in the way where she's not really joking.

She called me lame, and a total pansy. I told her that we were going to go to college and she had better not do anything stupid to jeopardize that. She just rolled her eyes.

I know I'm in the right here, but... I'm also not that much of a loser, really. I can be cool too. I know Summer doesn't see it, but.

I wish she would.

I might have an idea.

Theo
9/14/2014

The next three days passed by in a steady rhythm for Summer. The same rhythm as before, mostly. Wake up, share time and breakfast with Theo. Watch her leave for work. Work out and kill time before her shift. Work at the gas station. Come home, and spend time with Theo again.

It had been their pattern ever since Theo moved in. But now there was a melody accompanying the rhythm. Kisses in the dark. Morning showers together. Long text conversations during work hours, punctuated with numerous kissy emojis. Passion when they met up again, hot and heavy and deeply fulfilling. And then maybe what mattered to Summer the most; the quiet moments they shared together, cuddling, drawing, watching a show, and otherwise enjoying each other's company.

It all came together to create a much sweeter song, one that filled

Summer's heart, and drowned out the constant dread of how limited their time together would ultimately be.

"Yo, delivery trucks here," Minha said as she made her way through the store. "Can you go help them unload?"

Summer looked up from her phone, from where she loitered at the checkout. "Shit. Forgot it was Thursday." She sighed and stretched. "Isn't it your turn with the truck?"

Minha shrugged. "I've got a game tomorrow, I don't wanna risk twinging something in my back again."

"You gotta lift with your knees."

"I'm real short, remember? Those guys drop the boxes on me from up top on the truck."

"Fine, fine. I've got it. You gotta clean up tonight though."

Minha grinned, then moved past Summer to take over the register.

Summer made her way outside, greeted the drivers, then started hauling boxes from their truck. She was glad her workout earlier today hadn't been arm focused.

After about thirty minutes she'd finished, and she sat down on a nearby crate, wiping her face off with a towel.

She pulled out her phone, and found a few notifications in the group chat.

Riley: Quick summary of the testing I did on BTKC21 last night:

Riley: Made a bunch of wishes, both trivial and profound. None of them came true, at least not in easily observable ways.

Riley: Set up various measuring devices around the telescope to see if the mere act of observing the comet created some sort of observable or measurable effect. I thought I maybe had something with electrical fluctuations but that turned out to be some poor shielding on the telescope itself. It's not exactly a sterile lab environment.

Riley: But yeah. Nothing conclusive yet. Sorry.

Theo: lol that's okay! You're really going all out on this. Never would have thought of any of this myself.

Riley: I'd like to repeat some of the tests with you at some

```
point, see if it's related to you specifically in any way.
```

Theo: Sure, let me know when!

Summer added a thumbs up reaction. It was past six, so Theo was definitely home by now. As always, the thought that she'd be returning home to her brought a smile to Summer's face.

Summer made her way back into the store.

"Oh, yeah, it's gonna be awesome! You should totally come to my game tomorrow." Minha said, her boisterous voice carrying through the store.

"Oh, um. Maybe. If I can find the time. I'd like that a lot, actually. It's been a long time. I always loved watching you play."

Summer blinked. That voice. Wasn't it...

Sure enough, she rounded one of the isles and saw Theo at the counter, talking to Minha.

"Hah. I'm even better now. Honestly, I kind of choked on the last game, even if we still won. But I'll nail it this time for sure."

"Your... last game? When was that, again?"

"What do you mean? Like, last Saturday? Or, wait, the Saturday before that."

"Hmm. Minha, about that. Those pictures you sent me, I wanted to ask about those."

Summer made her way over, her heart filled with warmth. What an utterly delightful surprise. "Hey," Summer said, stepping up behind Theo and placing her fingers against the back of her neck. "This day just got a whole lot better, with you here."

Theo stiffened under her touch, then slowly craned her neck to look at Summer. Her eyes widened, then her face scrunched up in fury. With a wordless scream, she shoved Summer, hard.

With a crash, Summer stumbled into one of the displays, knocking bags of chips all over the floor.

"Woah, holy shit!" Minha exclaimed helpfully.

Theo stood there, looming over her, fists clenched, shaking, her face bright red. "What the fuck made you think that was appropriate?"

Summer stared, utterly confused. She shook her head, trying to orient herself. "I, uh. I'm sorry? Thought we were cool with that, but if you don't want me to, that's fine. I don't want to trigger anything."

"Don't want to…" Theo's expression twisted to confusion of her own. She stared down at Summer, eyes squinted through her big round glasses. Then she barked out a short, bitter laugh. "Can't say I ever imagined a reunion happening like this. God. Fuck."

"Uh…" Minha rubbed at the back of her head. "Are you two doing alright? I can watch the store if you need to go hash things out or whatever. No quickies in the bathroom though."

Theo stared at Minha in incredulity. "Minha, what? Come on, don't be disgusting."

Uh oh. An icy feeling snaked through Summer's guts. She made her way to her feet, a bit unsteady, a bag of chips rolling off of her shoulder. "Hey, uh. Sorry about that, Theo. But uh, weird question real quick. When was the last time we saw each other?"

"My name," Theo hissed, and took a step closer to Summer. "Is Theodora. Only friends are allowed to call me Theo."

Fuck. Fuck fuck fuck.

Summer's phone buzzed in her pocket. She pulled it out to check.

Theo: Do you want pasta with red sauce or white sauce for dinner?

Fuck.

⌒

Panic filled Theo as she sprinted down main street.

She clutched her phone tight in her hand, the text message she'd received still pulled up on the screen.

Summer: hey can u come down to the gas station real quick its an emergency

A prompt like that left Theo very little room for rational thought. Was Summer okay? She had to be, right? If it had been a dire emergency, Summer would have asked her to meet at the hospital. Or someone else would have texted on her behalf.

It probably wasn't the kind of emergency that left Summer lying in a pile of junk at the bottom of a basement, bleeding out onto the floor while Theo desperately prayed for an ambulance to get there faster.

On some level, she knew that everything was probably fine.

But that didn't stop the adrenaline coursing through her veins, didn't stop the thundering of her heartbeat, didn't stop the feel of bile rising in her throat. She ran faster than she'd ever run before, not even bothering to stop at intersections, earning more than a few angry honks in the process. Her sandals threatened to trip her with each step, her skirt got caught between her legs. She hadn't dressed properly. She wasn't in good enough shape.

It didn't matter.

Theo burst into the gas station, skidding to a stop on the tiled floor.

Summer stood there, seemingly whole and healthy. Her face flooded with relief as she saw Theo. "Oh, thank god. See? I told you."

Black dots swarmed across Theo's vision and she trembled, her breath coming in heaving, shaking gasps. She tried to still her heartbeat, calm her panic, let her muscles relax.

"What the fuck?"

A voice spoke. A familiar voice. An unfamiliar voice, uncanny and wrong.

Theo turned, tugging her eyesight away from Summer with herculean effort, her brain wanting nothing more than to tunnel vision onto the woman she loved, and never look away. But she did so anyway, only to stare into a mirror.

Only… it wasn't a mirror, was it? It was another flesh and blood human person.

Another Theo stared back at her in wide eyed horror.

Theo threw up on her.

~

Theo sat in a corner of the gas station, taking sips from a bottle of water, washing the taste of vomit out of her mouth.

Minha grumbled to herself as she poured cat litter over the vomit on the floor, and started cleaning it up.

Summer crouched in front of Theo, holding her hand, gently rubbing her fingers over Theo's knuckles. "I'm sorry about that. I wasn't thinking when I sent that message."

"It's fine," Theo said automatically. "You were right, this is kind of an emergency. It's my fault for getting caught up in my own head."

With a wince, Summer shook her head. "Coulda put more detail into the text message. Theo—Theo*dora* kept yelling at me though, so it was hard to get off."

Theo took a deep breath. Her body was finally starting to reset to some sense of default. "What do we do?"

"Be honest and forthcoming?" Summer shrugged. "It worked with Riley, right? Maybe we'll be lucky twice."

"Maybe." Theo glanced towards the bathrooms. "She seems kind of pissed though."

"I still want an explanation too, y'know," Minha added, pausing her cleaning to lean on her mop. "Which one of you is the Theo I know, and which one is the evil twin?"

Theo glanced over at Summer, and shrugged. "It's slightly more complicated than that. But... I'd never actually met you until the other week at the soccer game. I kind of went along with it because it was easier to pretend. I'm sorry. I guess that makes me the evil twin."

Minha pursed her lips as she stared down at the two of them. There seemed to be genuine pain in her expression. "Summer?"

Summer rubbed at the back of her head. "Yeah, I knew the whole time. Told you it was complicated. Sorry."

"That... fucking sucks, dude."

"Yeah. I know."

They were saved from one form of awkwardness by the return of Theodora, who stepped out of the bathroom. She'd removed her cardigan, washed the vomit off of it, and it was now tied around her waist. An entirely different bout of awkwardness awaited.

Theodora adjusted her glasses, and let out a quiet sigh. "Was really hoping I'd come back out and this would all be a bad dream, or the world's worst tiktok prank."

It was so uncanny, staring into the face of herself. Did identical twins feel like this all the time? Or maybe it would only be the ones who got separated at birth, and reunited as adults. "Hi," Theo said, taking Summer's hand for support and then standing up. "Um. Sorry about the mess earlier."

Theodora came closer, and circled Theo, inspecting her from every angle. "It's uncanny. I wonder if all identical twins feel like this. Or I guess, maybe only the ones who got separated at birth and meet as adults. But Summer said some bullshit about alternate realities. Doesn't look like you have a goatee, though."

Theo did her best to suppress a giggle, hearing her own thoughts so quickly verbalized. "Me being from an alternate reality is the best guess I have, and the fact that you're here in front of me seems like way more evidence for that theory."

"Mmm." Theodora turned her gaze towards Summer. "And your first action upon traveling to a separate dimension was to hook up with the woman who bullied the shit out of us in middle school? I mean, I kind of get it, we've got a kink about it now, but... still. What the hell?"

Well that was interesting. Theo cleared her throat, and decided to move past that bit of trivia about her alternate self. "That's... kind of the main thing, actually. In the universe I come from, Summer didn't bully me. We were best friends."

Theodora reacted as if she'd been struck, and took a step back. "Oh," she said, her voice quiet. She was silent for several long moments, her hands clasped together in front of her, fingers fidgeting. When she finally looked up, her gaze directed towards Summer, there was a deep pain reflected in her features. "So... are you also from another dimension? You were *her* best friend?"

Summer winced, and shook her head. "No. This is my home dimension. I'm the one who bullied you, when we were kids." She let out a long sigh. "I am sorry about that, for what it's worth. I know it doesn't make anything better, but I deeply regret the hurt I caused you back then."

Theo elbowed Summer gently. "You should give the apology you gave to me, back when you thought I was her. I remember it being way more poignant."

"Hey, come on." Summer pursed her lips, her cheeks coloring slightly. "I don't remember exactly what I said."

A bell rang, and a middle aged man walked into the store, immediately stopping and staring, the weird tension in the room easily sensed even by an outsider. But he shuffled up towards the unmanned counter, eying the cigarettes behind it.

Minha let out a quiet sigh, and then put on her customer service face. "Sorry about that, be right there!" She shoved the mop into Summer's hands, then ran over to the checkout.

Theo laughed. "This is a really awkward place to be having this conversation, huh?"

Theodora grunted. "Yeah. Can we get out of here, go somewhere else?"

"No can do." Summer finished the cleaning, and started wheeling the mop and bucket to the back of the store. "I've got a few more hours left in my shift, and I can't leave Minha here to deal with it all alone. Besides, she's a part of this conversation too, at least a little."

"She thinks of you like a sister, and misses you a lot, I think," Theo added.

"I… see." Theodora glanced towards Minha. "This is all so much. I have so many questions, things I want to know. I think I need some time to clear my head, sit and think. Can we meet up after your shift is over?"

Summer glanced over at Theo, and she nodded back. "Yeah," Summer said. "We're cool with that."

"Okay. Good. This is all so…" She gestured vaguely. "Right. Later."

Theodora turned to go, briskly walking towards the exit. But then she stopped, hovering in the doorway, before turning around.

"If you and the Summer from your reality were best friends… why are you here?"

Ah. She should have clarified that earlier. "Because, she died, when we were sixteen. And it was all my fault."

~

Summer sat with Theo at a circular picnic table, in the central plaza of the town. Even this late, they could still see occasional passersby, groups of students heading to bars, returning to campus.

She had texted Theodora, using Theo's old number, and received a thumbs up emoji in response. But they'd been waiting for an hour now after Summer had gotten off of her shift. Minha had decided to head home, rather than stick around for the drama. She'd been… distant.

Yet another important relationship Summer had blown up by being an asshole.

Theo let out a long sigh, resting her palm on her chin. "Do you think she's actually going to show up?"

"Starting to get the impression we might have gotten stood up," Summer said dryly.

"Guess I can't blame her. I mean, how could I? She's me."

"Yeah." Summer bit her lip. "Even though I knew she was out there somewhere... definitely wasn't prepared to see both of you in the same place at the same time. Surreal."

A mischievous smirk blossomed on Theo's face. "Which one of us do you think is hotter?"

"You," Summer answered immediately.

"Oh." Theo laughed. "Not even going for a funny answer?"

Summer shrugged. "I know a trap when I see one. But more importantly..." She pursed her lips, and drummed her fingers on the table. "The way you look at me is gentle and kind. She looks at me with disgust and hatred. I know which one I prefer."

Theo reached across the table and took Summer's hand in her own. It was cold. "Sorry. It must be hard."

"Yeah." Summer stared into Theo's eyes, idly squeezing her hand. "What you said, earlier. That it was your fault that... What actually happened to the other me? If it's too painful to talk about, I understand, I just..."

Silence hung in the air between them, and Theo averted her eyes. Her posture became stiff, her breathing measured.

"Sorry," Summer said, rushing to backpedal. "Seriously, we don't have to talk about it, I was just curious. Should have kept my mouth shut."

Theo squeezed her hand, hard. "It's fine," she said, her tone clipped. "I understand wanting to know. She's you, after all. What if I got *you* killed? Maybe this isn't some sort of weird blessing for me, but some terrible curse, forced to live out your death in every reality."

Summer blinked, and tried to choose her next words carefully. "That's uh, definitely not what I was thinking about. I'm not going anywhere, I promise."

"I know, I know." Theo groaned, and pinched the bridge of her nose. "Sorry, I'm catastrophizing again. I brought the other Summer to an abandoned building for her birthday so she could break stuff to her hearts content. I... we..." She sucked in a sharp breath through her teeth. "The floor gave way, and she fell."

"Fuck," Summer muttered. She tried to picture it. Hell, she'd done similar stuff as a kid. Though it had mostly been alone. "I'm so sorry you had to go through that."

Theo pulled her hand back, and used it to pinch the skin on her other forearm. "Yeah, well. It was a dumb accident. I've told myself that a million times. But it was still my idea to take her there, because I wanted her to think I was cool, that I would be willing to break the rules occasionally, that I was more than a sheltered goody-two-shoes. I thought it would be fine as long as we were careful. And it wasn't."

Summer thought back to the photos on Theo's phone, all the snapshots of a long gone friendship. She still couldn't imagine herself being okay with that, at that age. "Did you... feel like you needed to impress the other Summer, a lot?"

"Yeah." Theo lowered her head, and remained silent for a long time. "I don't like to think of it much but... Ugh. I dunno. You're not supposed to speak ill of the dead, and all that."

A sinking feeling settled in Summer's gut. "Look, if there's anyone who will understand, it's me, y'know? I can handle it."

Theo looked off into the distance, her expression blank. "I just... she was kind of mean, you know? She was always talking shit about everyone else. And there was always the sense that if I disappointed her in any way I'd be her next target. I was desperate to stay on her good side."

Too easy to picture. Summer didn't know how to respond.

"I know it was a bit unhealthy and codependent. I do now, anyway. But there were good bits, too! We genuinely had a lot of fun together. It's all just..." Theo sighed, and rested her forehead against the picnic table. "Sorry."

"Nothing you have to apologize to me for," Summer murmured.

"I don't think you're like that at all, for the record."

Summer looked up, and propped her chin on her hand. "Are you sure you could tell even if I was?"

Theo opened her mouth, then closed it, and shook her head. "Probably not. I'd like to say I'm mature enough to notice those patterns if I fall into them, but the truth is I'm not. I've had other relationships with similar dynamics. Easy to fall into."

"I get that. For what it's worth, I do my best to not be like that anymore. But... I'm always worried I'm fucking it up anyway. Shit, I feel really bad about lying to Minha. Dunno if I can make it up to her."

"I'm sure she needs some time to process. We'll do it together, okay?"

Theo reached out and took her hand again, squeezing gently.

"Okay."

Theo took a deep breath and released it slowly. "Well, I really don't think she's coming. Now what?"

"Guess we go back home, try again tomorrow."

"Yeah." Theo pulled out her phone, and glanced at it. "I know you said you bullied her a bunch, but… what exactly did you do? Like, specifically?"

"It's… complicated." Summer groaned, trying to figure out a way to even put it into words. "I—"

"She pretended to be my friend," Theodora said, stepping out from behind a nearby tree. "Before revealing that it was all a big lie."

Dear Diary,

I have the perfect plan.

There's an old house in the countryside scheduled for demolition.

For Summer's birthday, I'll take her there, and let her absolutely wreck the place to her heart's content.

It'll show her that I can be cool and break the rules together, and I'm sure she'll have a lot of fun.

I'm gonna take every precaution that we don't get caught, but even if we do, I'm pretty sure we can get off with a warning.

I hope so.

It'll be fine, I'm sure.

Summer will be so happy. And she really needs it, too.

Theo
7/19/2014

Theo's heart caught in her throat, mostly in shock from the sudden appearance of her doppelganger. "Oh, uh. Hey?"

Theodora came to a stop near the picnic table, and crossed her arms over her chest, looking down at the both of them. It was a gesture Theo had seen from her mother a million times. Did Theo do that?

"Were you waiting behind the tree for the perfect moment to dramatically enter the conversation?" Summer asked, raising an eyebrow.

"I, uh." Theodora's intimidating aura immediately vanished, and her cheeks colored pink. "Look, I got close enough to hear, and you were talking about stuff and I just… this whole situation is really fucking awkward, okay? *Excuse* me for not handling it perfectly."

"I get it," Theo said, doing her best to smile. But god, it was *so* weird!

Seeing her own movements, her own patterns of speech, inflections of tone. Worse than watching a video of herself, even. She felt goosebumps prickle on her skin, and she suppressed the urge to shiver.

Summer grunted, then gestured to the open third of the picnic table.

Theodora looked between the two of them, took a deep breath, and then sat down.

"So. Um." Theo rubbed her hands together, not wanting to look her other self in the eye. "What was that you were saying?"

"You mean she hasn't already told you?" Theodora scoffed, and shook her head. "Why is that, *Summer*?" The emphasis she put on Summer held a considerable amount of venom.

Summer looked away. "It's... complicated."

"Is it?" Theodora sneered. "Sounds like an excuse to me. But go on. Tell her what happened. I'm curious to see how you'll try to soften the blow."

Theo could see the pain and guilt in Summer's expression. A part of her wanted to reach out, comfort her. But another part... the idea that Summer had only been pretending. The thought of it filled her with a deep, existential dread, that she wasn't fully sure how to push through.

Summer puffed out her cheeks, slowly letting out a long breath. "Alright. Just... I was a little kid too, you know? My memory of what happened isn't the best, I can't fully recall my thought process or what led me to do anything. So I apologize in advance if I get something wrong."

"Go on."

"Well, it started when we were assigned together on a group project. Fourth grade? Fifth? I forget. I hadn't interacted much with Theodora before that. She was super excited about the project, all bright and bubbly and cheerful. I found it super annoying. I pushed all the work onto her."

Theodora clenched her fists, but didn't comment.

Summer glanced towards Theodora, but mostly kept her gaze focused on Theo. "After the project she kind of kept... following me around, talking to me. Acting like we were friends. I... I dunno. I remember being irrationally angry about it. Maybe it was something along the lines of 'how dare she be so carefree and happy when im so fucking miserable, and then come and rub that in my face.' But it's so hard to tell, thinking back. Did I really think like that? Am I projecting what I know now about therapy and coping mechanisms and childhood abuse? Shit's all a big mess. But… I kept telling her to do things for me, and she did. So I started taking advantage of that. Making her do my homework. Fetch me stuff from the vending machines. Carry my books. Little stuff, at first."

Theo winced. How often, had Summer just… casually ordered her to do a minor chore? How often had Theo eagerly jumped to do so?

Theodora looked at her, briefly seeming smug, but it vanished, and her expression was replaced with sympathy.

"It kept up like that for a while. Till middle school, at least. Puberty was rough. Stuff at home got worse. I kept escalating my requests, to see how much I could get away with. I had some… *friends* is the wrong word, but other girls who were shitbags like me. They kept egging me on, thought the little girl following me around like a puppydog was the funniest thing. The stuff I asked her to do got way more arbitrary and humiliating.

"I just wanted you to like me," Theodora said, her voice clipped.

Summer nodded, her expression dark. "I know. It all came to a head with one final prank. I locked her on the school roof. Convinced that I was going to go get help, to not call out to anyone because we'd both get in trouble. Left her there all night. It was autumn. She got hypothermia. Had to go to the hospital. That's when it all came out, and I got suspended, and Theodora moved away."

"Jesus fucking christ," Theo whispered.

Theodora's fists were clenched, her eyes shining with unshed tears. "*Why?*"

Summer shrugged. "I've thought a lot about that. Dunno that I have a real and honest answer. Best I've got is that wielding power over you made me feel better about the power I lacked elsewhere in my life. At least, that's what I've talked about with my therapist. I dunno. It's not an excuse. It doesn't change anything. I'm deeply, deeply sorry. I've spent a long time trying to become a better person, to work on my issues, to treat people better. But that doesn't erase the harm I did to you."

Theo thought back to her own relationship with Summer. It *had* been different. Right? They'd started from a different place. Sure, Summer had been pretty bossy. But they'd actually been friends. Theo had watched her warm up, break out of her shell, bit by bit. It was different.

"You…" Theodora took a deep, shuddering breath. "It hurt. It hurt, Summer. So fucking bad. I genuinely thought you were my friend. I know now I was a stupid baby lesbian with a crush, but still. It wasn't even the dumb roof thing. It was when I talked to you afterwards. I could have still forgiven you. But you told me you did it on purpose, that you couldn't believe I was that stupid. Hey guess what, fun fact, I have trust issues now in relationships, can't imagine where those came from."

Summer lowered her head, her hands shaking.

Theodora wiped at her face and sniffed. "And now you're here, and I guess you're literally dating me? What the fuck am I supposed to think about that?"

Nobody had any answer for her. Theodora turned towards Theo. "Is she worth it? Is it everything you ever hoped for?"

Theo winced. "I… my baggage with Summer is a bit different than yours. Sorry. If she was pretending… then she made it a lot longer, and the truth never came up. But I did wonder, sometimes. Especially after she died, I… went over every moment over and over and over. Would wind myself up to the point where I was convinced it was all some cruel joke."

Theodora grunted. "How can one woman fuck up the same life in so many different ways?"

"She's pretty talented."

That made Theodora snort with laughter.

A small smile pierced Summer's gloom.

Theo reached out and took Summer's hand again, squeezing. "My past is the biggest mess imaginable. It sounds like yours is too. But we've already decided to try to focus on the present, right?"

Summer glanced towards Theodora, but swallowed, and nodded.

"Theodora. God, feels weird to say it." Theo took a deep breath. "In the time I've known this Summer, she's been very self flagellating. If you wanted to take some kind of revenge on her, she'd probably let you. But I… really care for her. And would highly appreciate it if you didn't do that. You don't have to forgive her or anything, but…"

Theodora met Theo's gaze, her expression twisted. "I thought about it for a long time. Revenge. Some sort of epic prank. But I also had therapy, and I learned better ways to think of it. And then I met Seoyun, and… made new friends at my new school, and it all kind of faded into the past."

"Guess I'm two for two on unexpectedly opening up old wounds," Summer muttered.

"Be careful what you wish for, I guess," Theodora muttered.

Theo's ears perked up instantly. "What was that?"

"What was what?"

"You said something about a wish?"

Summer's raised an eyebrow, and her full attention turned towards Theodora.

Theodora blinked, and her cheeks colored slightly. "It's nothing, just an idle comment."

Theo leaned closer. "No, really. This whole alternate dimension thing. Uh, best theory right now is that it's vaguely wish based. If you've had any weird experiences lately, then…"

"That's…" Theodora shook her head. "No way. That's stupid."

"Please. If there's anything even slightly relevant, I wanna know. It could be important."

"Fine. I, uh." Theodora rubbed her arms together. "I was visiting my parents, had recently turned down a job here at the university, had this town on my mind, and I guess Summer. And I was out back in the treehouse, stargazing and… I dunno. I saw a comet. It was cool. But I wasn't really enjoying it because I was thinking too much and I kind of said like, 'I wish I could see what it would be like, if Summer had actually been my friend.' I dunno. I was in a bad place."

Theo and Summer glanced at each other.

"Why are you grinning like that?"

"We're going to have to introduce you to a friend of ours named Riley."

~

Summer arrived at the observatory the following evening, having headed straight there after her shift ended. Theo had already been here for a few hours already.

Unfortunately, Theodora arrived at the exact same time as her.

"Hey," Summer said.

Theodora bit her lip, her eyes full of venom. "Just go in ahead of me. I don't want to arrive together with you."

"Do you even know how to get there?"

"Uh." Theodora looked away. "There's probably signs, right?"

"Well, I'm going in. You can follow me at any distance you want." Summer opened the door, not holding it but pushing it far enough open

Theodora would have a chance to slip in if she wanted. "We didn't give Riley the heads up about you though so I'm glad I get to see her reaction in person."

The door behind her didn't close, and Theodora fell into step behind her.

As expected, the look on Riley's face when they walked into the observatory together was priceless. It made their efforts at subterfuge worth it.

Theo was standing over a desk, sorting through some papers, and looked particularly smug as she gave a little wave. "Hey you two!"

Riley looked between Theo and Theodora, her mouth hanging open, her eyes wide. "Wow. I, uh. You know I believed you before but this sure takes the cake. Hmm."

Theodora fidgeted uncomfortably. "Hi. Uh, nice to meet you, I guess? We were going to be coworkers before I had to turn the job down last minute. I'd say you can call me Theo, but... Theodora is fine for the current situation."

"Uh-huh. Uh-huh." Riley continued looking between the two of them, her cheeks faintly pink. "Could one of you put your hair up or something? This is going to drive me insane."

"I don't really like putting my hair up, it's kind of brittle and breaks easily," both Theo's said simultaneously.

A brief moment passed before they both laughed, shaking their heads. "I'll do it," Theo said. "I'm the interloper, after all."

Riley absentmindedly handed Theo a scrunchie, her gaze fixed on Summer. "Hey Summer I have a question for you."

"What's that?" Summer asked, trying her hardest not to think about how fucking good Theo looked with her hair up, and about how she wanted to leave hickies on the back of her neck.

"What the actual fuck?"

Summer laughed, then shrugged. "Hey, I wasn't expecting this one either."

"You could have given me a heads up!"

"Yeah, but it was funnier if we didn't."

"You know what? Fair." Riley pinched the bridge of her nose, then finally closed the gap between them and properly shook Theodora's hand. "Anyway, it's nice to meet you. Apologies in advance if I'm in any way weird about this."

"That's okay," Theodora said with a smile, and a familiar warmth she hadn't yet seen out of the other woman. Which made sense, there wasn't a scrap of it that Summer deserved. "I'll probably be kind of weird about this too. It's a weird situation. I'm told you're something of an expert?"

Riley snorted and shook her head. "I'm an overworked grad student with access to a big telescope. If that's what qualifies as an expert in this situation y'all are probably fucked. But, I at least know how to apply the scientific method to whatever weird sci-fi bullshit you've got going on. Theo said she'd uncovered some new information, and I guess it's something you know?"

Theodora nodded, then launched into the explanation she'd given last night.

Summer made her way over to Theo, and gently squeezed her hand. "Hey."

"Hey," Theo whispered back.

"Huh. Interesting." Riley turned away from Theodora, and started pacing. A small cubicle near the big telescope was filled to the brim with sticky notes, and Riley paused to look over them. "What was the date when you made that wish?"

"Uh." Theodora scrunched up her face, then pulled up her phone and the calendar app. "Sunday, August 25th."

"Do you remember the time?"

"I dunno. Late? Maybe around midnight or one."

"I see." Riley scribbled something down on a new sticky note. "And you, Theo?"

Theo frowned, and was silent for a few moments. "Same day. Pretty sure the same time."

"And you specifically, wished that Summer could see this comet together with you?"

Theo looked away. "Yeah. I think that's what I said."

Summer frowned. Something about that felt off.

"And you wished to see what would have happened if you and Summer had actually been friends."

Theodora shook her head. "This all sounds so stupid."

"I mean, maybe, sure, but also like it's all starting to come together?" There was a bit of a manic energy to Riley that Summer had rarely had the chance to see. "Two wishes, made at the same time, on the same comet. Both could be granted by bringing Theo here. It seems plausible."

"I dunno that I'd describe anything about this as plausible," Theo said. She glanced over at Theodora, lips pursed. "But I guess there's a certain amount of narrative sense to it."

"Well, that's why we can test some things! Gimme a second." Riley sat down at the computer, furiously typing. The position of the telescope started to move, gears clicking and grinding as the massive piece of machinery adjusted its position.

After a few minutes, it finally settled. "Alright," Riley said. "Theo, you take the telescope. Theodora, you'll have to watch the output on the monitors. Once you can both see the comet clearly, I'll count down to three and then you'll both say 'I wish there was a baked potato here on this plate' simultaneously." Riley held up a dirty plate.

"Why a baked potato?" Theodora asked.

"Because I'm hungry."

Theo snickered. "Should we order food?"

"Maybe if the potato thing doesn't work."

Summer crossed her arms over her chest. "Is this really a good idea?"

Riley raised an eyebrow. "It's science. Gotta test it somehow, right? Might as well do something silly and simple. I honestly don't think this is going to work, but it can establish a nice baseline."

"It's Friday the 13th, though."

Silence hung in the air after Summer's words for several long moments.

"Shit, really?" Both Theo's said at once.

Riley rolled her eyes. "Come on, Summer, don't tell me you're superstitious."

Summer shrugged. "You're literally trying to summon a potato with comet magic. Who the fuck even knows?"

"It's... probably fine?"

"I mean I think so too, just wanted to bring it up."

Theo gently bumped into Summer's shoulder, before moving towards the telescope. "Let's see what happens anyway."

Once everyone was in position, Riley led the countdown.

"On three. One. Two. Three!"

"I wish there was a baked potato here on this plate!"

Tension in the air hung with bated breath.

No potato related miracles occurred.

Everyone burst out laughing.

~

Theo helped Riley with every experiment she wanted, attempting to wish together with Theodora for all sorts of things, big and small. No magic had yet to present itself, but it was kind of fun to try anyway.

They were all taking a break now, sitting around a small table covered in various papers, and eating pizza straight out of the box.

"So," Riley said in between bites, a bit of pizza grease leaking onto her hand. "I think it's safe to say wishing for trivial nonsense isn't going to work. Honestly, I'd be willing to discount the methodology here entirely, but there's still the big stuff we haven't tried yet."

Theodora raised an eyebrow, finished chewing, then swallowed and took a drink of her soda before finally saying, "What big stuff?"

Riley gestured to both Theo and Theodora. "You know. The reason you're both here. Wishing for you to go home. Or fulfilling the obligation of Theo's original wish. You haven't actually looked at the comet *together* with Summer yet, have you?"

A piece of pizza got stuck in Theo's throat, and she was sent into a coughing fit. Summer slapped her on the back a few times before she finally got it under control, and drank a long gulp of water. "Sorry, uh." Theo cleared her throat a few more times. "No, I haven't done that yet."

Summer stared at her, lips pursed. Theo couldn't meet her gaze.

"Now that I'm thinking back," Summer said, her voice carefully even. "I don't remember wishes coming up when we first landed on the comet thing. When did that get added to the equation, anyway? Wasn't there something about Mars and Venus being in alignment?"

"Mars and Venus?" Riley asked, sounding confused.

Theo's mouth felt dry. "I, uh. I put a few extra things together when I explained the story to Riley? I guess maybe I didn't fully explain that, sorry, uh…"

Summer's gaze pierced through Theo, unbelieving.

"No, this is too stupid. I lied. I'm sorry." Theo hung her head, staring at her lap.

"Why?"

Deep breaths. Was it really that bad? "I… I figured out the connection right away. Me wanting to see the comet together with Summer, that was what I wished for. But if that's really the case, if it's really that simple, then we would have gone and done it and then… this would all be over. I wasn't ready to leave. I'm still not ready to leave. And… I couldn't just say that, back then. It would have been too desperate and pathetic and needy."

Silence, hung in the air, punctuated by the low electric hum of the telescope. Theodora and Riley shuffled awkwardly in their seats, an unwilling audience to this drama.

Summer let out a soft sigh. "Do you actually want to go home?"

Theo looked up. Summer's expression was unreadable. "I don't know. I should, shouldn't I? That's the right thing to do. My family is probably worried sick about me. I'm a terrible person, for making them wait for this long already."

"But do you *want* to?"

"No," Theo whispered.

Theodora coughed. "Not to interrupt whatever this moment is supposed to be, but I'm pretty sure there are some significant logistical difficulties to staying in this dimension. Like… you probably used your social security number to get this job, right? That's gonna show up on *my* taxes."

"Sorry about that. I didn't realize the whole dimension thing when I first came here and accepted the job."

"It's… probably fine for now?" Theodora shrugged. "But I imagine it will get more complicated if you actually stick around."

"All of this," Riley said, spreading her arms wide. "Still requires the assumption that the comet had anything to do with it at all, or that it's even possible for Theo to go home at all."

"At the very least," Theo said, wrapping her arms around her stomach. "I'm not ready to go back yet. The comet is still visible for another week and a half, right? If nothing else… I want that time. Is that… okay?"

Summer smiled at her softly, though there was a distant sadness in her eyes. "Yeah. Of course."

Riley pursed her lips. "Very romantic and all, but… if we try to save this for the last minute, there's a chance we'll be screwed due to weather, or if it doesn't work at all, we might not have enough time to figure out an alternative solution before the comet is gone."

Something occurred to Theo and she snorted with laughter. "Sorry.

Just had the thought that… if I avoid dealing with the problem, eventually I'll be stuck here no matter what, but it will have happened on its own, and I'll be able to blame fate instead of it being my choice. Pretty terrible of me."

Theodora winced. "That's… a mood, alright."

Riley drummed her fingers on the table. "Well, there's nine days left total. I understand if you want to make them count. Maybe we reconvene next Friday, to give enough of a buffer in case things go wrong? If you want, Theo, you can go ahead and quit, give yourself some more quality time together."

Not a bad idea, honestly. Theo nodded. "Maybe. You'll be okay without me?"

"Eh, we'll manage." Riley paused, then glanced over to Theodora. "Unless Theodora here wants to take your place. Do the ole' switcheroo."

"I guess maybe that's an option? I'll think about it," Theodora said, before stretching and letting out a big yawn. "Well, maybe in the morning."

"I suppose we have been at this for awhile." Riley moved over to her computer. "I have some notes I wanna finish adding, but y'all can head out."

Theo nodded, doing her best to suppress her own yawn. "Later. Don't stay up too late now."

"No promises."

Summer eyed Theo up and down, before offering up an arm. "Shall we?"

Theo took it, leaning in close against Summer's side. "Lead the way."

They made it to the door of the lab before Theodora called out, "Wait."

Theo glanced over her shoulder. Theodora stood there, arms wrapped around her stomach, looking unsure, nervous. Was that how she looked, when she felt like that?"

"I, uh…" Theodora licked her lips, then took a deep breath, clearly steeling her nerves. "I'd like to borrow Theo for a bit."

"Oh! Um…" Theo glanced at Summer, who shrugged. "I guess, sure? What for?"

"I dunno, I just… how often do you really get a chance to pick your own brain, you know?"

"Honestly I was kind of thinking the same. Summer, you mind going ahead?"

Summer shrugged. "Sure. Text me if this is going to be a really late thing."

"Will do."

With a wave, Summer pulled away, the lack of her warmth suddenly noticeable.

Theo watched her go, out the lab doors, and down the hall. "So, what's the plan?"

Theodora shrugged. "Wanna go for a walk?"

~

The two of them walked through the town in silence, passed closed up shops and bars, through the residential neighborhood, and all the way to Theodora's childhood home. Aaron's house, now.

Theodora seemed fully prepared to tresspass, but Theo sent a quick text to Aaron anyway.

"It really is the same," Theodora muttered, as they crested the top of the hill, the fort coming into view.

"Looks like we both had the same penchant for silly riddles," Theo said, gesturing towards the clock face carved into the wood.

Theodora knelt down and retrieved the key from under the correct rock. "What's the point in having a secret hideaway if you don't have to solve a puzzle to get in?"

They both giggled, then stepped inside.

"Less dusty than I expected."

"Oh, right. I uh, already came here with Summer, a few weeks ago."

"Hmm."

Theodora walked around the room, looking over things, her expression clearly pained. She stopped at a certain spot, looking up at the ceiling.

"You know I carved something incredibly embarassing into that beam up there."

"Yeah, I uh, saw it already."

"Of course you did." Theodora let out a long sigh, then let herself fall back onto the beanbag.

"I'm sorry."

"Don't be. It's not your fault."

Theo bit her lip, then sat down on the floor next to her.

"What..." Theodora paused, swallowed, and continued, her voice wavering. "What did you do, with Summer, that I didn't? That she was actually your friend?"

"I don't know. Summer said you met in a group project? What grade again?"

"Fifth."

"Ah. See, I met her in fourth grade. Happened to walk next to her on the way home, and we talked about some stuff. So it might really just have been a matter of timing."

Theodora clasped her hands in front of her mouth. "It really is something that small, huh?"

"Guess life is funny like that."

"Mmm."

She remained silent for a minute or two, before taking a deep breath. "Was it good? I know you said you lost her, but... was it good?"

Theo felt the old ache of grief as memories stirred inside her, and she let it wash over her. "It was. For the most part. Summer was a troubled kid. She wasn't always the most considerate friend. But we had fun. I... yeah. We had fun."

A thought occured to her, and Theo pulled out her phone, pulling up her old photos. "Do you want to see?"

Theodora nodded, took the phone from her, and began scrolling through Theo's old memories.

Theo sat back, staring up at the ceiling, letting her thoughts wander as Theodora processed whatever she needed to.

What a truly messed up tangle she'd found herself in.

But even now, Summer wasn't all that far away, and she was looking forward so when she'd be able to go back to the apartment, and fall asleep in her arms.

Eventually Theodora sniffed, wiping tears from her eyes, and handed the phone back to Theo. "Thank you."

"Of course. Can, uh. I ask you some stuff too?"

"Sure, what is it?"

Theo bit her lip. "Can you tell me about Seoyun?"

Theodora blinked. "Did you know her in your reality too?"

"No, never met her."

"Then why do you care?"

There was an edge to Theodora's voice that made Theo wince. "You don't have to talk about her if you don't want to, it's just…"

Theo sighed, and buried her face in her knees. "I've fucked up a lot of my relationships, because of, y'know. The trauma. Or at least, that was my excuse. So if things didn't work out for you, without that excuse, than…"

Theo left the final part ouf, the idea that maybe some core part of her was fundamentally broken, but she could see understanding in Theodora's eyes anyway.

"Ah." Theodora laid back on the beanbag and raised her hand into the air, staring at the ceiling through her fingers. "Would you believe me if I said the relationship just naturally ran its course? We were highschool sweethearts, and made it through college together, and then things just kind of fizzled out."

"I mean I guess I'd believe you, you're me, but also it makes me think you're about to tell me more of the story anyway."

"No hiding things from myself, I guess." Theodora let out a long sigh. "We were living together after college, had an apartment together. She was driven, ambitious. Eager to spread her wings and experience new things. Make new friends."

"She didn't—"

"No, of course not. Not that I know of, anyway. But I was struggling a bit at the time. Couldn't really find my footing in the job market. Couldn't seem to gel with her friends. We'd go to these fancy parties with all of these snobby intellectuals talking about the world over glasses of wine. While I sat in the corner and glowered."

Theo tried to picture it. It definitely wasn't her scene.

"She never forced me to go. Knew I didn't like that, always offered to cancel and stay home instead. But I insisted, I didn't want to hold her back, I'd try my best, I didn't hold any of it against her."

"But resentment has a way of sneaking up on you."

Theodora clenched her teeth. "Yeah. She was so good to me. I felt like I was holding her back, ruining her life. That she deserved to be with someone better."

A sinking feeling settled into Theo's gut. It was an all too familiar mindset that she had found herself in on more than one occasion.

"There weren't any big dramatic blowups or anything. I made the decision to end things before that could happen. She… accepted it, quietly and easily. A part of me wished that she'd gotten angry, or cried about it, or anything. Instead, we cordially and efficiently detangled our lives from each other. I moved back in with my parents, and she continued on her rise to the top, without me holding her back."

Theodora took off her glasses, wiping them on her shirt. "That a good enough explanation?"

Theo nodded. "Yeah. Thanks for sharing." She waited a moment, then leaned forward. "Can I give you a hug?"

"…Yeah. Sure."

They leaned forward, embracing each other, pulling each other tight.

"You know, I always wanted a sister," they both said simultaneously.

Theo pulled back, grinning, and both of them burst out laughing.

"It was really nice talking to you like this," Theo added, after they'd both calmed down a bit.

Theodora grinned. "Yeah, well. How often do you get the chance? Wanted to make sure to get this in before I head back home. Wasn't really planning on staying that long in town anyways. Only reason I came here at all was because Minha sent me those pictures of her hanging out with you."

Theo smacked herself in the forehead. "That explains it. But wait, weren't you going to take the university job? How come you turned it down, anyway?"

"Oh, right." Theodora scratched at her chin. "Mom got diagnosed with breast cancer. I decided I wanted to stick closer to home to support her, at least for the time being."

"Wait, what?" Theo's blood ran cold, and she leaned forward. "Is she okay? What's going on?"

Theodora shook her head. "They said because it was caught pretty early, should all be fine. Doesn't mean I'm not worried, though. And Mom's really bad at medical stuff. Only reason she even got checked out is because I badgered her into it."

Did that mean… her mom also had cancer? Theo hadn't been badgering her about it. Did she know? Would she check it out on her own?"

"Wait, did you not know? Shit."

Theo took a deep, shuddering breath, her mind racing. "Um. Fuck. I don't know. Please, can you tell me everything?"

Dear Diary,

Tomorrow is the big day.
  I've memorized the route, packed all the supplies.
  Everything will be perfect.

Theo
9/21/2014

Theo lay in bed, staring up at a darkened ceiling, on what should have been a perfectly lively Saturday morning.

The bedroom door opened a crack, a pool of light spilling in from the kitchen. "Hey," Summer's voice came through, soft and concerned.

All Theo could manage was to grunt noncommittally in response.

"Paint the Square is starting, pretty busy out there. Faith is actually downstairs painting the window for the donut shop. Peter has switched things up and is offering deep fried oreos and funnel cakes. Can smell it as soon as you step outside."

"Sounds nice," Theo mumbled.

A long pause. "Do you… want me to stay here, with you? We can sit and chill together," Summer said, with a slight edge to her voice that meant she didn't actually want that at all.

Theo shook her head. "No. Go have fun, please. I just… need to be alone for a while. Sorry."

"Hey, I've been there, believe me. Do you want me to bring you back anything?"

"Deep fried oreos do actually sound nice."

"Sure thing." Summer took a deep breath. "Just… remember I'm here for you, okay? Whatever decision you need to make or conclusion you come to just… let's do it together."

"Mmmhmm."

The door clicked shut, leaving Theo alone in darkness once more.

Decisions. Conclusions. That was the core of the problem, wasn't it?

Her mother had cancer. All Theo had to do was go back, make sure she got tested and help her through treatment, and she'd probably be fine.

And give up on this world, on the friends she'd made here, on Summer.

Had staying ever been a realistic option in the first place? Even beyond the logistical difficulties, it was already pretty monstrous to doom her family to never know what happened to her.

She wanted to stay, so, *so* badly. The thought of saying goodbye to Summer again filled her with a tearing agony that would rip her apart from the inside, old scabbed over wounds becoming infected and swollen. Could she survive that, a second time? Somehow she doubted.

And now the cost of staying might involve her mother's life.

It felt like a test. Maybe it was a test. That made the most sense out of anything else, right?

It wasn't some benevolent wish granted for seemingly no reason. But a test of moral character. For Theodora it was probably some bullshit about forgiveness. But for Theo, it was about temptation. The ultimate temptation, dangled in front of her, so easy to grasp. And now, the moral. The chance to turn away from it, to sacrifice her twisted desires for the sake of doing *the right thing*.

That was how the stories always went. Hell, this one felt downright biblical. Theo didn't believe in God. If he existed, she would spit in his eye. She'd always hated stories like that.

Why did it have to be like this? It wasn't fair. Couldn't Theo just be happy?

Of course, she knew the answer to that one already. How could she possibly deserve something like that? Summer was dead because of her, rotting in the ground. Her blood on Theo's hands, pouring out of a punctured artery, far, far too much. Her face, so pale, light fading from her eyes. Desperate screaming to the 911 operator, begging for an ambulance that would never make it in time.

What did Theo think she was doing, chasing after this ghost, this shadow, this twisted facsimile of the woman she'd killed? Touching her, loving her, fucking her. As if that was okay, as if it was normal? It was disgusting. She'd already ruined one Summer's life. Would she keep going until she ruined this one too? Would she move on then, to another reality, until that Summer died as well? Stuck forever in a Sispheyean tragedy?

Down, down, down, Theo spiraled, alone in the darkness.

Somewhere, in the back of her mind, Theo knew it was all pointless. It was all an exercise in self flagellation, a punishment she believed she needed to inflict upon herself.

Because at the end of the day, she already knew what she was going to do, and no amount of deliberation was going to change that.

~

Summer stepped out of her apartment, shielding her eyes against the bright sunlight. It was hot today, especially for mid September.

The din of the crowd wafted up towards her, punctuated by the occasional delighted shriek of a child. Paint the Square was an event that drew out the whole town, and quite a few people from outlying towns as well. From her vantage point she could already see masterpieces in the making.

Hundreds of three by three squares were dotted all over the central plaza. Kids and families and college students gathered at each square. Some kids got more paint on themselves than they did the ground, making art that could more accurately described as a mess but still captured a sense of unrestrained childish joy. Others worked more diligently to draw out the lines, mix the correct colors. To paint their favorite cartoon character, a simple flag, a cute animal.

Summer wished she had been able to actually enjoy this event as a child. Her mom would never take her, and she'd convinced herself it was stupid anyway. But rediscovering it as an adult still brought her joy. Food carts lined the outside of the plaza. Live music played, that same obnoxious steel drum band that had been playing here for the past twenty years.

It was vibrant, fun, and beautiful.

And Summer wished Theo was by her side to enjoy it with her.

But, well. Theo had her own demons to face. Summer would wait, and support her as best as she could. Even if the time they could spend together was constantly dwindling.

Summer made her way down the stairs to the street below. Immediately she saw Faith and Gloria. Gloria sat on a fold out camp chair, eating some sort of gelato out of a styrofoam cup. Faith stood on a step ladder, paint smudged on their cheeks, paintbrush clenched in their teeth as they studied their work on the window.

"Hey," Summer called out as she approached. "What's the masterpiece going to be?"

Gloria smiled broadly and waved. "Hey, Summer. You'd have to ask Faith, I can't pretend to understand their vision."

Faith turned to see Summer's approach, and waved, before signing, "Hey! What do you think so far? I've only kind of got a basic outline so far, but I think it's getting there!" They paused, then frowned, an awkward gesture with the paintbrush still in their mouth. "Where's Theo?"

"She's feeling a bit under the weather, unfortunately."

"Oh." Faith finally took the paintbrush out of their mouth, setting it on the step ladder. Their face twisted into a pout. "That sucks. Do you think she can make it down for a little bit, to see the painting when I'm done?"

Summer winced. "Uh. Probably. I'll be sure to get a bunch of pictures, at the very least. In fact…" She pulled out her phone, and snapped a quick picture of the work in progress. "Gotta capture the process too, right?"

As she lowered her phone, she took a moment to actually study the picture in question. Right now it was a bit blobby, flat colors in the vague shapes of people. To be filled in with more detail later. Two vaguely feminine figures stood on opposite sides of the window, reaching towards each other. A crack splitting the window in the center separated them, and had been outlined and highlighted with paint. An excellent use of the medium.

"Looking forward to seeing this when it's finished," Summer signed, finishing with a thumbs up. "It's really cool so far."

Faith beamed.

Gloria grinned. "They've been so worried about your opinion, you know. They've been fretting about 'oh no I hope Summer and Theo think it's cool!' over and over for the past couple days."

"Moooom!" Faith's face flushed, and they turned, picking up their paintbrush and got back to work.

Summer chuckled, and smiled at Gloria. "Well, I'd better get to it. Lots of stuff to see."

"You remembered to put on sunscreen, didn't you?"

"Oh. Uh..."

Gloria sighed, and pinched the bridge of her nose. "Sorry, force of mom habit. I don't mean to be nosy."

"No, you're right, I totally forgot. I need to grab Theo some oreos anyway, I'll put some on when I head back upstairs."

"See you around!"

Summer turned and made her way into the bakery, which had its door propped open.

There was a fairly substantial line, but it was moving fast, and Summer got in position to wait.

When she finally made it to the front, she looked up from her phone to find Aaron behind the counter.

"Hey, Summer," Aaron said, looking tired.

"Order of deep fried oreos, please. Didn't know you had ambitions to become a baker."

Aaron chuckled sheepishly. "One of Peter's employees called out for a family emergency. I offered to help for the day."

"Uh-huh." Summer grinned. "Very magnanimous of you. Nothing quite so romantic like baking together, right? Working side by side, flour in the air, a bit of extra frosting on your cheek that he offers to lick off for you?"

"You've got quite the imagination," Aaron deadpanned. Though he fidgeted a bit where he was standing. "It's mostly been me working the register, dealing with an endless stream of customers. Busiest day of the year."

Peter burst out of a door to the back, a little basket of deep fried oreos in his hands. "Oh, hey Summer! Here you go, later!" And then he vanished just as quickly.

Summer took the oreos from the counter, and stepped out of the way. "I'll leave you to the hell of retail, then. Later."

After eating one for herself, Summer took the remainder up to Theo. She hadn't changed much. Summer left the oreos on the bedside table, kissed Theo softly on her forehead, squeezed her hand, and stopped to put on sunscreen before making her way back outside.

It took a bit of wandering, but Summer eventually found Theodora and Minha. Theodora was crouched on her hands and knees, painting something abstract onto the pavement. Minha sat nearby, a small cooler stuffed full of beers next to her.

"Hey," Summer called out as she approached.

Theodora stiffened, glanced her way, then sighed, and returned to her painting without otherwise acknowledging her.

To be expected.

Minha reached up and adjusted her sunglasses before responding with a clipped, "Hey."

The anger in Minha's voice hurt a lot more, by comparison. Summer winced, but tried to keep smiling. "What're you working on?"

The square had been painted fully black, and Theodora was in the process of painting thick yellow lines. "Painting."

Summer stood there awkwardly, waiting for any further reply or conversation. None came. Eventually she let out a long sigh. "Hey, Minha? I get you're still pissed off. Do you want to talk about it? I'll buy you some food."

Minha stared up at her for several long moments, her expression mostly unreadable behind her sunglasses. She shrugged, then stood up. "Theo, you want anything?"

Theodora paused for a moment, then nodded. "Walking taco."

"Oh shit, that sounds awesome, now I want one too," Minha added.

Summer nodded. "Walking tacos it is."

Together Summer and Minha walked through the crowd, weaving between people and paintings.

"So where's fake-Theo?"

Summer sighed, and shook her head. "Lying in bed having an existential crisis, mostly."

"Damn, that sucks."

A kid covered head to toe in paint nearly barreled into them, shrieking and giggling as he ran.

Minha dodged smoothly. "You know what else sucks?"

"Me lying to you about Theo?"

"Oh hey you do know."

Summer hooked her thumbs into the loops of her jeans, staring forward as she walked. "Sorry."

Minha tugged at the brim of her baseball cap. "I know that the situation is really fucked but like. I thought we were bros."

It felt like she'd kicked a puppy. What could she actually say, to make this better? Were there any words at all that would do the trick? Summer always seemed to drop the ball in her relationships at some point, romantic or otherwise. Sometimes she could smooth it over, say the right words, apologize the right way, and everything would be fine.

And then sometimes she couldn't, and her life would become a little emptier.

They reached the walking taco cart, and got in line, waiting for several minutes. Summer bought three. Ground beef served in a bag of crushed up doritos, along with whatever additional toppings you could stuff into the bag, and eaten with a fork. A quintessential midwestern delicacy.

Summer took a bite, enjoying the flavor. Minha was stuck holding both her own and Theodora's, so she couldn't eat and walk at the same time.

"Is there anything I can do to make it up to you?"

Minha let out a long sigh. "I dunno, man. Like, I get it? It's crazy and weird and why go around explaining it when you barely understand it yourself and can't really prove it? But like… the fact that I was talking to and trying to hang out with Theo, thinking we were friends but she was pretending, like… fuck. I dunno. It hurts. Makes me feel like I'm stupid."

"I'm sorry. And you're not stupid."

Was that true? She'd always considered Minha to not be very bright. God, she really was an asshole.

"I mean I am dude, I know it. I get mostly get C's and D's and manage to scrape by because I'm good at kicking a ball. But that doesn't bother me like this does. And I don't know if I'm supposed to be more mad at you or at fake-Theo. You, probably."

Summer nodded. "Yeah, I'll take it. Theo was confused and trying to bluff her way out of an awkward conversation, at first. I encouraged her to keep going later."

"Mmm."

"But she…" Summer let out a soft sigh. "She did really like hanging out with you. And she was really interested in… well, Theodora, and how her life went differently, that she got to be friends with you. I mean, I can't fully speak for her, obviously, but I'm sure she'd love to keep being your friend, if you'd let her. I mean, hey. Two Theo's, right?"

Minha snorted and rolled her eyes. "God, you wish, don't you."

Summer pinched the bridge of her nose. "That is *definitely* never a thing that's ever going to happen."

"But you want it to?" Minha asked with a shit eating grin.

"Of course not." Summer paused, then sighed. Maybe giving Minha a little bit of ammo to tease her with would help smooth things over more. "I mean, like, sure, the thought *occurred* to me, the same way it does when you see twins or whatever, but still knowing the actual reality would be weirdly incestual."

Minha burst out laughing, then kicked Summer hard in the shin.

"Ow! Motherfu—" She kept cursing under her breath, hopping on one leg.

"There," Minha said, looking smug. "We're even now. Don't do that shit again."

Summer grimaced, then gave a shaky thumbs up as she flexed her ankle.

If that was all it took to keep being Minha's friend, then she was getting off easy.

The rest of the day passed with one less weight resting on Summer's shoulders. She hung out with Minha and Theodora for a little while longer, though Theodora definitely didn't want her there. And then she was off to wander.

Riley was easy to find, working together with some of her sorority sisters on painting some logos. They chatted for a bit, Riley asked how Theo was doing, Summer deflected, told her to go say hi to Theodora instead.

Afterwards she met up with various kids from the youth group, along with various other friends and acquaintances she didn't get to see that often. It was a great social event, where you could wander in any direction and be likely to spot a familiar face somewhere in the crowd. An environment where Summer thrived the best.

Where she could bounce around from connection to connection, brief, but never deep, never staying for long.

Later in the evening, when the sun was setting and the crowd had thinned out, Minha found her again, and convinced her to join her in bar hopping. It was rowdy, busy, and noisy, but there was more fun and friends to be had.

The whole time, Summer stayed in constant contact with Theo. She texted her updates, questions, sent pictures. Most of the responses she got back were emojis.

Finally, late at night, Summer climbed the stairs back up to her apartment, tired, sore, and a little buzzed. Her phone buzzed in her back pocket, probably a text from Theo, but no point in checking it now.

She pushed open the door to her apartment, and knelt down to greet Chester, as she always did. Her normal ritual for years now. Except now she had a plus one.

"Hey," Summer called out, loud enough that it could hopefully be heard through the bedroom.

There wasn't any response, but maybe Theo was asleep, or she wasn't up for responding. Not too surprising.

She made her way over and cracked open the bedroom door, peering into the darkness. "Hey. You eaten anything yet?"

Still no response. Summer squinted, trying to make out the bed in the darkness. Was it empty?

She opened the door all the way and turned the light on. The bed was empty.

Fuck.

"Theo?" Summer called out, loudly, pointlessly. It wasn't like there was anywhere to hide in her apartment. Theo wasn't in the bathroom. Summer checked the closet to be sure. But nothing.

Had she gone out to get food? To go talk with someone else? Maybe, but why wouldn't she have…

Summer pulled out her phone, and saw her most recent text from Theo.

Theo: I'm sorry.

Summer immediately texted back, "Where are you?"

It immediately pinged as read, which sent a wave of relief flooding through Summer. Then about a minute and a half followed of the typing notification appearing and disappearing, before Theo finally texted again.

"You know where to find me."

Stupid. Vague, pointless, frustratingly stupid. Made all the more so by the fact that Summer in fact, knew exactly where Theo must be.

~

Summer's boots crunched against dry grass as she made her way through Aaron's backyard. She'd texted him to inform him that Theo was going through some stuff right now and was probably up in the fort, and that she'd take care of it. He'd been understanding, and wished her the best.

All sorts of conflicting emotions warred in her as she climbed the hill. Anger. Fear. Concern. How could Theo do this, now? Was Summer going to be alone again? Was Theo okay?

The light was on in the fort. Summer pushed the door open, and stepped inside. Theo wasn't there, but the trapdoor on the roof was open. Somewhere on the ceiling T+S was carved inside of a heart. Not a consequence of a reality shift, but the wishful thinking of Theodora, pining after someone she should have stayed far away from. Summer climbed up the ladder, and closed the door behind her.

Theo stood at the edge of her roof, her hands resting on the railing, looking up at the sky. A vast portrait of stars stretched across the sky, the twinkling lights of other worlds looking down on them. Somewhere amongst them was a comet, that would take Theo out of Summer's life, forever.

"Let's just get this over with," Theo said, her hands gripping the rail tight. A small telescope sat on the roof next to her.

Summer took a step forward. "Theo, hey. Please. Let's sit down and talk about this, alright? I know you're scared, but together we can—"

"No!" Theo shouted, the sharp sound of it carrying across the countryside. She sucked in a sharp breath, shaking. "I've already made my peace with this. It's what I have to do. Don't make it any harder than it already is."

Of the various emotions raging through Summer, anger won out. She clenched her fists. "Did you ever stop to consider that maybe I *haven't* made peace with this? If you have to leave then you have to leave, but... like this? So dramatically and suddenly? Give me a chance to say goodbye. Give me closure. I deserve that much."

Theo snorted, and shook her head. "What does it matter? I'm just a summer fling to you. You'll have some new girl within a month."

The words cut Summer deep, her blood dripping onto the wooden roof below. "That's not true," she said, her voice shaky. "I'm not—Theo, you crashed into my life in a big way. And this last month with you has been amazing. Whatever connection we have, it's special. It means something. You can't pretend that it doesn't."

"As if." Theo finally turned to face her, the starlight reflecting off of her glasses. "I'm a creepy weirdo obsessed with her dead best friend, using you to live out my teenage fantasies. That's not special. It's fucked up. Riley was right. This was all a huge mistake."

More wounds. Summer took another step forward. "I knew that. I accepted that. It's something we could work through together. You're spiraling, Theo. I know you're scared for your mom, your family, your world. That's fine! You should be scared for them. I understand if you need to go back to them. But please, don't push me away. Like it all meant nothing."

Theo pinched the skin of her arm, hard, and tears streaked down her cheeks. "You don't get it. I'm a creep, Summer. I knew from the start, how to get back home. I lied to you about it, because I wanted to stay by your side, sleep in your bed, seduce you. If this reality represents my greatest temptation to fall then I full on sprinted off the edge and did a flip while diving into hell."

"I'm not your temptation, Theo. I'm a regular person, same as you. You have baggage, sure. So do I. But we're people, who care about each other. That's it. It's not some grand narrative of sin and redemption."

"You don't know that," Theo said quietly.

She didn't know that. Maybe the two of them really were just cosmic playthings. Maybe Summer existed as an object lesson for Theo. That would be some bullshit. Summer closed the distance between them, and took Theo's hands in her own. "I know that I care about you. That means something."

Theo pulled away, walking over to the corner instead, her back to Summer. "You care about me, huh? Well, I am desperately, madly in love with you. I love you, Summer Sullivan. A woman I've known for less than a month. That's normal. That's how relationships work, right? Surely you feel the same way, don't you?"

Summer's heart pounded in her chest, her mouth suddenly dry. "I, uh."

"What's the matter?" Theo looked over her shoulder, a manic look in her eyes. "That's what this all is, isn't it? Some grand declaration of love?"

"Look, I have a bit of my own baggage around saying stuff like that, but we can talk about—"

"Let me guess. Too many girls, can't let yourself be tied down by one?"

Summer clenched her teeth, and looked away. "Because every time I've ever told someone I loved them, they took some time to reconsider and decided that they didn't want a future with me. Which I guess you're trying to do right now so... why bother."

Theo blinked several times, and her face fell. "Sorry. That was uncalled for."

Deep breaths. She could get through this without crying. "Maybe you're right. Maybe we should get this over with."

"... Yeah." Theo wrapped her arms over her chest. She moved over to the telescope, and sat down next to, and started looking through it.

Summer made her way over and sat next to her.

Theo fiddled with the telescope, and they sat there in silence for several long minutes. "Here," she finally said. "The titular comet. I wished to see it together with you, Summer. A wish that's gone ungranted for far, far too long already."

Summer stared down at the telescope, fear gripping her heart. "Gonna feel really stupid if this doesn't work."

Her words made Theo laugh, which made Summer laugh a little in return. A little bit of the tension that had been hanging over them bled away.

Summer took a deep breath, squeezed Theo's hand in her own, then looked through the telescope.

There it was. A comet. A ball of rock and ice, hurtling through space, close enough to the sun that the ice melted behind it, giving it its signature tail. It was awesome to see, a fascinating astronomical phenomenon.

Something seemed to shift inside of Summer. It was actually happening. She pulled away from the telescope, shared a glance with Theo, fear in her eyes.

They came together, pressing their lips together, holding on to each other tight.

"I love you," Summer whispered.

And then Theo was gone, nothing in Summer's arms but empty air.

A chill breeze rustled through the surrounding trees, biting deep inside and making her shiver.

It seemed like summer was finally coming to an end.

Dear Diary,

Summer is
    I fucked up and
    Its my fault

Theo sat cold and alone on the roof of her fort, a place that should be warm and full of happy memories.

She wasn't sure how long she stayed there, huddled up in a ball, sobbing. Even long after she had no tears left to cry, she remained, a useless lump of grief.

She'd done it. Her wish had been granted. It was beautiful, amazing. The best time she'd ever have in her life.

And now Summer was gone again.

Theo took a deep breath, and forced herself to sit up. If she'd learned anything about grief, it was that life kept going even when your whole world stopped. No matter how much a part of her for wished it, she couldn't stay here on this roof until she got hypothermia and died. Even if she deserved it.

Was she even actually in her own reality? With numb fingers, Theo pulled her phone out of her pocket. No signal. A good sign. She'd remembered to bring her old SIM card with her, and she swapped it back into the phone with some effort.

It didn't take long for the phone to go ballistic. Hundreds of missed calls and texts, most of them from her mother, but from pretty much every member of her family, her friends, even her ex's. She'd vanished from her world completely, leaving behind chaos and grief.

A part of her thought it was worth it now, but would she feel the same when trying to explain it all to her mother? Could she explain it at all?

Would it all be a grief filled fever dream?

But no. She had proof. She opened up her phone, and they were still there. Pictures of Summer. Videos of Summer. Too much to be fake, to deny. It was real. It had all happened.

Another wave of crying threatened to overtake her, but Theo hardened her heart. She'd have plenty of time to wallow in her memories later. For now she needed to face up to her cruelty.

She made her way back down the hill, towards her old house. She could see it, now. The chain link fence surrounding the backyard. To contain the dog that didn't exist in the other world.

Said dog came bounding towards the fence, barking his head off. What was his name again? She couldn't even remember.

"Buddy, what are you doing! Inside!" Peter's voice came from inside the house. He stood in the doorway, silhouetted by the lights inside. "It's too late for this, and—"

He froze, as his gaze fell on Theo. He probably couldn't actually see who she was, with this distance, in the darkness.

She opened the gate to the backyard and slipped inside. Buddy stopped barking, sniffing her furiously and wagging his tale.

Theo stepped into the pool of light and smiled. "Hey, Peter. Don't suppose my room is still available?"

The mug of tea Peter had been holding fell to the ground, shattering.

~

"You should really try smiling more."

Summer stared blankly at the middle aged man in front of her, trying to remember whatever interaction she'd been completely zoned out for. There was something she was supposed to say, wasn't she? A generic phrase of customer service, ruts scored into her brain over thousands, millions of repetitions.

Nothing came to her. She continued staring.

The customer rolled his eyes and walked off, grumbling under his breath about kids these days.

"Take care, have a nice day!" Minha called out, raising both middle fingers behind the man's back.

Once the door was shut behind him she turned around to face Summer, eyebrow raised. "Jesus, dude. Let me handle the register, go stock shelves or something."

Summer blinked her eyes several times, trying to focus on the moment, the present. "No, no, it's fine. It's not like I haven't gotten dumped before. I can handle it."

"C'mon, man. This is clearly different."

It had been a week already, since Theo had vanished from her arms into thin air. It was nice, at least, that Riley and Minha knew the truth. She didn't have to come up with some weird bullshit lie with them. They knew and understood what had actually happened.

Did that actually make it better? She wasn't sure.

"Hey. Hey!" Minha snapped her fingers in front of Summer's face. "For fuck's sake, Summer. Go home already."

Summer pursed her lips, staring down at Minha. "It's not like I can afford any time off, you know that."

She could afford it a little bit longer, technically, because Theo's last paycheck was still sitting in her bank account. But even that wouldn't go very far.

Minha sighed and pinched the bridge of her nose. "You're supposed to be the responsible one here, you know? I'll cover for you as much as I can but like… you gotta do whatever you can to deal with it, y'know? Or like, quit. I mean, fuck this place anyway."

Since when had Summer ever been the responsible one? She certainly didn't feel like it. But Minha was right, to an extent. Summer closed her eyes and took a deep breath, pushing it all down.

"Sorry, sorry," Summer said, putting on her best reassuring smile. "I'm good, I promise. We can hit up a bar or something later."

Minha looked a bit skeptical, but eventually shrugged. "Sure, yeah. Get your mind off things."

Summer would find something else, someone else, to fill the yawning emptiness in her heart. She always did.

～

Theo stared up at the constellations of stars on the ceiling of her childhood bedroom.

As it turned out, returning from being a missing person was a complicated and exhausting affair.

She'd come up with a lie, to tell the cops, and anyone else she wasn't

close to. That she'd had a bit of a breakdown when confronting her childhood memories. That she'd turned off her phone and decided to hitchhike
around the country on a journey of self discovery.

It was total bullshit. The cops knew it was total bullshit. But at the
end of the day she was alive and well, there wasn't any evil kidnapper to
blame, and she was an adult who could go where she pleased. All they
could do was give her a stern lecture about safety.

To her family, however, she told the truth. All of it. Both the beautiful
and the ugly. And they loved her, and while they were certainly skeptical,
the evidence she'd brought back with her was more than convincing
enough. Something inexplicably supernatural had happened to Theo.

So then, a week had passed, full of explanations and emotional break-
downs and familial love. She'd opted to stay here, despite her mother's
insistence that she return to Minnesota, and managed to convince her
mom to schedule a cancer screening. Hopefully it wouldn't be too late.

At the end of the day, she couldn't wallow in grief forever. She would
have to move on with her life.

But what would that even look like, for her? She'd come to this town
to get a new job, but also to face the ghosts of her past. She'd done that,
in a big, impossible way. Had her relationship with Summer brought her
the closure she needed? She didn't know, honestly. It was still too close, it
still hurt too much. A raw, ragged wound. But it wasn't the same kind
of pain, as when Summer had died. Because this Summer was still out
there, somewhere. Theo would miss her terribly, but there was a comfort
in knowing that she lived on, and could go on with her life, her friends,
and find love again.

Theo knew she could accept it, eventually.

But what was she to do in the meantime? The job she'd come here for
was definitely gone. Was there any actual reason to stay?

Theo sat up in bed, took up her glasses and rubbed at her eyes. There
was a point, after wallowing in self flagellation for days, where she simply
got restless. She needed to get up, to move, to do something, anything.

She stood up stretched, then caught a glimpse of herself in the mirror
hanging from the closet door, and she winced.

First, she needed to clean herself up a bit.

Theo stepped through the doors to the astronomy building, same as she had every weekday for the past month.

She wasn't entirely sure what brought her here. To beg for her job? To see a friendly face? Maybe to apologize in person.

But right away, it seemed like she wouldn't be quite so lucky.

Riley wasn't sitting behind the front desk. Instead, a young man sat there, with short brown hair, wearing a hoodie, hunched over and staring blankly at his phone.

Who knew what small differences there were between realities?

Theo approached anyway, standing in front of the desk.

The man looked up, his eyes dead as he put on a plastic smile. "Hi there. How can I help you?"

Something about him looked and sounded uncannily familiar. Did Riley have a brother? "Hi there. My name is Theo Smith. I uh, was hoping to speak to your manager, Jerry? I was supposed to start a job here a few weeks ago but... some stuff happened. And I wanted to apologize in person."

He blinked slowly several times, looking her up and down. "Oh, you're that Theo. I remember that. The cops came and asked us a bunch of questions. I guess you're alright?"

Theo winced. "Sorry about that. It was... something extremely personal and complicated. But I'm okay now. I don't expect to get the job or anything, I know that's not happening.

The man shrugged. "I mean, position's still open. I'll send Jerry a message." He typed on his keyboard for a few moments, then turned back to her. A hint of genuine warmth entered his eyes, and he smiled slightly. "I'm glad you're okay, though. It was really scary to think that a kidnapping or something had happened so close to home. Half expected some true crime podcasters to come sniffing around."

There it was again. In the shape of his eyes, the curve of his smile. The familiarity was so, so striking, it was almost like he really was—

"Riley!?" Theo whispered in awe.

Utter, sheer panic filled his face, his eyes wide, his mouth dropping open. "What? I... how do you... I've never—"

Theo clasped her hand over her mouth, her heart racing. This was Riley, she was sure of it. But how? Some weird quirk of alternate dimensions, boy in one, girl in another? A different set of genetic code led to

XY instead of XX? But that didn't make any sense. There would be an entirely different person, in that case.

Summer's words echoed in her mind. She'd helped Riley figure out a lot of things. Nearly every boy she'd dated had turned out not to be one. A little cartoon sticker that said Egg Breaker.

"Oh, Riley," Theo whispered, her heart breaking, her eyes brimming with tears. "I'm so sorry."

Riley shook her head, her face pale. "That's impossible. I've never told anyone that name, I… who are you?"

What was she supposed to do? There didn't seem to be any way to approach it gently, not after she had already fucked up. Theo pulled out her phone, opening up the camera app. Found a picture of her and Riley, posing in front of the telescope. Handed the phone over to Riley.

Choking sobs escaped Riley at the sight, tears streaming down her face in earnest.

"I spent the last month in an alternate dimension. In it, I met a wonderful woman named Riley. She'd accepted who she was years prior, with a bit of a helping hand that didn't exist in this dimension. She was a great friend to me."

Riley looked between Theo and the picture, shaking her head. "That's… insane. Impossible. Sci-fi bullshit."

"I know. But it's the truth, anyway. I'll be happy to tell you the whole story, but… I think maybe you'll need a minute."

"I… I'm really…" Riley swallowed, tapping the picture of herself on the phone, as if she could reach into it. "If she did this years ago, then it's too late for me, I'm—"

"You're only twenty-three, Riley," Theo said, with a hint of amusement. "It's definitely not too late."

Riley clutched the phone, her knuckles white, her whole body shaking. "Of course you know how old I am."

"Well hello there!" Jerry said, stepping out from the back office and waving. "You must be Theo! I'm glad to see you're—uh, is everything okay here?

Theo wiped the tears from her own eyes, and turned to smile at Jerry. "Sorry, uh, a bit of an emotional moment. Sh—mm, needs a minute."

Jerry frowned, turning to Riley. "You good?"

Riley took a deep, shuddering breath. "I, um. I… I'm really sorry, but

I think I need to—I need to go home for the day. I can't, I've got to…"

Theo winced, easily recognizing the beginning of a panic attack that she'd caused. "Terribly sorry. I'll walk them home, okay?"

"Sure…" Jerry said, looking confused. "I'll keep an eye on things. Let me know that you're okay, alright?"

Theo nodded, helped Riley gather her things, and walked with her, silently staying by her side as she let Riley process the sledgehammer that Theo had slammed directly into her psyche.

Maybe there would be something good to come from this whole ordeal after all.

Summer sat on her bed, staring at her phone, watching short video after short video, letting the algorithm drip feed numbness directly into her brain.

She barely even noticed when her front door jiggled, then opened. Footsteps clicked against the tile of the kitchen, and then someone stood in the door frame to her bedroom, a shadow cast over Summer.

"I could've been masturbating, you know," Summer said, not looking up from her phone. "Going to town with the magic wand. I forgot you still had a key."

"Not like I haven't seen it before," Riley said. She crossed the distance to the bed, quickly snatched Summer's phone from her hands, and dodged back away from the counter-swipe. "Come on, I've got some homemade lasagna for you, still warm."

Summer closed her eyes, let out a deep sigh, and knocked her head against the wall behind her. "I don't need your pity visit. I know I'm kind of a bummer right now, but I'll get over it eventually, at my own pace. Lord knows how many times I've done it before."

Riley crossed her arms over her chest. "Too bad. I'm pity visiting anyway. You're going to eat my lasagna and like it."

There probably wasn't any point in being obstinate about it. It wasn't a fight Summer could win. Besides, Riley's cooking tended to be top tier. With a groan, Summer rolled out of bed, stretching, popping her back, trying to blink the haze from her eyes, from her brain.

"See? That's not so hard." Riley moved back into the kitchen.

Summer shuffled her way out of the bedroom, then froze.

Theo sat at the kitchen table, looking anxious.

No. It wasn't Theo. It was Theodora.

Her heart pounding in her chest, Summer, licked her lips, trying her best to calm down. "You tricked me."

"Sure did," Riley said, without a hint of guilt. She cursed when she realized that there weren't any clean dishes, then started washing some.

Theodora really was beautiful. Of course she would be, when she was identical. It was hard to look at her.

But she wasn't Theo.

Summer sat down across the table from Theodora. "Got more to say, I guess?"

Theodora rubbed her hands together, not looking up. "I do."

"It can wait," Riley said, setting three plates of lasagna down onto the table. "No sense being all dramatic on an empty stomach. She sat down and started eating herself, not waiting for a response.

Summer took a bite, and, damn. She'd forgotten how good Riley was at this.

"This is really good," Theodora said, looking up with a genuine smile directed towards Riley.

"Thanks!"

They ate in silence for several minutes, until Summer had finished her plate. She got up to give herself a second serving.

How many nights had she shared a dinner with Theo? The two of them across from Summer's little plastic kitchen table, talking about their days, joking around, flirting? Hardly any, objectively. Ten? Fifteen? Twenty? The number was specifically countable. But some part of it already felt like it had stretched out into an entire lifetime.

"You really loved her, didn't you?" Theodora said, her voice soft.

Summer let out a long sigh. "Yeah. I did. Do. Sorry."

Theodora bit her lip, and stared at her empty plate for several long moments. "I'm not... *jealous*. That's the wrong emotion. But it is really damn weird, seeing how things could have gone differently."

"Yeah."

"I..." Theodora took a deep breath, and shook her head. "I hated you for a long time, Summer. Blamed you for everything that went wrong in my life. Sometimes it was justified, sometimes it wasn't. But time passes. People change. We grow up, and gain more perspective about ourselves and the world.

"For a while I was… really angry whenever I looked at you. Filled with fury for the absurdity and injustice of it all. But… I dunno. It just feels sad, now."

Riley leaned forward. "I get that too. I was mad at you for quite some time. But you make it hard to stay mad, Summer. You've got that wet cat energy sometimes."

As if to punctuate the point, Chester meowed, and rubbed against Summer's leg.

Theodora nervously tugged at the wrist of her sweater. "The point is. I don't really want anything to do with you. I've made peace with that, and am ready to move on with my life and leave that behind me. But the other me did. And it really seemed like the two of you had something special together. And… I want her to be happy. I want the justice of knowing that things could have been better."

Summer blinked slowly, processing her words. She took another bite of lasagna, taking the her time with it, thinking. "I hope she finds happiness too."

Riley pinched the bridge of her nose. "Really, Summer? Come on. What about you, in this equation?"

"What about me? Theo went home. I started the relationship knowing that was the inevitable outcome. So did she. It sucks, maybe a bit more than I expected it to, but… I mean you know my dating history. I'll get over it."

Riley looked down at her, expression full of condescension and pity. "I've had a front row seat to most of your dating history. Theo was different. You know it, I know it, even Theodora knows it."

Summer looked away. "Doubt it. It was all the rush of a new relationship, and me filling in for her dead best friend. If we'd actually continued as a couple, the excitement would have worn out, and she would have realized she doesn't want to share a life together with a loser like me. Probably better that it ended like this, as something dramatic and magical, rather than sad and small and mundane."

"Be nicer to yourself," Riley commanded, gently kicking her under the table. "If Theo only liked you because of her baggage, then what drew you to her?"

"I dunno." What was she supposed to say, with Theodora right there?

"She's smart, and funny, and hot. And the proximity helped too. It's hard not to fall into someone when you're sharing your space so closely."

Riley shrugged. "I'm smart and funny and hot. I don't remember you being this mopey when we broke up."

"I mean, you are a lot more now than you were back then." Summer thought back to their relationship, what was it… four years ago? Riley had been nineteen, Summer twenty-two. At the time, she'd thought it was a relationship with a depressed, moody boy. A good match for her attitude at the time. But Summer had said a few key things, helped her experiment, saw her crack through her shell, helped her figure out who she really was. And she'd watched a spark glisten in Riley's eyes, a joy and wonder and euphoria for life that was dazzling, radiant. And Summer knew that if they stayed together, she'd dry up and evaporate in that brightness.

"I appreciate the sentiment. I work really hard to look this good, after all." Riley smiled softly, and gently rested her hand on Summer's and squeezed. "But I never saw you look at me, the way you looked at Theo. Or anyone else I've seen you date, for that matter."

Summer swallowed, her throat dry. Riley's hand was warm. Too warm. Hot, scorching, like fire. Almost painful to the touch. "I… I dunno. I liked being around her, you know?"

"What else? Try spelling it all out."

"She…" Summer paused, thinking, trying to put it into words. "I mean, it was magical, right? Literally. It made it all feel special. That it was something grand and cosmic, that it meant something."

Riley nodded. "I get that. Your very own fairy tale. Feels like it should come with a happily ever after. What else?"

What else? What else was there? Summer looked away, her chest tight. "I… the way she looked at me. Like I was the most important person in the world. I know, *I know* she was seeing the other Summer, and not me. But I wanted that for myself all the same."

"When you look at Theodora here, do you see Theo? Could you imagine falling for Theodora instead?

Theodora looked away.

Summer opened her mouth to immediately deny it, but she forced herself to stop and genuinely think it through. "I… do see her. A bit. It's hard not to. But no. I don't want that, even if it was an option."

"I also don't want that, to be clear," Theodora said, her voice clipped.

"If you could, would you go to her dimension? To be with Theo?"

Summer blinked, tilting her head. "I don't think that's possible."

Riley rolled her eyes. "I didn't think there were alternate dimensions a few weeks ago. Who the fuck knows anymore. But seriously. Would you go to her dimension?"

That… she hadn't even considered the thought. "I… I'm legally dead over there. It would probably cause a lot of problems."

"Could probably overcome them."

Summer opened her mouth, then shook her head and closed it again. She took another bite of her lasagna. It was starting to get cold. "I'd be leaving you behind. Minha. Faith. Peter. All my friends. And for what? That's assuming she'd even want me there. She probably wants to wrap a nice bow around the whole experience and pack it away."

"I'd miss you, for sure. But friends come and go."

The thought was tempting, but… "I dunno. That's the big, dramatic, romantic move, right? Throw away my entire life, everything and everyone I care about, all for a chance to be with her? I mean… she couldn't do that for me. And look at me, here hesitating over the same thought. And this is just a hypothetical. It's not like there's any way for me to actually go there."

Riley looked her dead in the eyes, her gaze intense. "The last night the comet will be visible is tomorrow night. Should be clear skies."

Summer stared, eyes wide. "No, that's… we don't know how it works. And doesn't there have to be a wish on the other end too?"

"We don't know how it works." Theodora interjected. "Even the dual wish thing is only a theory. But… don't you think the other me gave up a little too easily?"

"What do you mean?"

Riley gestured vaguely towards the sky. "Theo seemed convinced it was all for this specific purpose, this specific narrative, but what if it wasn't? What if you could ask for more? A way to move back and forth? Why does it have to be one or the other?"

Summer bit her lip. "You couldn't even get a potato to appear."

"And yet, Theo vanished from your arms. Maybe something big and grand is possible anyway. Isn't it worth trying? One last hail mary. You want to be with her, don't you? Fight for it. Ask for more."

Insane. There was no way it would work. But Summer's heart pounded in her chest, her mind racing, as the possibility flowed through her. A thought, a possible way to connect to someone on the other world, clicked in her brain. A silly plan, filled with mysticism and wishful thinking.

But what did she have to lose?

"Okay," Summer said, her voice shaky. "I think I have an idea. But I'll need your help."

It felt good to help Riley. Theo had walked her home, told the whole story, shared pictures, videos. Walked Riley through her fears, and doubts. Helped her come up with a plan of action, to come out, to get hormones.

Riley would be able to move forward, to become the person she was meant to be.

And Theo had a job again. Once she had gotten a chance to talk to Jerry, now with Riley's glowing recommendation backing her up, she'd be starting her new old job on Monday. Wouldn't even have to worry about the adjustment period.

She'd move on, start a new life, settle back into a routine.

A life without Summer.

She could accept that. It was beautiful. It was perfect. And now it was over. Not the tragedy of an early death. Just the simple loneliness of two people going in separate directions.

But something was still missing. The reason she'd come back to this town in the first place. To reconcile with her past. And playing around in an alternate reality hadn't changed that.

She still needed to face Summer, and to properly say goodbye.

Summer drove down empty country roads, past cornfields and dilapidated barns. The sunset cast streaks of orange and purple across the horizon. She hadn't put on any music, the little bluetooth speaker Theo had bought her stuck to her dashboard, unused. It felt inappropriate somehow. So she drove in silence.

Finding this place hadn't been easy. Theo hadn't exactly given her a lot of specific details, when she'd talked about how the other Summer had died. She'd fallen while exploring a condemned old farmhouse, on Summer's sixteenth birthday. That gave her a timeframe to work with.

So with Riley's help, they'd looked up old town records for approved demolition permits.

Address in hand, Summer had prepared. She'd grabbed Theo's old telescope from the backyard fort. And all sorts of supplies that might help with something occult. Candles. Chalk. Incense, herbs. It wasn't like she had the slightest idea what she might be doing. She was relying on vague impressions from horror movies, whatever she could scrounge up online.

But Summer had to try. She'd try anything, give it one last shot. No matter how stupid or silly or insane it all seemed. To bridge a gap between worlds. To fight for a connection she desperately wanted, even if she didn't think she deserved it.

~

Theo's boots crunched on gravel, and she tried to fight back the rising nausea and panic from coming here again.

The house wasn't still here, of course. Just an empty lot, full of tall grass, occasional pieces of rubble and foundation hiding within. The oranges and purples of oncoming twilight gave everything an almost dreamlike haze to it.

Or maybe that was because Theo was used to seeing this place in her nightmares.

Taking a deep breath, she steeled herself, then walked into the lot fully. Ten years ago, Summer had died right beneath her feet.

She'd been cremated, and didn't have a grave. Theo didn't even know what had happened to her ashes. Summer's mom had never responded to her. So she came here, instead, to where it all happened.

Kneeling down, Theo set the case for her telescope on the ground, alongside a small bouquet of flowers, and pulled out her childhood diary, long abandoned in a hidden storage compartment in her clubhouse. And for the final touch, she removed a small photo of Summer from her wallet. It was of her as a teenager, smiling radiantly, standing in front of the setting sun.

"Hey, Summer," Theo said, her voice shaky. "It's uh, been awhile. Kind of. You're never going to believe what I've been through."

~

Summer had no way of knowing if this was the right place. It fit the timeframe, and was close by. But if Theo had gone a few municipalities over, if there were random differences between their two realities, then it wouldn't matter.

She would hope she'd gotten it right. Summer stood in the center of an empty lot, old foundation buried beneath her feet. Carefully, she set up her candles, her telescope, her occult paraphernalia. She watched as it grew darker and darker, the stars appearing above one by one. A chill breeze caressed her, and she clutched her jacket closer around her shoulders.

"Hey," Summer said, her voice sounding too loud in the emptiness of this space. "Uh, hi. I'm Summer. I don't know if my words will reach you. You're dead, after all. And in an alternate dimension to boot. I don't know if ghosts are real. I don't know if heaven is real. I don't even know if I want either of those things to be real. But hear me out anyway, okay?"

The wind rustled nearby corn. Her candles flickered.

Summer took a deep breath, steadying her nerves. "I'm you, but another you. In my life, I met a girl named Theodora. And... I was afraid of her. Because she was weak, and I was afraid that her weaknesses would reveal my weakness in return. So I lorded my power over her, in an attempt to feel strong. I hurt her, bad. I doubt she'll ever forgive me."

She'd gotten to apologize, at least. She didn't need forgiveness, but. She hoped the apology had helped Theodora in some way anyway. Swallowing, she continued. "But from what I understand, it was different for you. Or maybe it was pretty similar. I guess I don't know what was on your mind. But for whatever reason... you accepted her. You took her hand, and followed her into her life. She showed you warmth, and love, and affection. Maybe you were prickly, and bossy, and kind of mean about it. But I could see it in your eyes, in your pictures. You cared."

~

"I loved you, you know." Tears streamed down Theo's cheeks, and she wrapped her fists into her sweater, squeezing tight. "I've been re-reading my old diary. Soaking in the old memories we made together. Some bad. But mostly good. Our friendship, forever captured on these pages. It's kind of funny, looking back at it, how monumental it all seemed at the time. It all seems so childish and silly now, but at the same time, so earnest and true.

"Maybe my feelings couldn't really be called love. I was sixteen. What did I actually understand about being in love? I'm not sure I understand it even now. But I definitely had a crush on you. I wanted us to be something more than friends. And I was so desperate to impress you that I k—" Her words caught in her throat, and she shuddered. She was here, baring it all, to the stars and the wind and the corn and to Summer. "I took you somewhere dangerous, you fell, and you died."

No response came, of course. It was strange, staring at the photo before her, of the teenaged Summer, after spending so much time with her as an adult. Theo swallowed. "I don't know what you thought, before the end. Maybe you hated me. Maybe you were disgusted with me. Or maybe you were confused and terrified and in pain. I'm sorry, for everything that happened. I'm sorry I took you here. I'm sorry I couldn't be normal about that stupid diary. I'm sorry I didn't know what to do afterwards, I didn't know how to apply a tourniquet." Theo took a deep, shuddering breath. "I'm sorry. I hope, wherever you are, you can find it in your heart to forgive me."

Theo sniffed, her snot running down her lips. She wiped it off on her sleeve. "But I've said all this before. Apologized, begged for forgiveness. Torn my soul apart with blame. The real reason I came here today… is because I wanted to tell you about Summer."

~

"I'm a little jealous of you, you know?" Summer sat on the ground in her circle of candles, knees held close to her chest, as she stared up at the sky. There was the slightest glimmer there, that might have been the comet. "Which probably isn't fair. I'm sure things were plenty hard for you, as well. But I was just… so lonely as a kid. And so angry about it. I can only imagine how much actually letting Theo into my life would have improved it. Mortality rate notwithstanding."

Summer snorted, and shook her head. "Did you fall in love with her, the same way I did? You'd have been pretty stupid not to. But I mean, I was pretty stupid at your age. Didn't have my shit figured out yet. I'm sure you felt it, though. The way her smile makes me feel, every time, is just… fuck.

"I want to see her smile again."

~

"…And the way her smile makes me feel. It's a lot like your smile, really but it's… gentler. More mature, I guess? I dunno. I'm sure you could have grown into it."

Theo sniffed again, and pulled off her glasses to rub at her eyes. "God, this feels so fucked up. Me bragging about finding a better, hotter you in another world. Am I the worst? It feels like I'm the worst. But… I don't want to hate myself, for loving her. And I know I'll never know, but I don't want to believe that you'd hate me for loving her, either."

The sky was full of tiny pinpricks of light. One of them, a comet, streaking through the cosmos. "Maybe that's willful self delusion. But sure, alright. I'm a master of that anyway."

Theo reached her hand up, as if she could hold the stars in her palm. "I wish…"

Summer fell back, staring up at the sky, a million stars stretching in every direction. This was all stupid, and silly. It was no seance, there were no ghosts, no amount of candles and salt and honeyed words would let her speak to the dead.

But still, she *wanted*.

She reached her hand up to the sky, grasping for something just out of reach. "I wish…"

""'That there was a way we could be together.'""

Theo's whole world was darkness. She stood in an empty void, not a single speck of light available anywhere for her eyes. Everything was still. She couldn't even see her own body.

"Hello?" Theo asked, her voice deafening in this silence.

A hand slipped into her own, slender, cold, wrapping around her fingers, and tugging her forward.

Theo stumbled, letting herself be pulled forward. What was happening? Where was she? She'd been on the ground, talking to—

"Summer?" Theo asked, her voice raw.

The hand holding hers squeezed twice, but no other response came, other than to continue drawing her forward.

Tears streamed down Theo's cheeks, and her breath came in ragged gasps, but she let herself be led forward in the darkness.

She wasn't sure how much time passed. Minutes? Hours? Was she in a void of pure darkness? Had she gone blind? Was this all in her head? She didn't know.

Eventually, whomever was leading her stiffened their arm, and they both came to a stop.

"What are we…?"

The hand slipped out of hers, and for a brief moment, Theo was struck by the terror of being utterly alone. Then the hand patted her chest twice, and a cold finger booped her on the nose.

If there was a meaning Theo could take from the gesture, Theo interpreted it as, *wait here.*

She wanted to reach out, to touch this figure that made no sound, seemed to have no weight. She didn't want to be alone.

But Theo waited, anyway. She crouched down, sitting on the floor beneath her. What was the floor? It felt rough, like stone. Cold, like ice.

Almost on instinct, as a way to pass the time, Theo reached for her pocket, to pull out her phone.

It was only then she realized she wasn't wearing any clothes at all.

So this was some kind of dream.

Time passed, ephemeral, uncountable. Theo waited in darkness, for someone, something to happen.

Eventually, she heard footsteps. Slowly approaching her, hesitant, stumbling.

Before she could call out, a glimmer of light appeared in the sky. A comet, streaking across an infinite void of darkness.

And in the faint light of the comet, Theo could see again, and Summer stood before her. The adult, whom she'd come to know so intimately over the past month. Just as naked as her.

Theo's words died in her throat, and all she could do was stare, overwhelmed.

Summer licked her lips, looking unsure. "Theo? I... someone led me here. I think it might have been..."

Deep pain inside of Theo, that threatened to overwhelm her. Her eyes brimmed with tears. "Y-yeah. I... felt it—I felt her too."

"I see." Summer took a deep breath, closing her eyes. "Thank you," she murmured under her breath.

They stood there like that for several long moments. Awkward. Unsure.

That was stupid. Reality itself was creating a miracle so they could be together. Theo threw herself forward, wrapping her arms tight around Summer. A part of her feared that Summer would be just as ephemeral as the rest of this place, but she was solid, and warm beneath her touch. "I missed you."

Summer shuddered, and squeezed Theo back, so tightly that it hurt. "I missed you too," she whispered, her voice raw.

Theo buried her face in Summer's shoulder. She never wanted to let go. "I'm sorry. I'm so sorry I left like that. I mean, I had to, but... it wasn't fair to you, the way I did it. I was scared, and confused, and panicking, and god I forgot how much actually having my meds makes a difference."

A snort of laughter escaped Summer. She wrapped her fingers into Theo's hair. "I get it. It's fi—" Summer trailed off, and then she shook her head. "It hurt, a lot. I tried to be cool with it, to be casual, but the truth is I'm a pathetic loser who falls in love too easily. I wanted more.

And maybe that wasn't actually possible. But the fact that you gave up so easily... hurt almost as much as you being gone in the first place."

"I'm sorry," Theo said again. "And you're not a loser, Summer. You're kind, and thoughtful, and you care about others so much, and even if you screw things up sometimes, you always try to make it right."

Summer closed her eyes, her lips trembling. "I love you," she whispered.

Warmth and happiness bloomed in Theo's chest, and she reached up, cupping Summer's cheek. "I love you too. And I mean that. It's *you* I've fallen in love with, Summer. I promise. I don't know if you'll believe me, but I'll do my best to prove that to you, every single day and—"

The distance between them closed, and Summer pressed their lips together. She tasted like tears.

Theo couldn't help but smile through the kiss, and she held onto Summer even tighter, never wanting to let go.

Eventually they broke apart, foreheads resting together, breath low and heavy.

Theo looked at Summer, and smiled.

Summer smiled back.

They both burst into laughter, light, airy, the tension finally releasing.

"Now what do we do?" Summer asked, lifting her head up and looking around.

"I'm not sure." Theo looked around, at the void around them, at the comet above. "Can we even get out of here?

A shimmer of light traced through the air, behind Summer, forming the shape of a door.

"Woah," Summer said, pointing behind Theo.

She turned to see an identical door shape behind her.

"Your world or mine, I guess," Summer said, looking between the two.

Theo bit her lip. "Same choice as we had before." She took a deep breath. "I'm ready this time. I'll stay with—"

"No." Summer put a hand on Theo's chest. "I'll go with you. I'm making this choice to chase after what I want, and I can't ask you to give up on your family."

"But what about all of your friends? Your life?" Theo shook her head. "And there's the whole legally dead thing..."

"As opposed to you butting up against Theodora? Both will have their difficulties. I'll miss my friends, but let's be real. Half of them were going to move out of that town eventually anyway. We'll figure out the legal issues. Can't be that hard."

This was all... Theo fidgeted, looking between the two doors. "Are these really the only options? To give up one side of everything, forever?"

Summer pursed her lips, and looked up at the comet. "Hey, you! Whoever you are! The ghost of the other Summer, or some god or whatever. I know we're already experiencing an incredible miracle here, but... is this really it? One reality or the other, a choice made here and now for the rest of our lives? I know it's romantic to sacrifice everything for the one you love, but fuck that. Why should either of us have to? Give us something better."

"Summer!" Theo hissed, her eyes going wide. Should they really be provoking whatever this was?

There was a brief pause, then a movement of air, a faint touch on her back, a whisper in her mind, and then Theo understood.

As long as the comet shone in the sky, the door would remain open.

Summer let out a soft gasp, as she presumably received the same information. Then she shook her head. "So great, a couple extra hours then? If even that? What does that get us?"

"No," Theo said, smiling. "Riley mentioned it to me. This comet is annual. It'll come back around again, next August."

"Oh." Summer blinked, then her eyes went wide. "*Oh!*"

"Yeah."

Summer grinned, then looked up at the sky. "Okay, yeah. I think we can work with that. Um. Thank you?"

Theo wrapped Summer's hand in hers, and squeezed. "I want to come to your world. I... really liked the life we were building there, together. And if I can come back to visit in a year then... it's not so scary, you know?"

Summer looked down at her, eyebrow raised. "Are you sure? What about your mom's cancer?"

"I made her schedule an appointment. And my brother will make sure she actually follows through. And I told my family the whole truth. They already know that I might come back here."

"One step ahead of me," Summer said, shaking her head. "Although I mean, I guess Riley and Minha kind of already know too. But still. To leave without saying goodbye?"

"Well…" Theo glanced back at the door behind her. "If we've got a few more hours… I could go out and say a few goodbyes, and grab some stuff to bring with me. I uh… may have packed everything into the trunk of my car already."

Summer nodded, then took a step back, pulling out of their embrace. "Okay. Yeah, sure. Let's do it."

"I'll be back soon, I promise." Theo turned away from Summer, took several steps to the door, then paused.

She looked back, up at the comet, into the darkness.

"Thank you," she whispered. "For being my friend."

~

Summer sat on the grass, staring up at the comet in the sky.

Back in her own reality again. The candles she'd brought had all flickered out. Had they helped at all? Probably not.

She'd been waiting here for an hour now, her jacket zipped up tight, chill seeping into her jeans from the cold ground below.

The comet was getting low on the horizon, almost out of sight. How long did it take, really? Surely Theo would be here any minute, wouldn't she?

Assuming that what she'd experienced was even real, and not some weird sort of stress induced hallucination.

Summer pulled her knees closer to her chest. She'd have to trust. She'd have to hope. She'd have to believe.

Something crunched on the gravel behind her. Summer turned her head only to be blinded by a headlight directly in her face.

Scrambling, she dove out of the way, rolling onto the grass, as a car pulled forward, that definitely hadn't been there before.

The car came to a stop, the engine shut off, and then the door opened, and Theo stepped out, looking rather smug.

Summer stared up at her, dumbfounded. "You're here."

"Sorry," Theo said. "I got pulled into a video call with my family, to say goodbye. And had to draft a big text to Riley. But yeah. I'm here."

Summer took Theo's outstretched hand, and let herself be pulled up to her feet. "And you brought your car? How?"

Theo grinned. "I dunno. I tried driving through where that door was. Doesn't seem like there's any specific reason it only had to be person sized, you know? And otherwise that meant my car would be sitting there abandoned for a year, and having two cars would probably be helpful."

"Smart." Summer looked the car over, which was considerably nicer than her own. "And you've got all your stuff?"

"Yep. In the trunk."

A moment of silence passed between them as they stared into each other's eyes, in the darkness of the stars.

Summer closed the distance between them, grabbing Theo's face, kissing her as deeply and passionately as she could.

Theo let out a contented little murmur, her hands wrapped tight around Summer and pulling her close.

"I love you," Summer whispered, in between kisses.

"I love you too," Theo said, smiling as she said the words.

Summer pulled Theo into a hug, burying her face in Theo's hair. "Is it really okay? You actually want a life with me? There's still time to turn back, you know."

Theo laughed, and shook her head. "It's too late for self sabotage, Summer. You're stuck with me, okay?"

"Okay." Summer took a deep, shuddering breath. Maybe she could actually believe it. "What now?"

Theo pulled out of the embrace, taking Summer's hand in her own. "We go home. Together."

The wind rustled the nearby cornfields, bringing with it the scent of damp earth and decaying leaves. "We've got two cars though. We'll have to drive separate."

"Oh. Right." Theo scratched at her chin, looking sheepish. "Little less romantic that way, huh? But I'll meet you there?"

"Yeah."

Dear Diary,

I never imagined that I'd write another entry in here. This will probably be the final one I do, if only to provide an endnote here beyond tragedy.

So much has happened in the last month. More than I'd be able to recount on these pages without writing an entire novel.

So I'll instead simply dedicate this entry to Summer. You were my first friend, my first crush, my closest companion. Despite everything, I'm glad for every moment we got to spend together. And I know in my heart that you felt the same, no matter how much my self loathing tries to tell me otherwise.

And I will dedicate this entry to Summer. A woman I know, and don't know, and wish to know better. A woman who's stuck with me through all of my bullshit, and I hope to make many more memories with together.

I love you both. In different ways, in different times, with all of my heart. And I will do my best to continue to accept that love, and the path I've chosen, and ignore the doubts and fears.

Goodbye,
And See You Tomorrow.

Theo
9/24/2024

"Morning!" Theo called out, stifling a yawn as stepped into the work.

"Heya," Riley called out from the front desk. "Didn't sleep well?"

"Not really." Theo took off her glasses, and rubbed at her eyes. "Was too nervous."

Riley grinned, and leaned forward on her elbows. "Today's the big day, after all. You excited to see your family again?"

A whole year now, since Theo had decided to stay in this world. Tonight, the comet would finally be visible again. And hopefully, she'd be able to visit her home once more. "I'm a bit worried about my mom."

"I'm sure she's fine. Theodora's mom is doing great, so I'm sure there's no worry on the other end."

The sentiment didn't quite still the anxiety in Theo's heart. "You're probably right. I hope so, anyway."

Riley nodded, and drummed bright, patterned nails onto the desk. "So how's Summer holding up? Always a bit nerve racking meeting your girlfriend's parents, you know?"

Theo raised an eyebrow. "I mean, you met Theodora's parents. How did it go for you?"

"That's, uh, well." Riley scratched at the side of her cheek, presumably blushing, though it couldn't be seen under her makeup. "I mean, sure. They're nice enough. There was a lot of other crazy stuff going on at the time though, so I dunno that I got to make the best impression."

"Ugh. Tell me about it." Getting Theo settled in this world had involved a bit of a crazy scheme, which required the cooperation of Theodora and her parents.

They'd come up with a story that Theo and Theodora had been identical twins separated at birth, and accidentally given the same name and social security number. With the help of a lawyer, they'd managed to get Theo a new number issued, so she could finally open up her own bank account, and live as a separate person without causing any more problems.

"Still. Once you get back I really want to check this portal out, okay?"

"Ehhh…" Theo looked back and forth, lips pursed. "I still dunno about that. It's a literal miracle. I'm not sure trying to study it is such a good idea."

"Oh come on." Riley clasped her hands together. "I'll be as respectful and unobtrusive as possible. Just a *little* bit of science. Pretty please?"

As always, Riley had a smile that was hard to say no to. Theo sighed. "We'll see once we get back, alright? I'd better get to work."

"Thanks, you're the best!" Riley beamed, and then turned back to her own computer.

Theo made her way down the hall, towards her office.

"Oh, um. Theo?" Riley called out, her voice uncharacteristically hesitant.

"Yeah?"

"You are going to show her the video, right?"

Theo clutched her phone in her pocket. Riley had recorded a video of herself, a message for her alternate self.

"I will. I promise."

~

"Alright class, we'll stop there for today. Next week we'll be discussing the impressionist movement, so please read from pages 372-394."

Summer stood up, loading her books back into her bag, and joined the flow of students making their way into the hall. Finally done with classes for the day. She could get back home, meet up with Theo, and then together they could—

Footsteps pounded towards her from behind. Summer gritted her teeth, and braced herself.

Minha crashed into her, slinging her arm around Summer's shoulder. "How's it going, frosh?"

Summer sighed, and shook her head. "For the last time. I'm taking a few art classes part time. That doesn't actually make me a freshman. I'm still six years older than you."

"Doesn't matter!" Minha slapped her on the back, then pulled away. "You done for the day? Wanna go grab something to eat?"

"Nah. Got stuff planned with Theo tonight."

"Booo." Minha kept walking with her anyway, keeping pace. She frowned, then her eyes lit up. "Wait, is that today? All the portal shit or whatever?"

"Yup. Get to go visit a whole other world. So y'know. I won't have cell service."

Minha laughed. "Dude, that's still so fucking cool. Can I come?"

"No."

"I wonder what other Minha is like? Wonder if she even came to this school?"

Summer shrugged. "Theo never intersected with her life, so possible there's some divergences. I'll see if I can find anything out while I'm over there."

"Wild shit." They passed through the doors leading outside, the sky overcast.

Minha looked up, her expression pensive. "You're coming back though, right? You're not gonna stay over there?"

Summer glanced over at Minha, sensing vulnerability there. She smiled. "We're not planning on it, no. There's a small chance, I guess. If Theo's mom really needs help. Or if the whole portal thing doesn't work as promised. But we like our life here."

"Cool, cool." Minha grinned, though it lacked her usual enthusiasm. "I've missed you over at the gas station."

"Yeah, same. But, y'know. Can't stay stuck in the same rut forever. Gotta actually try and better myself, move forward, accomplish something."

Minha raised an eyebrow. "That what Theo expects from you?"

Summer laughed, and shook her head. "Nah. This is all on my end. She just… makes me want to actually try."

"Hell yeah." Minha raised her hand for a fist bump.

"What about you, anyway? This is your last year, right? What comes next?" Summer returned the fist bump.

Minha's face fell, and she shrugged. "Dunno. Only thing I'm good at is soccer. There's been a little bit of interest from teams scouting and stuff, but nothing concrete. And even then…"

"Not sure if you actually wanna go pro?"

"Yeah." Minha tugged at her ponytail as she walked. "Pay is shit, nobody actually comes to watch the games, you destroy your body, and gotta constantly be traveling. It's… I dunno. Not sure what else I'm gonna do though."

Summer's hands twitched, fighting an old urge to reach for a cigarette. Never quite gone. "Ain't that a mood. Not like there's much money to be made in art either, but… only thing I'm good at. Still, you've got some more time before you make a decision. And you know I'm here to support you with whatever you wanna do. Theo too. We got your back."

Minha looked relieved at that, and smiled. "Cool. I'll see you in what, like a week?"

"Yeah. Later."

"Later!"

Minha jogged off towards the soccer fields, and Summer turned to head back to her apartment.

As she walked, her phone buzzed repeatedly in her pocket, and she pulled it out to find several texts from Faith. Mostly several exclamations of joy, followed by a link to an article.

Summer pulled it up, scrolling through it. It was a short bit about an upcoming art exhibition by local youths, and Faith's name was there and proudly featured.

It was hard not to smile as Summer put her phone away.

The people she cared about were going to be alright.

~

On her way back to the apartment, Summer decided to swing by the bakery, for old times sake.

Like usual, she found Peter there behind the counter, and his smile became radiant at the sight of her.

"Hey, Summer!" he called out, waving cheerfully. "Feels like I lost half my business when you moved out from upstairs."

Summer laughed. "Probably didn't need that many carbs anyway. That being said, I'll take two dozen donuts."

"Going somewhere with them, or are you just very hungry?"

"Gonna meet Theo's folks, might as well make a good impression with the best baked goods I know."

"Aww. That's really sweet!" Peter beamed at her, then started gathering up the requisite donuts. He paused, halfway through. "This the first time you're meeting them?"

"Yeah."

"I see." Peter frowned, his brow furrowing.

Summer raised an eyebrow. "Something wrong?"

"No, no, nothing's wrong, I just..." He sighed, then looked around furtively, and leaned in close. "Can you keep a secret?"

"Sure. What's up?"

"I bought a ring."

"Oh shit! Congrats man, Aaron's gonna be so happy."

Peter's face flushed, and he rubbed at the back of his head. "I'm not so sure... I've been dating Aaron the same amount of time as you and Theo, but I'm scared that maybe I'm moving too fast."

Summer opened her mouth to offer reassurance, but nothing came out. Shit, was that something she should be thinking about? Everything was so hectic and unsure and had been changing and she'd largely been focused on living life day by day. But planning for a future was something else entirely, wasn't it?

With a sigh, Peter finished up with the donuts and handed the box off to Summer, and started ringing her up.

"You two are perfect together," Summer said, trying to put on her best reassuring smile. "I know you'll be very happy together."

"You really think so?" Peter asked, his eyes sparkling.

"I do. I promise."

Theo practically vibrated with energy and anticipation as she rode the elevator up to her apartment.

It was a modern one, built to support the influx of people coming into town with the success of the university. And a lot nicer than Summer's place had been.

Theo liked the extra space, but more than that, she liked that it was a place they could make a life together, more than a place where they struggled to get by.

When she opened the door to the apartment, she saw a box of donuts lying on the kitchen counter. The open plan of the kitchen gave way into a proper living room, with a couch, and a TV. Enough space to entertain guests.

She found Summer in their bedroom, half of her wardrobe currently splayed out across the bed. A nice bed, with a proper frame and every-thing.

"How was school?" Theo asked, resting one hand on her hip.

"Eh." Summer stared at two shirts on the bed, one a band t-shirt that was her usual style, and the other a nice blouse, which was Theo's. "Which of these should I wear, to meet your parents? How do I make a good impression?"

Theo rolled her eyes. "Just go as yourself. It's fine."

"Yeah, but..." Summer turned back to their closet, frowning. "Why don't I own a good suit? I'd look sharp as hell in a good suit, wouldn't I?"

"I mean, yeah, obviously." Theo took a moment to picture it, and decided she needed to make that happen, eventually. "But this isn't a formal thing, you know. It's mostly going to be super awkward and there's going to be a lot of crying, since, you know. They remember the other Summer."

"Right." Summer winced. "Sorry, I'm just…"

Theo stepped forward, resting her hands on Summer's shoulders. "It's okay to be anxious. I've been feeling it all day too."

"I know, I know." Summer bit her lip, looking back and forth. "There's so many what ifs and what should I do and also like, do you wanna get married?"

Well that stopped Theo's heart in her tracks. She stared at Summer, eyes wide.

Summer continued on, seemingly oblivious. "I saw Peter earlier and he talked about how he was buying a ring, or had already bought a ring? I forget, but I've never really given that any thought but now I feel like I probably should have and—"

Theo squeezed Summer's hands hard enough to get her attention. "Summer? Are you asking me as a hypothetical, or are you proposing to me right now?"

A beat of silence hung in the air, and Summer's face filled with horror as she presumably realized exactly what she'd said. "I, uh, that is—"

"Because either way the answer is yes," Theo said, then leaned in to gently kiss Summer on the lips.

When they pulled away from each other, Summer still seemed to be somewhat in shock, and she sat down on the bed. "I, uh. Fuck. Sorry. Did I mess that up?"

Theo sat next to her, resting her head on her shoulder. "Don't worry about it. If you want to make a big spectacle of it, you can try again later. Being with you is all that really matters to me."

Summer was silent for a long, long time, her weight pushed against Theo, brow furrowed in thought.

When she finally spoke, her voice was hesitant. "Is it weird that… I'm really excited about being introduced to your family as your fiance?"

Theo laughed, and nudged Summer gently. "I really like the sound of that too."

Summer looked over to her, her smile radiant, tears in her eyes. "Sorry, uh. Shit. This is a lot really fast and I've got all this other shit to be stressed out about but… really? I mean, wouldn't it make sense to wait until after this trip, in case anything changes?"

"Nah." Theo matched her smile with one of her own, all of the love inside of her bubbling to the surface. "No matter what happens, no matter what's changed, whatever we face, I know I want to do it by your side. As long as you'll have me."

"Yeah." Summer took a deep, shaky breath. "Okay. As long as you'll have me."

Theo grinned, stood up, and pulled Summer to her feet. "So come on then, *future wife*. We've still got to finish packing, right? We've got a comet to view, and a whole other world to travel to."

Summer leaned in and kissed her once more. "As long as we do it together."

www.ingramcontent.com/pod-product-compliance
Lightning Source LLC
Chambersburg PA
CBHW050149120726
47903CB00002B/557